DIVE BOMBERS IN THE MED!

'Here they come again!'

'Hard a-starboard!'

Impi was turning at full speed as the Stuka came in low over the stern. The barrage of flak seemed overwhelming and impenetrable. The guns' crews were working like madmen, their weapons blotching the sky with shell bursts, but the aircraft still came on . . .

The bomb seemed to hang below the aircraft as it was released, poised over the ship for what seemed an age, growing larger and larger as it came nearer, as if it were a balloon being blown up by a child.

Siggis' guns were hammering away and he saw the Stuka lift away with pieces falling off the wing. Kelly was watching the bomb. Half-consciously he saw the splash in the corner of his eye as the aeroplane went in, then the deck jarred under his feet as the bomb struck with a shattering explosion that jarred his spine and made his teeth feel loose . . .

Also by Max Hennessy in Sphere Books:

THE LION AT SEA
THE DANGEROUS YEARS

Back To Battle

MAX HENNESSY

SPHERE BOOKS LIMITED
30/32 Gray's Inn Road, London WC1X 8JL

First published in Great Britain by
Hamish Hamilton Ltd 1979
Copyright © Max Hennessy 1979
Published by Sphere Books Ltd 1982
Reprinted 1982

TRADE
MARK

Printed and bound in Great Britain by
Cox & Wyman Ltd, Reading

Characters in *Back to Battle* who appeared in the two previous books of the trilogy, *The Lion at Sea* and *The Dangerous Years*.

George Kelly ('Ginger') Maguire	
Rear-Admiral Sir Edward Maguire, Bt	Kelly's father
James Caspar ('Cruiser') Verschoyle	Kelly's term-mate at Dartmouth and enemy turned friend
Charlotte Kimister	Kelly's former girl-friend, married to a term-mate but widowed after the Invergordon Mutiny
Mabel Dunbar	Charley's sister
Christina Verschoyle	Kelly's former wife, now married to Verschoyle
Hugh Withinshawe	Christina's son by her first husband and Kelly's stepson
Albert Rumbelo	Kelly's coxswain
Biddy Rumbelo	Rumbelo's wife and Kelly's housekeeper
Albert Kelly Rumbelo	Rumbelo's son and Kelly's godson
Patricia Rumbelo	Rumbelo's daughter
Admiral Corbett Admiral Orrmont }	Former captains of ships in which Kelly served
William Latimer Arthur Smart Archibald Fanshawe Seamus Boyle }	Former shipmates of Kelly's

Part One

1

The Atlantic was always moody and September storms had blown up from nowhere so that the great grey rollers had smashed constantly against the cliffs round Cape Trafalgar. Today, however, the sea was calm, with a soft north-westerly wind bringing up cloud that dropped a gauze veil along the coast. For once the sea looked sluggish and, as it nibbled at the land, in the villages of the Algarve and round Cadiz the fishermen began to prepare their gaudy trawlers and load them with the chocolate-coloured nets.

Off the coast to the east of Tarifa, the two ships were lifting and rolling gently to the slow undulations of the swell and as the destroyer, *Badger*, came round towards them, leaning to the sea, Commander George Kelly Maguire lifted his glasses and settled himself to study them. Behind him on the bridge, *Badger's* commanding officer, Lieutenant-Commander Arthur Smart, waited for instructions, ready to act on them at once because he knew Kelly Maguire, and Kelly Maguire was known throughout the Navy for his lack of hesitancy; even the crisp red hair beneath his cap seemed to indicate a quick temper and a no-nonsense attitude to his job.

Badger's bows lifted as she thundered towards the two ships in the distance. Laid down in 1931, she was relatively new and her 1400 tons clove the water at her full thirty-five knots. After the eighteen years of peace in Europe since 1918, cruises off the coast of Spain were no longer steamed at 'economical speed' but at 'full speed,' because a civil war had broken out in the Iberian peninsula and British ships were being threatened. Her decks cleared for action, her 4-inch guns and torpedo tubes manned, she had come at racing speed through the Straits of Gibraltar at the squawk for help they'd heard on their radio,

3

the thin quivering hull pitching into the swell in a spray-drenched salt-sticky wetness.

Every eye was on the two ships ahead. The farther of the two was a small coaster, high-sterned with a funnel like a Woodbine. She was about 8,000 tons and ancient, and she looked grubby and ill-found, with joints that creaked and groaned in heavy weather. Down below, the engine room crew laboured in gloomy caverns painted rust-brown for cheapness, and stinking of damp, coal dust and the bushy-tailed rats that infested her. Her cabins would be the same – brown-black with age, and as cramped, ugly and narrow as her alleyways.

'That her?' Kelly Maguire lifted his glasses again and settled himself to study her.

'That's her, sir.' The answer came quickly. '*Jeb el Aioun.* Plies regularly between French Morocco and Gib. She was Spanish but since the Civil War she's been registered as British. Owned by Barbes and Co., Gibraltar.'

Placing his elbows on the bridge coaming, Kelly stared for a long time at the old ship. Then he shifted position and turned the glasses on the nearer vessel. She was also unprepossessing, with tall old-fashioned stacks that made her cruiser stern seem curiously anachronistic, and sides that were rust-streaked and dirty-looking. Alongside *Jeb el Aioun*, however, she looked like the Fairy Queen.

'And her?'

'Spanish cruiser, *Ayala,* sir. *Pero Lopez de Ayala,* to be exact. Spanish writer, I believe.'

'I'm glad we don't call our ships after writers.'

'Imagine *HMS William Makepeace Thackeray.*' Smart grinned. 'Or *Percy Bysshe Shelley.*'

The navigating officer decided to show his literary knowledge. 'How about *Oscar Fingall O'Flahertie Wills Wilde*?' he suggested.

He'd expected Kelly to laugh but, still leaning on the bridge-coaming, his glasses on the Spanish ship, Kelly was concentrating, and the smiles died. As one of the most decorated officers in the Royal Navy, 'Ginger' Maguire was used to a great deal of respect, especially since he was also considered to be a little 'regimental' at times. They all knew his reputation. Decorated for the first time in 1911 for saving life, he had never

4

seemed to stop gathering gongs even during the drab years since the Great War when there'd been remarkably little opportunity for anybody to distinguish themselves anywhere. But it wasn't just the ribbons that graced his breast which gave him his reputation; there was a hard core of technical knowledge under the gold-laced cap, and the steely grey eyes missed nothing, and they all knew it.

In a period when big ships and big guns – despite their repudiation before his death by Jacky Fisher, the man who had created them – still remained the sworn credo of the Royal Navy, and the specialists who manned them were in the ascendant, many small ship men had been condemned because they didn't fit the standard pattern. And Kelly Maguire, who had always been a confirmed and unabashed destroyer man, had been left behind a little by the gunnery, signal and torpedo experts who had gained their distinction solely by serving in the monolithic vessels about which he was so often virulently expressive. Since the beginning of the Spanish Civil War that July of 1936, however, he seemed to have found his feet again, because the sea round Spain was suddenly a place where unhesitant decisions were demanded and there was nobody better at that than Kelly Maguire.

Although the British government still appeared unable to make up its mind what its attitude ought to be towards the two belligerents, the navy had always seen its duty quite clearly and its work these days consisted chiefly of protecting British interests, evacuating British subjects and acting with strict neutrality. Ships had spent their time lifting Socialists from the Balearics, which were under the fascist flag and Fascists from Catalonia, which was held by the Socialist Spanish Government, so that they were constantly in the front row of the stalls when it came to viewing the fluid and vicious struggle ashore.

And, as often as not, Kelly Maguire had been there to handle the arrangements. He spoke fluent French, some German and Italian and, after two years in Gibraltar, solid if uninspired Spanish, and when the request for help had come, his had been the name that had sprung to the mind of Rear-Admiral Cuthbert Corbett, Chief Staff Officer (Intelligence), Gibraltar.

He studied the Spanish ship again, the limp red and black flag at her mast-head, the cluttered decks and the men between

5

the guns watching *Badger* as she pounded up, a white wash of foam at her bows. He didn't have a very high opinion of Spanish warships; so far they seemed good only at bombarding defenceless towns.

'Looks goddamn grubby,' he growled contemptuously, and again the eyes met behind his back because he'd always been noted for calling a spade a bloody shovel. 'Position, navigator?'

'Thirteen and a half miles from the coast, sir. The Republicans claim territorial waters up to twelve.'

Kelly grunted. 'We recognise 'em only up to three,' he said briskly. 'It's a clear case of piracy. I don't suppose the International Code contains anything about that, does it?'

The signals officer grinned. 'No, sir. We could use X, which means "Stop carrying out your intentions and watch my signals."'

'I know my International Code. Very well, give 'em X.'

Again there were a few sidelong glances. The Spanish ship was twice the size of *Badger* and, if it came to an altercation, they could well come off worst by a long way. On the other hand, there was still a lot to be said for skill and determination, and there wasn't a man aboard the destroyer, from Kelly Maguire down to the youngest boy seaman, who didn't believe they couldn't wipe up *Pero Lopez de Ayala* and not even get out of breath. The Royal Navy was still the Royal Navy.

'You sure of the position, Navigator?' Kelly asked.

'Absolutely, sir.'

'Right. Yeoman, make "Cease interfering."'

'"Cease interfering," sir.'

There was a long pause. The jocularity had vanished now because they were all aware that within an hour they could be involved in an international incident that could well lead to war.

'They're answering, sir,' the yeoman of signals called out. 'They recognise our signal.'

'That all?'

'Yes, sir. They don't say they'll cease.'

Kelly rubbed his nose, studied the Spanish ship again for a long time, then he straightened up. 'I think we'll board,' he said.

There was another exchange of looks, sharper this time and

6

with more alarm in them. 'Ginger' Maguire seemed to be enjoying himself and, with all those ribbons on his chest, they were beginning to wonder if he was itching to earn another.

'Large party of seamen, sir?' Smart asked.

'Don't be a damn fool, Arthur,' Kelly said mildly. 'You ought to know me better than that. Me, my petty officer and, with your permission, your navigator and signals officer. We'll be wearing Number Tens and let's make sure they're spotless, even if we have to borrow 'em.'

Staring at himself in the mirror as he changed, Kelly Maguire frowned. It was difficult to comprehend a civil war where the revolutionaries were smart and well-equipped while the government forces were scruffy and ill-found. But, for once, the war had not come as a total surprise to the rest of Europe because it had been obvious when the Spanish king had abdicated in 1931, that the generals who'd taken the oath of loyalty to the new republic had had no intention of keeping it. However, in a situation complicated by strong separatist movements in Catalonia and the Basque provinces, the Socialist government had managed to hold a balance but, by the spring of that year, the plotting had grown stronger, and one of the generals, Francisco Franco y Bahamonde, had finally established a military government in the Canaries, while revolts had broken out in Spanish Morocco and Andalusia, and the first troops of the Spanish Army of Africa had been ferried across the Strait to Cadiz. Unfortunately, when the Spanish Navy had tried to follow suit, the plan had misfired and there had been a widespread slaughter of officers. *Pero Lopez de Ayala* was one of the mutinous ships.

Struggling into his high-collared white jacket with its triple row of medal ribbons, Kelly stared again at himself. The ribbons didn't mean much to him except to mark his years of service but he decided they might impress the Spanish. He knew exactly what he had to do.

It was a pretty sick sort of world. Only three years before he'd stood on the deck of the destroyer, *Actaeon*, in Alexandria as the Italian troopships heading for the war they'd started in Abyssinia had passed towards the Suez Canal, the Italian soldiers singing fascist anthems and jeering at what they considered the old and mangy British lion. With the Suez Canal a private company registered in Paris, it had not been possible to stop them, but any government worth its salt could have made things a whole lot more difficult for Mussolini, and it had not been the politicians but the ordinary British matelot who had put the thing in its proper perspective. With the Chiefs of Staff in London pessimistic, the Mediterranean Fleet had remained ebullient and when an Italian soldier had peed over the stern of his ship to show his opinion of the Royal Navy he had been greeted by a shout from a British seaman. 'Do it while you still can, mate,' he had yelled. 'Them Abyssinians'll cut it off when they catch you.'

While British and French ministers had tried to sell their countries' honour for the sake of peace, the Navy had spent a whole year applying League of Nations sanctions (as valueless as they were difficult) and, with a world moving rapidly away from the old days of civilised diplomacy, events had always moved too fast for the democracies. Japan was at war with China and, with Abyssinia conquered, Mussolini clearly now intended becoming involved in Spain. Things were tense, especially as everybody in the service knew the Navy was ageing. Yet they could do nothing because the men in Whitehall were still hoping to put off what looked remarkably like an approaching war with the fascist states in Europe merely by keeping their fingers crossed. The fleet review at Spithead in 1935 to mark the King's jubilee, thanks to the machinations of maladroit politicians, had been a shop window full of obsolescent goods. As Winston Churchill had commented, it was a fine fleet but it was wearing out and the fascist dictators were growing too bloody big for their boots. There was already talk that they'd sent 'experts' to Spain to help the insurgents.

He jerked at his collar. The Spanish Civil War, he thought savagely, had not only brought to an end the Navy's smug feeling of supremacy, it had also brought to an end his own promising courtship with a Spanish girl. He had found it lonely living the bachelor life of a divorced man and had just been considering asking her to marry him when the first shots had been fired and she'd disappeared towards Bilbao, where she'd been born. Having probably read too much into the things she'd said, her disappearance had shaken him, but for a naval officer there was

8

no such anodyne as letting off steam and becoming emotional. He had simply coped with it, closing his teeth against a cry of protest, and accepted it.

As he fastened on his sword, he took a final look at himself in the mirror. He was still young enough to look lithe and sinewy, with a strong jaw, far-away seaman's eyes and only a sprinkling of grey in his red hair. He frowned, deciding that the possession of more than one language was sometimes a disadvantage. If he weren't careful he'd find himself condemned to Intelligence for the rest of his career. Admiral Corbett's assertion that in his present job he was an asset to the Navy and was learning a lot that would stand him in good stead was poor consolation for not having a ship of his own. Jerking his belt into place, he picked up his cap, jammed it angrily over one eye, and slammed the door behind him just to show what he felt.

A few minutes later, his temper under control again and dressed in dazzling white with his sword at his side, he headed for the deck. The navigator and the signals officer were waiting for him, with Petty Officer Albert Rumbelo just to one side. Good old Rumbelo, he thought warmly. He'd been in more unpleasant situations with Rumbelo than either of them cared to remember and Rumbelo had always reacted as he was reacting now, with his potato face devoid of expression, his thick body relaxed. By contrast, the two officers seemed on edge, the signals officer distinctly nervous.

Kelly paused, moving with deliberation so that both the Spaniards and the British should see him as unperturbed and in command of the situation. He stared about him. *Badger*'s guns were trained on *Pero Lopez de Ayala*. They seemed to be jammed almost up the Spaniards' nostrils and he wondered what it felt like to look down a lethal four-incher at that distance.

'If there's trouble, don't hesitate to let 'em have it,' he said. 'We're not playing ring-a-roses.'

'Aye aye, sir.' Smart smiled. 'How about you if we do?'

'It'll be up to us to jump over the side and up to you to pick us up.'

Clambering into the whaler, they were lowered down the side of the ship and rowed across the surge of the swell.

9

'Hope the Spanish react with good manners,' the officer of the watch said dryly. 'After all, these people butchered their officers at the beginning of the war.'

Smart grunted. 'I'd like to see anybody try to butcher Ginger Maguire,' he observed. 'I reckon he's about the most unbutcherable officer in the Navy.'

The Spaniards gave the whaler a bowline and lowered a jumping ladder. As they bumped alongside, Kelly began to clamber up the hull of the ship. It was grubby, he noticed, and he was forcibly reminded of the German ships at Scapa Flow in 1919 after their surrender, dirty, unkempt and uncared for, their crews mutinous and ugly. Then another unhappy memory jogged at his mind, as he recalled almost pleading with the ship's company of the battleship, *Rebuke* – his own men! – at Invergordon. Was it only five years ago? But for a bit of luck and a lot of understanding on both sides, he thought, *Rebuke* might just have gone the same way then as *Pero Lopez de Ayala* had now. It had been a shattering experience.

There was a tense atmosphere of expectation as he reached the deck, followed by the signals officer, the navigator and Rumbelo. The Spanish crew were unshaven and dressed in a mixture of clothing, among which only occasional scraps of uniform were visible. Spanish Republican soldiers fought in overalls and braces so perhaps the Republican navy felt they ought to show their oneness with their comrades by following suit.

To his surprise, a bosun's pipe twittered and he was pleased at the sign of normality. The Spanish sailors crowded round, pressing forward to see him and his party, those at the front leaning back in order to avoid rubbing their grubby clothes against the spotless white drill which seemed to leave them somewhat awed. Then an older man, dressed indifferently like the rest but wearing a petty officer's cap, pushed through the crowd.

'*A quién está buscando Usted?*'

There was no indication of respect but at least they were getting somewhere and Kelly was grateful for the hours he'd spent studying Spanish. It was still far from good Spanish but it enabled him to speak directly.

'I wish to see your captain,' he said.

'We have no captain. We shot him.'

If the Spaniards had expected to see any change of expression on Kelly's face they were mistaken. He remained wooden, but polite.

'Who's in command then?'

'I am.'

'Then we'd better get on with it, hadn't we?'

As he explained why they'd come, Kelly could see the navigator's eyes skating hurriedly over the surrounding Spanish sailors. He remained rigidly stiff, however, while the signals officer, a precise young man, seemed to be edging backwards all the time as if he was afraid of having his whites dirtied. This business of dealing with mutinous Spanish sailors was new to the Navy but, Kelly felt, it was something they had to cope with and, when they were back aboard, the signals officer might well benefit from a few sharp words. He decided to suggest it to Smart. Naval occasions weren't always social and sometimes it was necessary to get dirty, something the signals officer clearly needed to learn. Rumbelo was Rumbelo, blank-faced, immovable and quite imperturbable.

'The ship's now being run by a committee of forty sailors of all trades,' the man with the petty officer's cap was explaining, as if he felt democracy, his type of democracy, was something not easily understood.

Kelly remained polite. 'Don't you find it difficult getting things done?' he asked blandly.

The petty officer smiled and shrugged. He had a curiously likable smile. 'Sometimes,' he agreed. 'It's a good job the committee are all big and strong.'

Kelly smiled back, putting on a show of affability when everything connected with mutiny roused a feeling of black hatred in him. 'I'd like to speak to your navigating officer,' he said.

The Spaniard shrugged. 'We haven't got one,' he pointed out. 'Only me. I've done some small boat sailing so I'm acting as navigator.'

'I see.' Kelly smiled again. 'Well, you're a bit out in your working, I think.'

'Never.' The Spaniard was certain of himself. 'We're well inside Spanish waters.'

'Suppose we go to the chart room.'

The petty officer pushed a way through the crowding sailors towards the bridge. The decks were littered with cigarette ends and the paintwork was dirty, and the chart room was so untidy it took him what seemed ages to find the correct chart. Spreading it on the table, he jabbed his finger at it.

'There,' he said. 'That's where we are.'

'May I see your workings?' the navigator asked.

The petty officer produced his workings willingly enough and they pored over them together, the navigator polite and interested, taking his lead from Kelly.

'We don't recognise a three-mile limit,' the Spaniard said. 'For us it's twelve miles.'

'Still no good,' the navigator said cheerfully. 'You're a mile and a half outside it. *Jeb el Aioun*'s thirteen and a half miles from the coast. She's in neutral waters.'

The Spaniard stared and scratched his head. 'Well,' he admitted, 'I'm not an expert.'

'Must make it a bit difficult at times,' Kelly said cheerfully.

The Spaniard changed his stance. 'Anyway,' he said, 'it makes no difference. She's a British vessel from Gibraltar gunrunning for the revolutionaries.'

Kelly smiled. 'Nothing of the kind. She's on her normal trade run, cleared by the authorities in Gibraltar to proceed on her lawful occasions. If you check her log book, you'll find she does the run regularly.'

He smiled again, seeing the funny side of the situation. *Pero Lopez de Ayala*, representing the government of Spain with a crew who'd revolted against their officers, was trying to oppose another revolution ashore and being frustrated on the technicality of accurate navigation. He took a cigarette case from his pocket and raised his eyebrows. The Spaniard gestured to him to go ahead.

He offered the case and they lit up, peering at the chart as they smoked, while the signals officer stood at the back of the chart-room, wide-eyed at the sight of an immaculate British commander with gold on his cap sharing cigarettes with a scruffy and mutinous Spanish petty officer. Knowing Kelly and having known him since 1911, Rumbelo still remained totally undisturbed.

The navigator found the Spaniard's mistake and Kelly

12

leaned over the chart. 'You'll have to let her go,' he said.

The Spaniard grinned and nodded.

'Otherwise we'll be forced to sink you.'

'Think you could?'

'Before your people could get your guns to bear. You haven't even bothered to man them.'

The petty officer grinned again. 'It's harder than you think being part of a social revolution when everybody thinks they're equal.'

He showed them round the ship. It was drab and uncared-for, the decks dirty under the grime of hundreds of feet. Breech mechanisms, sighting instruments and range-finders looked rusty and unclean, and Kelly suspected even that magazines and shell rooms were only half full. In the wardroom they were shown the bullet holes in the panelling where the officers had been murdered. The signals officer winced slightly but the others remained totally blank-faced. In the captain's cabin they were joined by several other men, all full of political catch-phrases and all over-earnest and lacking the petty officer's humour. But there was no hostility and one of them even produced a bottle of brandy and glasses.

The petty officer indicated the chair alongside the desk. 'The captain was sitting there,' he said, 'when he was shot.'

They were pressed into accepting long Spanish cigars and when they'd finished their drinks, they were escorted back to the ship's side. Kelly noticed at once that many of the sailors, if they hadn't put on uniforms, at least had put on uniform caps, and as he turned to climb down the ladder, he stiffened and saluted the petty officer. The Spaniard looked a little disconcerted and he guessed that saluting had been done away with. Then he saw one of the sailors nudge him and he stiffened to attention and saluted back. Immediately, there were so many salutes they looked like waving corn, and someone shouted 'Vivan los marineros ingleses.'

Kelly smiled, feeling the initiative was still his, as it had been throughout the interview. He had stamped his own presence on the opposition and that, surely, was the way to success. Master of your fate. Captain of your soul. Nobody pushed Kelly Maguire about. Not even the Spanish government.

As he began to climb down the jumping ladder back to the

whaler, he was aware of dozens of heads hanging over the rails above him. As the boat began to draw away, there were even a few friendly waves but he kept his gaze firmly ahead and showed no signs of having seen them.

Back aboard *Badger*, he climbed to the bridge where he was met by Smart. As he nodded, Smart turned to the voice pipe. 'Half ahead both.'

As they passed the old freighter, they could see a fat man wearing a peaked cap leaning on the bridge. The bridge messenger handed over a megaphone and Kelly shouted into it.

'You may carry on,' he said. 'They've accepted that you're outside territorial waters.'

The man in the cap waved and, a few moments later, they saw the water churning at her stern as she began to move off.

'I'll go and change,' Kelly said.

As they watched him go to his cabin, Smart turned to the navigating officer.

'How did he do it?' he asked.

The navigator looked bewildered for a moment, then he grinned. 'Talked to 'em like a Dutch uncle,' he said. 'At one point, I thought he was even going to put his arm round that bloody Spaniard's shoulder.'

Smart smiled. 'I bet he had the other behind his back, though,' he said. 'Wearing a knuckle-duster.'

2

Gibraltar lay like a crouching lion across the sea, a vast lump of limestone on the southern tip of Spain, dominating the narrow stretch of water that was a cross-roads for ships hurrying east and west, to and from the Mediterranean, and north and south on the North African trade route.

It was never entirely foreign. The beer had a different label, sherry was a novelty and the brandy sometimes produced disastrous results, but the pubs and cafés were much the same as in Portsmouth, dispensing egg and chips for the sailors and providing pianos so they could thrash the keys in a sing-song when they felt like it.

Since the *Ayala-Jeb el Aioun* incident, the war had grown. In the early days it hadn't been a real war at all, just a comic opera with an occasional death, run by the grandees of the Right against the dozens of parties of the Left, all known by a different set of initials – POUM, PSUC, FAI, CNT, UGT who couldn't even agree among themselves. The whole thing had been ruled by '*mañana*' – tomorrow – that single word that seemed to regulate the whole of Spanish life, while the artillery shells that were fired were said to be so old and useless the belligerents just fired them back; there was even said to be one which had been going backwards and forwards for months.

It was different now. Russian support for the government had increased, and international brigades had been formed from volunteers from every country in Europe – many of them young men of wealthy families out to show their disgust at their parents' indifference to the poverty and misery of the Depression by fighting for the wrong side. The reaction, of course, had been strong German and Italian support for the fascist revolutionaries which had brought their soldiers, aeroplanes and

15

ships into the conflict. A policy of non-intervention was still being followed by the French and British Governments but with international meddling had come increased bitterness, and in a savage war of ideologies, it was now far from abnormal for women teachers to be stripped, marched about with shaven heads or even shot, and for priests to fight against priests and not hesitate to kill. To the Fascists the Republicans were 'anti-Christ Marxist *canaille*,' while to the Republicans, Franco's men were 'anti-Marxist priests' bastards.' It was hard to tell which were the most virulent in their hatred, with prisoners taken in arms shot out of hand and officers shot whatever the situation.

In February, the Nationalists had eliminated the Republican pocket round Malaga, with the Italians helping on land and the new German pocket battleship, *Graf Spee*, standing by in support. In April, the Kondor Legion of the German Luftwaffe had wiped out Guernica, the Basque market town. In May the destroyer, *Hunter*, had struck an Italian-made Nationalist mine off Almeria, with eight killed and nine wounded – and a fortnight later, *Graf Spee's* sister ship, *Deutschland*, had been bombed by government aircraft off Ibiza, and after landing her wounded at Gib, had bombarded Almeria in revenge.

By this time, General Franco's forces controlled the west and south coasts of Spain with part of the north, while the government held the east coast with the great ports of Barcelona and Valencia. Though a fascist blockade had been declared and considerable efforts had been made to enforce it, it had not been recognised by the British government and, attracted by enormous profits, British shipowners were now operating whole lines of small steamers to break it. Like *Jeb el Aioun*, they were constantly in trouble, and merchant ships of all nationalities continued to be sent to the bottom, while one British destroyer, narrowly missed by a torpedo, had not hesitated to call up her flotilla mates so that the Italian submarine which had fired the torpedo had only just escaped, damaged and unnerved. Nobody in the Navy was kidding themselves any more that the Spanish Civil War wasn't the prelude to a major conflict. The gathering storm was just off the quarterdeck.

Walking home to his flat in Main Street under the Rock, Kelly stared round him at the towering fortress, wondering if it

16

could be held. If war came would there be another great siege? Those whose job was the strategy of the British Empire had probably already abandoned it in their plans because a siege would be a useless piece of heroics.

It was clear the Germans were treating the Spanish war as a rehearsal for a more serious conflagration and, with the powers constantly trying to draw military lessons from it, Kelly himself had been involved in drawing up reports on the influence of the air on land and sea warfare. It had not been difficult to notice that, in air attacks on warships, though no ships had been sunk, many had been damaged and every endeavour was now being made to improve anti-aircraft armament.

Stopping by his door, he wasn't looking forward to spending another evening alone. Yet he'd spent too many dining with people who had wives to feel he could impose any more. Even Rumbelo had gone now, his time in the Navy finished, and was back at Thakeham, near Esher, where his wife, Biddy, looked after the vast empty house Kelly owned. He'd gone with no regrets because, contrary to the romantic legends about the pull of the sea, there weren't many long-serving sailors who didn't happily give it up.

His hand in his pocket feeling for his key, Kelly wondered what he'd do when his own time came to retire. It couldn't be far off because, unless something happened soon, he could see himself being passed over for captain's rank in favour of the experts who'd built such a reputation in capital ships. Would he marry? He didn't think so. Not again, though judging by the people who kept pushing their daughters at him, he supposed he must still be a good catch.

You, Kelly Maguire, he thought as he took out the key, are a bloody fool.

It was a thought that often came to him these days. Ten years before he would have believed that his life had been laid out for him: a steady climb up the ladder and a happy home provided by Charley Upfold, the one woman he'd loved all his life. But he'd been too involved with the Navy, and she'd escaped him to marry his term-mate, Kimister, and on Kimister's death, had vanished to America – so he understood, to marry an American. He'd never heard from her since, while his own wife, Christina had left him for another naval officer, James Verschoyle.

He was just pushing the key into the lock when he was surprised to hear a voice calling inside the flat.

'It's open!'

Throwing the door back, he was confronted by a young man in grey flannels and tweed jacket.

'Hugh! When did you arrive?'

'This afternoon.' The boy smiled. 'The caretaker let me in.'

Kelly's face was pink with pleasure. Out of the whole sorry business of his broken marriage, the only worthwhile thing that had come to him had been his stepson, Christina's son by her first marriage. Twenty now, and on indifferent terms with his mother, he had spent all his time away from school or university with Kelly, visiting his ships with an enthusiasm that led Kelly to hope he might eventually join the Navy himself.

'How long are you here for?'

'I pick up a ship tomorrow for Naples. I'm doing some research at the university there.'

Kelly grinned and the boy mixed a pink gin for him. 'Mind if I join you?'

'You're old enough now. How'd you get here?'

'James Verschoyle brought me. We came by car.'

Kelly made no comment. Though he and Verschoyle had spent all their youth at loggerheads, the dislike had disappeared in the muddled years of the thirties and had not returned even after Christina's remarriage. It was curious, but Verschoyle was Verschoyle and nothing could change him.

'What's Verschoyle doing here?' he asked.

'Appointment to the admiral's staff, I understand.'

'Good for him. He might relieve me.' Kelly finished his drink briskly. 'Been to Thakeham lately?'

'Yes,' Hugh said. 'Everybody sent their regards.' He passed across a photograph. 'That's the house. I thought you'd like to have it.'

'Who's the sailor in the background?'

The boy laughed. 'Your godson. Kelly Rumbelo.'

'In uniform already? God, that makes me feel old!' Kelly paused. 'How about you, Hugh? Have you ever thought what you're going to do for a living?'

'Not really. In fact, it seems funny to be thinking of work with a war coming.'

18

'You think one is?'

'Don't you?'

Kelly paused. It was certainly rapidly becoming clear that, despite Russian help, the Nationalist superiority on land was growing decisive, and when it finally did, doubtless the Germans and the Italians would persuade Franco to raise the old cry of 'Gibraltar for the Spanish!' as a trigger to start another war in which they could legitimately take part.

'Yes,' he agreed. 'I do. In which case you could always join the Navy.'

Hugh looked faintly guilty. 'Isn't the navy a bit out of date?'

Kelly's face grew red. But then he hesitated. The politicians had always seemed more concerned with the expediency of party political ends than with long-term national interests and their subservience to the Treasury made them spoil every ship they touched for the necessary extra ha'p'orth of tar.

He took refuge in indignation. 'Just let those buggers, Hitler and Mussolini, start something,' he growled, 'and you'll soon see if we're out of date.'

Hugh grinned at his expression. 'I meant, hasn't the Air Force become more important?'

The boy had a point, Kelly thought. If a war came, then certainly the Air Force would count for a great deal. Air power was going to be a decisive factor in the next bunfight, and that was something that had never been understood by the clots in Parliament or by the War Office and the Admiralty, probably not even by the bloody Air Ministry, come to that!

He pushed the thought aside.

'Never mind the Navy for tonight,' he said. 'We'll find somewhere good to eat. How about your mother? Seen her lately?'

Hugh shrugged. 'Yes. But I don't think she's desperately interested in me – even now.'

'How is she?'

Hugh looked up, puzzled. 'She seems content enough.' He clearly couldn't understand how any woman who'd married her first husband out of pure selfishness and been the cause of the break-up of her marriage to the second, could possibly be content with her third. He hadn't yet learned that things didn't fit into neat patterns.

'How about James Verschoyle? How do you get on with

him?'

'Surprisingly well really.' Hugh frowned. 'Do you hate him, Kelly?'

Kelly thought about it. Whatever else 'Cruiser' Verschoyle was – and, God knew, he had a soul that was still a dark tinge of grey at times! – he was always his own man, shrewd, clever, cynical, well aware of what was going on and determined to manoeuvre it to his own advantage.

'No,' he said equably. 'Occasionally we even bump into each other professionally. We just don't talk about our private lives and, as a naval officer, he's among the best.'

Hugh looked puzzled and Kelly tried to explain. 'As you grow older,' he said, 'you realise everything isn't just black and white. There must have been something wrong with your mother and me because we never did anything but quarrel.'

Hugh frowned. 'She never does anything but quarrel with James Verschoyle.'

'But she's stayed married to him, old son,' Kelly said gently. 'That's something she didn't do with me.'

They ate at the Rock Hotel. The place was full, and Kelly noticed more than one woman with her eyes on him. It didn't bother him, because he often found people watching him, perhaps to see if a man with his country's highest decoration for courage ate from his knife or was rude to waiters. They all knew him. Quite a few of them didn't like him even, because it had always been his habit to say what he thought – especially about big ships. Forthrightness, he liked to think it was, though he knew that at times it bordered on downright rudeness. But at least people knew where they were; he'd never sought popularity, and he was far too old now to change.

'Ever thought of marrying again, Kelly?' Hugh asked.

Kelly's head jerked up, as he realised his thoughts had been far away. 'Once,' he said. 'No, twice. Once with Charlotte Kimister. You'll remember I once took you to her house for tea when you were a boy.'

'And the second time?'

'A Spanish girl.' Kelly's smile was faintly embarrassed. 'Bit younger than me but not so young as to be improper.'

'What happened?'

Kelly took a sip of his wine. He'd noticed the girl several times when he'd visited Algeciras, just over the border in Spain. He'd thought at first she was one of the growing army of German and Italian agents watching the Rock, but then it had dawned on him that it wasn't the Rock she was interested in but himself. She'd been introduced to him as Teresa Axuriaguer-rera but it had turned out that she was the widow of the Conde de Fayon, who had been murdered in Madrid by Fascist troublemakers in 1936. It had been a warm, satisfying relationship, but after her disappearance there had been only one brief letter indicating that she'd thrown in her lot with the Basques in their fight for autonomy, and he'd been forced to suppose that her political beliefs were stronger than her need for a husband.

'What happened?' he said. 'The war got in the way.'

He realised that the boy was watching him closely and had been all evening. 'You've got something on your mind, old son,' he said abruptly. 'Don't you think you'd better spit it out?'

Hugh frowned, ill at ease and uncertain. 'Yes,' he agreed. 'I really broke my journey here to talk to you.'

'What about?'

'Well –' Hugh met his gaze '– Paddy and I –' 'Who?'

'Paddy. Pat Rumbelo. The Rumbelos' daughter.'

'Is that what you call her?'

Hugh affected surprise. 'Don't you?'

'Not really. Mostly it was "Wally". After Wally Hammond, the cricketer. She never failed to clout my leg-breaks over the fence.'

'She's decided to be a nurse. As soon as she's old enough.'

'Has she now?' Kelly hadn't missed the change of tone in the boy's voice.

Hugh raised his head and stared him in the face. By God, Kelly thought, that's his mother, because whatever else Christina was, she was no coward. 'Well,' he said, 'Paddy and I were wondering –'

' – if I thought you should get married.'

Hugh grinned. 'How did you know?'

Kelly smiled. Hugh had spent far more time at Thakeham than with his mother, sailing with the Rumbelo children, playing cricket, teaching Pat Rumbelo the finer arts of rugby

21

football, cricket and wrestling. Kelly had been cutting the lawn the first time it had dawned on them that they were adult and he'd seen them untwine their young bodies from the half-nelson they'd been demonstrating and stare at each other, a lanky fair-haired boy and a petite dark-haired girl, both suddenly a little startled at their discovery.

'Stuck out a mile,' he said.

'She suggested I should ask your opinion.'

'Shows her good sense. It's an indication of the Rumbelos' intelligence that they have such clever children.'

'Well, should we?'

Kelly smiled. 'She's a bit young still. Come to that, so are you.'

Hugh made a gesture that was faintly irritated. 'A man's got to think ahead a bit, ain't he?'

Kelly smiled, pleased. And there, he thought, is me. Often he heard little inflections, small phrases he knew had been picked up from himself, and it was flattering, because it indicated the boy wished to emulate him.

'I don't mean now,' Hugh went on. 'I mean when we're old enough.'

'Which, I imagine, will be soon.'

'Yes.'

Kelly paused. Charley Upfold had been only thirteen when she'd decided to marry *him* and she'd never once changed her mind until his own thoughtlessness had finished it all.

'Age don't really make much difference,' he said slowly. 'And females know their own minds much better than men. I'd certainly say marry her. But not until you can afford it.'

Hugh was smiling. 'Thanks,' he said. 'I didn't think you'd see it my way.'

Kelly smiled back. 'Oh, yes,' he said. 'Every time. If only for the fact that when I was your age I didn't.'

The following morning, Kelly drove Hugh to the quay for the steamer to Naples, then headed slowly back to his flat to pick up his brief case. As he entered, the telephone was ringing and he snatched it up fiercely.

'Admiral's secretary, sir. I've been trying to get you for some time. The admiral would like to see you.'

22

'What about?'

'There's a job he wants doing, sir.'

Kelly put the telephone down slowly. He'd grown used to being Corbett's hatchet man. His languages dispensed with interpreters, which was no bad thing, and, he suspected, he'd become known for his cool cheek. He'd been sent into Bilbao in April because the British Government had been dodging its responsibilities to eager British shipping with the claim that the approaches were mined and the coastal guns insufficient to deter Nationalist warships. He'd found that the mines were 1914–18 types, all useless and all swept, anyway, while the approaches were controlled by batteries of modern guns crewed by men trained by one of the finest artillerists in Spain, and Westminster had had to climb down. With *Hood* waiting outside the place with her fifteen-inch rifles, the supply ships that had slipped in had kept the town's resistance going until June, when he'd gone in a second time to bring out what was left of the British residents.

It was Verschoyle who met him as he appeared in Corbett's office. He hadn't changed much and was as languid and good-looking as ever.

'Hello, Cruiser,' Kelly said. 'What are you doing here?'

'Being groomed to take over your job, I suspect.' Verschoyle smiled. 'You're away so often fixing things, the admiral thought he needed another assistant.'

'How's Christina?'

Verschoyle looked faintly sheepish. It was an odd expression for one who was normally so arrogant. 'All right. She gives me hell a lot of the time but I'm no angel either and somehow it works.'

Kelly felt no resentment. There had been a time when he'd hated his former wife but he'd long since recognised that his marriage had been a disaster and as much his own fault as hers. He glanced pointedly at Verschoyle's thickening middle. 'You're getting fatter,' he said. 'More of a battle cruiser than a light cruiser these days.'

Verschoyle smiled. 'Fleshpots are too easy to come by with a wife like Christina,' he said. 'She has too much money.'

'What am I wanted for?'

'Seems Santander's about to fall to the Nationalists and

23

there are a bunch of nuns there whose lives are in danger. They're being held as hostages, but it appears there's an unidentified local authority up there who's willing to exchange them for two "loyal" generals who've been held in custody in Mallorca. The British vice-consul's sorted out the details with the aid of a Roman Catholic priest called Father Eufemio. It seems we have the generals in Gib now, and we have the name of a woman who knows where to find him.'

Admiral Corbett was perusing a report as Kelly opened his door and he waved wordlessly at a chair. For the Navy, there was plenty to worry about just then because the Germans and Italians were parading in the Spanish waters big new ships that made the British vessels look as outdated as the dodo.

He put the report down at last. 'Sorry to drag you out, Kelly,' he said. 'You've heard what it's about?'

'Is Santander in our diocese, sir?'

'As much as Bilbao was,' Corbett said. 'Home Fleet's asked us to help and you've become a sort of naval Scarlet Pimpernel. There doesn't seem to be any other choice.'

Kelly drew a deep breath. 'Sir, I don't think Intelligence is my strong point.'

Corbett looked up. He'd had a high opinion of Kelly ever since the trouble in *Rebuke* at Invergordon. 'You're pretty good at it all the same,' he pointed out.

'I'm best at sea, sir, and that's where I think I ought to be.'

Corbett stared at his fingers for a moment, deep in thought. 'Intelligence,' he insisted, 'is finding out what you don't know from what you do. It's what the Duke of Wellington called guessing what's at the other side of the hill, and if the Germans and Italians remain as awkward as they are at the moment and a war comes out of it, then we'll need a few good guessers.'

He paused, as if he'd said his last word on the subject, then went on quickly. 'You'll know about the nuns,' he said. 'And there are also a few other odds and ends to be collected. Fortunately, there's a woman called Jenner-Neate who runs the Child Relief Fund and she knows them all. It'll take you three or four days, I imagine, so fetch 'em out, Kelly, and I'll see you go back to sea.'

Kelly grinned. 'How do I get there, sir?' he asked.

'We have the hostages in *Badger*. She's up there waiting for you.'

'And me, sir?'

'You're a pilot, aren't you? You'd better fly. There's a woman at the Presidencia who has all the details, but just be a bit diplomatic how you ask for her because it seems she's already being watched, and the police chief's a fanatic called Neila who used to be leader of the Santander Socialists, and takes his victims for what he calls a "paseo" at night or in the early morning. "Paseo's" a euphemism for a ride *à la* Al Capone. So, make sure you keep your nose clean. We don't want to have to use diplomatic pressure to make sure it doesn't happen to you. You were asked for by name, by the way. The woman seems to know you. Teresa Axuriaguerrera. Know her?'

Kelly's heart gave an unexpected thump. Did he know her? Not half he didn't! It was like something coming out of the past, what had been a pleasant dream suddenly becoming flesh and blood in front of him.

'Yes, sir,' he said briskly. 'I know her.'

'Then – ' Corbett knew Kelly well and he shot him a sidelong glance ' – you'd better get on with it, hadn't you?'

3

They flew him up at once to Biarritz where a Frenchman called Leduc was standing by to pilot him into Santander. The arrangements had all been made ahead of him and *Badger* was already inside Santander Bay waiting for him to send her the refugees.

It was a risky flight, and a regular service machine had been shot down only three days before by Italian fighters, but in the first light of the day the little Beechcraft skimmed over the water at only three hundred feet, level with a filmy cloud bank, tattered, thin and insubstantial as a cobweb. It was easy to identify *Badger* in the bay, and with her, her sister ships, *Blanche*, *Brazen* and *Beagle*, all lying close to the Spanish nationalist cruiser, *Almirante Cervera*, with the German battleship, *Graf Spee*, half a mile away, holding a watching brief. Leduc gestured at the sky.

'Keep your eyes open,' he said.

There appeared to be a panic at Santander, because Nationalist machines had bombed the aerodrome only a few hours earlier and men were busily filling in the craters. Leduc took a look at it, laughed, seemed to shut his eyes and landed between the holes, wriggling like a snake. Parked at wide intervals round the perimeter of the field were Russian monoplane fighters like grasshoppers, their stubby fuselages on bow legs. They were said to be the fastest fighters in Spain.

The game was already clearly up, though. The advancing enemy troops were Italians and Moors with a formidable artillery support of 65 mm weapons, German ack-ack, and six-inch and three-inch guns, an artillery orchestration twice as powerful as Kelly had seen even when he'd been a spectator from the Senior Officers' War Course at manoeuvres in England. There

26

were also said to be plenty of Fiat-Ansaldo tanks, with machine guns and cannons, and plenty of air cover from Italian Fiat fighters based at Villarcayo. The bombers were German, escorted by new German Messerschmitt monoplanes operating from Aguilar del Campo. In reply, Santander had the eighteen Russian fighters, a random collection of worthless bombers, chiefly old French Bréguets and Potez, and seventeen even more worthless Gourdoux which were supposed to be dive bombers. They had hardly any automatic weapons, a few six-inch guns from Bilbao, a few 75s, and one four-inch battery. The guns were of all nationalities, ammunition was faulty and there was a shortage of telephones.

The newspapers, marked by vast blank spaces where the censors had been at work, seemed to consist largely of slogans and the sayings of demagogic politicians. Nobody seemed to take much notice of them and Kelly suspected that the men who thought them up were keeping well out of the firing line. One day, he thought cynically, there might be a war in which they would see the unprecedented sight of a politician with a bullet hole in him.

Finding a room at the Hotel Jauregui, he was just brushing his teeth with a mouth full of peppermint foam when the tap water failed. Flinging his toothbrush into the bowl in a fury, he managed to clear his mouth and, going outside, found militiamen and girls washing, shaving, making up their faces and collecting water by an artificial lake, watched by the swans that inhabited it. Already long-range machine gun bullets were flitting through the trees, and as he left the hotel, aeroplanes came over and dropped bombs. A house was blown to pieces and a fine thick dust came floating down to dull the tram-lines and lie in the folds of clothing. Nobody was hit but a girl collapsed in a hysteria of fear, her skin damp and puffy, her limbs jerking, her lips forming terrified words.

Wearing khaki trousers and a bush jacket he'd bought in South Africa three years before with no sign of his rank or profession, he set off for the Presidencia. There were several soldiers on guard, but none of them stopped him – chiefly, he suspected, because they couldn't think of any grounds to do so.

Then he saw Teresa Axuriaguerrera. She was standing near the entrance talking to one of the soldiers. She was wearing a red shirt and blue cotton trousers, the uniform of so many of the Republican men and women, and his heart gave an unexpected knock against his chest because she didn't seem to have altered much, with the same dark hair and blue eyes that had always reminded him of Charley Upfold, and a dignity that came from the upright carriage that every young Spaniard, male or female, seemed to possess.

It seemed stiflingly hot and there was a smell of dust in the air, and he noticed that the flowers by the gate were coated with a thick white powder. Above him, the sky was a scalding blue, shining with a brilliance that was reflected from the white walls in a way that hurt the eyes, and there were a lot of kites about, which he'd been told had been attracted by the bodies in the fields outside the city.

Lighting a cigarette to show a self-confidence he didn't feel, he began to march forward. One of the soldiers stepped in front of him immediately, holding his rifle breast-high.

'*Quière algo?*'

The girl looked round and addressed a few words to the soldier. He laughed and she turned to Kelly, no sign of recognition on her face so that he was on his guard at once against a trick. Did they suspect him for some reason? Was she being used to trap him? Had she so changed her spots with the civil war she was no longer to be trusted?

'You are not a Basque?' she asked quietly.

'No. English.'

'From one of the British destroyers?'

'Yes. I'm looking for someone.'

She put a hand on his arm. 'You won't find her here,' she smiled.

She spoke again to the soldier, who grinned and waved them away, then, putting her arm through Kelly's, she guided him up the shabby street towards the centre of the town.

'*Quière usted beber?*'

Kelly nodded. 'Yes, I'd like a drink.'

They found a bar and sat outside under a dusty umbrella. She lifted her glass to toast him.

'*Tengo el gusto de beber a la salud de Ustedes. Quière usted verme?*' Then, dropping her voice, she spoke again in English. 'I am so pleased to see you again, George Kelly.'

There was no mistaking the warmth in her voice and he placed his hand over hers. 'Why did you disappear, Teresa?'

She gave him an anguished look. 'My country was suffering. To the Basques there is such a thing as honour.'

'To the British,' Kelly said, 'there's such a thing as love. I was on the point of asking you to marry me.'

'Oh, no!' Her face fell. 'I can't believe it!'

'Why not? I thought it was what you wanted, too.' He frowned, remembering an old hurt that was connected with Charley Upfold. 'Somebody once said that as a sailor I was terrific but as a hearts and flowers type I was a dead loss.'

'Dead loss?'

'*Fiasco. Falla. Fracaso.*' He tried to explain. 'I'm a slow starter.'

She looked at him with suddenly shining eyes and he found the magic worked again just as it had the previous year. Being with her was like looking through a magnifying glass that made everything sharp and clear and colourful. He was bewitched at once. The only other woman who'd ever had the same effect on him had been Charley Upfold and he determined not to let her get away again.

'I asked for you,' she said quietly. 'But not because of that. I didn't even know.' Her fingers tightened in his. 'I couldn't have known. You never showed what you felt.'

Kelly frowned. 'Englishmen don't go in for singing serenades with guitars under balconies!'

She gave a little laugh. 'I always loved you when you were stiff and British, George Kelly. I heard what you did at Bilbao and asked for you because I knew I could trust you.'

'You couldn't in a dark corner,' he said, and she laughed.

The streets were full of marching men carrying rifles and flags, the red, yellow and purple Republican colours contrasting with the black streamers they added for the dead. They wore overalls and berets, forage caps and steel helmets, with clattering rifles, pans and aluminium cups hung about them. A few of them had their girl friends with them at their head, scarlet-lipped and trousered, because the Anarchists liked to shock the pious Basques. They were carrying their wounded because it was said that most of the hurt in this war died from the jolting of the ambulances on the appalling Spanish roads, and Kelly noticed that though no one was supposed to believe in the church any more, bells were still tolling for the dead.

Many of the buildings had been wrecked by bombs and were still smoking, and on the walls were slogans – '*Arriba España,*' '*Viva la libertad*' and the more earthy '*Vino y aceite.*'

'The bombers came last night,' Teresa said. 'The German volunteers. The troops outside the city are Italians. Why doesn't the British government send soldiers to help us?'

Probably because they're a gutless lot, Kelly thought. Or probably because, with half the country in favour of the Republicans and the other half – that half which got its faces in the society magazines – undoubtedly supporting Franco, it was hard to know who to favour.

The priest, who was wearing civilian clothes, had a flat near the cathedral which consisted of a living-bedroom and a kitchen. He was an old man, shabby and with a shaking voice, but his resolve was firm.

'The sisters are all in hiding,' he announced at once. 'Have you found a ship to transport them?'

'She's in the bay. I still have to find the means of getting them on board.'

It was decided that the old man should warn the nuns to be ready while Kelly sought means to get a message to *Badger*. As they parted, Teresa took his hand to touch his fingers with her lips.

He managed to find a small ship which had been Greek until a few weeks before but had now started flying the Union Jack and called herself – somewhat hastily, Kelly guessed, so there'd been no time to forage in a dictionary of names – *Jimmy*. Even that was spelt uncertainly on her stern as *JIMY*.

Her captain was obese and moist with anxiety, but he agreed to help and had one of the ship's motor boats lowered into the water to carry messages to *Badger*. Because he was due to leave in three days time, he agreed to carry any evacuees Kelly wished to lift off, but he was in constant need of reassurance that the British warships would protect him when he left. On board already were five hundred badly-wounded Basque soldiers due to go to Santoña further along the coast. They were dragging their way along the decks to get soup, candles, matches or cigarettes in the light of flickering oil lamps. In the shadows, the bandages they wore made them seem as if they'd been in a snowstorm.

Returning to the priest's flat, Kelly found Teresa there with the old man. All the messages had been delivered and the nuns would start appearing the following day. There was still the question of the dozen or so British nationals remaining in Santander, however, and they borrowed an old French Citroën which they used to drive to the British Club near the museum. It had been wrecked by a bomb and then by looters and there was only one British woman there.

'Jenner-Neate,' she introduced herself briskly. 'Of the Child Relief Fund.'

She would have been recognizable as British at once from her sensible skirt and shoes and the pearls she wore round her neck. But she also had a sensible straight back and a splendid figure and she'd already performed wonders getting Spanish children to safety along the Basque coast.

'The people who're left are such a silly lot,' she said angrily. 'There's an elderly major and his wife, and Mrs. Fotheringay –'

'She sounds formidable,' Kelly grinned.

'She has a dog and she won't leave without it. There are nine altogether, with two Spanish, one Frenchwoman and one Albanian.'

As they left, Teresa was wearing a troubled frown and he knew there was something on her mind. Pulling her into a café for a drink, he made her tell him what it was.

'Will you accept one more?' she asked. 'For me?'

'No political figures. We're supposed to be neutral.'

She gave a little laugh. 'I doubt if there's a politician in Spain of either side worth helping. It's my old professor. He was always inclined to air his opinions and he's been talking too much. He's had to hide from Chief of Police Neila.'

By the time Kelly returned to the city centre, shells were dropping in the streets, and police vans, Red Cross ambulances and journalists' cars were moving in the murk of dust they raised. The city swarmed with movement and seemed bowed under the noise of the sirens of the trawlers which had been brought into the harbour to pick up the refugees. It was impossible to separate individuals, and he could only count hundreds of excited heads as women, children and old men

31

piled uncontrollably aboard. The streets were stacked high with chairs, bedsteads and sagging bundles, and the sound was of marching men, the roar of motors, and the cries of awakened children.

Troops were coming in from the front as Kelly reached the hotel, and the look on their faces showed what they thought of their chances. There was no longer any line, they said and they were retiring without a struggle, bombed mercilessly by the Germans and Italians whenever the mist lifted, so that they'd had to leave their wounded to die in the highlands behind them. A division of the Basque Army corps had resisted immovably for thirty-six hours, but the Santanderinos, who were not made of the same stuff, had left them to it and gone home in a steady stream across the coverless hills, until finally the Basques had also had more than they could take and were on their way in, too.

By evening, most of the nuns, all dressed in ordinary clothes, had appeared in twos and threes and been ferried in *Jimmy's* motor boat out to *Badger*. There had been no sign from Teresa and there was still the problem of the two hostage Republican generals. Kelly had been unable to find anyone in authority who was interested in them and, in desperation, he tried the sentries on the quay.

'Who's your superior officer?' he asked.

The man grinned. 'Anybody with a bigger gun than I have,' he said.

In the end they brought the two men from *Badger* and turned them loose on the quay. It seemed a bit like pushing them out of the frying pan into the fire because it was clearly not going to be long before Santander fell, and the Nationalists weren't noted for showing much mercy.

Back aboard *Badger*, a sherry party for the nuns was being thrown in the wardroom and they appeared to be thoroughly enjoying themselves.

'Ought to try 'em on gin, sir,' Smart suggested. 'They'd probably be quite lively.'

'I'm going back for the British contingent now,' Kelly said. 'If there's bombing, don't wait. *Jimmy*'ll bring 'em out.'

There had still been no message from Teresa and he was growing worried, but he knew that if he went to the Presidencia again it could cause trouble for her.

The following day the weather was like summer in England and nobody seemed to have accepted that the place was dying. The offensive had started three days before and the Nationalists were already half-way to the city, but, though the government had ordered the shutting down of all industries so that workers could help construct fortifications, organisation seemed to have fallen apart and most people seemed merely to be enjoying the time off while the army squabbled among itself, first the Santanderinos refusing to fight, then the Bilbainos who had arrived to help them.

At the British Club, Miss Jenner-Neate was worried. She'd been unable to contact several of the British residents who'd gone into hiding in safer parts of the city.

'They're all a bit stupid,' she said. 'They think because they're British they're untouchable.'

'Tell them the destroyer, *Hunter*, was mined only a fortnight ago,' Kelly suggested. 'That might convince them that the might of the British Empire doesn't necessarily reach out to them here.'

He took several addresses and set off to unearth them. The day was exhausting in the heat, because the British residents were not anxious to move and many of them were elderly people who'd spent their savings buying what they thought could be a safe retreat from English winters. Bullying, cajoling and extracting promises, in the end he had them all agreeing not to let him down, and he returned to the Hotel Jauregui hoping against hope he'd hear something from Teresa.

The tap water was still not running so he found a large bucket and went to the ornamental lake to get enough to wash, carrying it back with the spatulate leaves from the trees floating on the surface to stop it slopping over. When he poured it into the wash basin, fifty per cent of it had solidified as mud on the bottom.

There was a constant drone of aeroplanes overhead and scarlet flashes in the sky at the other side of the city. It looked as if everyone was out in the streets but the heart seemed to have gone out of them. Christ, he thought uneasily, he'd been in more dying towns and cities in his life than he cared to remember.

33

The planes came again after dark, German Junkers and Heinkels and Italian Savoias and Fiats, and as the bombs dropped he could hear the wails of terror outside. The hotel seemed to have emptied of staff but the ground floor was full of terrified people. He took one look at it, pushed his way to the bar, bought a bottle of brandy and headed back to his room. If he were going to die, he thought, he might as well die with a bit of elbow room to do it in, not trampled to death by a panic-stricken mob.

The artillery fire sounded closer now and he heard there had been a last infantry attack which had left a mountain of corpses on the rocky slopes outside the city. Going downstairs again, he questioned a group of Basques.

There was something about the Basques that appealed to him. They were a religious, deep-drinking lot who all seemed to be good sailors and detested regimentation. To the Spanish they were '*brutos*' and '*bestias*', but to them the Spanish were intriguers and political parasites who lived off other people's industry, and their whole history had been one of trying to obtain autonomy for themselves. By this time, they'd lost every foot of their country and were simply hoping now to reach the wild Asturias to fight a hopeless rearguard action.

They were all well-armed with rifles, while revolvers, those most dramatic and useless of weapons, dangled from all ranks, to say nothing of grenades which swung in bunches from their waists like the bananas that Josephine Baker had used in her nude shows. They were exhausted but far from dispirited.

'*Hay una vida mas barata*,' one of them said to Kelly, '*que no vale la pena de vivir*. There's a cheaper life but it's not worth living.'

It seemed a better attitude than that of the British government as it crawled at the feet of the dictators.

During the night the bombing seemed to stop. Expecting Teresa's professor at any moment, Kelly decided to leave the bed for him and merely lay on top of it, a glass of brandy by his elbow. He had just dropped off when the door rattled and he was off the bed in an instant. As he unlocked it, it flew open in his face and Teresa flung herself at him. All the mischief, all the taunting had gone from her face and her cheeks were covered with tears.

34

'What's happened? Where is he?'

'Neila took him,' she sobbed. 'Neila took him last night. They took him to the Cabo Mayor wireless station near the Miramar Palace. They shot him and threw his body into the sea.'

Her fingers clutched his, tense and hard, and she began to cry in soft muted whimperings. Holding her tight, trying to comfort her, harrowed by her tears, all he was able to do was say 'Please don't cry' and stroke her hair. Then, with her crouched against him, his lips in her hair, they slipped down against the pillows, clutching each other. Lifting her head, he laid his lips on hers and suddenly he found they were exchanging racking kisses that left their mouths numb. At last she seemed to relax and he saw she was staring at him with a strange, wondering look. For a second, they remained like that, their faces only an inch apart, then his hand slipped under her shirt above the trousers she wore, and he felt the warm skin in the hollow of her back and the sudden quivering tension of her body.

She shuddered in a spasm of pain and there were new tears on his cheek, then she was moaning softly against him, her face hidden in the curve of his neck, her fingers digging into his muscles, and he reached up and pulled the sheet over them.

When they woke the following morning, Kelly could hear the thudding of shells in the distance and somewhere not far away the tap-tapping of a machine gun. It sounded slow and old, as though it were a relic from the Great War. Then he became aware of Teresa's head against his shoulder. He felt faintly guilty, feverish and absurd, but, as he turned to look at her, he saw her eyes were open, large and wondering and blue. As his lips touched hers, her arms went swiftly round his neck.

'Marry me, Teresa,' he said.

'We are already married, George Kelly,' she said. 'As married as we'll ever be. More married than my professor will ever be now.'

He tried to extract a promise but she remained wary and noncommittal as if she had no confidence in the future.

'I wonder if it's all been worthwhile,' she said, as though she doubted even her own beliefs. 'I wonder how much difference it

35

will make when the war's over who won. Who'll be any better off in all the poverty and debt? People don't meet these days as they should, and falling in love is like being on a bicycle back-pedalling. You put in a lot of hard work and get nowhere. Love includes having a future, too.'

'There *is* a future,' he insisted. 'Come with me when I leave. We can be married in St. Jean de Luz.'

She smiled in a way that seemed to imply willingness but she still made no promises.

They left the hotel together. It was clear the end was near because the guns now seemed to be only at the end of the street. Teresa looked tired but she seemed to have recovered her spirits.

'I'm glad what happened between us did happen,' she admitted. 'With all the world dying about us, it makes it all the more sensible that the rest of us should go on living.'

They spent the day in the old Citroën trying to contact people and send them to the British Club. They were all ready with what they could carry, all save Mrs. Fotheringay, who had disappeared from the address where Kelly had found her the previous day, and they decided she'd gone alone to join Miss Jenner-Neate.

When they reached the club in the evening it was drizzling a little and the streets were empty. 'Looks a bit like Liverpool on a wet day,' Kelly said. 'With the shops shut, the Irish away at Blackpool and the Protestants staying at home and keeping the King's Peace.'

The smashed rooms contained thirteen depressed-looking people and Miss Jenner-Neate was in a fury.

'Mrs. Fotheringay's dog's disappeared,' she said, 'and she insists on looking for it.'

They led those who'd arrived down to the jetty and aboard *Jimmy*. The Greek captain was almost in tears at the delay, and unless the missing people turned up in the next hour or two, it was clear they were going to be delayed until the following evening because, with the Italian guns now able to cover the harbour and the German bombers constantly overhead, it would be impossible to move except under cover of darkness.

'Perhaps there are others we can persuade to leave,' Teresa said.

Kelly was unwilling but she was insistent. 'We have twenty-four hours,' she pointed out. 'And Neila is still arresting anybody who's ever indulged in defeatist talk or done anything to harm the cause.'

It was impossible to argue with her. She seemed lost in a morass of her own thoughts, and he saw there were tears in her eyes as she drove off in the old Citroën.

The city seemed fuller and the people more terror-stricken than ever. The Italians had occupied Torrelavega, cutting off the retreat of the Basques to Asturias, and there was wild firing in the streets. Two battalions came stumbling through, exhausted and defeated.

'*Estamos copados*!' they were shouting. 'We were surprised!'

A battery of 75s followed to protect the city centre but the gunners clearly had no wish to stay long because they were without ammunition. A squadron of Doniers came over, invisible in the darkness, and the 75s fired their last shells. A few men knocked out windows and made holes in walls for a last stand, and as night fell it was possible from the Jauregui Hotel to see flames and smell the smoke.

There was no sign of Teresa returning and once again Kelly grew worried. A lorry went past, crammed with typewriters, files and desks, a guard sitting on the back, his heavy boots dangling. A rash of new posters had appeared on the walls, carrying a crude political appeal to every Republican to denounce defeatist or rightist talk, but they were ugly, lacking in style and totally devoid of skill.

Worried, as soon as it was light Kelly went to the British Club, hoping that Teresa had gone there. But there had been no sign of her. There was a message from Smart in *Badger*, however, warning him that the bombing had forced him to take the ship to the safety zone for neutral ships at the other side of the bay.

It was beginning to look difficult now, and, guessing Teresa would turn up later, Kelly headed for the quay to make sure the Greek captain held to his promise. It was dawn and the water was lapping against the steps. Even the gulls had not yet roused themselves, and in the early morning freshness there was a curious kind of foreboding. When he reached the waterfront, he found that *Jimmy* had disappeared. The Greek had finally thrown in the sponge and bolted without waiting for the last of his passengers, and, livid with fury, Kelly returned to the British Club to count noses. There were still nine British nationals left, together with the Albanian and Miss Jenner-Neate. There were also one or two Spanish sent by Teresa, and Mrs. Fotheringay had turned up, in high spirits at having recovered her dog. He told her icily that she'd risked everybody's life for her bloody dog, and she promptly burst into tears.

There seemed nothing to do but find a launch and get them out to *Badger*, but the harbour was full of confusion. The mine-sweepers which had kept the bay clear of mines were just heading away from the quay for Santoña, packed with people. The terms for the capitulation had just been received and there was little doubt now that they'd be accepted.

The August sun polished the closed and level waters of the harbour until they shone like silver. By this time the first of Franco's troops were pushing into the city and the balconies were already full of hangings in the colours of the monarchy, and even fascist songs were being heard. Every boat in the place with an engine and a great many without were following the minesweepers, packed until the gunwales were only just above the water with suitcases, bedding and people. Even as he watched, he saw a rowing boat capsize and the people fished out of the water by a following launch, wailing about their lost belongings.

In the end, he found a whaler and with the greatest of difficulty an ill-matching set of oars, and, with the Albanian, carried them to the boat. Then, leaving the Albanian guarding their prize, he went to fetch everybody from the British Club.

When he arrived there was still no sign of Teresa and Miss Jenner-Neate handed him a letter. He recognised the writing on the envelope at once and as he opened it he saw it was on notepaper headed 'Office of Chief of Police.'

'*I am being allowed to write this note to you, George Kelly,*' he read. '*Because I have helped people out of compassion, I am accused of treachery and informed that I must pay for it. I am not afraid. I am a good Catholic, despite my Republicanism, and the step into the darkness is really only a step into another life beyond. Perhaps we shall meet again. I send you my love and my life. Your Teresa.*'

For a moment he stared at it disbelievingly, then slowly, his hand crushed the paper into a ball and he swung round on Miss Jenner-Neate.

'Get everybody together,' he said. 'I'm going to the Chief of Police's office. When I return we'll be leaving.'

The Presidencia was calmer than the town. Basque guards wearing berets watched by its garden wall but inside they were preparing to hand over to the advancing Franco troops. The man Kelly spoke to was nothing but a clerk and he seemed already to be afraid of death. 'Colonel Neila flew to France this morning,' he said.

'What about prisoners?'

'There are no prisoners, señor. The last were released when the Colonel left.'

Kelly placed the letter he'd received on the desk and smoothed its crumpled surface.

'This woman,' he said. 'Where is she then?'

The clerk took the letter and studied it. Then he slowly lifted frightened eyes to Kelly's face and pushed a sheet of paper across. It bore the previous day's date and was scored across by a stroke of red ink.

'They were shot last night, señor.'

The paper contained seven names and the last one was 'Condesa de Fayon.'

That night, with the town sporting fascist colours and emblems and the Falangists firing from the balconies, Kelly led the group from the British Club to the harbour. His face was taut and bitter and he was filled with loathing for his charges. They had risked the necks of sailors, and finally taken Teresa's life. She was now only a cherished image to be hugged to himself like a secret. He'd been full of an irrational and indefensible belief that he'd only had to speak to her to claim her, but war, politics and the ambitions of ruthless men had snatched her away into the darkness, and he felt he couldn't even bear to think of her.

Between the blocks of flats and thick rows of sandbags were motor lorries, the pavements packed with men and women holding children or lying down with them to sleep on the ground. On the quays, men were throwing arms into heaps – rifles, revolvers, machine guns, cartridge belts – and more men were marching into the port to disarm and disperse. There was a mist like milk on the water as they climbed into the whaler where the Albanian was sitting shivering.

Tersely, Kelly explained to people who'd never handled a large sweep before what they must do and they pushed off in the dusk, the oars crashing against each other. Gradually they got the hang of it, and in the mist picked their way down the harbour to the open sea. There were empty and capsized boats everywhere, floating oars and what seemed to be dozens of bodies, but by the grace of God they made it to the neutral zone and finally bumped alongside *Badger*. The other British aboard greeted them rapturously and in his cabin, staring at himself in the mirror, Kelly heard a tap on the door.

It was Smart. 'It's the evacuees, sir,' he said. 'They'd like to have you in the wardroom. They'd like to propose a toast.'

Kelly lifted his head. 'Tell them,' he said slowly and coldly, 'to go to hell.'

He was still lying wide awake in his bunk when they struck the mine. The crash flung him to the deck and he picked himself up, shedding the books, papers and other articles that had fallen from the shelves on top of him. As he hurried on deck, still dazed and stunned, the ship lay dead in the water, steam roaring into the darkness. Men were running in all directions, but there was order in the confusion. Crash mats and hoses were being dragged forward, and he was pleased to see that orders were being given calmly. A centuries-old discipline had taken control and *Badger's* crew were getting on with their jobs quietly.

'Them fucking Spanish!' someone said, but it wasn't a cry of panic or even of fury, just one of disgust.

The ship was taking in water forward and amidships. 'A' gun was useless, the boiler room was flooding and the wardroom a shambles. By the grace of God, the party for the refugees had just finished and they'd been led to one of the mess flats where they'd been given hammocks. They clustered on deck now near the torpedo tubes, frightened, tired and bewildered, and Kelly saw the indefatigable Miss Jenner-Neate bullying them into some sort of order.

The engineer was just reporting to Smart. Number two boiler had just gone out and there were no electrics and no

40

hydraulic power. The engine room had been only superficially damaged, however, and the engine room staff were struggling to shore up the bulkhead and pump out the boiler room.

'How about casualties?' Kelly asked.

'So far four killed,' Smart said. 'But we think there may be a couple more. Seven injured, two seriously. We'll be towing her into St. Jean de Luz. We've already radioed and *Brazen's* answered. More than likely it was a German mine laid by an Italian ship. It's as bad as being at war.'

Kelly turned. 'As bad as?' he snapped. 'Dammit, we *are* at war! Here, it's just started a little early.'

4

The late March dawn came wet, cold and grim, the waves changing gradually from night-time black to iron-blue and eventually to a cheerless green-grey.

The war had come exactly as Kelly had predicted. With disarmament and pacifism rampant in Britain, the will to withstand the bullying of the dictators had been sapped. Appeasement wasn't just the will of the politicians, it was the will of the nation – something that had become obvious from the tumult of joy when Chamberlain had returned from Munich after knuckling his forelock to Hitler – and the Czechs, the Austrians and the Albanians had been sacrificed to the dictators in the hope of buying them off. Unfortunately the dictators had asked for more and, shamed at last into standing up for the Poles, a nation they couldn't even reach, London and Paris had finally been edged – 'shoved' was perhaps a better word – into war. And Kelly, with the bonus of an extra stripe on his sleeve, had been snatched from the shore job at Portsmouth, where he'd found himself after a year on the staff of the C.-in-C., Home Fleet, given the Flotilla leader, *Feudal*, and a group of ill-assorted escorts and thrust into convoy duties across the Atlantic. Like everybody else, he knew little about the job and was having to learn as he went along, but it was better, by a long chalk, than Portsmouth where the house he had occupied – wired like a battleship with naval-type switches and plugs and shades like plantpots – had been furnished by a predecessor with the imagination of a cockroach.

As the light increased, the first things visible were the white crests of the waves, then he picked out the veins that marked where the wind had clawed them down the lee side. The sky was filled from one horizon to the other with close banks of cloud that looked like old hard-packed snow, grey, dirty and ugly, and the rain fell in squally flurries in a steep, slanting drizzle that blew across the ship, blurring the horizon, so that the point where the watery sky met the sea was ill-defined, as if the two elements ran into each other and they were steaming into a sombre moving mass that curved down ahead of them and swept back below.

From *Feudal*'s bridge, Kelly stared back at the convoy he was leading. As the long steely waves from the south-west swept by in a never-ending succession, the ships bobbed their heads, bowing in obeisance to the gale before lifting them again and falling once more, to raise their sterns as they slid into the trough ready for the next act of obeisance. The smaller ships seemed to vanish entirely in the vast valleys of water until only their funnels and mastheads were visible and they seemed at times to be on their last long journey down to the immemorial ooze two miles below.

Behind *Feudal*, beyond the commodore ship, there was a forest of moving masts, funnels, samson posts and cargo booms, as freighters, tankers and passenger ships rolled and pitched and danced eastwards towards Britain. As the convoy executed its change of course, it was not at first noticeable, just that the ships appeared to be showing a different profile, and where Kelly had been looking at their bows now he was on the starboard beam as they swung to port. Every ship did the same thing, swinging slowly, adjusting position so that they simply changed lines and faced the stern of a different ship.

As the watery sun sent an unexpected ray down from the packed clouds, the light caught the curve of wet bows. The change of course put the wind in a different direction and instead of the spray swinging back on either side of the bridge, it now slashed directly across it, soaking the men who stood there so that they hitched at the towels they wore round their necks as scarves.

Though to other ships her decks seemed empty and she seemed to be devoid of crew, in fact *Feudal* was humming with activity. Throughout her length, auxiliary machinery, dynamos and ventilating fans filled the alleyways with background noise, and the cooking smells that pervaded the ship mingled with the smell of oil, vomit, and that curious acrid blend of steam and electricity which was always present where there was marine machinery.

Despite the curious passivity of the front in France – what the Americans with their gift for apt phrases were calling the Phoney War – nobody aboard was kidding himself that Britain had taken advantage of the lull. At home there were still plenty of holidays, and even with the war privilege had not vanished. Though the wealthy younger elements were rushing to the services, their parents were carefully establishing themselves in comfort in safe areas, determined to survive, and there had been little increase in war production. The Air Force was still short of aeroplanes, and the Army was still short of tanks, and there was a story, probably apocryphal, about a staff course at Camberley where an officer had been criticised for an overdeveloped sense of humour for mounting an imaginary anti-tank gun up a tree. He had defended himself briskly with the information that he had no idea what the weapon was like because he'd never seen one and, so it seemed, neither had anybody else.

The Navy was as short of ships. Though Britain had the largest and most professional navy in the world, it was desperately in need of reinforcements. Its strength on paper was misleading because half its ships had been designed for the earlier war, and though some had been refitted, many were obsolescent and some positively obsolete. Of those commissioned between the wars, some were magnificent but there were others, designed in a penny-pinching era, that were useless for fighting yet too slow to run away.

Though the Navy still remained the darling of the British people, who considered it its bulwark against aggression, the men in it knew that out of fifteen capital ships only two were of post-1918 vintage, and Kelly had long suspected in any case that battleships' bulk and low speed made them vulnerable to air and undersea attack, so that they could never be exposed without a fleet of smaller vessels as escort. Yet, because only a battleship could confront a battleship and since the Germans had built them too, blue-water admirals, who believed that ack-ack was better for ships than fighters, had been glad to build them in reply and they would have to be housed in secure anchorages until needed, absorbing thousands of men who might usefully have been employed on escort duties. It had not even been a battleship which had scored their only real success to date, the crippling of the pocket battleship, *Graf Spee*, in December, but three cruisers, every one of them outgunned.

It was a far grimmer war that was being fought by the lighter forces – and even they were far from perfect for their job. A destroyer was not an efficient escort vessel because her torpedoes were pointless for that duty, her low-angle guns valueless against aeroplanes, and her tremendous speed rarely needed. Her enormous engines occupied space that was needed for fuel and she required an unnecessarily large crew. The new escort sloops and corvettes that had been planned, though slower and smaller, were not only less cramped, but also less complex, and they could be built much more easily, while their armament laid stress chiefly on anti-aircraft weapons and depth charges.

From *Feudal's* bridge, Kelly could see the ship's company closed up at action stations. There were many newcomers among them, still going through the shocks of the changeover from peace to war. This war was a different one from the last, with different problems, though war itself remained the same and still brought out the same old human imperfections. The Hostilities-Only men were still struggling to become part of a crew. There still weren't many of them, but to them everything was horrifyingly new – the sea, the ship, even seasickness – and, with the battle fleets taking all the best destroyers, only the old ones were left for escort duties, so that they were all desperately tired, desperately dirty and desperately overstretched.

His mind busy, even as he was alert to what was going on around him, Kelly glanced to starboard. The old W-class ship, *Wrestler*, now converted to escort vessel, was just heaving herself out of a trough. To port was the armed merchantman, *Sappho*, formerly a Lampert and Holt ship. Bringing up the rear of the convoy was another converted destroyer, *Vandyke*, together with the corvette, *Sanderling*. By the standards of the day the convoy was well-protected.

To Kelly and everybody else who had taken the anti-submarine course at Portland, it had always seemed that a defensive policy was the only one that could be applied to convoy work: make the U-boats come to the escort, rather than form escorts into hunting groups to search the vast ocean spaces for the enemy. Perhaps the desire to assume the offensive had been implicit in everything the Admiralty had done since the signal, 'Winston is back,' had been sent out in 1939, but at a time when the submariners were also still learning, not only were the hunting groups achieving negligible successes but they were certainly not using their new radar sets properly by thundering about the sea after stale scents and false periscopes sighted by aircrews, trawler skippers and old gentlemen fishing from the ends of piers. Judging by the reports that had to be investigated, the sea was teeming with German U-boats, and the radar operators – still nervously believing their sets made them impotent – were new enough to the game to be regularly sick over their dials.

Kelly's own group had originally included the destroyers, *Firebrand* and *Fortunate*, the escort vessel, *Wheeler*, and the corvette, *Dunlin*, but these four had been snatched from him to oversee a convoy from Nova Scotia which was supposed to have joined them and never had. But, as everybody knew, when an escort group was named, the only thing that was certain was the leader, while the rest depended on what was available.

There had been a brush with a U-boat during the night. It had come to nothing, but Kelly was in no doubt that other submarines would have been called into the assault, because the Germans were beginning to realise that, against the new devices being used against them, it was necessary to contribute numbers. As full daylight came, he began to relax. It might be possible now to go below, change, and perhaps even snatch a little sleep. He had got over Teresa's death more quickly than he could have imagined possible, and had wondered uncomfortably more than once if his feelings for her sprang merely from the fact that she looked like his long-lost Charley. It had become still easier when it had dawned on him that she'd never intended to leave Santander with him. She'd gone back again and again into danger because she'd had to, afraid to live and because of her faith unafraid to die. He'd been angry at her sacrifice and bitter at what he felt were her muddled beliefs, but the anger and the bitterness had finally died, and in New York, lonely as he watched his officers and men stream ashore to enjoy themselves with the bright lights and the girls, his thoughts had turned again to Charley Upfold.

Was it six years, or was it seven since she'd sailed in *Maure-tania* for a job in New York? He'd looked her up in the telephone directory under her married name of Kimister and again under her maiden name of Upfold, but there had been nobody who could possibly have been her. The only person he knew who could still have been in contact with her to give her address was her sister, Mabel, but she was in England and married to a retired colonel of the Devons, who had somehow got himself back into the army and across the Channel to France.

'I'm going below for a wash, Number One,' he said to the first lieutenant. 'But don't for a minute imagine we've thrown him off because I dare bet our particulars have been passed to every U-boat in the area not wearing an ear trumpet.'

As he reached his cabin, Rumbelo was waiting for him. The same old Rumbelo, recalled to service and happy to be back with Kelly. With a son serving in the destroyer, *Grafton*, it was hard on Rumbelo to have to return to sea, because he'd just got used to being settled at Thakeham. But he hadn't grumbled, accepting it as normal, and grateful to be back with Kelly instead of in some unrewarding job ashore. The gap that had appeared between them when, to Rumbelo's disgust, Kelly had married the wrong woman in 1927, had happily disappeared when the marriage had broken up, and Rumbelo and Biddy and their children had taken the place, with Hugh Withinshawe, of the family that Kelly had never had.

He was just reaching out to take Kelly's cap when the buzzer went, and his hand changed its direction automatically to lift the instrument and pass it to Kelly.

'Sir! Bridge! *Wrestler* has a contact!'

Snatching his cap back, Kelly hurried for the ladder. Below him, as he reached the bridge screen, was the four-inch gun and the forecastle streaming with water, the chain cables rising and falling as the bow drove into the sea.

'Where's *Wrestler* now?' he demanded at once of the officer of the watch.

'She's moved astern, sir.'

'Very well, we'll join her. Bring her round to starboard.'

There was silence among the men alert at their action stations. Most of them were peacetime regulars with seven, twelve or twenty-two-year engagements, many of them enlisted in the years of the Depression to avoid unemployment. A lot of them had been awaiting their release when the war had broken out and among them were recalled men like Rumbelo, often middle-aged and in no condition for the spartan regime of a destroyer's mess decks in the Atlantic. There were also a few Naval Reservists, trawlermen and merchant seamen, who, if not very good yet at their drill, were skilled seamen, and one or two Naval Volunteer Reservists, the Saturday afternoon sailors, mostly pure amateurs with more enthusiasm than expertise. But even they were learning fast, and they all of them – from the captain downwards – belonged to a small and closely-kept community, from which they could never escape. Aboard a destroyer, there was little time or room for pleasure and never freedom from noise or movement. Perhaps it was the one thing that held them together and made them a team.

As *Feudal* came round on the starboard side of the convoy, they saw that *Wrestler* had hoisted a signal and the yeoman of signals sang out. 'Wrestler in contact, sir!'

Kelly's eyes narrowed. William Latimer, the captain of *Wrestler* was well-known to him. He had met him in 1927 up the Yangtze, when they'd stood alongside each other at Chinkiang with a small group of sailors holding off a mob of Chinese intent on murdering every white in sight. Kelly had been a lieutenant-commander then and Latimer had been a midshipman. He'd done well in the intervening years, though *Wrestler* was his first ship and he was still young enough and enthusiastic enough to want to depth-charge everything from a clump of seaweed to a shoal of herring.

Wrestler was steering away from the convoy now, pitching drunkenly, huge sheets of spray lifting over her bridge. She was steaming full ahead and it seemed that Latimer was going to drop something, if only for luck. At that moment, another flag fluttered to *Wrestler*'s yard arm.

'*Wrestler* attacking, sir!'

They all watched, wondering how good the contact was, and saw the depth-charges go down. After a few moments the sea bulged and huge columns of grey-green water rose high above them. As the spray settled, they waited with their glasses trained.

'From *Wrestler*, sir. "Lost contact."'

As they came round, the spray slashing across the bridge to coat it with a thin sparkling crust and fill mouths with the taste of salt, they were close to the other ship, and Kelly leaned on the bridge coaming, his eyes narrow and glittering as he watched from under the tarnished gold of his cap.

'Call her up, yeoman. Tell her to continue her search and ask her the nature of the contact.'

As the stream of flags shot up and the lamp flickered, the yeoman called out. 'Contact firm, sir. Classified as U-boat, moving to port.'

'Ask 'em what they think now?'

'Still think it's a U-boat,' Latimer replied. '"I can call spirits from the vasty deep."'

Kelly smiled. Where most naval officers relied on the Bible for their clever signals, Latimer used Shakespeare. He'd quoted *The Merchant of Venice*, he remembered, as they'd stood on the bund at Chinkiang under a shower of brickbats from the Chinese mob.

He guessed Latimer was right. If the submarine had been on the point of attacking the convoy when she was contacted she would certainly have moved in the direction Latimer had indicated.

'Make "Continue the search!"' he said.

Together, the two ships watched the convoy pass them, moving slowly through the water, suspecting that the U-boat would continue to follow the merchantmen. As *Feudal* swung in a wide circle towards *Wrestler*, the Asdic-repeater's note was monotonous, thin and featureless above the thump and crash and hiss of the waves, then suddenly it changed to a solid echo that made the operator jump. In his tiny soundproofed compartment, his straining ears were almost deafened.

'Asdic to bridge! H.E. reciprocating engines green oh-one-oh!'

Kelly spoke over his shoulder to the yeoman of signals. 'Make to *Wrestler* "Have strong contact."'

The Asdic echo sharpened. 'Contact moving slowly right!'

'Starboard twenty!'

As the speed dropped, the Asdic's note came more clearly. Ping-ping-ping-pong.

'Good God, we're almost on top of him!' Kelly snapped. 'Full

49

ahead both. Depth charge crews stand by – fire pattern. All guns prepare to engage to starboard.'

'Target drawing away right.'

As the amatol-packed canisters exploded, the sea was split apart with an effervescent roar. Hundreds of tons of foam-white water rose slowly, hung motionless against the sky, then dematerialised into spray to fall back to the surface in a scum of dirty froth. As it settled, the Asdic operator called out.

'Lost contact, sir!'

Even as his voice died, however, the yeoman of signals came in again. '*Wrestler*'s signalling, sir. "In contact."'

'Good for *Wrestler*!'

The excitement was intense, everybody holding his breath. *Wrestler* was coming round like an express train now, the waves lifting over her bridge in a vast cloud of spray, and they saw the depth charges arc outwards from her stern and drop into her wake. A few moments later, the sea domed, lifted in a colossal mushroom and disintegrated in spray drifting over the foamy circle where the explosive had disturbed it.

'Contact, sir! Moving left!'

Somewhere below them, the submarine was trying to squirm to safety, and, weaving in at right angles to complete the lethal pattern, *Feudal* dropped her own charges, and they saw the sea erupt once more.

'Contact lost, sir.'

But *Wrestler* was hurtling past at full speed, bunting fluttering at the yardarm.

'*Wrestler* still in contact, sir.'

As *Feudal* swung, *Wrestler* lay over on her beam ends and they saw the depth charges go again.

'U-boat surfacing, sir! – port bow!' The yell came from the bridge look-out, wild and excited, and as the sea settled, from the blur of spray a black shape like a pointing hand rose at a steep angle to the surface, exposing sixty feet of the U-boat's bows, with the jumping wire and the dark holes of the torpedo tubes and a belly streaked with rust and weed. All round it the sea boiled with the escaping air.

Immediately, X-gun fired and the first shot struck at water level as the lifting steel tube steadied. Then the pom-pom crew got going and, enveloped in smoke and spray, the great helpless metal whale lurched, lifted higher, paused, as though suspended from the sky, then began to slide slowly back. As it went, there was a heavy underwater explosion and it vanished in a swirling whirlpool of water.

This time, as the sea resumed its place, they saw it was black with oil and in it things were floating – bits of wood, clothing, a life jacket. *Wrestler* stopped, her bow dipping as her speed dropped, and lay surrounded by wreckage, her crew crowding the rails busy with buckets and grappling hooks.

'*Wrestler* reports a body, sir. They have it on board.'

As they surged past on the side away from the debris, the two ships looked like wooden horses on a fairground roundabout, moving up and down, one against the other, as they lifted to the waves, two old grey horses with sides that were streaked with rust and caked with salt. Men on both ships were cheering each other and waving congratulations and Latimer was on the bridge of *Wrestler* as they went past, yelling into the loud-hailer.

'We now have *two* bodies!'

As they drew ahead, Kelly waved. 'Make "Well done,"' he said to the yeoman of signals. Though the submarine would be credited to the group, it was undoubtedly *Wrestler*'s victory.

The lamp clattered and it was without surprise that Kelly heard the yeoman sing out.

'*Wrestler* replying. "I have done service to the state. Othello."' Trust Latimer to come up with something clever, Kelly thought. 'Make "Resume station and confine signals to facts."'

That ought to shut him up, he thought with a grim smile. There was no point in squashing enthusiasm but, given a chance, Latimer would be sending sonnets. He'd buy him a drink when they got home to show there was no ill-feeling.

5

Inishtrahull and Kintyre vanished into the mist astern and dawn was just breaking over the mountains of Argyllshire as *Feudal* led the convoy into the Clyde. The channel opened in front of them, with the silent pinnacle of Ailsa Craig, the jagged summit of Arran and, beyond, the softer outline of Bute. Strung along the shore were the coastal resorts of Ayrshire and Dumbarton, then they passed the Cloch light into Greenock. To the north the tawny and purple mountains lifted, and finally the coast crumbled into a rubbish heap of ugly tenements and warehouses.

Mail came aboard, mostly bills, but there was a letter from Hugh to inform Kelly he hoped to see him shortly. He had joined the Fleet Air Arm before the war was a fortnight old and he was now finishing his training on Sea Gladiators. He'd not swerved in his belief in air power, but it had pleased Kelly that he'd chosen the Navy.

Below decks, the sailors were still swearing to the Customs men that the nylons they'd bought in New York were personal gear, and a furious stoker was drinking himself silly on bourbon rather than let the government officials have it, when the Rear-Admiral (D)'s barge was seen approaching from the pier.

'Hello,' the Sub said. 'Something in the wind!'

The Admiral was in a hurry and not inclined to mince words. The prevailing mood as they'd tied up to the buoy had been light. They were due for a boiler-clean and a boiler-clean meant leave, and the feeling of relief had been clear throughout the ship. The first lieutenant had had his little joke with the coxswain and the cook with Jack Dusty, and somehow they were all together. But now suddenly, the sky had clouded over, because an admiral didn't appear alongside a ship at full speed

52

and scramble over the side just to inform them that a boiler-clean was all right with him. There was something unpleasant in the offing; and in a moment, the lighthearted jokes became bitter, and the word 'bastard', which had been a term of affection up to that moment, suddenly had a sharper edge.

The Admiral pulled no punches. 'You'll have to put off your boiler-clean,' he said. 'It's hard, I know, but there it is. We're short of ships. Between 'em, the politicals have just about done for us and I don't know which I detest most — the ancient glittering eyes of the reactionaries or the joyless dogma of the left wing intellectuals.'

Rumbelo passed over a drink and, as the Admiral swallowed it, Kelly probed gently. 'What's the job, sir?'

The Admiral grunted. 'We suspect the Germans are up to something in the North. Max Horton stationed his submarines down the Norwegian coast weeks ago and they were in a position to stop the Germans, but those asses in Westminster wouldn't have it and they've been withdrawn.'

'And us, sir?'

'We're making up a new flotilla. You'll lose *Sappho* and *Sanderling* but you're getting *Freelance*. They're sneaking ore ships down the Inner Leads and we think there's going to be trouble because we have reports of capital ships moving in Kiel and Wilhelmshaven. You're to take station off Narvik and keep watch. And while you're there, you're to keep a look out for *Köldom*. She's an old freighter but she's believed to be carrying German naval and military experts from the Argentine. They've been there ever since we got *Graf Spee* in December, and some of them are important. She's probably even armed and we think she's making for home, because she was reported up near the Denmark Strait, heading for Bergen. Admiral Whitworth's up there with *Renown* and four destroyers, and the Twentieth Destroyer Flotilla's been ordered to join him. You'll be attached for orders.'

'When do we leave, sir?'

'At once. *Freelance* will join you from Scapa en route.'

The nylons remained on board as the Customs men were shooed off at full speed and the stoker who'd polished off the bourbon was heard complaining drunkenly that he'd sunk his bloody booze at the rush for nothing. On the whole, though, they took it quietly, almost too quietly, because so long as the lower deck had a drip on the Navy was all right. There was a minor brush forward when the chief buffer ticked someone off for leaving his dhobying about, and when the officer of the day went to attend to it, an unidentified voice from the back shouted 'You can chew my starboard nipple!'

In the end Kelly cleared lower deck and explained the situation, talking quietly and avoiding resounding phrases. They accepted it in good spirit. He'd once considered he was no good with any words but swear-words, but he'd since learned he was considered an excellent speaker. He tried it man to man on them and insisted that he'd get them leave as soon as he could, but for the moment it was felt that the Germans were on the move and they had a job to do. As he turned away, the ship was as still as a church, but within half an hour from his cabin he heard a raucous voice singing. 'Officers don't worry me – not much – !'

He smiled. It was going to be all right.

They slipped the buoy at nightfall and steamed south for Kildonan, Sanda and the Mull of Kyntyre, the very route they'd just covered in the opposite direction. But then, instead of turning south-west, they turned north and headed towards Islay and Tiree. The next morning, *Freelance* joined them off Cape Wrath and they headed north round the Shetlands.

As they headed into the North Sea, the flotilla signals officer handed Kelly a signal.

'KOLNDOM PASSED NORTH OF ICELAND AND FAEROES. NOW BELIEVED OFF NARVIK MOVING SOUTH INSIDE NORWEGIAN TERRITORIAL WATERS.'

'Let's just hope that by the time we arrive,' Kelly said, 'she's *outside* Norwegian territorial waters.'

Making their landfall off Trondheim, the four destroyers swept north in line astern. What they might expect, Kelly had no idea. He didn't think *Kölndom* would cause much trouble, but German destroyers were said to be operating off the coast of Norway to protect German ships carrying Swedish iron from Narvik. And the German destroyers were bigger than the British, while with two converted V/W class ships, his flotilla could hardly be called a strong one.

It was bitterly cold, because spring hadn't yet shown any signs of arriving in these northern latitudes, and the land – towering walls of black rock and snow, with patches of green and the darker verdure of pine trees – was faintly depressing. There were also large coils of thick mist that made visibility uncertain and worried him in case he missed his quarry. There was a lot of traffic in the Leads and, with the mist growing thicker, the look-outs were warned to be doubly alert.

'We'd look fine if we ran into her,' the first lieutenant said.

'There's nothing like a collision,' Kelly agreed, 'to ruin your entire day.'

Nobody knew what *Kölndom* looked like but someone found an old copy of *The Times* in the wardroom which showed her alongside *Graf Spee* in the harbour of Montevideo. It wasn't a good picture because she was half obscured, but she seemed more modern than they'd expected, about eight thousand tons with a high bow and a flaring billet-head. She didn't look desperately fast but Kelly was under no delusion that even if she didn't carry a gun there would be arms on board.

It was as dusk approached on the second day that the navigator spotted her making south, a grey-hulled ship hard to see against the misty background of the land. As they closed, it was possible to pick out the German ensign and finally the name on her stern.

'There are two torpedo boats with her, sir,' the officer of the watch called out, his binoculars to his eyes. 'Norwegian, I think.'

'Signal her to stop.'

As they drew closer, the Norwegian vessels ranged themselves alongside *Kölndom*, preventing the destroyers from going close, and abreast Sebring Fjord, she swung abruptly to port, increased speed and vanished through the narrow entrance, with the Norwegians close behind, blocking the channel.

Kelly beat softly on the bridge coaming with his gloved fist. 'Bloody Norwegians,' he muttered. 'Their idea of neutrality seems to be curiously weighted in favour of Hitler.'

Feudal lay off the entrance to the fjord, with *Freelance*, *Wrestler* and *Vandyke* further out to sea watching the escape route. They had reached an impasse. The naval and military experts on board *Kölndom* made her a legitimate target, but so far they were only suspected, and if they were not on board *Feudal* had no right to interfere. But what if they *were* on board?

Kelly was just wondering what to do when the signals officer handed him a signal.

'Home Fleet's out, sir,' he announced. 'They must be expecting a break-out of German capital ships, because we've got two battleships, a battle cruiser, four cruisers and twenty-one destroyers at sea.'

Kelly grunted. 'Last time the Home Fleet went looking for the Germans twenty-two years ago,' he said, 'it mustered thirty-five battleships and battlecruisers, twenty-six cruisers and eighty-five destroyers.'

He frowned, wondering if the break-out of German capital ships made it possible to push the matter of *Kölndom* a stage further. He was just considering the possibilities when one of the Volunteer Reserve officers by the name of Harstatt appeared on the bridge. 'Sir,' he announced. 'My father was a Norwegian who became a naturalised Englishman. I speak fluent German and Norwegian. Can I help?'

'I'm damn sure you can,' Kelly said, making up his mind at once. 'My German's very dubious and I have no Norwegian at all. Hail the Norwegians and invite the senior officer on board.'

The Norwegian commanding officer, a big man with hair as red as Kelly's own, was clearly unhappy at the situation but stiff with pride. 'Norway is not at war with Germany,' he insisted, 'any more than she is with Britain. My orders are to ensure our rights over our own waters.'

'Germany shows scant regard for your rights,' Kelly argued. 'I have reason to believe *Kölndom* has German naval and military experts aboard.'

The Norwegian shook his head. 'She has twice been examined since her entry into Norwegian waters and there are only German merchant sailors aboard. My instructions are to resist entry by force. My torpedo tubes are already trained on your ship.'

It appeared to be a deadlock and, as the Norwegian returned to his command, Kelly retired to his cabin with the flotilla signals officer and Harstatt.

'I dare bet the bugger never examined her,' he snapped.

56

'They're scared stiff of upsetting the Germans. What's your opinion, Harstatt?'

'I'm inclined to agree, sir.'

'Right. Then let's make a signal to the Admiralty asking for instructions. This seems to be a case for the Foreign Office, because any hurried action on our part might push Norway into the arms of the Nazis and nobody wants that.'

Taking the ship beyond the entrance to the fjord, they waited for the reply. Close under the bleak shore line with its high steep mountains and hidden inlets, it was bitterly cold and, as the early darkness came, the men on deck shivered, flapping their arms against the wintry weather. It was late in the evening and pitch dark when the reply came. Its text seemed to suggest that Churchill himself had had a hand in it.

'UNLESS NORWEGIANS WILLING TO ESCORT KOLNDOM TO BERGEN WITH JOINT ANGLO-NORWEGIAN GUARD ON BOARD YOU SHOULD TAKE POSSESSION PENDING FURTHER INSTRUCTIONS. SUGGEST YOU WARN NORWEGIANS HONOUR COULD BE SERVED BY SUBMITTING TO SUPERIOR FORCE.'

It seemed to cover everything and, closing the Norwegian torpedo boats from where *Feudal* could rake their decks without their torpedoes being able to reply, the sense of the signal was made clear.

There was a long wait, with them all grey-faced and red-nosed with the cold, then eventually the first lieutenant appeared at the door of Kelly's cabin, grinning.

'The Norwegians appear to have decided honour *is* satisfied, sir,' he announced. 'They're withdrawing.'

'Good.' Kelly reached for his cap and made for the bridge. The men by the guns and torpedo tubes looked expectantly at him, their faces pale in the shadows.

'Half ahead both. Navigator, keep your eye on that chart. Let's have the look-outs alerted.'

Slowly they picked their way into the dark fjord. It was faintly awe-inspiring in its silence and loneliness, with only the low hum of the turbines and the wash of the oily water alongside. Rounding a bend, they saw *Kölndom*, her bows facing shorewards, her hull black against the snow.

'Is she aground?'

'No, sir, up against the ice so that if they have to, their "guests" can escape across it.'

Kelly nodded. 'We'll board. Harstatt had better do it since he speaks German.'

The first lieutenant drew attention to packing cases lashed on *Kölndom*'s deck. 'She's supposed to have hidden six-inchers, sir. Could they be behind the cases?'

Kelly grunted. 'If they are, we'll just have to see who shoots faster. Have the guns trained on them and at the slightest movement from them, they're to fire.'

As he turned, he bumped into Rumbelo, waiting by the ladder. He was clad in gaiters and steel helmet and was armed with a revolver.

'Where the hell are you going?' Kelly demanded.

'Reporting for the boarding party, sir.'

Kelly grinned. 'Take 'em off, Albert,' he said. 'Tin hats always did look like tits on mountains on you.'

'Aren't we going aboard her, sir?'

'No, we're not. War's a young man's game and you and I are too bloody old these days.'

Rumbelo looked hurt, then he grinned. 'I thought I might as well try, sir.'

Clearly the only way to handle the business was to go alongside *Kölndom* as fast as possible. Her captain had trained his searchlight on *Feudal*'s bridge in the hope of blinding her officers and, as they approached, she suddenly went astern at full speed in the hope of ramming.

'Full astern, both!' The navigator spoke calmly into the engine room voice pipe. 'Hard-a-starboard!'

Kölndom's blunt stern scraped *Feudal*'s bow and, as they slid alongside, Harstatt leapt like a stag for *Kölndom*'s deck. The petty officer who followed him missed by a yard and fell into the icy water from which he was only rescued by a hastily thrown rope. As the rest of the party scrambled across, there was a hurried scuffle then a shot crashed across the silent fjord and *Kölndom* slid slowly ahead, her bows crunching into the ice, until she was brought up sharp with a jerk, her nose aground. Another flurry of shots came and one of the boarding party fell, then the German crew began to scramble over the side.

'You all right, Harstatt?'

Kelly's breath hung frostily in the air as he shouted. Harstatt appeared from below and waved. 'Yes, sir. One of the Jerries attempted to move the ship's telegraph. We have the experts, sir, two of them naval captains. There's also a German general as well, to say nothing of reams of documents and instruments that look as if they've come off *Graf Spee*. I had one man wounded as the crew got ashore.'

The Germans who had escaped ashore were sniping at *Feudal*'s crew now but, easy targets against the snow, they were quickly silenced. Kelly made up his mind quickly.

'We'll tow you off,' he shouted. 'And put a prize crew aboard. See that your prisoners are shoved below hatches. You'll be sailing her back to England.'

They had just seen *Kölndom* off to the west with her secrets, when the signals officer appeared with a long signal.

'Intercepted message from *Glowworm*, sir,' he announced. 'She appears to have sighted German heavy ships. *Repulse* is going to her assistance with four destroyers. We're ordered to join *Renown*.'

Half an hour later, as they turned west, the signals officer was back. '*Glowworm*'s stopped signalling, sir. It looks as if she's run into the enemy and been sunk.'

Kelly frowned. If *Glowworm* had indeed run into German heavies, the contest must have been short and sharp, and there would be little chance for her ship's company in the icy northern waters in the blackness of the night.

Outside the fjord a wind had got up from the north-west and as it increased they had to reduce speed. A signal arrived to indicate German ships were entering Oslo Fjord and approaching Bergen, Stavanger and Trondheim, and Kelly swore.

'This isn't a break-out!' he said. 'It's a bloody invasion!'

Their speed further reduced by the increasingly bad weather, they continued to head north and the following morning they learned that *Renown* had met and engaged the German battle-cruisers, *Gneisenau* and *Scharnhorst*, and that Admiral Forbes' group had been attacked by bombers and the destroyer, *Gurkha*, sunk. Half-way to their rendezvous, another signal ordered them to Narvik to support the Second Destroyer Flotilla. As they crashed northwards, the signals officer brought an intercepted signal from the Second Destroyer Flotilla itself.

NORWEGIANS REPORT GERMANS HOLDING NARVIK IN FORCE. SIX DESTROYERS AND ONE SUBMARINE. CHANNEL POSSIBLY MINED. INTEND ATTACKING AT DAWN HIGH WATER.

'Full revolutions,' Kelly ordered. 'I want to be there, too.'

With *Vandyck* and *Wrestler* trailing behind in the heavy seas, *Feudal* and *Freelance* arrived off the fjord in the early hours of the next day. As the revolutions dropped and the crashing of the water diminished, they could distinctly hear the sound of gunfire from deep inside the fjord.

'Second Flotilla seems to have found the Germans,' Kelly commented. 'Make to Admiralty, C-in-C, Home Fleet, and the Second Destroyer Flotilla: "Am going in, in support." Warn *Wrestler* to wait in the entrance as guard ship. *Freelance* and *Vandyke* to follow *Feudal*. They will operate independently.'

Through the mist, near the pilot station at Tranöy they caught sight of a large freighter heading north-east and a glimpse of the German flag at her stern, then the mist closed again and she was gone.

'Leave her,' Kelly ordered. 'We can pick her up on the way out.'

They passed the entrance to Tjeldsundetfjord, picking their way carefully through the swirling tendrils of smoky vapour, catching brief glimpses of the land as they went. It wasn't hard to guess that the Second Flotilla had done a lot of damage and was now on its way out. Hamnesholm, Tjellebotn and Djupvik slid past to starboard, the high hills covered with fir trees that were black against the snow, then, as they rounded the corner to where the narrow waters of Ofotfjord opened out, they saw a running fight approaching them, British destroyers retiring at full speed, followed by the bigger German vessels, which appeared to be coming from Herjangsfjord and Ballangenfjord opposite. The retiring destroyers seemed to have been caught between two forces, and one of the British ships was already disabled and drifting towards the shore near Virek, another was sinking and a third appeared to be out of control. Narvik harbour behind, in front of Framnes, was a shamble of sinking ships, the houses obscured by rolling clouds of black and yellow smoke where fires were burning, and through the confusion the Germans seemed to be firing with light field guns.

One of the fleeing destroyers was laying a smoke screen and it seemed a good idea to add to it.

'Full ahead both,' Kelly said. 'Make smoke. Hoist battle ensign.'

They were flying through the water now. Inside the fjord there seemed to be no wind, but the water was turbulent with the washes of swiftly-moving ships, so that *Feudal* kept lurching savagely, thumping into each small wave as if it were made of concrete, and they could hear the crash and rattle of crockery and tinware below. In the engine room, a red light had glowed on the bulkhead and valves were being adjusted to admit just too much oil and shut off just too much air to allow complete combustion. As the black coils began to pour from the funnels the first lieutenant looked up.

'Greasy hydrocarbons,' he said. 'Known as smoke.'

Kelly clung to his bridge stool as it bucked beneath him, unaware of the motion as the reflexes of years adjusted to enable him to keep his seat. With three minutes of smoke, they could lay a bank a mile long for the retreating ships, and the Germans weren't going to be in a hurry to plunge through it after them without knowing what was on the other side. As they crossed the paths of the oncoming ships at full speed, he turned to the voice pipe.

'Guns, I'm turning to starboard in a moment. We shall then be going through the smoke and you'll find the Germans just about red five as we come out. It'll take us just about two minutes. Open fire when you're ready.'

As they came round on to their own wake, they saw the British destroyers emerge from the smoke, tearing it into wisps with the speed of their passage, and a light flashed a message of thanks.

'Now for the Germans!'

'They have five-inchers against our four-point-sevens, sir,' the first lieutenant pointed out, not nervously but matter-of-factly.

'With a projectile twice as heavy,' Kelly agreed. 'Thank you,

Number One. I expect we'll manage.'

What little wind there was carried the smoke to port and, as they resumed course, they plunged into a darkness that stank of unburnt fuel oil. It filled their nostrils and lungs and made them cough, and the ship became silent with the silence of alertness.

For a while they endured the smoke, their eyes smarting, trying to hold their breath, then they were leaping clear of it into the daylight again just opposite Bogen Bay. Directly ahead was a large merchantman wearing the German flag. Her decks were crowded with soldiers and, as *Feudal* swung, her torpedoes plunged into the stirred water like swimmers in a racing dive. As they came round they saw a flash that completely obscured the German ship, then a second later there was a shattering crash that echoed and re-echoed among the surrounding hills.

A sheet of flame ran along the German's decks, flinging out scarlet tendrils as it went, then a coil of black smoke began to lift and swell, its centre filled with brilliant light. From the smoke, huge dark objects lifted up, whirring outwards to splash into the water, and momentarily Kelly saw the clear shape of a man, arms and legs flailing as he was flung high into the air. A colossal mushroom of brown smoke climbed upwards, spilling flaming debris. Beyond it the German ship had vanished, and beneath the pall the sea seemed to swirl under a shower of burning cordite, splintered lifeboats, wood, mess-stools, hammocks, oil-drums, even a funnel gyrating in the sky, and unidentifiable fragments that could have been clothes or men. The German ship had gone like a burst bubble in a single instant.

There was a stunned silence then the first lieutenant spoke. 'Ammunition,' he said.

The German ship had been torn apart and, as the smoke cleared they saw it had split in two, with the two halves, surrounded by swimming men, standing on end and sinking lower in the water as they passed them.

'Good old Ginger,' someone said with deep satisfaction just below the bridge. 'That's stopped the buggers coughing in church.'

As they swept through the smoke, they almost collided with *Freelance*, coming round from the other side. A light flickered from the other ship's bridge, and the yeoman of signals called out.

'*Freelance* signalling. "Do you come here often?"'

Kelly's mouth moved in a taut smile. There wasn't much wrong with morale when hard-pressed men could make signals like that. Resisting the impulse to reply in the same vein, he gave himself wholeheartedly to the job in hand. Beyond the sinking wreck of the ammunition ship, three German destroyers were just turning and they took them from the quarter. One of them reeled away, her after-deck smothered in flame; then, one behind the other, their guns blazing at point-blank range, *Feudal*, *Freelance* and *Vandyke* burst through the line. As *Feudal* swung again, however, leaning to the turn, the first lieutenant pointed and, swinging round, Kelly saw three more Germans coming from Bogen Bay on their own quarter, not more than two miles away. They had been lying at anchor behind the large island that filled the western half of the bay, and they were coming down now at full speed. Caught up against the islands of Lilandsgrund, *Feudal* had been trapped exactly as they had trapped the Germans, and she caught the full force of their vengeful fury.

It was a fierce encounter as they tried to hit back, conducted at lightning speed and with scant regard for science because they were too close. There was only time for the voice of the director-layer to reach the sweating guns' crews, then shells were bursting on either side of *Feudal*, the near misses rocking her, the stench of explosives sweeping down on her with the falling spray, the fragments clattering against the hull.

The guns were roaring furiously, their crews, unmoved by the tumult, aiming at the first enemy they saw in the murk of smoke, spray and mist. Another German reeled aside trailing smoke and flames as the guns recoiled, brass cylinders smoking, and the breeches clanged shut again. Two more hits sparked along the enemy hull, followed by a cheer that was drowned by an explosion abaft the bridge that hit home like a hammer and set *Feudal* staggering from the fight in her turn.

Another shell struck, then another, cutting off all communications systems and wrecking the electrics. A fourth smashed into her boiler room and she lost way at once, shuddering, and came to a stop, her nose bowing to the water, escaping steam roaring from her bowels, a shower of soot from the funnels coming down across the deck.

The ship was a shambles, gaping holes fringed by jagged edges of shining metal that lifted like the petals of a steel flower round her wounds. Among the debris were the scorched bodies of men, their blood draining into the scuppers. A blaze was roaring abaft the bridge, where cordite charges had caught fire, a shrieking white flame lifting up towards the masthead, its glow reflected on the dark water. The damage control party was already running forward with hoses, however, flinging the debris overboard and dragging the bodies aside, and badly wounded men were being placed in a row near the bridge ladder.

The Germans had vanished into the smoke and the guns had fallen silent, the guns' crews clearing the deck of the shell cases. One of them vomited over the side and, as the smoke cleared, propped up against the bulkhead in the glare of the flames, Kelly saw the remains of one of the torpedomen minus arms and legs and with his inside spilling out. Straightening up, the nauseated gunner began to yell hysterically but he was immediately grabbed by his friends and quietened. As the magazine parties emerged, grimy and puffy-eyed from the stinking darkness, the engineer lieutenant appeared to report, his face streaked with someone else's blood.

'What's it like?' Kelly asked.

'Pretty rough, sir. I've lost a lot of men. Given half an hour, though, I think I can get her moving.'

Kelly turned to glance towards the smoke. Second Flotilla had vanished seawards, accompanied by *Vandyke*, which appeared to be on fire aft, and *Freelance*, chased down the fjord by two of the German ships.

'I don't think we've *got* half an hour,' he said, and as he spoke, one of the Germans re-emerged from the smoke, her guns blazing. The torpedo gunner tried to hit her but, stopped as they were, he had neither swing nor spread and against the fast-moving target it was a vain hope.

The guns' crews tried to hit back, each gunlayer having to judge his own range and fall of shot, but the German ship had been joined now by two more from further up the fjord and A gun was the first to go. Then a fire broke out under B gun and it was clear *Feudal* had not much time left to live. The searchlight platform went and a fire started aft, stopping the supply of ammunition. The engineer lieutenant reappeared, sweating and faintly apologetic.

'I'm afraid it's no use, sir,' he reported. 'The water's gaining.'

The Germans had moved further up the fjord now to the help of their own shattered ships. It was quite clear *Feudal* was not going to move and, with a last salvo into her, they vanished into the smoke. As the shells struck, Kelly heard the clatter of metallic objects crashing to the deck, and saw the water stirred alongside as fragments whipped into it. The whole centre section of the ship was ablaze now and the smoke was so thick it was hardly possible to see. From the dark coils, he could hear men yelling, but even now there was no panic and the men emerging from below were all dragging wounded shipmates with them. Alongside, some of the men in the sea had become silent, floating with their heads fallen back, but torpedomen and engine room ratings were still struggling to lower a Carley raft and one of the leading seamen appeared on the bridge.

'Depth charges rendered safe, sir.'

Kelly looked at him with admiration, wondering at his calmness. 'Thank you. I'm glad to hear it.'

The ship's list was pronounced now. It didn't seem to be quite real. Rafts were drifting round the hull and more wounded men were being brought from amidships. The ship hadn't much longer to live and, with the Germans gone, Kelly was frantically searching his mind for something that would enable them all to escape. He'd been a prisoner in the last war and the idea of another spell didn't appeal. He glanced to the deck below him and saw Rumbelo there. His face was quite calm as he waited with Kelly's life jacket, and Kelly wondered what he was thinking and whether he were wishing he were back at Thakeham with Biddy.

The men on the deck were shivering as they stripped off their clothes. The water was so cold he knew that a lot of them wouldn't survive long, and with the shoreline covered with deep snow, even if they made it they'd freeze to death there.

He had almost resigned himself to a German prison when, through the smoke, he saw the shape of another destroyer approaching.

'Here we go again,' the navigator said in a flat resigned voice, and they were bracing themselves for the *coup de grace* when Rumbelo spoke.

'That's *Wrestler*, sir,' he announced quietly.

As *Wrestler* emerged, it was possible to recognise her by the four-incher that had been removed to make room for more depth-charges. She was coming down the fjord fast and, as she swung to come up astern, Kelly saw Latimer on the bridge giving orders.

He laid *Wrestler* alongside *Feudal* as neatly as if she were a ferry at the cross-channel berth at Dover, and men began to jump the gap.

'Go on, Rumbelo,' Kelly said. 'Get cracking.'

Rumbelo looked stubborn. 'I'll go when you go,' he said.

Wrestler had her outer scrambling nets down and on her quarter *Feudal*'s sole remaining boat was moving alongside. As the survivors clawed their way up her hull, the boat moved away again among the bobbing heads in the water, picking up swimming men. By this time there appeared to be no sign of life near *Feudal*'s bridge and the upper deck was deserted except for the huddled figures of the dead. The list had increased and she was well down by the bows.

'I think we won this bit of the war, sir,' Latimer called across. '*Vandyke* took a hit but she's making her own way home.'

Suddenly the fjord was very silent except for the splashing and the shouts of men in the water. Somewhere guns were still firing but they sounded muted now.

'Better come now, sir,' Rumbelo said as calmly as if he were suggesting that they crossed the road.

Kelly nodded and stepped across the gap between the two ships. Rumbelo waited until he was safe aboard before following himself. Willing hands grasped them. By this time, most of the men in the water had reached the nets and were being dragged aboard.

'Look slippy,' Latimer shouted.

As *Wrestler* went astern, they heard *Feudal*'s death rattle, a violent convulsion that ran through her slender hull, then a swirl of water spread from her bows and she began to plunge. For a moment, as her stern rose steeply, she seemed to hang, half-alive and half-dead, her bow deep in the water, her propellors silhouetted against the white sky. Then, with what sounded like a tired sigh, she slipped below, going swiftly, the angle of her descent steep. The last they saw of her was her stern still sticking out of the water and the tip of her mainmast with the white ensign still at the gaff.

6

The war had come to life with a vengeance.

The Navy had been at battle stations from two days before the declaration of hostilities and the areas of sea they had covered were vast. The advantage had always been with the enemy, however, and naval intelligence had often been incomplete, but, at least, unlike the army, the Navy was still virtually a force of regulars, trained to the last degree in the use of its weapons and the handling of its ships. Judging by some of the soldiers Kelly had seen heading for Norway, the army could not boast the same.

Intervention in Scandinavia had proved a disaster. The country was not only unprepared for war but it didn't even know how to fight it. Troops had been landed without their equipment and requests for information had only brought more questions so that, with everybody asking what in God's name was going on, orders had invariably proved to be out of date. Nevertheless, the Navy had not let the country down and the German seagoing forces had limped home battered, with the cruisers, *Blücher* and *Karlsruhe*, sunk; and the pocket battleship, *Lutzow*, the heavy cruiser, *Hipper*, the battle cruisers, *Scharnhorst* and *Gneisenau*, and the cruisers, *Köln* and *Bremse*, all damaged, to say nothing of a whole fleet of destroyers sunk or damaged at Narvik.

Perhaps it was as well, because after eight months of silence in France, with most of the casualties coming from road accidents, and most of the country feeling that the war, like an old soldier, would simply fade away, Hitler had launched across Holland, Belgium and Northern France the *blitzkrieg* that had devastated Poland the previous year. With the Allies still – despite Poland, despite Norway! – painstakingly building up the traditional forces of 1918, by May 20th they had reached the sea and split the allied armies in two.

At Thakeham, it was hard to believe that men were dying and that the remnants of the British Expeditionary Force were penned with units of the Belgian and French armies, into a tongue of land no more than forty miles deep and the same distance wide. People were still taking long week-ends and half-days off work, still planning their summer holidays, still playing cricket and working out whether they could hunt when the winter came. As the facts became known, they produced only a numbed disbelief and the country still sat back, content that the British Empire could come to no harm. It was not surprising. The newspapers had perpetuated the legend that the Luftwaffe was out of date and even the Prime Minister had said that Hitler had missed the bus, so that wishful thinking and self-deception had continued to hang over the country like a miasma.

The only good thing that had come out of the disasters was that England had at last got a new leader. Churchill, who had conducted the affairs of the Admiralty since the previous year with his usual aggressive élan, had become Prime Minister and was offering only blood, toil, tears, and sweat, a daunting prospect that was at least realistic. In his impulsive way, Kelly thought, Winston would undoubtedly make mistakes as he always had, but at least he had a habit of doing *something*, while the recent government, fighting the war with committees, had only been able to display the certainty of good committee men trying to avoid positive action.

Seething with fury without a command and, still devoid of a hundred items of kit and uniform which had disappeared with *Feudal*, he stamped about the house in a frustrated fury. Though it had been the family home since his mother had moved from Ireland to be near her husband and sons at the beginning of the 1914–18 war, he realised he hardly knew it. He had spent so much of his life abroad, he'd rarely lived there, not even after his mother had let him have it for his home after he'd married. It had been transformed by his wife's money, modernised and filled with the treasures she'd acquired, but it had still meant little to him because she'd always preferred London and, as Biddy's children had grown, Kelly, enjoying their noise and their laughter with the pleasure of a childless man, had managed to bring life to the place only by encouraging them to use it for parties.

As he brooded about the garden he was watched anxiously by Biddy. Rumbelo had disappeared mysteriously to Dover on some job but the Navy seemed to have forgotten Kelly. When he'd been sunk in *Cressy*, in 1914, it had been the cause of great indignation to him then that he'd been snatched back to sea before he'd had his survivor's leave; this time, survivor's leave left him cold. The Britain of 1940 wasn't the Britain of 1914 and he needed to be where things were happening.

Unexpectedly, his father arrived from London where he'd lived ever since Kelly's marriage. He was looking his age at last, because he'd done *his* stint in the Navy as long ago as the heyday of Queen Victoria. In the whole of his active career he'd never heard a shot fired in anger and to Kelly, who'd heard too many, he belonged to the big-ship-polo-playing navy that had died before 1918 but had steadfastly refused to lie down.

"Made a bloody mess of Norway, didn't you?" was his first greeting.

He seemed to be dropping hints about needing money but Kelly firmly set his face against them because his father had always been selfish and spendthrift, and he couldn't remember his ever helping him in the days when he'd needed help. Everything he'd ever possessed as a child had come from his mother while his father had indulged himself with fast women and slow horses in and around London.

Realising he was getting nothing, the old man, frail, demanding and selfish as ever, stayed for only two days before returning to London, and it was only when he'd gone that Kelly realised he'd taken a suitcase full of treasures belonging to his mother or Christina which he clearly intended selling. He was glad to see the back of him, and there were no farewell waves from either of them.

Buying a paper in the village, Kelly sat in the garden to read it. It was full enough of disaster to be depressing. Young British airmen in outdated machines that had been wished on them by men like his father were committing suicide bombing bridges to stop the Germans, and the whole Channel coast of France was ablaze. In London, it seemed, instead of being concerned with victory, thoughts were suddenly dwelling on the possibility of defeat.

The day was hot and there was a scent of crushed grass in the air from the fields at the back of the house, and somewhere, faintly, from one of the nearby houses, the strains of '*Deep Purple*' came through an open window. The German Army was trying to force its way into Boulogne and Calais and, from what it was possible to make out, the French Army was in ruins.

It was clear that the BEF was about to be pinned into a narrow strip of land round La Panne, Nieuport and Dunkirk. Nobody was talking about evacuation yet, of course, but among the vague references to 'interior lines', 'pincer movements' and 'pouring in reserves' that he'd been hearing on the wireless, Kelly had not failed to notice one item the previous week which even then had appeared to be of great significance.

'The Admiralty has made an order requesting all owners of self-propelled pleasure craft between thirty and a hundred feet in length, to send all particulars . . . within fourteen days . . . if they have not already been offered or requisitioned.'

The request had gone largely unnoticed in the plethora of gloom coming from France and Kelly had recognised it only as a move by the Small Vessels Pool to acquire harbour craft, but it had soon become clear to him that the Small Vessels Pool was now taking advantage of it as a precautionary measure for the evacuation of the Army.

He was still glowering at the paper and had just decided to head for London the following morning to bully someone into giving him a ship when Hugh arrived. He'd finished his training and was waiting to be posted to an aircraft carrier. He looked staggeringly handsome in uniform with his pale face, sensitive features and fair hair, and unbelievably like his mother.

His arrival provided a touch of light on a gloomy horizon, and Kelly smiled, delighted to see him.

'Naval uniform suits you,' he said. 'Should fetch the girls.'

Hugh blushed a little. 'Only one girl I want to fetch, sir,' he said. 'She's outside.'

By the grace of God, Rumbelo's daughter resembled not Rumbelo but Biddy, and she was blue-eyed, dark-haired and dainty in a way Kelly remembered her mother in 1914 when

Rumbelo had fallen for her. She came in with Hugh and they had about them that indefinable rapport, that unity, that sets a man and woman in love apart from the rest of humanity. Paddy looked so heartbreakingly young and so much like Charley at the time of the last war, Kelly felt as old as God, because it only seemed like yesterday when he'd been bowling leg-breaks to her on the back lawn and watching her wallop them into the next field.

She gave him a grin that was a mixture of friendliness and shyness. He'd known her since Biddy had first presented her to him within a few days of her arriving in the world and he'd grown to accept her as much a part of his proxy family as Hugh was. Without his godson, now at sea somewhere in the destroyer, *Grafton*, and this slip of a thing, he'd often felt he'd have grown middle-aged too quickly. She was wearing a nurse's uniform and he eyed her up and down as she stood in the doorway with Hugh.

'She'll do,' he said. 'Wheel her in. What's on your minds?'

They glanced at each other and he knew exactly what their reply would be. 'We want to get engaged.'

Kelly's smile died. 'Seen your mother about it, Hugh?' he asked. 'After all, I'm not your father and it's really nothing to do with me.'

Hugh frowned. 'I saw her,' he said. 'She had no objection.'

'It seems to me she's getting a jolly pretty daughter-in-law. What do you want for a wedding present when it comes off? I'm not very wealthy, but I could probably run to a small cottage somewhere.'

'That's generous, sir,' Hugh said. 'But we were wondering –'

Paddy tugged at his hand and as he became silent she spoke. She had inherited a touch of the Irish accent that had never left Biddy and there was a great deal of her mother in her forthright manner.

'We were wondering,' she said, 'if, while the war's on at least, we could convert the stables into somewhere to live. They have two or three rooms above that used to be used by the grooms.'

'And it's handy for Portsmouth, Chatham and Devonport,' Kelly smiled. 'To say nothing of London.'

'I'll still be working at the hospital, so I'll be able to get home and I can be here whenever Hugh comes on leave.' She paused.

'We'd pay properly, of course, because neither of us has any call on you.'

'Don't make a scrap of difference,' Kelly said. 'You'd better start getting on with it at once. In the meantime, I think we ought to celebrate, don't you? And, with your brother at sea and your father doing mysterious things in Dover, I think we'd better have your mother in to join us.'

The following morning Kelly took the train to London. Somehow the Admiralty had come to life. It had always hummed under Winston but until Norway it had always had the dead hand of the Chamberlain administration over it. Now, there was a new confidence because at last someone had recognised that the British people had sufficient intelligence and courage to face facts, and the battle in France was finally being spoken of as the major disaster it surely was. It was suggested immediately that there was work for him if he wanted it, and he was told to report to Dover Command.

Because it was Sunday, the trains were running at their usual peace-time half-strength, and he had to wait what seemed ages. Young servicemen with their girl friends and wives filled the station, and he felt old and lonely. Thinking of Charley, he wondered what it must be like to be in America when your country was at war, and if it would be possible next time he was in New York to get in touch with her through one of the welfare organisations who sent comforts to British troops.

He was still waiting at the gate when the Dover train came in and almost the first person he saw coming towards him was Mabel, Charley's sister. She seemed to have shed a lot of the artificiality which had been part of her personality and there was a solidity about her he'd never seen before.

'Well, I'm damned,' she said. 'Where did you spring from?'

He told her what he'd been doing and her face changed. 'It looks bad, Kelly, doesn't it?' she said. 'George's in France. I hope to God he's all right.'

He tried to pump her on the subject of Charley's whereabouts, but she was giving nothing away. 'I can't tell you, Kelly,' she said. 'I don't even know if she'd wish me to.'

He accepted the rebuke. 'Well,' he said, 'just give her my love when you're next in touch with her.'

She gave him a curious look, but said nothing, and he was aware of her watching him as he turned away and headed for the platform.

As the train left London, Sunday cricket was still being played, and every road was full of small cars heading for the countryside. It seemed unbelievable that there was a war on, let alone a British army fighting for its life only a few miles away, and it reminded him of the indifference he'd seen in Santander. Would people still be so indifferent when the 'last trump' came?

It was evening when he arrived in Dover and he was aware at once of the war intruding. The place was packed with people, and they all seemed bent on some urgent task. There were policemen and uniformed women welfare workers everywhere, and it was obvious they'd arrived from other towns and cities in response to an appeal for help. The town seemed totally inadequate for what was going on, and it was clear the minute he stepped from the train that the place was being geared up for the evacuation of the Army from France. The station was full of lines of communications troops, footsore men with harrowing tales of being bombed and shot at all the way from Brussels to the coast, and the station entrance and forecourt were filled with more of them, standing in lost groups waiting to be told what to do.

Every taxi in the place seemed already spoken for and he set off on foot for naval headquarters. Oddly enough, the first person he met was Rumbelo, plodding out of the gates with an envelope in his hand.

'What the hell are they using you for, Rumbelo?' he asked. 'Messenger boy?'

'Yes, sir.' Rumbelo's face was sullen. 'As if I was a newly-joined boy seaman or a bloody old barrack stanchion having to lean on his broom to stop himself falling down. Taking messages. That's what I'm doing. How about getting me out of it, sir?'

Kelly grinned, and told him of the celebration they'd had the night before. Rumbelo's potato face lifted.

'Honest, sir, I'm that pleased. How about you? Don't you mind?'

'It's nothing to do with me, Albert, old son. He's not my boy, and even if he were, it still wouldn't be any of my business.'

74

'I mean, me being only –'

'Dry up, you old fool,' Kelly said. 'We've known each other too bloody long to worry about what we are. Biddy's looked after my mother and then me, and you and I have been getting each other out of trouble ever since 1911. I can't think of anybody better to be related to.'

Rumbelo's face went pink with pleasure. 'I reckon you'd better see Admiral Corbett, sir,' he suggested conspiratorially. 'He's here and, if anyone can, he ought to be able to do something for us – both of us.' He was just on the point of moving away when he stopped again. 'By the way, sir, Mr. Boyle's on his staff, and *he* looks down in the mouth, too.'

Boyle was talking urgently into the telephone when Kelly pushed into his office. They'd served together in the destroyer, *Mordant*, and again in the battleship, *Rebuke*, after Boyle had switched to the paymaster branch. His wife was French; her family had bought a house at Dunkirk when her father had retired from the Consular Service and he was trying to find out what had happened to them.

Corbett was deep in conversation with three other senior officers when Kelly was shown in, but he broke off at once. 'Just the man I'm looking for,' he said.

He looked tired and admitted he hadn't slept for three nights. 'It's just beginning to be difficult,' he pointed out. 'We've just heard Boulogne and Calais have gone, but Gort's had the guts to decide to bring out the Army. And thank God, too, because if he doesn't the war's as good as lost. We haven't another. Let's go along and see Ramsay.'

Admiral Ramsay, the C.-in-C., Dover, who was organising the evacuation, was a man of medium size, quiet, and so unemotional he'd always been considered rather a cold fish. Before the war, he'd even been regarded as a failure because he'd disagreed with his chief and, throwing up his appointment, had been on the retired list when the demands of the war and his unquestioned ability had brought him back. His headquarters were in the galleries hewn by French prisoners during the Napoleonic Wars in the cliffs below Dover Castle, and as Kelly was ushered in, the adjoining rooms were full of grim-faced men trying to bring order out of chaos. With the rumble of gunfire clearly audible, they were planning for emergencies.

As they waited, Ramsay was sitting on the edge of a desk talking to his chief of staff. 'We can no longer expect an orderly evacuation,' he was saying. 'What ships are available?'

'*Keith* and *Vimy* both hit at Boulogne, sir.' The chief of staff looked at a list in his hand. 'Both captains killed. *Venetia* also hit. *Vimiera* brought out one thousand four hundred men. The French lost *Orage, Frondeur* and *Chacal*.'

Ramsay's face was expressionless. 'What about Calais?'

'We lost *Wessex*, with *Vimiera* and *Burza* damaged.'

Ramsay nodded. 'Better get me a list of all available personnel ships, and we might even have to consider the all-out use of destroyers as lifting vessels.'

As the chief of staff turned away, Corbett introduced Kelly. Ramsay stared at him in his expressionless way.

'Maguire,' he said. 'I've heard of you. You were at Bilbao and Santander in 1937.'

'He was also at Chinkiang in 1927,' Corbett pointed out. 'And Odessa in 1920 and Domlupinu before that. He knows a bit about evacuations. In 1914 he brought a couple of hundred Marines out of Antwerp after the Germans arrived.'

Kelly began to see the direction the conversation was heading. 'Nearer a hundred,' he said quickly.

'You seem to have spent a remarkable amount of your naval career rescuing people from on shore,' Ramsay commented. 'Understand you speak good French.'

'Yes, sir.'

'Well, Winston's a bit worried that the French are hanging back and he wants them bringing out in equal numbers. Unfortunately, they're not very organised and we need to know why.'

'Probably,' Corbett said, 'because there's nobody over there who can speak their language. We're not noted as linguists.'

Ramsay looked at Kelly. 'I'd like you to go and sort it out,' he said.

'I'd hoped for a ship, sir.'

'It's everybody's wish to distinguish himself at sea,' Ramsay said dryly. 'Unfortunately we're more in need at the moment of people who can distinguish themselves on land. Tennant's going across tomorrow as senior naval officer ashore. We need another.'

Kelly bowed to the inevitable. 'I'll go, of course, sir, if that's where I'm needed.'

'Good. You'll need some staff. Any ideas?'

'There's a petty officer here, sir. He was with me in Antwerp and Domlupinu and Odessa. I know him well.'

'He's yours.'

'Anybody else?'

'Lieutenant-Commander Boyle, sir.'

'He's my secretary!' Corbett protested.

'He was at Odessa and Domlupinu, too, sir. Moreover, he speaks excellent French because he has a French wife and he knows Dunkirk.'

Ramsay rubbed his nose and gave Corbett a cold little smile. 'It looks as if you've lost him, Cuthbert,' he observed. 'Very well, fix yourself up with transport across the Channel. Your job will be to contact the French Army and direct their men to the ships. You'll find a bit of resentment all round because our people think the French have let 'em down by giving way and the French think we're letting them down by pulling out. It's up to you to sort it out.'

The harbour was packed with shipping. It had been designed originally as an anchorage for the old Channel Fleet, yet at the berths at the Admiralty Pier Kelly could see as many as eighteen or twenty ships moored in trots two and three deep. A hospital ship was unloading into a row of ambulances, and exhausted khaki-clad figures were stumbling ashore across her from other vessels. As he watched, a tug began to butt at a ship whose yellow bridge paintwork was scorched by a great black scar where the steelwork was wrenched back like the lid of a sardine tin.

The office of the Director of Shipping was crowded and the naval commander behind the desk seemed to be at his wits' end. When Kelly appeared, he simply waved him to the inner office where a naval captain was standing in front of a map, sticking flags into it, with a list in his left hand. Alongside him was a remarkably pretty girl in the uniform of a Wren.

'Captain Verschoyle's busy,' she said immediately.

'Not too busy to see me,' Kelly retorted.

Verschoyle turned, stared at Kelly and began to smile.

'Ginger Maguire, as I live and breathe,' he said. 'I heard they'd sunk you at Narvik.' He gestured at the girl. 'Beat it, Maisie. I'll let you know when to come back.'

As the door closed, Kelly grinned. 'I see you still know how to pick 'em.'

Verschoyle gave his superior smile and stuck another flag into the map. 'I'd be a bloody fool if I let them fob me off with one with buck teeth and breasts like clockweights,' he said. 'Maisie used to be an actress, but patriotism or lack of plays drove her into uniform and she picked the Navy because her father was a chief petty officer in *Nelson*. She glosses over her background and she's mastered her accent but I've noticed when we go aboard a ship she still tends to turn forward rather than aft at the top of the gangway.'

He saw Kelly looking round the office and gestured. 'Don't let this fool you,' he said. 'It's only until this little bunfight settles down. After that, I suspect they'll be needing everybody at sea who can handle even a pram dinghy because somebody seems to have made a proper balls-up of things, and we've finished up with the final socialist dream of plenty of money for social welfare but no fighting services.' He jabbed another flag into the map, this time as if it were into a politician's backside. '*Si vis pacem para bellum*. Well, now we're up to the necks in the bellum we haven't para'd for. What are you doing here?'

'Just been landed with the job of naval liaison officer to the French Army.'

'I hope you can run fast.'

'I want a lift across with my staff, Cruiser.'

Verschoyle smiled. 'You have an incredible gift for diving in at the deep end. How many have you got?'

'So far, two. Seamus Boyle and Rumbelo.'

Verschoyle grinned. 'I saw Boyle yesterday and Rumbelo a couple of days ago, so I had a feeling in my bones you'd turn up before long.' He glanced at the list in his hand. 'You'd better go across in *Wolfhound*. She'll be leaving tomorrow. Tennant's already booked a passage aboard her. You under him?'

'No,' Kelly said briskly. 'I'm under me.'

7

They spent the night searching for French speakers among the sailors arriving in Dover to offer their services, and before morning had found seven men and five officers from the training establishment, *King Alfred*, plus one of Verschoyle's staff and a middle-aged Guernseyman called Le Mesurier, who had once had his name in the newspapers for sailing single-handed at the age of seventeen to Malta during his school holidays. Running out of funds at Malaga on the way back, his boat impounded, his charts confiscated, his credit stopped and a guard put on his boat, he'd traced a map from an atlas at the library, floored the guard with a sack of oranges he'd pinched from a market for food and reached home literally on his last orange pip. Since he spoke fluent French and claimed to know Dunkirk and the surrounding countryside as well as Boyle, with the aid of one of Verschoyle's staff they fitted him up with a reserve sub-lieutenant's uniform to give him authority and attached him to the group.

'I hadn't really intended to join up,' he bleated. 'In fact, when I volunteered for the army they turned me down.'

'You haven't joined up,' Kelly said shortly. 'Just been disguised. If you find you like it, you can join when we get back.'

When they arrived at Dunkirk, steel-helmeted, their uniforms dragged out of shape by webbing belts and revolver holsters, the place was burning and most of the harbour facilities were in ruins. The bombing appeared to be continuous and the information they received was alarming to say the least because the Belgians had just surrendered, leaving a huge gap in the Allied lines.

There were hundreds of them at the station with more hundreds of French, standing among heaps of rifles, packs and helmets, bewildered and prepared to lay down their arms. There were a few who were not prepared to march meekly into captivity, however, and Le Mesurier managed to persuade them to head for the beaches where a slow lifting had started by ships' boats. Eventually, even those who had been prepared to give up began to straggle off.

It was a beginning and they set up an office close to that set up by Tennant, but it soon became clear that out of the five officers Kelly had picked, two had so little French they were useless and one was so frightened he refused to move from the harbour. Kelly sent them home on the ferry, *Queen of the Channel*, and recruited instead two army Intelligence officers and a French naval captain called D'Archy with a title and a grand manner to go with it. D'Archy was only part of his name and the rest went on for so long, 'Archie Bumf' was the nearest they could get to it and that was how he was known.

Enlisting the assistance of a few sailors from bombed ships, Kelly posted his men at strategic points leading to the beaches and left Boyle to look after them while he set off with Rumbelo and Le Mesurier to find out what conditions were like. The town had already descended into chaos and telephones were not working. The streets were full of rubble and burning vehicles and dazed French soldiers, too far gone in shock to be able to help themselves, stood in groups, watching as the British poured in. Some of the British units had also disintegrated and thrown away their equipment and rifles, but there were still some with long histories, great traditions or simply good officers, who appeared complete with kit and arms, their heads up and marching in step. The chances of getting them to safety already seemed problematical and it was becoming increasingly obvious that an idea Tennant had had to embark them all from the beaches was the only way to do it.

It was too late to do much that night beyond seeing Abrial, the French Amiral Nord, so Kelly sent Boyle off to try to trace his in-laws.

'Find 'em, Seamus,' he said. 'We'll get 'em on a ship somehow.'

Admiral Abrial looked exhausted because he had been conducting his operations for a week before anybody had thought of evacuation, but, though the French Navy seemed to be functioning well, the French military staff seemed to have lost all control of the situation and were still calling for an all-out attack southwards to cut off the German spearheads, something which was quite clearly impossible.

'They seem to know nothing of the decision to evacuate,' one of the British liaison officers informed Kelly. 'It doesn't appear to have been passed down by the High Command.'

There was a great lack of co-ordination, and a chaos of rumour and uncertainty, but they managed to make a start by getting a few shocked *poilus* to join the queues on the beaches.

Boyle returned about midnight. He looked tired and strained, and was dirty from clambering across ruins all evening.

'There was no one there,' he said. 'The house was full of British soldiers. They were sleeping in all the rooms – even in the garden – but they knew nothing, and there were no neighbours to ask because they'd disappeared too. Thank God, my wife's in England. She'd had it in mind to bring the kids over for a summer holiday.'

It seemed important to contact Gort so, leaving Boyle in charge of the operations round the docks, the following morning Kelly acquired a small Austin staff car with a faltering engine and, taking Rumbelo, Le Mesurier and D'Archy, joined the endless queues heading for La Panne. He didn't expect any problems because he knew Gort well and had worked closely with him in Shanghai in 1927.

The town, a favourite place for painters for years, had been a pretty place of parks and gardens, but now houses were burning and there were charred wrecks of vehicles about the streets. Air raid wardens were collecting bodies, and civilians stood at their doorways jeering at the soldiers as they tramped past the small hotels and boarding houses, their rooms still locked after the winter, their windows shuttered and barred. Thousands of men waited on the sand, a few digging shelters in the dunes, more standing bootless in the shallows to cool their aching feet. A few were trying to construct rafts from planks and barrels, absorbed in their task and indifferent to the danger.

British Army Headquarters had been set up in a château surrounded by pink and white apple blossom and the green of

81

young corn just outside the town. There were soldiers everywhere and lorries and pennanted staff cars were parked down the gravelled drive and round the ornamental pond that fronted the building. A French horse artillery regiment clattered past as they arrived, the drivers shouting and lashing at the horses, the gunners clinging grimly to the limbers, ammunition trailers, mess carts and waggons. The whole area seemed to be seething with movement, and there was a constant flow of figures towards the sea. Grey-faced with tiredness, they tramped silently past, dragging their lurching stragglers and wheeling their wounded in barrows, their sergeants chivvying them like sheepdogs. 'Keep the steps, lads, it'll help! Keep the step!' Exhausted despatch riders, their strained faces blank as zombies, roared up and down the columns, and alongside the road French soldiers were digging trenches for their final stand and covering them with branches from a nearby orchard to hide them from the German dive bombers.

The château was filled with worried-looking officers. Of them all Gort seemed by far the calmest. He looked a lot older than when Kelly had met him in Shanghai, but he still had the same sturdy figure, his thick legs astride as if rooted to the ground. There had been a tendency among the intellectuals of the army to regard his appointment as C.-in-C. with dismay because he fussed over detail and ran his headquarters in spartan style. 'Oh, Gort, our help in ages past' Kelly had heard several times, and it hadn't been uttered without sarcasm.

As they shook hands, Kelly explained his mission and Gort gestured. 'Well,' he said, 'the French have distinguished themselves in the fighting, but hardly in other ways. They've ignored instructions to destroy their vehicles before entering the perimeter and they're now disregarding orders for beach and road discipline.' He frowned. 'They always were arrogant enough to believe they knew best, of course, but until the 29th nobody seems to have received any orders about embarkation at all, and Abrial seems to be showing signs of obstructing the departure of all fighting troops. Understandable, I suppose, because he feels they belong in France.'

'How many are we expecting to bring out?'

'Thirty per cent of all troops engaged. At least, that was the first estimate but I'm inclined to be more optimistic now. I've given orders that all the best-trained men and officers are to go first. Originally I sent non-combatant troops but now I'm sending key men of all ranks and all units because we'll need them to rebuild. Pownall's gone, and Brooke will go before long. Alexander stays with the rearguard, because I've been informed that I've got to go, too. The PM says it's in accordance with correct military procedure and that on political grounds it'd be silly to be captured.' He frowned. 'All the same, I can't say I like it.'

He agreed to provide a document enabling Kelly to cut through orders to try to move the French. 'So long as it hasn't been agreed that they're part of the rearguard,' he pointed out. 'We've assigned the Guards and our best troops to the job, and the French have agreed to do the same. There'll obviously be little chance of getting them all out, but that's something we have to face.'

With the aid of Archie Bumf, one of the staff officers drafted a document in French for Kelly to use that would satisfy French consciences and, borrowing typewriters and carbons, they spent the next hour pecking out as many copies as they could.

'Try Gyseghem,' the staff officer suggested. 'The place's full of troops. It's the headquarters of General Guyou and he's been nothing but a bloody nuisance. If you can get *him* moving north, you'll be doing us all a favour because he's not doing a scrap of good where he is and he's blocking the escape route of the rearguard. He's got some good people who've done well and are worth saving, but he himself doesn't seem to know his arse from his elbow.'

The Germans started dropping shells in La Panne as they left. The sound of them approaching seemed to fill the air and everybody started to run. French drivers began to lash at their horses and swing off the road among the trees, and the place emptied of human beings in a flash. Feeling conspicuous, Kelly's party flung themselves over a wall, thinking they would have the other side to themselves. To their surprise it was occupied by dozens of soldiers, who moved up to make room. The explosions threw up dust and clods of earth in the fields beyond the château, then the shelling stopped again and everybody began to appear from holes in the ground and from behind trees and walls. Vehicles began to move again and the whole countryside seemed to come to life.

As they drove from La Panne, they found themselves in countryside that was flat with miles of marshy fields, each one below the level of the network of canals that cut up the area. The whole of the BEF was streaming into it, every road jammed with khaki-coloured transport and great columns of troops, stretching back to the horizon, all of them heading towards the single point on the coast. Ambulances, lorries, trucks, Bren gun carriers, artillery columns, everything except tanks, was crawling north over the featureless landscape in the early sunshine, like slow-moving rivers of mud from some far-off upheaval of the earth.

'They've been having a day of prayer for us back in London,' Rumbelo said conversationally as they pushed past.

Kelly grunted. 'That'll be why the whole bloody thing's falling apart, I expect,' he said.

It was easy for the church dignitaries to make their announcements and equally easy for the politicians to turn up in their top hats and frock coats and bow their heads before the altar, but it wasn't as simple as that. War contained a wealth of grief and pity and those people in London getting down on their knees and saying a few easily-uttered prayers were a world away from this grimness and fear, this mounting weariness of body and spirit. For some of the men passing on their way north it was a fortnight since they'd had a decent sleep and some of the drivers had feet so swollen they drove without their boots and fell into unconsciousness every time the column came to a halt at one of the paralysing road blocks, so that they had to be hammered back to life as the military police got it moving again.

Among the hordes of men heading north were French troops who had tossed away their rifles and helmets and were forcing their way through the rows of horse-drawn and motorized vehicles. They looked the sort of men you didn't argue with. Their drivers were unshaven, their clothes muddy, and there were no officers or NCOs. As they passed, they gave sheepish smiles that sent a cold chill through Kelly's heart. They were the ruin of an army and their commanders had thrown in their hands.

Gyseghem was a dull red-brick little town largely centred

round a factory making motor car accessories. The factory had been bombed into stark smoke-blackened spires of brick and twisted girders, and mirrors, fenders, and hub caps lay everywhere in the square. Firemen and soldiers were still dragging the dead and injured from the ruins, and from every house and cottage – even the church steeple – white flags of tablecloths, sheets, towels or handkerchieves were hanging. A few people stood in their doorways, watching, their expressions apprehensive at the thought of what the arrival of the Germans might bring.

The town was full of troops and at the French headquarters in the *Mairie* they split up, Le Mesurier taking the car and heading out of the town with Archie Bumf to find out what the situation was, while Kelly looked for General Guyou. Outside the *Mairie* an intact regiment was waiting in the square. Several buildings were burning, and the soldiers were backgrounded by broken walls and blackened brickwork. They had lost their colonel and the major in command was thin, spare and greying, a regular soldier who in Germany would probably have been a general but in the confusion that had gripped France since 1918 had remained only in a junior rank. His men were bewildered but they still had weapons in their hands and their heads were high, and there was something in their faces that showed they were unbeaten. The old major's face was drawn with weariness and it was also full of disgust.

'We are doing nothing, you understand,' he told Kelly angrily 'We are neither fighting nor retreating. We have been here twenty-four hours and the command structure has atrophied. There must be four thousand men in this place who don't know what to do and have no orders. We would welcome evacuation, so we could fight again elsewhere.'

While they were talking, a staff car drew up and General Guyou climbed out. He was small, plump and petulant-looking and when he learned what Kelly's mission was, he started to work himself up into a passion. In reply, Kelly put on his Royal-Navy-In-Adversity act – cold, arrogant and bullying. It didn't work.

'I have no orders,' Guyou insisted loudly. 'And German tanks are approaching.'

'My information,' Kelly said, 'is that you're unlikely to receive any orders, and that it's imperative that you move to the coast and leave Gyseghem clear for the rearguard to move through.'

'My men are exhausted!'

'Surely not too exhausted to be incapable of movement,' Kelly snapped. 'The French government has agreed that their troops shall have the same facilities for evacuation as the British.'

'I have not been informed.'

'I'm informing you now! There are ships waiting to take your men to safety!'

They were still arguing when the old Austin drew up with a shriek of brakes and Le Mesurier fell out, yelling.

'Tanks,' he screamed. 'About three miles away! And coming fast!'

The square emptied, and Kelly saw some of the old major's soldiers setting up machine guns, their faces grim. Then his eye fell on all the hub caps lying about the square and he caught the eye of D'Archy.

The Frenchman smiled. 'You are thinking what I am thinking, I believe,' he said.

Rounding up a party of men, they set one half of them placing the hub caps in rows along the road, while the other half brought ashes and pulverised earth and scattered it to hide the shiny crome. They were all out of sight when the tanks appeared. They stopped by the row of hub caps, the commander of the leading tank clearly worried by what he suspected were land mines. As they watched, a hatch opened and an officer climbed from the turret and moved slowly forward, accompanied by one of his crew and the commander of the second tank.

They were still watching when the turret lid of the third tank lifted and the commander's head appeared. Climbing out, he sat on the edge of the hatch, watching as the other Germans moved closer to the scattered hub caps. Kneeling, one of them probed carefully under the scattered earth with his fingers, then they heard him say something and saw him straighten up and take a kick at the hub cap. As it skated away, rattling, he turned back to the tank, and immediately, every machine gun round the square opened up. The Germans were flung aside like rag dolls and the commander of the third tank fell backwards, draped across the hatch as if he were full of straw, his body sprouting crimson flowers.

The French soldiers were letting fly with everything they had, with so little regard for direction they were in danger of shooting each other. Bullets clinked and clicked against the walls to whine off into the distance, and a young corporal ran forward and tossed a grenade into the open hatchway of the rear tank. The muffled thump as it exploded was followed by screams, and a crimson horror pushed the body of the commander aside and began to drag itself out. At once every weapon in the place was turned on it and, shredded by the lash of the bullets, it flopped silently back out of sight.

With their retreat blocked by the third tank, the first two tanks began to move forward over the bodies of their own commanders, but the Frenchmen, infuriated and humiliated by their defeat, were swarming all over them, shouting and cursing, almost fighting each other for the privilege of thrusting a rifle or a grenade through the slits. Within a minute, there was no sign of life from inside them and Kelly stared at D'Archy in astonishment at the unexpected success of their scheme.

At first, Guyou still refused to withdraw but D'Archy's title finally overawed him and, catching the angry mutterings from the weary officers and men behind him, he changed his mind. The burning tanks were filling the air with oily smoke as the old major's men formed up and began to tramp away. As the last man moved off, Kelly noticed that Guyou also turned his car north and drove after them.

Watching silently, D'Archy turned to Kelly and smiled gravely.

'It's a measure of the weakness of the general staff,' he explained, with all the contempt for the army that all naval men, whatever their nationality, seemed to imbibe with their mother's milk, 'that sixteen generals have been removed for failing in their duty.'

Without Guyou, his staff were much more realistic and willing to help, and within an hour they had rounded up the rest of the French troops and had them heading north. They were unshaven and out of step, because the French had never set much store by smartness, but they still managed to look like soldiers.

'What'll happen when it's over, sir?' Rumbelo asked as they watched.

'France will surrender, I suppose,' Kelly said.

'And then, sir?'

'And then it will be the Germans marching down the Champs Elysées,' D'Archy said. 'And those *bougres* who have bank accounts and mistresses and apartments in the Avenue Foch making terms to get the best they can out of it. There are a few in England, too, I have no doubt.'

Rumbelo looked alarmed. 'They'll not get to England, will they, sir?'

'Not on your life, Albert, old lad.' Kelly's face was grim as he spoke. 'But if France goes, then it'll be a bloody sight more difficult for us in the navy, because they'll hold every scrap of coastline from north Norway to Spain, and probably that, too. Think of that in terms of U-boats and bases for commerce raiders.'

8

As they returned to Dunkirk, military police were forcing everything on wheels into enormous car parks in fields outside the town, and all along the road an orgy of destruction was taking place under a vivid blue sky.

Engineers were handing out blocks of gun cotton and detonators for artillery officers to place in the breeches of their guns to destroy them, and in a beet field, where thousands of new vehicles were parked – Scammells, diggers, buses, engineering plants, limbers and lorries – men were smashing their petrol tanks and cylinders with sledge-hammers in a steady crunching sound.

As the jam of vehicles ahead brought the Austin to a stop, a provost lieutenant stepped in front of their bonnet, waving a revolver. 'In here,' he said.

'I'm going into Dunkirk,' Kelly explained.

The officer lifted the revolver. 'In here,' he repeated.

Kelly climbed out of the car, followed by Rumbelo and the other two, expecting that the four stripes on his sleeve would overawe the officer, but the lieutenant was adamant.

'In here,' he said once more.

Without arguing, Kelly pulled out his own revolver and pointed it at the officer's stomach. Rumbelo did the same.

'I have the authority of the admiral in charge of the evacuation and of Lord Gort,' he said. 'And I'll happily shoot you if you try to stop me doing my job. And if you should just manage to shoot me first, my petty officer will do it for me. Now – do we go into Dunkirk?'

The officer blinked, startled, then he scowled, pushed away his weapon and waved them on.

The destruction stretched all the way back to Dunkirk, every dyke jammed with abandoned vehicles that stuck out of the water among the floating straw and the bodies of drowned animals, every road littered with cast-off equipment, caps and helmets. Dunkirk seemed to have grown more battered even while they'd been away and tall skeletons of buildings were silhouetted against a sword-cut of opal sky. Among them fierce fires raged.

As they drew to a stop, they could hear the hammering of guns from near the harbour, then another sound intruded, rolling in iron waves round the sky. As it increased, blending with it, they heard a growing howl.

'Run!' Kelly yelled and they all dived from the car for an open doorway. As they flung themselves down, the scream of the bombs grew to a shriek and the crash as they exploded seemed to lift the ground and hit them in the face. The air was filled with dust and acrid smoke and they could hear metal clanging to the cobbles. His face tight, the skin pulled taut, Kelly found his jaws were aching with the clenching of his teeth.

Unharmed but shaken, they scrambled to their feet to find the old Austin lying on its side against a wall, half-demolished and with its hood licked by small tongues of flame. The din was tremendous and the water of the harbour and canals was dotted with splashes as shell splinters dropped from the sky. There were a few good omens, however. The French had started to join in the evacuation, though the town major's office was bedlam, with what appeared to be dozens of officers all shouting the claims of their own units.

'I must have the numbers,' an officer at the desk was yelling. 'I've got to know how many men there are!'

'For Christ's sake – ' the officer who yelled back at him was filthy-dirty, grey-faced and red-eyed with fatigue – 'I don't know the bloody numbers myself!'

As the dive bombers returned, the arguing stopped while everyone tried to assess where the bombs would fall and then, according to what they'd decided, took cover or remained where they were, flinching at the crashes. The town major, an exhausted-looking colonel, didn't even look round as the bombs exploded, and as Kelly explained what he was up to, he managed a thin smile.

'Well, you blue jobs have got the destroyers coming across

now like Number Eleven buses,' he said. 'And some chap's found a pier we can use and we're sending everybody along there.'

By now, the dock area was full of wreckage – a burning train, cranes knocked out of true by bombs, ambulances punctured like colanders with bullets and shell fragments, splintered carts with dead horses in the shafts, and torrents of scattered brickwork where buildings had fallen. The situation had clarified a little, however, because Tennant had got a wooden mole working and a control system had been set up with berthing parties, a pier master and sailors in the town to act as guides. Redirected from the beach, men began to arrive in large numbers and there were ships alongside the pier, with hundreds more men queueing to go on board them. On the beaches, there were more queues on the hard wet sand among the litter of equipment and abandoned greatcoats. There was no sign of the disorganisation they'd seen among the French, however, and everybody was patient. Nobody seemed to be terribly worried even and, though their attitude was one of disgust that they'd been beaten, they all seemed certain it wasn't their fault and that, given another chance, they'd put it right.

Smoke from the burning town filled the air with an appalling stench of dead and decomposing farm animals. The beach was dotted with wrecked vehicles but among them, amazingly, soldiers were playing football as they waited for ships to arrive, and despatch riders were putting on dirt-track races round a marked perimeter.

A chaos of rumour and uncertainty existed. In some parts of the beach, there were no French, yet in others small boats arriving to lift men to the ships waiting in the roadstead found nothing else. In one area, the *poilus* behaved steadily and intelligently, while in another inland Frenchman, unaccustomed to the sea, stood in the shallows wearing motor car inner tubes as lifebelts, shouting for help and working themselves up into a fury as they failed to understand that human beings crowding into a boat could set it so firmly on the sand nothing on God's earth would move it until they all climbed out again.

'One would think their precious boats were made of paper!' one officer yelled in fury. 'They are so afraid of them turning over.'

They were totally indifferent to the appeals of the British who, since few of them lived more than a hundred miles from the sea, had some knowledge of boats, and only D'Archy's awesome hauteur damped their fury.

It was a babble of tongues, order, counter-order, rumour and counter-rumour, with the problem of languages increasing wherever the French predominated. With discipline all too often broken down, it was impossible to stop them rushing the boats but, as rumour piled on exhaustion to create confusion, at least they were beginning at last to arrive in a continuous stream. The chief problem, Kelly found, was keeping sufficient hold of enough of his staff to be able to despatch them to the points where the delays were occurring, to explain to the furious French officers what was happening and what was expected of them.

By the third day it was clear that Le Mesurier was drunk. Where he'd obtained the brandy he was drinking no one knew, but he stayed on his feet, red-eyed, unshaven and verbose with the Frenchmen with the verbosity of someone who had a perfect command of the language. It was obvious why he'd been free to join their party, because he was clearly on the way to being an alcoholic and some sharp-eyed doctor had spotted it when he'd offered himself for the army.

The queueing was continuous, not even stopping with darkness, and they obtained meals of bread and cheese from the ships that arrived and tried to snatch sleep in turns.

There was a monument on the promenade that seemed to separate the two armies. On one side were the British and on the other an enormous crowd of Frenchmen, among them many Moroccans who were resentful and bitter because they felt they were being left behind. Taking D'Archy, Kelly tried to bully them into moving to the mole, which seemed now to be working at tremendous speed, but they had set up a line of men with fixed bayonets and informed him that from that point on the promenade was reserved for the French. A Grenadier Guardsman was arguing with them, apparently willing to take on the whole of the French Army, but Kelly pulled him away and sent him into the city.

'Get yourself aboard a ship,' he said. 'Leave that lot to me.'

But the French didn't trust him and one of them even took a

potshot at him. When D'Archy addressed them in their own language, however, a few broke away and headed for the town, but the rest remained firmly where they were, many of them drunk, and they had to leave them.

Tennant's organisation was working well now, with a naval commander doing wonders as piermaster and Kelly's group bringing in French units in increasing numbers. But the bombers were constantly overhead, operating at low altitudes, dropping their bombs and machine-gunning, and occasionally, where they'd been caught, there were swathes of dead soldiers propped against walls or stretched on the pavements, their big boots limp, helmets, gas capes or groundsheets over their dead faces.

All day a pall of smoke from the burning town and the blazing oil tanks at St. Pol had covered the harbour but, as the wind changed, it drifted inshore, exposing the activity round the mole, and the bombers came in again and again, appearing from nowhere, stepped up in flights one above the other. Already, out in the roads, a ship which had brought landing craft to help with the loading from the beaches lay smoking and on fire, sinking slowly with a destroyer alongside trying to take off the troops she'd embarked. On the eastward side of the mole, two big paddle steamers, *Fenella* and *Crested Eagle*, were loading and against its inside face, opposite them, were the destroyers, *Grenade* and *Jaguar*, with six trawlers inshore of them and, astern, the personnel ship, *Canterbury*. Farther in were three more destroyers, *Malcolm*, *Verity* and *Sabre*, with the French destroyers, *Mistral* and *Sirocco* at the guiding jetty and *Cyclone* at the Quai Felix Fauré.

D'Archy had mustered some five hundred French soldiers on the mole. Judging by the motor inner tubes they clutched, they knew little about ships and D'Archy was holding up a whistle. 'When I blow this,' he said. 'You will squat down, with your steel helmets square on your heads. Do you understand?'

Despite the aeroplanes overhead, the loading went on and whenever any of them came near D'Archy blew his whistle and the French soldiers did as he told them with an orderly calmness that went oddly with the panic-stricken way they clutched their inner tubes.

But it couldn't last. With the smoke blown clear, the whole

group of shipping lay at the mercy of the *Luftwaffe*. *Fenella* was the first to be hit. One bomb went through her passenger deck to burst among the packed soldiers below and another hit the mole, sending lumps of concrete through her side below the water line. Jetties and gangways were blown away, and pushing among the crowding men, Kelly fought his way into the shambles past a gaunt-eyed man who was clutching the shreds of his right arm and who stumbled against him leaving a shining smear of red across the front of his uniform. Rumbelo, his face as impassive as ever, his helmet perched on his huge head like a pimple, was dragging a man with burning clothes ashore. More men, desperately wounded, scorched or burned, sometimes simply shrieking with shock, stumbled out of the holocaust but, despite the continuous machine-gunning that felled them in their tracks even as they struggled to safety, all the troops and stretcher cases were disembarked and placed on board *Crested Eagle*.

They had barely completed the job when *Grenade* was hit and swung away out of control to sink in the fairway. Then two trawlers were sunk alongside, and *Canterbury* and *Jaguar* were hit, and with ships trying desperately to move to the safety of the roads where they could manoeuvre, *Crested Eagle* was also hit in her turn.

Watching *Crested Eagle* blazing furiously as she was driven on to the beaches at Malo-les-Bains, Kelly felt numb. Stupefied with weariness, he could hardly make his mind function. They had pushed hundreds of Frenchmen aboard *Fenella*, promising them a passage to safety, then, as she'd been hit, had marshalled them all off again, hating and distrusting the British, and got them aboard *Crested Eagle*. God alone knew what they would think now; in the best French tradition, they'd doubtless claim they'd been betrayed.

Among them were the last of the seriously wounded. Even as they'd pushed them aboard *Crested Eagle*, it had occurred to Kelly that all these wounded they were struggling to save could help nobody, and certainly couldn't help Britain. Most of them would never fight again, many would never even walk again. They had to forget them to save the fit and able-bodied. Even as he debated with himself what to do about it, instructions arrived that no more wounded were to be placed aboard ships and that preference was to be given to unwounded men or men who could get aboard under their own steam. It must have been an agonising decision to take but he knew it was right, though it was received with taut faces by Le Mesurier and the others.

'These men have served their country well,' one of the army officers argued.

'They'll serve it well again by not standing in the way of whole men who can carry on the fight,' Kelly said. 'It's not a decision anybody wants to take, but a wounded man lying down takes up as much room as four men standing upright, and twice as long as ten unwounded men to put aboard. They've already stopped them coming off the beaches because they can't climb nets and it takes too long to rig slings.'

The stretchers were now being placed in warehouses and shelters wherever they could be left out of the bombing, and a medical officer with a barrow loaded with champagne, watched over by a sergeant with a revolver, was moving among the wounded, offering drink and cigarettes, as though he felt there was now nothing else he could do for them. Behind the town, the convoys of ambulances had been stopped and temporary hospitals had been set up in schools and halls, where more RAMC men were working alongside French Sisters of Mercy.

Though the decision meant that the unwounded could now move more freely to the ships and the congestion the wounded had caused disappeared, it was still hard for Kelly to convince himself they'd done the right thing. When you were involved in a catastrophe, you inherited its grief and became part of it because it was a shared thing, a shared sorrow, a shared anger and a shared guilt.

Yet, despite the horror and the unbelievable fatigue, there was a strange elation as they saw the soldiers carried away. Destroyers were coming in, as the town major had said, like Number Eleven buses, handled by their captains like pinnaces run by drunken midshipmen. By this time, French colonels were coming to Kelly for instructions, and he considered it a measure of their success. The very fact that they were succeeding beyond all their hopes kept them on their feet. Most people went to their graves without ever pulling out all the stops, and to work at full throttle for so good a cause as the survival of their country kept them all going – even Le Mesurier – long after they should have fallen exhausted. Fear, excitement, anger and impatience produced different results from different people but responsibility simplified the problem, and success added the spice of comfort that condensed it to simplicity, so that there could never be any doubts about why they were there.

After the bombing, all movement on the mole had ceased. The harbour seemed to be out of action again and ships and men were being diverted to the beaches once more. The thought of throwing his hand in never occurred to Kelly, and it was obvious it hadn't occurred to anyone else either. Calling in at Tennant's office, he picked up the list of tragedies. Even the ships off the beaches hadn't escaped.

'*Normannia, Lorina, Waverley* and *Gracie Fields* sunk,' he was told, '*Pangbourne* damaged, *Wakefield* and *Grafton* sunk –'

In his weariness, Kelly had hardly caught the name. Rumbelo's son – his godson – was in *Grafton*.

'*Grafton*?'

'Torpedoed. She was full of troops.'

'Casualties?'

'Heavy.'

Suddenly the elation vanished. First Boyle's tragedy, he thought, now Rumbelo's. Sorrow was bearable so long as it was somebody else's, but when it became personal, it was a different thing altogether. He tried to push it out of his mind and concentrate on what he was doing.

On the ninth morning, by which time the evacuation seemed to have been going on for a whole lifetime and beyond, he stood with Boyle in the doorway of their office drinking mugs of tea that Rumbelo had managed to beg from one of the destroyers. His face expressionless, Rumbelo had accepted the news of *Grafton* without the flicker of an eyelid. Lighting a cigarette, he'd disappeared about his business, pushing the dwindling group of sailors to greater efforts, making sure all the time that his officers were looked after, thrusting his private grief below the unperturbed demeanour that was the result of years of intelligent discipline.

His face gaunt, his eyes red-rimmed with sleeplessness, his feet swollen with standing, Boyle stared at Kelly wearily and, unable to look him in the face, Kelly turned to gaze at the dying city. Shells coming from the direction of Calais were bursting in the streets now and the beach was littered with wrecked ships and small boats. The sea front was a lurid study in black and red, a high wall of fire roaring with darting tongues of flame, the smoke pouring up in thick coils to disappear into the sky in a frightful panorama of destruction. The atmosphere had the stink of blood and mutilated flesh of a slaughterhouse. And still the Germans were pounding the ruins.

The losses continued to make grim reading. *Keith, Foudroyant* and *Basilisk*, with *Ivanhoe* and *Worcester* damaged – valuable destroyers that Kelly knew they'd miss desperately when it came to the battle against the submarines which would inevitably follow this debâcle. The men marching in now had been in heavy fighting. There were a lot of wounded among them, the blood bright on their bandages. They were the last regiments, both British and French, to pull back, proud regiments of both nations, and they still carried their weapons and gave Kelly a smart eyes right as they passed. There was something about them that stirred him almost to tears. He'd lost the two British army officers he'd picked up, and D'Archy, considering his job done, had formally requested permission to rejoin his admiral.

'What will you do, Archie?' Kelly asked.

The Frenchman's thin face cracked into a smile. 'Disappear,' he said shortly. 'We cannot evacuate the whole of France, you understand. Yet I don't intend to stay here to be sent to a prison camp. I shall find civilian clothes and make my way to the base at Toulon. France will need men of spirit to keep our ships out of the hands of the Germans and prepare them for when the time comes to hit back.'

The Frenchman's disappearance left only Le Mesurier, one of the naval officers and a mere handful of sailors. What had happened to the others nobody knew.

Troops still continued to trudge into the town through the Place Jean Bart and down the Boulevard Jeanne d'Arc past the ruins of the Church of St. Eloi. Most of them now were French. Inland somewhere, there were still others, with the gunners of the rear-guard who would never make it, because the Germans were now too close and Ramsay, at Dover, knowing how desperately they'd be needed in the future, had reluctantly withdrawn what remained of his destroyers.

The mob had emerged from the cellars of the city in hundreds. They clutched bottles and a few of them were singing, but the smell about them was the smell of fear. Unmoving, Kelly kept his group across the end of the mole, forcing a gap in the crowd for the last few men of the rearguard who appeared, to pass through.

'Thank you.' A tall Guards officer, shaved and polished as if he'd been on parade at St. James, but with eyes that were hollow with weariness, led his men through the line. 'It's nice of you to save us a place.'

Behind the Guards were French soldiers led by a colonel who looked like the major they'd seen at Gyseghem – thin with age and as smart as the Guardsman. As he passed, he saluted gravely.

Deaf to the yells of the mob, Kelly waited until it appeared there was no one else to come, then, forming his men up, the soldiers and sailors and three airmen he'd also acquired who were the survivors of a sunken RAF tender, he marched them down the mole and stood behind them with his revolver drawn to prevent them being swamped by the rabble that followed them.

Two hundred thousand soldiers had passed down the narrow plankway to safety and, despite the darkness, the wind, the sea and the enemy shellfire and bombing, the river of men had hardly ever stopped. The mole had been wrecked and repaired again and again and the loading berths were blocked by sunken ships, and still they'd come. Because the flow was now intermittent, however, the vessels arriving were only fishing vessels, motor-boats, and RAF rescue launches.

Rumbelo stood in silence in front of him. Boyle's face was drawn and agonised, and Kelly tried to imagine what they were thinking. Le Mesurier sagged against him. He had walked and run a hundred times to the beaches of Malo-les-Bains, even occasionally to La Panne, and he was clearly finished, his face exhausted and puffy with booze.

The queue edged forward and Kelly found himself jammed aboard an RAF pinnace as she edged from the pier and picked her way through the wrecked ships.

As they swung out and passed the end of the mole, they saw the last weary men of the rearguard who had made it halt on the end. There were tears of misery in his eyes as he realised there would be no ships for them. The last of the personnel carriers had gone, with the paddle steamers, the fleet sweepers, the trawlers, the drifters and finally the destroyers. These men, both French and British, had stumbled into the town expecting to be picked up, but the monstrous army of cowards, lines of communication troops, transport drivers and the men of ancillary services who had not put their heads above the earth for days had snatched their places. They had never had any intention of fighting but they had also had no intention of standing back to give up their places to the men who *had* fought. As the pinnace, crammed with men and top-heavy, headed for the sea, Kelly saw the pale faces watching in anguish.

A small motor boat had been sent in to take off a French general and his staff, and the picture burned itself into Kelly's mind. There were still about a thousand men on the mole, men of proud regiments, and they stood at attention in the faint light of dawn with the flames throwing the faces and helmets into sharp relief, while the general and his staff, tears on their cheeks, saluted. It was only a gesture but, Kelly thought, sometimes gestures could be bloody moving.

As they reached the open sea in the last of the darkness, the recriminations began. Who had been responsible? Who had let them down? Where had the RAF been? Kelly stared ahead of him with narrow eyes, knowing perfectly well that the responsibility lay with the politicians and do-gooders who'd felt it wrong to kill men with big guns and big ships and big bombs, and had allowed themselves to believe the words of Hitler and Mussolini.

He was cold and tired and the dirt had a strange mummifying effect on him, as if it stiffened his limbs and dulled his mind. Overhead he could still see the pin-prick flickering of anti-aircraft fire inland where the RAF was still trying to bomb German troop concentrations.

'I'm bloody hungry,' a Guardsman next to him said. 'I ain't had anything to eat for three days.'

'We could always eat each other,' Kelly suggested. 'But, as senior officer,' he said, 'I expect first bite.'

It raised a laugh but it didn't last long. Shells were still dropping in the fairway and, as they cleared the town, a fresh flight of Junkers 87s came down on them. For a while, the crash of bombs seemed to strip their nerves and leave them, in their exhausted state, shaking with fear. Vast splashes rose around them and the boats scattered in every direction. In the sea ahead was a mat of swimmers where a launch had been hit, then a bomb landed close alongside and the pinnace began to take in water. Discarding jackets and shoes, they began to slip overboard one after the other and swim to another pinnace which had avoided the worst of the attack.

Rumbelo was puffing badly and Kelly and Boyle dragged him along with them. Le Mesurier was swimming alongside them and he called out cheerfully that he was all right, but when they were dragged aboard and turned round for him, he had vanished.

Crammed with men, some of them wounded, most of them covered with oil, their faces haggard with weariness, the boat started to move off. Unaware of his rank, a worried sergeant snarled at Kelly to get a move on and he obediently edged further along the deck, huddling in the mass of exhausted men from the chilling wind that raced over the bow. They were all silent. Nobody felt like talking, all aware of the depression that came with the shattering knowledge of defeat. Above their heads loomed the black pall from the oil tanks of St. Pol, stretching up into the air for 11,000 feet and a mile wide, two millions tons of the stuff burning like a furnace. It had the look of doom itself about it.

Dover harbour was crowded to capacity, with loud-hailers squawking as officers in command of ships demanded permission to leave or go alongside. The quayside echoed to the shouts of red-eyed soldiers begging cigarettes and the barking of dozens of dogs which had attached themselves to them. On a wall someone had scrawled. 'Well done, BEF' and the man alongside Kelly sniffed audibly. 'I thought we'd *lost* the bloody battle,' he said.

They had transferred to a big motor launch as soon as they'd cleared Dunkirk, and when the launch's overworked engines had broken down, had been picked up by the trawler, *General Roberts*. Near the Kwinte Buoy they'd picked up the survivors of

101

a French fishing boat which had hit a mine. The survivors had had their clothes stripped clean away by the explosion and almost every one of them was suffering from a fracture of the legs, pelvis or spine.

The last ships were gathering outside the harbour as they arrived, personnel carriers and tugs, minesweepers from the North Sea and East Coast ports, coasters and short-sea traders, and boats with registrations from the Wash to Poole, while the destroyers whooped their way among them, setting the moored dinghies rolling and curtseying in their wake.

Getting the trawler in through the difficult tide stream and the press of boats required an intricate feat of seamanship which Kelly, as an inveterate bad handler of ships in harbour, had to admire even through his weariness. Men were still trooping ashore from the preceding vessels, and ships crowded every berth, many of them marked by fire or scarred by splinters. On their decks silent shapes lay covered with blankets, waiting for collection, and as the living streamed on to the quays, civilians clambered past with stretchers and first aid equipment. Air raid wardens, indifferent to the mess it made of their own clothes, were struggling to help men covered with fuel oil. Others were clearing ships of dirt, pools of blood and equipment; and women, some in the uniform of the voluntary services, some in summer frocks and hastily recruited, were passing round water bottles and telegram forms. They all looked hot because there was no wind and not a cloud in the sky, and many of them had faces that were wet with tears.

More women were running a mobile canteen with cups borrowed from local catering businesses, handing out food they'd acquired from the city shops, working at full speed and totally indifferent to the near-nakedness of some of the men. Despite the constant harassment, they all kept their heads. French-Moroccan soldiers were struggling with a group of sailors who were complaining loudly that they'd stolen their gear, and there was no order because senior officers were mixed with the lowest ranks, among them French and Belgian refugees – even a few German prisoners who had somehow got themselves captured in the chaos.

A squad of cavalrymen was forming up in threes, indifferent to the other soldiers.

'We,' their sergeant was informing them, 'are the Supple Twelfth and don't you forget it. We will not straggle, lose our 'eads or otherwise be'ave like ordinary soldiers. We are now going to the station and we will *march*. Is that understood?'

As they clanked off, every man in step, the quayside emptied a little. Boyle and Rumbelo had vanished and Kelly could only suppose they'd gone in search of somewhere to get their heads down, so he sought out Verschoyle to inform him that the officer they'd snatched from his staff had vanished in the confusion.

'I think he was killed on the mole,' he said. 'He was there when they got *Fenella*, *Crested Eagle* and *Grenade*.'

Verschoyle studied him. He'd not slept more than a few hours in a week and was haggard with tiredness himself. Even his Wren looked worn-out.

'Fish it out, Maisie,' he said and she reached into a drawer to produce a flask.

'I wish,' Kelly said, coughing as the spirit burned his empty stomach, 'that all those bloody politicians who spent the thirties cutting the services, all those dim-witted generals, admirals and air marshals who spent their time watching their pensions instead of watching the enemy, and all those bloody soft-minded buggers at the League of Nations who preached appeasement could just have been there.'

Verschoyle gave him a tired smile. 'You've obviously come out of it mentally unharmed,' he said. 'You still sound like Ginger Maguire.'

He produced a lift to the Castle and, still in shirtsleeves, his wrinkled clothes drying on him, Kelly reported to Corbett who assigned a Wren writer to him to take down his report. She looked about sixteen and, after what he'd seen in Dunkirk, breathtakingly beautiful.

As he left the office, somebody handed him a telegram and he read it dazedly, half-expecting it to inform him of the loss of Rumbelo's son in *Grafton*. Instead, it announced the death of Rear-Admiral Sir Edward Maguire, Bt., from a heart attack at his club in London. It had been sent by the club's secretary to Thakenham and re-addressed by Biddy. Just then it didn't really register.

Two hours later, he headed back to the docks. Rumbelo and

Boyle had appeared at the Castle, like himself still wearing the clothes they'd worn when they'd had to swim for their lives, but he was worried about Le Mesurier. Drunk or sober, he'd done a tremendous job and he was hoping against hope he might have turned up.

Somebody gave him a lift to the docks in a staff car. Tugs were moving ships whose crews were fast asleep, doing the whole job themselves because it was impossible to wake the exhausted men below, and there were rows of stretchers along the small boat stage which sweating helpers were hoisting into ambulances. Women bent over the wounded, fixing labels to their battle-dress blouses, and one of them was holding a mug of tea to a man whose head was swathed in bandages. For a while Kelly stared at her with red-rimmed eyes. I know this woman, he thought dazedly. I've known her all my life.

Despite his weariness, he felt a stab of pain at all the promise and pleasure he'd lost, and his thoughts scampered like frightened mice through his mind as he tried to make out how she came to be there when she should have been in America. Then, through a daze of exhaustion, he remembered meeting Mabel in London. She'd got off the Dover train, he recalled, and now he realised why.

He felt like a guilty schoolboy up before the headmaster as he stepped forward.

'Hello, Charley,' he said.

Part Two

1

Charley straightened up, frowning. At first she didn't recognise him because he was wearing a pair of borrowed shoes that were too big for him and someone else's jacket, then recognition came and, for a moment, there was anguish in her face. Finally her expression changed again to one that was devoid of both pleasure and displeasure.

'Hello, Kelly,' she said quietly.

'Where did you come from?' he asked.

She guessed he hadn't slept for a week. His face was grey and gaunt with fatigue, and he was stooping with weariness, but though her heart went out to him, she kept hold of herself and forced herself to answer calmly.

'There was a war on. America was no place for me.'

He had expected nothing more, felt he deserved no more, and began to turn away, but she put a hand on his arm.

'Where are you going?'

'I'm looking for a naval officer. Name of Le Mesurier. Don't suppose you've seen him, have you?'

In his weariness, his tongue stumbled over the words and her heart swelled with compassion. 'I think you need some sleep,' she said.

'Yes,' he agreed. 'I expect someone will find me a bed.'

She produced a key from her pocket and gave him an address. 'Go to my place,' she said. 'There's a bed there. If I hear of your officer, I'll let you know.'

He wasn't sure in his weariness how he found himself on the doorstep of her flat. The place was small with only a living-dining room, but it was neat and full of sunshine and chintz. On the window ledge was a silver frame containing the photograph of a man in an RAF wing-commander's uniform. It was a strong, intelligent good-looking face, but in his tiredness Kelly missed its significance.

Immediately opposite the door was a table bearing a whisky decanter and, in a daze, he sloshed half a tumbler of the spirit into a glass. Going to the bathroom, he splashed water into it from a tap and began to drink. Then, staring around him, he became aware of toothbrushes, face cloths and silk stockings hanging from a small clothes line. He gazed at them, only dimly aware that they belonged to Charley – *his* Charley – the Charley he'd wanted to marry all his life and who once had wanted to marry him. Then weariness swept over him. He couldn't remember when he'd last closed his eyes and he went in search of a bed.

Stumbling through a doorway, he found a small room where there was a double bed spread with a flowered cover, and it looked incredibly comfortable. As he emptied his pockets, he found the telegram he'd been handed at the Castle and stared at it dully. So the old boy had gone at last, he thought. He'd begun to think of him as immortal. Then he realised that it meant that he'd inherited the title. Unexpectedly, when he'd forgotten all about it, he'd suddenly become Sir Kelly Maguire, Baronet.

He tried to think about what it meant but he was too tired and he thrust it from his mind without much effort. Then he realised that the bed he was about to climb into was Charley's and, though he'd been in a few women's beds in his time, he'd never been in hers, and it seemed so wrong he turned round and headed for the settee. He was just about to sit down when he realised he was filthy dirty and stank of sweat and smoke and blood, so he found a blanket in a cupboard and lay down on the floor instead.

When he came round, he was in the bed. How he'd got there he had no idea, but somebody had stripped his clothes off and he lay staring at the ceiling, trying to remember what had happened. As he tried to recover his wits, the door clicked and he saw Charley looking at him.

'How did I get here?' he asked.

'I put you there.'

'Dragged me?'

'You walked. Sleep-walked would be a better description.'

She disappeared and returned, grave-faced and unsmiling, with a tray.

'I expect you could do with a cup of tea.'

It was a trite sort of remark and, under the circumstances, terribly English, but somehow, it seemed to steady a world in danger of whirling off its axis into insanity. And, after all the salt water he'd swallowed, the vast swig he'd taken from Verschoyle's flask and the enormous whisky that had followed, his mouth felt as if he'd been weeks in the Sahara.

'Yes,' he agreed. 'I could.'

As she poured the tea, he studied her under drooping eyelids. She was a beautiful, dignified woman, not very different from when he'd last seen her, but with a clear wariness about her that made him feel wary in return, and he didn't know what to say. It was seven years since he'd last seen her and thirteen since they'd ruined their lives by marrying the wrong partners.

He could see himself in the mirror opposite, gaunt with tiredness, his eyes circled by dark shadows, his chin blurred by a three-day-old beard. She didn't seem to notice, however, and sat on the end of the bed. She was wearing a blue dress that matched her eyes and she looked so beautiful he wanted to weep for all the wasted years.

'Your officer doesn't appear to have turned up,' she told him quietly. 'I'm sorry.'

He shrugged. 'He was a brave man.'

For a moment, they were silent, unable to find anything to say. It was as if they were strangers and it bothered him because once they'd shared all of each other's secrets. He didn't know a thing about her now, he realised, nothing beyond what he could see.

'What are you doing in Dover, Charley?' he asked quietly.

'I live here.' She answered his question but volunteered nothing further.

'In this place?'

'Yes.'

'What happened to the American?'

'He was killed. In an automobile accident. Six months after I arrived. We'd planned our wedding.'

There was nothing much he could say except that he was sorry.

Her shoulders moved in a slight shrug but there was still no expression on her face. Remembering the times she'd greeted him with delight, and the laughter he'd heard from her, he found her expressionlessness heart-breaking.

'So why here?' he asked.

'When the war started, I came home and got a job with the Navy. They employ a lot of civilians.'

There was an uneasy silence and he felt he had to say something. 'I saw Mabel at Victoria,' he said.

She managed a small smile at last, a ghost of a smile that made him think that perhaps he was getting through to her.

'She's got fat but she seems very happy,' she said. 'George was in France, but he was one of the first out. She telephoned. He's been sent to a depot near Cheltenham.'

'I'm glad,' Kelly said. 'And I'm glad Mabel's happy.' He paused before he went on. 'Did you marry again, Charley?'

'No.'

He couldn't believe that nobody had tried. 'Is – is there a man?'

'No,' she said quietly.

'Never?'

'I'm not a nun,' she said coldly. 'There was one in the RAF but he was lost in a raid on Kiel last year.'

Oh, God, he thought, remembering the photograph he'd seen, what had she done to have to endure so much unhappiness?

'I'm sorry.'

She shrugged again. 'I'm over it now,' she said. 'I think there must be limits to a person's comprehension of sadness.'

He found his mind was becoming hazy and, as the cup of tea tilted, he jumped and realised he'd been falling asleep.

'I'm afraid I've spilt it on the cover,' he said.

She said nothing but took it from him and pressed him down in the bed.

His eyelids drooped and when he wasn't expecting it, she leaned over and kissed him on the forehead. Automatically he tried to grab her but she'd gone before he could get his hands free and he lay back, disappointed, a little sad, unutterably lonely and desperately depressed still by what he'd seen at the other side of the Channel.

But he was also too tired to care, and as his eyelids drooped again, he allowed himself to drift into sleep.

He remembered waking up and seeing the room flooded with sunshine, but he was quite indifferent and allowed himself to drift off again. When he came round once more, it was dark outside and the curtains were drawn against the black-out.

He lay for a while trying to remember what had happened, then he wondered where Rumbelo and Boyle had got to and remembered that Le Mesurier had not turned up. He'd have to get the man an award of some sort, he felt. He'd been a tower of strength, civilian or not, drunk or sober, and he deserved something. The thought of his dying when they'd almost made it jerked at his heartstrings and he remembered seeing *Crested Eagle*, *Fenella*, *Grenade* and *Jaguar* hit by bombs, and *Crested Eagle* on fire and sinking in the fairway with all the French and all the wounded on board that they'd just rescued from *Fenella*. Unexpectedly, he found there were tears in his eyes and, as he blinked them away, he found Charley watching him from the doorway. She was wearing a neat skirt and a blue and white-striped linen blouse.

'Kelly! What is it?'

He tried to tell her but he choked over the words. She came to the bed and knelt beside it, with her hands on his.

'Oh, Kelly!'

He put his arms round her and they clung together like sorrowing schoolgirls.

'Don't say anything now, Kelly,' she said quietly. 'Just go to sleep.' She kissed him again and tried to draw away but he couldn't bear to let her go and clung on to her, pulling her to him. For a moment they stayed like that, their faces only an inch or two apart. It was impossible to tell her that she represented all the things they'd lost across the other side of the Channel. She represented peace, England, his youth, his whole life even, in a way nobody else ever had.

Her head turned uncertainly as he kissed her throat but she didn't resist, and as his hand came up to her breast he felt her tense and saw her eyes fill with tears.

She gave a little moan, still, after all the wasted years, crucified by her longing for him. 'Oh, Kelly!' she whispered again.

'Why did you go away?'

She turned a lost face towards him. Love, he decided, was a sort of self-immolation that left you dizzy but, with her in his arms again, he didn't care. There had been many times in recent years when there'd been a loneliness it had seemed impossible to endure, but suddenly, now, he felt he was no longer on his own. They kissed with a painful intensity and then she was crying, hard sobs with taut lips and clenched teeth, small and lost like a child, as if she were putty in his hands.

Their love-making was intense and left him shocked by its sheer carnality and passion. It was fierce and twice as powerful because it was a relief from the agony across the Channel, a relief from exhaustion and ugliness and misery. When he woke again it was daylight. There was a man's dressing gown over the end of the bed and he wondered if she'd borrowed it for him or whether it belonged to someone who stayed with her, some man who'd slept in her bed as he had.

He found her in the tiny kitchen, listening to the news on the radio and making coffee on an electric cooker. She was quite different from the previous night. She'd regained control of herself and was cool and distant. He moved to her and put his arms round her, but she slipped away and placed a cup, saucer and plate on the table. Moving to her again, he tried once more but again she slipped away.

'No,' she said. 'That was last night. It's different now.'

'Why?'

She turned angrily. 'What am I supposed to be, Kelly? Disappearing the way you did every time, you could hardly expect when we meet again that I should just hold the bed-clothes back for you to slip in beside me. Just because it happens to suit you and the Navy says it's all right. I was in love with you, Kelly. Always.'

He couldn't believe his ears. Her tones were sharp when he'd expected gentleness.

'You behaved last night as if you still were,' he said.

She refused to meet his eyes. 'I was carried away,' she said. 'It was all that agony at the docks. It seemed to demand some self-sacrifice. Call it my war effort.'

He watched her, baffled, his thoughts sad and splintered with pain, but she made no attempt to show any sign of

112

warmth. He didn't believe her, couldn't believe her. Their behaviour the night before could never have been the result only of the sweeping emotion that had run through the country, proud, giving – but still impersonal. She'd held him to her, moaning softly, whispering and calling out his name in ecstasy.

He sat down, uncertain how to react. She filled his cup and he sat smoking a cigarette from a packet she pushed across. After a while he became aware of the radio and realised he was listening to Churchill's words. They were from a speech he'd made and somehow they had more in them to stir the blood than he'd heard for years from the tradesmen of the thirties who'd masqueraded as diplomats and statesmen.

'We shall defend our island, whatever the cost may be. We shall fight on the beaches, we shall fight on the landing grounds, we shall fight in the fields and in the streets, we shall fight in the hills; we shall never surrender – '

As the announcer faded, she switched off the radio. In the silence, Kelly's voice sounded loud.

'What day is it?'

'Wednesday. You slept for two days.'

He sighed and moved uneasily. 'I think I'd better go and make my number with the admiral.'

She gave him a quick look. 'You always made sure you made your number with the admiral, didn't you, Kelly?'

He stared at her, disappointed with her reactions, angry at her attitude, and frustrated by the perplexed gropings of his mind.

'I'm still in the navy, Charley,' he said.

She looked at him steadily, accusing him for all the years of ambition, all the years of conforming when she'd felt he should have put her first. 'You always were, Kelly,' she said.

His brows came down. 'Dammit, Charley, there's a war on!'

Her eyes flashed and she went pink with rage. He'd always been brisk with her but now it acted like an electric shock. Reaching across him, she snatched up the photograph of the man in the wing commander's uniform and slammed it down in front of him, so that the dead man's face stared up at him, her sole souvenir.

'Do you think *I* don't know?' she snapped.

But the mole was working again now, despite the fact that it had been breached half a dozen times and repaired with planks and ladders again and again; offshore, small miracles were still being performed as men made sails with clothing and water-proof capes, and engineers stood waist-deep in waterlogged engine rooms to watch their gauges. The Casino was blazing and there were wrecks in the fairway circled by small boats on the look-out for survivors. Beyond those still on the mole, there were no known complete units left to be rescued, and Tennant had sent the signal, 'BEF evacuated,' the previous night.

The dead lay all over the town, in hastily-scraped graves in gardens and parks and among the sand dunes. They floated along the tide line and lay in the warm soil all the way back to the Belgian frontier and through the graveyards of the earlier war. They huddled in ditches, in the fields and in the streets of dozens of small towns and villages, among the wrecked guns and smoking vehicles of a defeated army. Hundreds more were entombed in the cold hulks of ships beneath the sea.

During the night, the shelling had grown more intense and the German bombers seemed to be hovering above the town all the time. The din was deafening and Kelly and his little party were still on the move among the shattered streets, climbing over piles of bricks and timber and dodging the fires to direct the last men towards the mole. They were stumbling with exhaustion by this time, and when daylight came, Kelly found his party had dwindled to Boyle, Rumbelo and Le Mesurier. The others had taken advantage of the confusion to step aboard a ship, and he felt he couldn't blame them, because no one could look forward to being a prisoner of war with equanimity. Officially the evacuation had ended. There was nothing to do from this point on but save themselves.

They were in the last stages now, and the French admiral was moving with his staff towards the sea. Behind them came an immense river of refugees and craven soldiers – French, Belgians, Moroccans, British – who had hidden in ruined houses from the bombing, to snatch the places of the desperate fighting troops. In a fury, Kelly mustered a group of Guardsmen, artillerymen, sailors and cavalrymen, and they formed a line at the end of the mole with two machine guns and their rifles at the ready.

2

By a miracle the country had come through. There was no army worth mentioning and survival depended on elderly gentlemen with Great War medals standing guard on cross roads armed with shotguns, pitchforks and – for God's sake! – pikes. Ageing generals were serving in the Local Defence Volunteers – the Look, Duck and Vanish Brigade, as it was known – under men who'd been their subalterns but had the advantage of being younger and more active, and Kelly heard that Admiral Tyrwhitt, his former chief, had enlisted as a private.

They had rescued over 300,000 men from France, when the expected total had been in the region of 20,000, and, though they had no weapons and there seemed to be not a single gun or tank in the whole country, they still had the nucleus of an armed force; moreover, an armed force with the skill and knowledge obtained from crossing swords with the Nazis.

It was clear they'd been lucky. Thanks to Gort and the Navy, the country had survived. If Dunkirk had failed, it was doubtful if Britain could have withstood the Nazis because Churchill still wasn't securely in the saddle and in the ranks of his ministers he'd been obliged to accept men who'd once been appeasers. But at least, now, for the first time, there was the feel of a strong hand on the wheel. Dunkirk had burned with self-sacrifice and high endeavour like an incandescent flame and had awakened something spontaneously all over the country, and the cricket, the half-days and the long week-ends had stopped overnight. Self-indulgence became something to be ashamed of, and men and women at last found the direction and the encouragement they needed.

Virtually unemployed, without a ship, Kelly found himself once more under Corbett. He had a room at the Castle and

Dover had suddenly become the front line. Yet there was a curious calm about the country so that he somehow couldn't imagine it panicking, perhaps even a feeling of relief that there were no longer any doubtful allies to worry about and they could go it alone.

With six British and three French destroyers lost and twenty-three others badly damaged in nine days, the Navy was stretched to its limit. To redress the balance a little and despite the horror it produced among those who could foresee a whole decade of bitterness and distrust, the French Fleet at Oran was destroyed by gunfire by Admiral Somerville's ships from Gibraltar to prevent it falling into the hands of the Germans. As a French expert, Kelly was flown to the Rock to act as interpreter, but the affair had been concluded before he arrived and he was promptly flown back, wondering if Archie Bumf had escaped and what he made of it all. Meanwhile, the government was negotiating with West Indian bases for fifty old American first-war vessels to take the place of the lost destroyers, because the U-boats had already begun to step up their assault on the convoys in the Atlantic.

In their efforts to subdue British resistance, the Germans had also started bombing Channel convoys, an operation that had soon changed to an all-out assault on RAF stations in the south, and everybody guessed it was the prelude to an invasion.

Slipping back to Thakeham to collect kit to replace that which he'd lost at Dunkirk, Kelly found only Paddy at home.

'Mother's gone to see brother Kelly,' she announced. 'They fished him out of the sea with nothing worse than a broken toe and a bad cut on his head.'

They hugged each other, thankful not to be in mourning, and sat down to a meal of bacon and eggs cooked by Paddy in Biddy's kitchen.

'How's Hugh?' Kelly asked.

'Doing his daredevil pilot thing,' Paddy said, suddenly becoming serious. 'He's converting to Hurricanes. The RAF's asked for volunteers from the Navy to help out.'

She gave him a quick look and, behind the smile, he saw the fear in her eyes. Young men were being killed every day along the south coast of England in an effort to prevent the Luftwaffe wrenching the command of the sky from the RAF, and he tried to anaesthetize her fear with distractions.

'How about you? When are you going to lead him to the post?'

'As soon as there's time.' She gave him a fleeting smile. 'We've all been a bit busy lately, haven't we?'

During the weekend Hugh telephoned to say he'd finished his conversion course and as Kelly, on his way back to Dover, kissed Paddy goodbye, he held her gently for a while.

'Take it easy,' he said quietly. 'It might never happen.'

'On the other hand,' she replied in her forthright manner, 'it jolly well might. I know what his chances are because we've had one or two pilots in the hospital and I've talked to them.' She lifted her eyes to his, steady and fearless and willing to face what lay ahead. 'But I'm ready for it. We've already been to bed together and I regret nothing, only the fact that the bloody war's somehow got in the way at a time when we need to be so close you couldn't shove a fig leaf between us.' She lifted her face to gaze frankly at him. 'I've applied to join the services.'

'Which one?'

'The Navy, of course.' She managed a shaky grin. 'Can you imagine what Hugh or Father, or Brother Kelly – or *you*, for that matter! – would say if I joined one of the less senior services?'

Back in Dover, Kelly found himself listening every evening to the news, wondering when he was going to hear that Hugh was no longer alive. The country's future hung on a thread as fragile as a spider's web. RAF pilot casualties were enormous and Hugh was already in action, he knew, because Rumbelo, informed from home via Biddy, had told him he was.

When work permitted, he saw Charley. But she'd changed from being an enthusiastic girl to a prickly woman. She seemed prepared to accept him in a matter-of-fact sort of way that he found difficult to accept, and they rarely talked about the life she'd lived in America and never about the past. She was friendly but never encouraging, and he found himself falling hopelessly in love with her again. When she'd always been available and he'd expected her to marry him, he'd taken her for granted, but now her very inaccessibility worked on his system like an aphrodisiac.

In September, he was sent to Harwich and from there to Felixstowe, to sort out problems at *HMS Beehive* and pick up information for the establishment of new motor torpedo boat bases at Portland and Fowey and the setting up of a new command to deal solely with coastal forces. The place was full of noisy young men, most of them Hostilities-Onlys, and his rank didn't bother them in the slightest, though they were somewhat in awe of his medal ribbons and once they found what they represented were inclined to shove enthusiastically with their elbows to make room for him at the bar.

Because they'd not been moulded by the long education and apprenticeship of the regulars, they had far less respect for their elders than the products of Dartmouth, but they also had fewer inhibitions. They were astute enough to show respect for what was admirable in naval tradition, but brought a fresh breeze of ribald derision into a service where conservatism was a common characteristic. Those recalled elderly officers who grumbled about their indifference to the niceties of dress when entering or leaving port or the way they made mating sounds at the Wrens from the ship's deck had been inclined at first to go red in the face with anger but by this time they were all growing used to each other, and as the newcomers tried to look like professionals and began to use King's Regulations and Admiralty Instructions as if it were a Bible, the older men became more and more amateur in appearance and used it to prop up the broken leg of a table.

The war was now in its second stage as they drew breath after Dunkirk. Slowly the country rearmed itself. Tank, field gun and fighter deliveries mounted steadily. The embers had only glowed after Dunkirk but, with Churchill blowing on them, they blazed into a fire of enthusiasm. With the Germans in possession of the Atlantic seaboard from Norway to Spain, however, the main problem remained the convoys and supplies from America, and Kelly knew that his time ashore was growing short.

His first leave since the war had begun took him to London to attend to his father's affairs. From there he went to Thakeham. Biddy greeted him warily and he guessed that Rumbelo had told her that Charley was around again. Rumbelo had never made any bones about his attitude. He'd never agreed with Kelly's marriage to Christina and, given the chance, Kelly suspected, he'd scheme to the limit to bring them together. Biddy

117

was more circumspect and careful to show neither doubt nor pleasure, concentrating solely on the pride she felt at her son being given a DSM in the rash of medals that had resulted from Dunkirk.

'Tell him to apply for a commission, Biddy,' Kelly advised. 'I'll push it with everything I've got.'

He spent the week going through his father's papers. As he'd expected, the old man had left him nothing but the title. He'd never really known him, anyway, and in the confusion after Dunkirk had not even been to his funeral. He suspected, in fact, that he'd still been asleep when they'd put the old man away, and all he had left of him were his old uniforms with their tarnished braid and a few relics of his service under Victoria.

The place seemed curiously empty with Rumbelo's family all away and he was wondering if he dared go back to Dover to see Charley when Biddy appeared with a telegram. This time he thought it was about Hugh but what it contained was totally unexpected.

'1130. OHMS ADMIRALTY LONDON AS OF LAST NIGHT. CAPT. GK MAGUIRE THAKEHAM – YOU ARE APPOINTED 23RD DESTROYER FLOTILLA IN COMMAND AUGUST 17. JOIN MERSEY FORTHWITH – FROM ADMIRALTY.'

It could hardly be called a step up.

He arrived in London in the middle of an air raid and had to waste two hours in the Underground at Victoria. The first person he met at the Admiralty was Corbett.

'Hello, Kelly,' he said. 'Hear they've given you the Twenty-Third Flotilla. They're I-class ships and pretty up-to-date. You're attached to C.-in-C., Western Approaches, but, make no mistake about it, it's only on a short-term loan because things are going to boil up in the Med now that Mussolini's come in on Hitler's side. Gibraltar's having her civilians evacuated and, as you know, Malta was hardly in a state to look after herself up to a month or two ago. But, with the Mediterranean Fleet in foreign waters and surrounded by foreign land at Alexandria, someone suddenly woke up to the fact that the place has advantages as an air base. It'll need supplying, though, and you'll probably find yourself doing it.'

As Kelly left, he met Verschoyle, who was quick to congratulate him.

'I think you and I had better go and have a drink,' he said. 'I've got the Nineteenth. Four Hunt-class ships – *Chatsworth*, *Hallamshire*, *Ashby* and *Rushden*, small and a bit older than yours, but a flotilla nevertheless.'

They took a taxi but, instead of getting out of it at their club, as Kelly had expected, Verschoyle stopped it at a Mayfair address.

'It's time you met Christina again,' he said.

Kelly was wary because Christina had never been noted for her kindness, but though she was beautiful and as hard as a diamond, this time she was subdued and even friendly.

'You grow more good-looking, Kelly,' she observed. 'Age becomes you.'

'You, too, Christina.'

She smiled. 'I no longer throw the crockery at James,' she said. 'And since the war started, I even try not to be too selfish. I don't suppose it'll last, though, especially as I can no longer go to the South of France for a change.'

'At least you haven't fled to America,' Kelly said. 'Quite a few have.'

Christina gave a snort of disgust. 'Whatever our faults,' she said, 'my family never dodged danger. If the Germans do make it across the Channel, you'll not find me Kowtowing to them, and I've dropped a lot of people who I know damn well would. I wouldn't be seen dead in a neutral country while England's fighting for her life.' She smiled. 'Hugh's written to say he's been given the DSC for killing Germans, by the way, and that ought to please him because he always thought you wore the most spectacular array of ribbons he'd ever seen' – she paused and tapped his chest – 'among which, incidentally, I noticed two new ones.'

There was no longer any feeling for his ex-wife and Kelly was not sorry to escape and catch the evening train to Dover. The first thing that had occurred to him when he'd read his orders had been that he had to see Charley, because he'd wondered more than once if he dared try to put their relationship on a more stable footing. When they were together, beneath the brittle shell of their conversation there were always strange

119

underlying currents and he knew she was as aware of them as he was. But he knew also that she was no longer awed by the mystique of sailormen and had never forgiven him for disappearing on duty from Shanghai when she'd arrived there in 1927 to marry him.

But, because they'd been too close to each other for too much of their childhood and youth, she also could not entirely put him aside, and she greeted him warmly enough, though with just enough wariness to make him doubtful. As he waited for her to give him a drink, he noticed that the photograph of the RAF officer had vanished, and he guessed that its disappearance had been attended with some thought and a decision to start again.

It gave him hope but, as she offered him his glass, he noticed she was studying him cautiously, with the suppressed excitement of a dog about to start a fight. His own excitement had not gone unnoticed and she'd already guessed why he was there.

Swallowing the last of his drink, he stood up and faced her. 'I'm going to sea again, Charley,' he said.

She looked up at him, the dark shadows under her eyes making her seem more fragile. 'I'm pleased for you, Kelly,' she said. 'I know it's what you want.'

He stared at her, faintly baffled by her indifference. His mood was a curious and uncharacteristic blend of defeat and confusion. He'd given orders so long he was almost physically uncomfortable in a relationship that required a democratic exchange of viewpoints. Besides, he loved his country and was prepared to fight for it and he resented her coolness that implied he was being put on trial for his attitudes and convictions.

He forced himself to continue, because he had to. 'Marry me before I go, Charley,' he said quietly.

Indignation flared in her eyes, then it vanished again and he saw an infinite pity and distress fill them for the merest fraction of a second. For a long time she was silent and his heart began to thump. He'd been in love with her all his life – despite Christina, despite Teresa, despite all the other women he'd known – and his love had returned undiminished since he'd bumped into her again. During his period with Corbett, he'd seen her occasionally about the corridors of Dover Castle and had often heard other officers commenting on her, even trying to invite her to dinner. She'd always refused them, however, and, because his reputation and quick temper were legendary, when they'd seen him with her the word had gone round quickly and she'd been left alone. She hadn't seemed to mind, existing in a quiet vacuum, her mind curiously secretive, and, though her expression had never been inviting, it had also always been friendly.

Because he'd convinced himself he had a chance, her answer rocked him. 'My answer to that one's simple, Kelly,' she said, looking him straight in the face. 'No.'

The proposal had not been impulsive and, not really expecting her to refuse him, he was aware of a sick disappointment.

'They've given me a flotilla,' he said. 'And now my father's dead I have the baronetcy.'

He'd hoped faintly that the news might change her attitude but he ought to have known better and she showed no interest whatsoever. Instead she gave him that faint smile he'd come to know so well.

'And you think you need a wife to go with them?'

'No! Good God, no, Charley!' He tried a different line, still curiously humble. 'When I came back from Dunkirk,' he said, 'we spent the night together.'

She had no idea what had prompted his surrender, and he couldn't know she was too afraid of him to let him come near her. Too many wasted years had gone by and, though she knew he blamed himself for them, she knew also that much of the blame lay with her, too. She'd expected to take first place in his life when naval wives never did. She'd been jealous of his ships and the devotion he'd given to his men.

'What difference does that make?' she said.

He was looking at her in bewilderment, feeling she might have had the detachment to feel some sort of compassion for him, then he thrust the feeling aside, knowing it was self-pity, something he despised.

She tried to speak calmly. She'd been too much alone over the years, aching for his love as he thought of his ships and the sea, frightened at the thought of him leaving her again – and again – and again. She was trying hard to control her emotions but the effort was so physically draining she felt exhausted. He

121

was not aware of the unbearable tension in her and that she was afraid that at any instant she might burst into tears. Her eyes were dark and haunted against the pallor of her face.

'Standards have changed,' she pointed out, forcing her voice to be steady. 'It isn't 1920 any more and there's a war on. People are concerned to get what they can out of life, while they still have it.'

What she said shocked him, but she didn't pursue the matter with accusations.

'I *was* in love with you once, Kelly,' she admitted coolly. 'That's true.'

'And now?'

'No.'

'Will you ever be again?'

Her shoulders moved tiredly. She felt she'd like to cry but crying had always come hard to her and her emotions left her confused and bewildered. 'How do I know? *You* haven't changed much, but I have. I've had to.'

'Charley – ' he paused. 'If anything happened to me, there'd be my pension. It wouldn't be insubstantial and I happen to know you're not well off.'

She gave him a sad little smile. 'You sound as if you're offering something from a bargain basement.'

'Perhaps I am,' he said quietly. 'Perhaps it's that important.'

She looked up at him quickly, catching the stillness of his expression, the sudden cold appraisal of his eyes. She experienced an uncomfortable twist of fear and need but she couldn't manage any effort to help him. She was giving nothing away because her own marriage – for which she'd always blamed him – had been a disaster and had tied her to a man she'd never even been able to respect.

Kelly was only sadly conscious of the difference in her, aware that something that had existed between them had gone and would take years to put back.

'I just wanted you to feel – ' he began. Then he stopped and shrugged. 'But it doesn't matter now. After all, your life's your own. I've no claim on it.' He managed a smile. 'You'll be able to see all those other people at the Castle without concerning yourself any more with whether I'll be jealous or not.'

'I didn't concern myself, Kelly,' she said sharply. Then she

122

realised she was being unnecessarily cruel and her voice dropped. She didn't meet his eyes. 'And there aren't any other men.'

'There will be when I'm not here.'

'No.'

He tried again, not with much hope. 'Then why won't you marry me?'

He was frowning and it pleased her somehow to find he was human enough to lose his temper. It made him more selfish and more real.

'Because the Navy has no time for women, Kelly,' she said. 'In the Army, wives are part of the regiment. The Navy's concern is with ships, and wives are merely indiscretions.'

There was an element of truth in what she said and there was a long silence before she spoke again, quietly, as if he'd never even mentioned marriage.

'When do you take over?'

'Tomorrow.'

'Where are you staying?'

'I expect I can find a room at the Castle.'

There was a long pause. 'You could always stay here,' she said.

He put down his glass. His hand was unsteady and it rattled against the mantelshelf.

'I thought you said—'

Her eyes met his, clear and unequivocal. 'I said I wouldn't *marry* you, Kelly. *That*'s what I said.'

It seemed a strange sort of agreement but he was afraid, now that he'd found her, of losing her again and was willing to accept anything that would allow him to be near her occasionally.

'We shall be based on the Mersey, I believe,' he said. 'That means Western Approaches. But not for long, I'm afraid.'

'The Mediterranean?'

He guessed she'd heard something at the Castle and he nodded. 'They're expecting trouble there.'

'And they want Ginger Maguire.'

The comment flattered him a little but he remained humble. 'Something like that.'

'I expect you're just what's needed.'

123

Hell on wheels as a sailor, Mabel had once said of him, but a dead loss as a hearts-and-flowers type. It seemed he still was.

'There may be odd week-ends before we go,' he said slowly, picking his way carefully through the shoals of thought that troubled him. 'I'd like to come and see you.'

His humility troubled her more than she'd thought possible. 'Why not?'

'Won't it make any difference?'

'None at all, Kelly. We've been friends far too long.'

Friends! It was like a jab in the guts from a marlin spike.

'There's only one bed, I'm afraid. And the settee's hard and not nearly big enough.'

She seemed to be dropping hints.

'Perhaps I can leave a camp bed here,' he suggested.

She looked at him unblinkingly, giving nothing away but not hostile either.

'Yes,' she said. 'Do that. You could put it in the living room.'

Her coolness almost broke his heart and he knew the hints he'd imagined weren't hints at all. Why did women feel they were the only ones who could suffer? Why did they feel that men, because they didn't show their emotions, because very often they'd been trained *not* to show their emotions, never had any? She'd clearly lost control when he'd come back from Dunkirk, and she was completely in possession of herself now.

'Yes,' he said. 'I'll do that.'

But he knew he never would.

3

Impi, Inca, Impatient and *Indian*, the I-class destroyers of the Twenty-Third Flotilla, had been completed in the year before the war and, like all the new destroyers, were bigger than their forbears. While Verschoyle's Hunt-class ships were only just over a thousand tons, slow, and carried only four-inch anti-aircraft armament and no torpedoes, the Is were almost 1500 tons and carried four 4.7-inchers and torpedo tubes and had a speed of over thirty-six knots. The flotilla leader, *Impi*, was even bigger, with quarters for the flotilla commander's staff, and she was an impressive sight butting into the seas at full revolutions. At this speed the vibration was heavy but she handled well and it was a pleasure to Kelly to bring her alongside in his usual fashion – like a midshipman with a pinnace – which had more than once in the past resulted in scraped paint, crushed whalers and a few sour looks from the mooring party trying to get ropes ashore. Never good with a ship in close conditions, for once he was pleased to notice he'd made a good job of it and as he rang down 'Finished with engines,' he was flattered to see relieved smiles all round and hear one of the mooring party below him whistling 'Anybody here seen Kelly?'

It did his heart good because it had been almost a signature tune in *Mordant*. In the sad years between the wars, when the Admiralty had lost touch with its sailors and the gulf between wardroom and mess deck had become enormous, it had disappeared from the lower deck's repertoire, but the Navy had rediscovered its soul since Norway and Dunkirk, and pride was visible again.

Impi was a well-run ship with a first-rate Number One and few names in the Captain's Report. Only one occurred regularly, that of 'Dancer' Siggis, a lantern-jawed Irish able-seaman who seemed unable to carry his beer.

'Well, sorr,' he liked to explain, 'me ma was a barmaid and she used to enjoy her Guinness, so mebbe I imbibed it with me mother's milk.'

They could never tell whether he believed it or was deliberately pulling their leg, but he was the ship's character and, though he took thirty seconds to write his own name, he was a dead shot with the twin Bofors and could work out in his head in a moment how long it took to close to a given range, so that the tendency was always to treat him lightly. 'After all,' Kelly observed, 'sailors aren't bloody spinsters.'

In October, the flotilla was sent to Liverpool and kept busy about the Irish Sea. It was a curiously remote kind of life and, except for odd days in harbour, they were out of touch with the world, their only home the lonely ocean and the winter gales. The ship seemed crowded by peacetime standards because extra experts had been pushed aboard and there were often complements of troops or even civilians, pressed on them by some authority able to bully the Admiralty.

Rumbelo's son, expecting his commission to come through any time, was aboard *Hood* at Scapa, while Hugh, newly in the Mediterranean, was flying from *Illustrious*. Paddy was still working in the hospital at Esher but was making threatening noises about leaving if Hugh didn't return to marry her and the Navy didn't accept her application to become a naval nursing sister.

At the end of November, Kelly attended the Palace to receive a bar to his DSO for the capture of *Kölndom* and the action in Narvik Fjord, and the CB he'd been given for Dunkirk. Because there was no one else and Biddy was already there with her son, he took Paddy. The press photographers were waiting outside as he left, taking pictures of all the recipients.

'Is this your wife, sir?' one of them asked, indicating Paddy.

She grinned delightedly at Kelly so that he almost wished she were. 'I haven't got a wife,' he growled and he knew the picture would appear the following day with him looking as if he were about to attack the photographer.

'You know what they'll think, don't you?' Paddy giggled as he pushed her into a taxi and took the lot of them to lunch. 'That I'm a tart and you're a dirty old man.'

126

At the beginning of December, he learned he'd been given Verschoyle's flotilla as well as his own. He didn't persuade himself it was for any other reason than that, after Dunkirk and Norway, there was no one else and it didn't seem to mean promotion.

By this time the vast majority of the men in the ships were Hostilities-Only sailors and Liverpool presented a warlike picture as the frontline base of the Atlantic operations. Cranes clattered and pneumatic drills yammered, while tugs scuttled up and down the Mersey, their whistles wailing, and destroyers, sloops and corvettes whooped their warnings as they moved in and out of the port. The C.-in-C.'s headquarters were at Derby House, and the ops room had a floor-to-ceiling map of the Atlantic, showing convoys, escorts and submarines. Wren plotters, their mouths full of tape and pins, were laying out the routes and, in the glass-fronted offices overlooking it all, duty control officers watched them at work. In that great room it wasn't hard to believe that the business of countering the U-boats was a simple matter for the men at sea.

Kelly's first job was to brief his new commanding officers in what he expected of them and try out the ships' companies. As they left harbour for working-up exercises off the coast of Scotland, he was determined there should be no individualists, but a single unit.

The working-up routine had been devised by an expert in the art of driving both officers and men to the limit, and all day they carried out anti-submarine and gunnery exercises and at night controlled imaginary convoys. By the end of November they were as trained as the brief course would allow and they returned to Liverpool to act as convoy escorts. As *Impi* went alongside the oiler in Kelly's usual hit-or-miss fashion, she wiped off *Chatsworth*'s whaler.

Going across to apologise, he informed Verschoyle that there was to be no leave.

'Pity,' Verschoyle said. 'Thought I might slip down to Dover to see Maisie. When Christina's having a bad temper, she always makes me welcome.'

To Kelly's delight, Paddy appeared, demanding that he take her out to dinner. At long last, she was wearing the uniform of a naval nursing sister and was waiting to go to Haslar near

Portsmouth to absorb naval methods, ideals and mannerisms.

'What about Hugh?' Kelly asked.

'Too far away,' she said bluntly. 'Still with *Illustrious*. And that's no good to me. I want him here in England, and alongside me.' She looked at Kelly with steady eyes. 'And I mean *alongside*,' she said firmly. 'Standing up and lying down. In bed or out of bed. I need him and he needs me, and that's the way it's going to be when he comes home, married or not.'

Too many attitudes had changed since the war and he wasn't shocked. Indeed, it only brought home to him once more his own loneliness.

The following day he was informed he was to take a convoy to New York and, clutching a brief case containing the Western Approaches Convoy Instructions, the convoy bible, he met the officers of the merchant ships at a conference to brief them on his intentions. To his surprise, the commodore was 'Gorgeous George' Harrison, the last captain of *Rebuke*, whose departure from the Navy had become inevitable from the day he started dodging his responsibilities during the mutiny at Invergordon. He was still a captain and still a dandy, but he looked a great deal older, more soured, and resentful of the fact that the man who had once been his Second-in-Command was now running the show.

It was to his credit that he had emerged from retirement to take his chance at sea but he was still too naval for most people's taste.

'I'd sell you a hundred of that bastard any day,' Verschoyle said. 'He makes me feel seasick.'

The merchant skippers came in all sizes and all types, from the elegant men of the big passenger vessels to those who ran ships that were little more than ocean tramps. There was an enormous amount of secrecy and no one was informed when the convoy was to sail.

'Orders stamped "To be destroyed before being read,"' Verschoyle commented sarcastically.

The voyage was marked by a sustained battle against three submarines, one of which was damaged and one of which was sunk by Verschoyle, but the small Hunt ships were never able to keep up with the I-class vessels in the emergencies and Kelly decided bitterly that somewhere in the thirties Britain had

128

betrayed the dead of Jutland now screwed down in their sailors' Valhalla. There'd been time and enough to provide for this war, but it had never been done, and now they were scraping the barrel to survive and praying that somehow the Germans would so infuriate the Americans that they, too, would enter the conflict.

Just before they reached New York, they ran into the worst gale to strike the Western Atlantic since the war had started. The sky darkened to reduce visibility to less than a mile, and life became wretched as the wind increased and they headed at three knots into mountainous seas that lifted like impenetrable green walls above their heads. Low overhead, black clouds raced past before a wind that screeched like dervishes on the rampage, and lifeboats, whalers, and motorboats were smashed, and galley fires were swamped so that food was cold and everyone forgot what it was like to be dry. Everybody seemed to be in a bad temper, from Kelly down through the first lieutenant and the master-at-arms, to the youngest boy seaman and the ship's cat.

For two days they lay hove-to in gigantic seas, behaving like double-decker buses on a big dipper. On the bridge, salt water penetrated the most tightly-wrapped scarf to irritate sore necks and, as everyone's sense of humour became strained, small things assumed magnified importance. Meals became tests of stamina because it required an acrobat to sit in a chair and tilt a cup of soup against a swinging and unhelpful ship. Below decks, hammocks bumped against each other and a constant rain of condensation dripped from the steel plates of the deck-heads into the foul air of closed compartments. Exhausted guns' crews and bridge personnel stumbled below to snatch some sleep, only to doze fully-dressed in hammocks, on bunks, tables and lockers, even on the hard steel deck.

At dawn on the third day, the storm eased enough to allow them to proceed at about seven knots, the stinging spray losing its bite and the great seas rolling under the ships instead of cascading across them, the spume and rain squalls thinning out to a mere heavy blow. As the battered, weather-scarred, rust-stained line of ships steamed into port, they all drew a breath of relief.

The welcome from the Americans was as warm as ever but

they found an even greater comfort in the feel of firm ground under their feet, the sound of birds, the land smell of the city, the blessed release from worry, and above all real sleep in steady bunks in quiet ships. *Impi* had come out of it with little worse than smashed crockery, but *Hallamshire* had had a huge wave smash a gun mounting and cock the barrels at full elevation, while a second had ripped out a steel ammunition locker and carried it overboard with a man who had been using the deck to go to his post instead of the gearing compartment and engine room; while *Chatsworth* had a crack in the quarterdeck plating which let water into the wardroom and caused the stern to move independently of the rest of the ship – 'until it was flapping like a virgin's fan,' Verschoyle said.

They returned with another convoy to Liverpool and, with the chance of several days in port, Kelly went to Thakeham where there was a telephone call from Paddy to say that Hugh was a survivor from the bombing of *Illustrious*.

'But he's safe,' she crowed delightedly. 'And he's coming home!' Then her voice sagged. 'I've almost finished at Haslar,' she wailed. 'What'll happen if I'm sent to the north of Scotland before he arrives?'

'That's one of the things in wartime that always produces a great deal of ill will,' Kelly said. 'I'll try to get your posting delayed or, failing that, get him sent to Scapa.'

He decided he'd better inform Christina and was surprised to hear the concern in her voice. Perhaps they were all growing more compassionate with age, he thought.

A disastrous year drew to its close with the bombing of Coventry, Bristol, London, and a dozen other places, while in Africa the Italians had captured Somaliland and invaded Egypt and Greece. On the credit side, the supply of arms mounted, President Roosevelt of the United States showed himself a generous-hearted friend, and a great strategic prize had been gained as the fine natural harbour in Suda Bay on the island of Crete had been occupied at the invitation of the Greek government as a fuelling base for naval operations in the central Mediterranean. Its value was proved almost immediately as Admiral Cunningham, C.-in-C., Mediterranean, launched a carrier-borne attack which crippled the Italian fleet at Taranto. Finally – at the end of the week – Hugh arrived home, flown from the Med in a Sunderland, and the day afterwards Paddy arrived, quivering with pleasure.

It was impossible not to be affected by her joy. Hugh was a little subdued, white and curiously tense, but happy because he was expecting to be appointed to a squadron operating from Macrihanish in Scotland, with a view to joining the new carrier, *Victorious*, as soon as she was ready.

It bothered Biddy a little that her daughter didn't sleep in her own room now that Hugh was home, but with death just round the corner, Kelly found he could hardly blame either of them.

The New Year – with another convoy and another visit to New York under their belts – saw the Italians tossed out of Egypt by Wavell, but Hitler, concerned with Italian failures, promptly sent the *Luftwaffe* – a very different proposition from the Italian Regia Aeronautica – to Sicily.

'And since the aeroplane's become the ultimate neurosis symptom of the age,' Verschoyle said as they received the news, 'like a virgin on her wedding night, it should give the Mediterranean Fleet something pretty weighty to think about.'

It was as if Churchill and Hitler were playing a vast game of chess covering the whole globe, with fleets and armies as kings and queens and men and women merely as pawns.

Almost at once, the battleship, *Rebuke*, was caught by two squadrons of Stukas near the entrance to the Kithera Channel off Crete. Nicknamed *Rebuilt* after all the alterations done on her, she'd been attached to Cunningham's fleet and because, in the stringent period of economy before the war, she'd never managed to be provided with the armoured deck she'd been promised, when she was hit, she'd turned turtle almost at once, taking with her to the bottom 740 men out of her complement of 1310.

Kelly was hardly surprised. He'd predicted some such fate for her as long ago as 1931. Not since Jutland, when he'd seen three massive vessels destroyed by German heavy shells plunging down on their unarmoured decks, had he had a high opinion of battleships.

The press published dirges but nobody in the Navy was surprised, and they'd barely accepted her disappearance when the dive bombers caught and sank the cruiser, *Southampton*. Almost immediately, they learned that German troops had arrived in

131

North Africa and they all knew that from now on it would not be the walk-over it had been with the Italians but a hard slog against tough professionals.

With two of his captains promoted and the Admiralty displaying a strange reluctance, that spoke of a foreknowledge of events, to send the Twenty-Third and Nineteenth Flotillas across the Atlantic again, Kelly took the opportunity to get hold of Rumbelo to look after him and acquire Latimer for *Impi* and Smart for *Impatient*. They'd doubtless have Shakespeare for breakfast, dinner and tea but at least the signals would be worth reading.

The time in port also meant it was possible to get home, but Thakeham remained lonely and, with the blitzes, London was no place to go for an evening out. Verschoyle had moved Christina out to Guildford, much to her disgust, as staying put in London had seemed to her the only way she could show her defiance of the Germans, and he knew she'd go back as soon as he was at sea.

With the centre of London full of still-smoking wreckage and the streets crunching with broken glass, Kelly went to Dover. During the invasion scare of September, guns and torpedo tubes had been mounted to defend the harbour, and plans to immobilise cranes, wharves and other port equipment had been made, and with control of the Strait lost, the Germans had mounted huge guns to command the narrows.

'Since they weren't needed to protect the flank of an invasion,' he was told, 'they've been used instead to bombard Dover. Our guns keep trying to knock them out, but, so far, neither side seems to have been very successful.'

Charley was friendly and matter of fact, but no more. He stayed at her flat – sleeping on the settee – but there was always something missing, and he had been in Dover only two days when Hugh telephoned him from Thakeham.

'Mother's dead,' he said.

'What?' It seemed unbelievable. 'When, Hugh?'

'The air raid last evening. I've just heard from James Verschoyle. She went back to London and he found her covered with debris. I don't think she suffered. He rang me first thing this morning. I thought you'd like to know.'

Kelly put the telephone down wonderingly. What a bloody

132

funny thing war could be, he thought. While he'd found Charley again, Verschoyle had been robbed of Christina.

He examined his feelings, trying to find some emotion. But there was none. This woman, who – if only for a short time – had been important to him – had gone, and the only feeling he could produce was sadness that she was a human being who'd been robbed of life. It was hard to think of her as dead because she'd always been so tremendously alive, but that was all. His sorrow was not for himself but for Verschoyle.

Heading back to London for the funeral, he found Hugh there ahead of him with Paddy, and Verschoyle looking desperately lonely.

'I shall miss her, Kelly,' he said slowly. 'God knows what it was that kept us together because we were both as selfish as hell. I just thank God Hugh's around with that pretty little chit of his.'

While he was with Verschoyle at his club, Corbett contacted him and they went to the Admiralty together.

'You'd better both start packing,' Corbett said. 'The balloon's gone up in the Med. Intelligence has it that the Germans are going into the Balkans.'

Telephoning Charley to say he wouldn't be going back to Dover, Kelly heard a long pause as his words sank in, but there was no indication as to whether she was sad or otherwise, and the following day a signal arrived ordering his ships to join the Mediterranean Fleet.

He thought of ringing Charley again to say goodbye but a curious doubt held him back and in the end he headed for Liverpool without seeing her.

4

It was strange to be back in Gib again, especially with all the lights glowing after the blackout in England.

'So this is Mussolini's *Mare Nostrum*,' Latimer said. 'It looks like the same old Med to me.'

'Sell the pig and buy me out,' Able Seaman Siggis wailed. 'I wish I was back in Wallasey.'

Everybody was talking about the coming joust with the Germans which they all knew was only just round the corner, but though the harbour was full of warships and bristling with guns, not a shot had yet been fired in anger there and the biggest concern was the German and Italian spies who everybody knew were watching from La Linea.

The whole area of the Med was changing. The Italian adventure into Greece had turned out to be the usual disaster and, with their army flung back across the frontier by the Greeks, they were now on the run everywhere. But while troop convoys were moving from North Africa in response to the Greeks' call for help, nobody felt that they'd stay there for long. The Germans had already occupied Roumania and Bulgaria and it was obvious that Greece and Yugoslavia would be next, if only because it was clearly policy to prevent the British regaining a foothold on the mainland of Europe. The latest funny story, in fact, consisted of what the sailors had shouted down to the soldiers as they'd disembarked at Piraeus and lined up before marching off. 'See you later,' they'd yelled. 'At the evacuation!'

With the Eastern Mediterranean suddenly the focal point of the war, Kelly knew very well that he'd be moving with his ships to Alexandria before long, and, in the middle of March, Nineteenth and Twenty-Third Flotillas were informed they

134

were to accompany a desperately-needed convoy to Malta before passing on to Alex. Intelligence had it that the Italian Fleet was contemplating a sortie against the Greek convoys while Admiral Cunningham, in Alexandria, was making dispositions to catch them at it, and the Malta convoy was to be the last for a while because he had no wish for such an important collection of ships to be caught at sea.

Getting his captains together on board *Impi*, Kelly explained what he intended and they worked it out carefully with model ships until everybody knew exactly how his mind was moving, what he thought would happen and what he intended them to do.

'The voyage will divide itself roughly into three parts of three hundred miles,' he pointed out, 'and if the convoy makes a speed of just over twelve knots, we can divide it roughly into three periods of twenty-four hours. If we leave at daylight we should arrive off Malta at daylight on D+3 and, with the early-setting new moon, we shall have only minimum illumination at night, and the hours of darkness on all three days will be almost equal to the hours of daylight.'

He paused to look at the men listening to him. Verschoyle sat alongside him, his hands clasped on a thick wad of papers, and directly in front were Smart and Latimer, as different as chalk from cheese; Smart elegant, unruffled and controlled, Latimer nervous and edgy and eager to get on with the job. The men about them looked unbelievably young.

'The major hazards,' Kelly continued, 'will occur during daylight and will consist, I imagine, of evening reconnaissances and air torpedo and bombing attacks. These might well be supplemented by the proximity of Italian heavy ships, with the most dangerous time as we go through the Sicilian Channel. However, the Long Range Desert group's expected to put on a diversion against enemy airfields, and cruisers from Alex have been ordered to bombard Soluk near Benghazi to keep the Luftwaffe busy. To gain early information, submarines will be patrolling off Taranto and the Strait of Messina.' He paused. 'We can't expect air support.'

He looked up again at the young faces staring at him but there was no sign of alarm.

'If enemy surface forces are sighted,' he went on, 'Twenty-

Third Flotilla's job will be to harass and threaten a materially superior enemy by repeated assaults and withdrawals, to prevent them reaching the convoy. Liberal use of smoke screens ought not only to prevent them sighting the merchantmen but will also conceal the imminence of short range gunfire action and – of even greater concern to them – of torpedo attacks.'

He saw the officers shift a little in their seats because what he was saying could well be condemning some of them to death.

'The ships will be split up to make a striking force, consisting of *Impi*, *Inca* and *Impatient*, who will harass enemy warships. *Indian* and *Hallamshire* will act to lay smoke between them and the convoy. Captain Verschoyle's remaining ships will be the close anti-aircraft escort. The disposition for surface action, to be assumed in place of the normal cruising disposition designed to meet air attack, will be taken up with the least possible delay. The Hunts will leave the night before to carry out an anti-submarine search ahead, and join on the morning of D + 1.'

He let that sink in, then went on slowly. 'If the Italians appear, the two rear groups will use their W/T as much as possible to give the impression of a larger force than there actually is. False names and false positions can be used, but let's be discreet; if we appear to be an armada the Italians will soon get suspicious.'

He paused, remembering the stress laid at Jutland on signalling and the rigidness it had produced, and recalled something Verschoyle had said then about the Grand Fleet.

'Apart from this,' he concluded, 'I wish to cut down signalling. From everybody's point of view it'll be safer. I suspect our general purpose weapons will be switching at full speed from aircraft to surface vessels and it'll require some pretty quick decisions about which target's the most important, so you won't want to be looking to the flotilla leader to know what to do.'

There were a few smiles and he concluded briskly. 'Too much signalling only results in tactical arthritis, anyway, and I prefer command to be more elastic and hope that apart from "Enemy in sight" and "Am engaging the enemy," there won't be need for much. If anybody's in any doubt, he can do no better than place his ship between the convoy and the enemy and I expect you to use your initiative. We're a band of brothers

136

not a flock of sheep; and initiative, like muscle, atrophies if it's not used, though there's always a well-tried course of action everybody in destroyers should have learned by now – "When in doubt, follow father."'

As the conference broke up, the officers left with serious faces.

'They look worried sick,' Kelly said, frowning.

'But of course,' Verschoyle agreed. 'They're terrified of not coming up to scratch, because you have a reputation for coming down on carelessness like a ton of bricks.'

It surprised Kelly. 'I have?'

'"Extremely efficient,"' Verschoyle quoted. '"Merciless with the inefficient and never one to hand out the chocolate."'

The weather was fair and visibility was good when the convoy, consisting of the fast supply ship, *Hoylake*, two freighters, *Youlgreave* and *Clan Mackay*, and the tanker, *Mons Star*, sailed with *Hallamshire* and the Twenty-Third Flotilla. But they were already deteriorating into a moderate swell and an increasing wind and, with the first problem the position and progress of any Italian ships that might be out, Kelly was almost indifferent to the air attacks which began almost at once. Verschoyle's ships appeared ahead on time, as the aircraft were reported – and just as it was discovered that *Clan Mackay* could make no more than nine knots. The attacks, delivered by high-level bombers, were neither heavy nor well-pressed home.

'Wind-up after Taranto,' Rumbelo suggested in a growl from the back of the bridge.

Despite the Italians' lack of success, they knew they were being shadowed all the time, and later in the day there were a few torpedo attacks by Italian S79s. But the torpedoes were dropped at extreme range and the attacks were futile, and, with the convoy opened out so that each ship could take avoiding action, no one was hit or damaged.

The aeroplanes appeared and reappeared throughout the afternoon but they were at extreme range from their bases and did little other than shadow them and the big problem still lay ahead. The second day was much the same as the first, not too dangerous but nerve-wracking in its tenseness. In a way, the

137

aircraft enabled everybody to let off a little steam, and the sound of the guns, though they weren't doing much but frighten off the Italians, at least were a sop to edgy nerves.

On the morning of the third day, the flotilla signals officer appeared with an intercepted signal from one of the submarines watching ahead.

'Italian heavy ships have left Taranto, sir. Submarines report their course as 270 and speed as 23 knots. They don't give number and class.'

'So they're out at last,' Kelly said. 'Repeat it to Nineteenth Flotilla and tell *Hallamshire*, *Indian*, *Inca* and *Impatient* to conform to our movements.'

Shortly after midday another signal was received: two battleships and six cruisers were across their path. For a moment there was a heart-stopping pause as the talk on the bridge quietened. Two battleships and six cruisers were too much even for the best of destroyers.

Then Kelly spoke dryly: 'They haven't got that many cruisers,' he commented. 'And they'd be bloody fools to risk them against us with Cunningham in Alex itching to catch 'em with their trousers down. Somebody's being too enthusiastic and mistaking destroyers for cruisers and cruisers for battleships. In the Italian navy, the silhouettes are the same.'

The sun was sinking towards the horizon now and the sea had become a deep navy blue. Eyes were turned towards the bridge in expectation. The buzz had already gone round that the Eyeties were out, and the attitude, despite the imminence of death, was not one of trepidation but of excitement and anticipation. They could wipe up the Eyeties easy. No one had the slightest doubt about it and it was strangely reassuring to be so confident.

The ship's cat, an enormous ginger tom, which spent half its time asleep in a miniature hammock made for it by one of the petty officers, had deigned to appear above deck and was stretched in the sunshine in a sheltered part of the bridge shield.

'Better remove Leading Cat Pluto,' Kelly suggested to Rumbelo. 'He's bad-tempered enough as it is and he'll be diabolical if the guns disturb his afternoon caulk.'

By this time, *Impi*, *Inca* and *Impatient* were steaming two miles ahead of the convoy which was guarded by *Chatsworth*, *Ashby* and *Rushden*, with *Indian* and *Hallamshire* in between ready to screen the merchant ships with smoke. The Mediterranean was looking more like the Atlantic than anything else by now, the ships rising and falling like horses on a roundabout, but the sky remained blue, and the tossing sea blended with it exquisitely, the white caps and the wake of the ships completing the picture. From *Impi*'s bridge, Kelly could see the guns' crews relaxed with the ease of veterans. Most of them had already seen eighteen months of war and they handled their weapons with the skill of professionals. Below decks, food was arranged for those who had to remain at their stations and men were already collecting it for their shipmates.

As the ship rolled in the quartering sea, Kelly glanced about him. Somewhere astern, Verschoyle was handling the convoy. It couldn't turn away because there was nowhere for it to run to. And it had to reach Malta. Since the arrival of the Luftwaffe, the situation there had grown perilous, and there were thousands of people who had to be fed. The island had become a thorn in the Italians' side and they all knew that when the tide turned, as turn it eventually must, it would become not merely a thorn but a huge battery directed at the Italian mainland. It had to be held just as surely as for the enemy it had to fall. If Malta fell the Italians would find it safe enough to tow barges across to North Africa.

A slash of spray across the bridge made them duck, and brought the realisation that they were protected neither from the weather nor from enemy shellfire, because the thin plating was heavy enough only to keep out the green seas. Nobody seemed nervous, however. There were still many Regulars in the ship's company, all trained – officers and men – for years for such a moment as this. Their actions were disciplined, sparing of effort and confident. Perched on his stool, Kelly felt quite calm and not in the slightest troubled by the weight of his responsibilities. He'd spent the whole of his life from the age of thirteen learning how to behave in the face of an enemy. He'd served in small ships and big ships, on shore stations and in offices in London, and had attended staff courses and listened to admirals laying down the law. He knew his job. He was confident in himself. What to do in any given situation was in his mind as clearly as the Lord's Prayer.

The sun was bronze-gold now and the sea was darkening to purple. He glanced at his watch.

'If they leave it much longer, we're going to dodge 'em in the darkness,' he said.

Even as he spoke, the buzzer went and the officer of the watch answered it.

'Radar has them, sir,' he reported. 'Eight vessels. They can't tell yet what they are.'

As he replaced the instrument, the masthead buzzer followed at once. 'Masthead reports smoke, green three-oh, sir.'

'Thank you.' Kelly settled himself more comfortably on his stool. 'So they've decided to have a go after all. We will now proceed to kick Mussolini's backside round the Mediterranean.' He looked quizzically round him at the expectant faces. 'How do you suggest we set about it? You're the staff and you're supposed to offer advice.'

There was a short, pungent and very earnest discussion with a lot of emphasis laid on caution. Kelly stared at them, his eyes amused.

'What a lot of lily-livered skunks you are,' he said cheerfully. 'Delay favours the defence. We'll go straight at 'em.'

There were a few grins. It was part of his job to make everybody feel they couldn't lose even though he had a pretty shrewd idea himself that they could. How many of the Italians there were and how big they were was something nobody knew, but he guessed they wouldn't come out after Taranto unless they were expecting success, and that meant they would be big and there would be plenty of them. If they appeared, he intended to attack them. A defensive role was objectionable to the deeply-rooted naval philosophy in him and alien to his closed world of unquestioned loyalties and rigid values. Retreat could be accepted only after the most unemotional calculation; and emotion, warlike and vengeful after Dunkirk, was strongly present in him.

He became aware of the officer of the watch speaking. 'Masthead reports smoke now green two-five.'

Lifting his glasses, Kelly saw it himself, heavy and black on the horizon. The Italians were moving across their bows and that meant they intended to bring him to battle, come what may. He glanced at *Impi*'s funnels and was pleased to note that

140

there wasn't sufficient smoke to reveal their position. The Italians had no radar worth speaking of, so perhaps they had no idea yet how close they were.

The wind lay in exactly the right direction for a smoke screen and, hidden by it, the British ships would be able to approach to close quarters. Behind them, Verschoyle's ships were already making enough chatter on the radio to draw the Italians' attention and convince them there were plenty of them and that they were bigger than they really were.

The destroyers were turning now and increasing speed to place themselves between the convoy and the Italians. They were too far ahead of the merchant ships by this time to expect Verschoyle to come to their assistance, and were rushing down on the Italians, whatever they were, at a combined speed of fifty-odd miles an hour.

Shortly afterwards, an Italian float-plane appeared, the last of the sun catching the underside of its wings. Despite the barrage that was thrown at it, it managed to drop a string of bright red flares over the convoy.

'Marking the line of advance,' Kelly said. 'Hoist battle ensigns!'

The masthead voice pipe buzzed again. 'Ships in sight – '

A few minutes later, Kelly saw them himself. There were eight of them, six of them destroyers, he guessed, and two larger vessels that were probably light cruisers. In the last of the day, they looked like minute silver models against the darkening sky, and it reminded him that, although he had the weather gauge, he also had the afterglow of the sun behind him with the horizon a bright lemon-colour that would throw up his ships in sharp silhouette.

'Make "Enemy in sight,"' he said. '"Concentrate in readiness for surface action." Steer oh-four-five. Revolutions for twenty-eight knots.'

As the ship swung north-east, Latimer stared ahead through his binoculars. 'Light cruisers, sir,' he reported. 'Probably *Condottieri* class. More than likely *Mazzini* and *Rienzi*. Seven thousand tons. Thirty knots, eight six-inch guns. Destroyers are probably *Vivaldis*. Bigger than us by a long way. Two thousand five hundred tons, thirty-four knots, five 4.7s.'

'Odds against us are only about a hundred to one,' Kelly

commented. 'We ought to be able to cope with that.'

Everybody knew what he meant. Cunningham had established a moral ascendancy in the Mediterranean that remained real and clear, and every man in the Royal Navy was aware of it. It gave them the advantage even before battle was joined, and one of Cunningham's signals, though it had been issued with his tongue in his cheek, summed it up: 'The right range for any ship of the Mediterranean Fleet, from a battleship to a submarine, to engage the enemy is POINT BLANK – at which range even a gunnery officer cannot miss.'

Despite the sun, the wind was cold and Kelly was just becoming conscious of it when Rumbelo arrived, unperturbed at the prospect of action, with cocoa, thick as liquid mud.

'Nothing like warmth in the stomach,' he said. 'It stops you getting scared.'

'Who's scared?' Kelly said.

Rumbelo grinned. 'Me, sir.'

Kelly smiled back at him, but there was an element of truth in his words nevertheless. Nobody could thunder towards an opposing force of superior strength without feeling twinges of dread.

'Italian radio's pretty busy,' the signals officer said.

'Battle orders.' Kelly jerked himself out of his thoughtful mood and decided to try a funny signal. The Navy had a reputation for funny signals and they always gave the troops something to think about in the run-up to action when butterflies were appearing under belts and men were beginning to wonder what the outcome would be.

'Make "Wait till you see the whites of their eyes."'

The lamp clattered and was acknowledged, then Smart, with the familiarity of years, made 'Italians asking, "Anybody here seen Kelly?"' to which *Impatient* replied. 'Just wait till they do.'

' 'Oo gives a fish tit for the Eyeties anyway?' Siggis' voice, shrill and defiant, came over the noisy crashing of the sea. It was flattering because it indicated high spirits and confidence but, even as Kelly smiled, he turned briskly to the yeoman. 'Make "Confine signals to events not to flattery."'

As the flags went up, he saw heads bobbing about round the gun platforms and Able Seaman Siggis grinning at the Bofors, as those who could read the signal translated for those who couldn't. It would keep them happy for a bit longer.

He knew what they thought of him. To the Hostilities-Only he was only one grade lower than God. To the regulars like Siggis, he was Ginger Maguire; Crasher Maguire who scraped paint going alongside; most of all, Maguire of *Mordant* – the name that had stuck with him ever since 1916 – and the rows of medal ribbons on his chest indicated that he knew something about his job.

It wasn't quite as easy as he made it out to be, however, because the Italians' six-inch guns could outrange his own four-inchers by around two miles. Nevertheless, it was already firmly in the Italian mind that the British always beat them, and a bold act of resolution might achieve a great deal more than caution. The Italians might even believe there were bigger ships behind him if he advanced as if he were not afraid of the consequences.

'Are the Italians picking up our signals?' he asked.

'Must be, sir.' The signals officer's reply came at once. 'We're picking up theirs.'

'Then let's hope they've got somebody handy who can read English.'

There was a quick grin. 'Must have, sir. Most of 'em have done a stint selling ice-cream down the Old Kent Road.'

The contempt was studied and deliberate because they knew the Italian naval officers were well-trained and their failures came chiefly from a chronic shortage of sophisticated equipment.

'Make a signal, yeoman,' Kelly said. 'Plain language. To Heavy Cruiser *Verschoyle* from *Kelly*.'

The yeoman glanced quickly at the signals officer who looked at Kelly.

'Sir?'

'Make "Italian fleet in sight. Am engaging. Would be glad of assistance."'

The signals officer looked puzzled. 'And the address, sir?'

'You have it: Heavy Cruiser *Verschoyle*."'

The signals officer still looked puzzled and Kelly smiled. 'We have a *Nelson*, a *Rodney*, a *Barham* and a *Hood*,' he said. 'It's a habit of the Navy to name its capital ships after its favourite admirals. We also have a *Kelly* – Mountbatten's ship – and where

143

Kelly and Mountbatten are, something drastic usually happens. If we're not big enough to sink the buggers, let's try to frighten 'em off. If *Chatsworth*'s operator has his wits about him, he'll know what's going on. I'm sure Captain Verschoyle will.'

'Very good, sir. Address "Heavy Cruiser *Verschoyle*."'

As the yeoman of signals vanished, obviously disapproving of this departure from established practice, Kelly lifted his binoculars. They still had more than a mile to go to be even within range, while the Italians had been in range for some time.

'Enemy due to open the bowling any time, I should say,' Latimer observed.

The range shortened, the three destroyers bucking the sea like wild horses. The tenseness on the bridge could almost be felt as they waited for the Italians to start the ball rolling.

'We're well within their range,' Latimer observed. 'Seems to be taking 'em a long time to hoist in the idea, digest it and fire at us.'

Even as he spoke, there was a whistle and a crack and a tall column of water rose out of the sea ahead of them, disintegrated and collapsed.

'Penny's dropped,' Latimer commented.

'They're trying to oblige.'

When the yeoman of signals reappeared he was followed by the signals officer.

'Captain Verschoyle's replied, sir,' he reported. '"Am on my way."'

'That all?'

'That's all, sir.'

'It's enough.'

'He's also making a lot of noise, sir. The signal was to "*Kelly*" and was signed "*Heavy Cruiser Verschoyle*."'

Kelly smiled. 'I bet the Italian admiral's put his sundae down to look through the list of long-dead British admirals,' he said. 'To find one by the name of Verschoyle.'

As they swung again, nearer to the Italian ships, a sparkle of flashes ran down the Italian line.

'Here it comes,' Latimer said. 'Let's hope they're not as good at gunnery as they are at making ice-cream.'

The chatter was light-hearted but, behind it, it was remarkably like Jutland all over again. The weather was bright and cold as it had been at the beginning of that battle, and they were now thundering down towards the enemy battlefleet just as *Mordant* had in 1916. This time, though, more depended on the outcome. Jutland hadn't had much effect on the strategy of that war, but the loss of Malta could have on this one. And this time, whatever they possessed in the way of moral ascendancy, the odds were loaded against them. Feeling a sense of unreality and fatalism, Kelly was conscious that his responsibility this time covered not just a job aboard a ship, but the safety of his own flotilla, Verschoyle's flotilla, the whole of the convoy, the lives of hundreds of men, and the security of Malta.

'Nineteen, eighteen, seventeen – ' Latimer was counting the seconds to the arrival of the Italian salvo – 'sixteen, fifteen, fourteen – '

The navigating officer stiffened, his head forward, peering towards the Italians. 'For what we are about to receive –' he said.

'Three, two, one – here it comes!'

5

The salvo arrived with a sound that was a mixture between a whirr and a rumble. Wailing like demons, the shells crashed like stones into the Mediterranean just ahead of *Impi* and, as the splinters flew, the mountains of water they threw up, yellow-tinted with high-explosive, broke and cascaded back into the sea, and they found they were wet through, blinded and coughing with the sharp smell of cordite.

'Bracketed, by God!'

The Italians were well in sight now, their upper works clearly visible under the smoke they were making, and as they thundered towards him, Kelly tried to put himself in the mind of the Italian admiral. He had three options – to interpose his ships between the convoy and Malta, to pull away to port so as to come on them from the east, or to split his force, sending one cruiser and half his destroyers to one side and the other cruiser with the rest of the destroyers to the other. Deciding he would simply try to prevent the convoy reaching Malta because, with night coming on, he wouldn't wish his ships to be scattered, he made up his mind to employ exactly the same tactics he'd used at Narvik.

'Make smoke!'

As *Impi* turned thirty degrees to follow a course across the bows of the Italian ships, *Inca* and *Impatient* turned with her. Smoke began to pour from the after funnels, nothing more than a wisp or two at first as the stoker petty officers in the engine rooms adjusted their valves, then the wisps came thicker and within seconds it was pouring out in thick cylindrical streams to sag to the surface of the sea and roll across it, pushed by the wind towards the Italians in front of the destroyers.

Latimer glanced up at it. 'Boiler room crews are going to love us,' he commented. 'With the chimney-sweeping they'll have to do when we make port.'

'Range four-oh-nine! Range four-oh-eight!'

The range-taker's voice came over the chatter, unemotional and matter of fact.

They were turning now, in a tight circle, one behind the other, back towards their own smoke. The Italian ships vanished astern as they continued to swing, turbines whining, the water crashing against the bows in the rush and rattle of spray-thrashed steel, and Kelly caught the smell of salt above the stink of oil from the smoke, and the sting of the wind on his cheek. The ship seemed like a living animal, the spray on the paintwork moving in little jerking runnels jarred along by the throb and quiver of the engines. Again, the thought of the danger came to him but he brushed it aside. Fear was a luxury and he was best keeping his mind on the job in hand. There was nothing else to think about. Everybody was at their action stations and the wardroom had been taken over by the surgeon who had stacked packets of bandages in handy corners about the ship.

He turned to the voice pipe. 'Captain to Gunnery Officer. We shall be making our bow in just three minutes and we shall then turn to starboard. You'll find the enemy about red four. Open fire as soon as you see them.'

He shifted on the stool and, glancing backwards, saw *Inca* on his port quarter, just a little out of position but clinging tightly to him, and behind her Smart in *Impatient* bringing up the rear.

The blood was tingling in his veins and, once again, as he always was, he was conscious of the excitement and wondered if he ought to feel more dispassionate, even concerned, and whether it was wrong to feel this tingling fervour at the prospect of a fight and the possibility of death.

The turbines were howling at full power as they plunged into the stinking darkness of the smoke, the smell of fuel oil making them cough.

Latimer was wiping his eyes. 'Rotten bad for white drill, sir,' he commented. 'Big laundry bill after this is over.'

A shaft of sunshine broke through, then darkness again. Latimer looked at his watch.

'One minute!'

147

The darkness seemed to thicken in a choking cotton-wool cloud about them, then they were out into the daylight once more. The two Italian cruisers seemed to be right on the bow, huge and grim in their pale Mediterranean paint that seemed dazzling against the darker grey of *Impi*, *Inca* and *Impatient*, which hadn't yet shed their Home Fleet colours.

'Range three-seven-one!'

The last of the light was catching the curve of the Italians' hulls and the edges of their turrets, and he thanked God his own ships, in their dark paint, were against the murky background of the smoke. The two cruisers were changing course slightly, their shapes lengthening as they turned to bring their turrets to bear. The movement of the guns was quite clear.

'Torpedoes, sir?'

'No.' Kelly shook his head. 'Let's keep 'em as a threat. Once they're gone, they won't need to be half so careful. We'll move as if to launch them but use the guns instead.'

As they rushed towards the Italian ships, he saw them continuing their turn, nervously expecting the torpedoes, and the Italian destroyers, up to now far out on the flank, rushing to join their consorts.

'Enemy turning away, sir.'

'Starboard fifteen.'

As the line of destroyers swung, the deck heeled abruptly and *Impi* began to shudder with her speed. The bow wave rose higher as the revolutions mounted, and Kelly watched the forward 4.7s moving. As they hurtled forward in a long curve, the guns crashed out, the din dying away to the ruffle of sound made by the shells as they lifted through the air. Long before they had arrived at their destination, the next salvo was on its way. Glancing round, not forgetting the ships astern of him, Kelly saw *Inca*'s first salvo even as she came out of the smoke. There was a flash as her guns fired and a curling ring of smoke, and almost immediately *Impatient* emerged behind her. They were performing the evolution faultlessly.

There was a line of splashes alongside the leading Italian cruiser, then they all saw a yellow flash just abaft the bridge.

'One for his nob!' Latimer said.

'With your knowledge of Shakespeare,' Kelly observed, 'you might have come up with something more memorable than that.'

'How about "A hit, a hit, a palpable hit", sir?'

There was a continuous roar of gunfire now and more sparkling flashes running along the Italian ships as their heavier rifles fired. The shells smashed into the sea to port, marking the water with scummy circles of foam.

'Starboard. We'll go round again, Pilot, and come out further down this time. That ought to keep 'em guessing, because they're bound to be stupid enough to expect us to appear where we appeared last time. We'll shorten the range again as if we're going to fire torpedoes before we turn away.'

The smoke lay on the water in vast greasy black coils, that Kelly guessed the Italians wouldn't attempt to enter. They'd inevitably expect torpedoes as they emerged on the other side and, not daring to risk their bigger ships, would try to make contact with the convoy by passing round the edge of the smoke bank.

The smoke looked like a vast dark cliff behind *Impi* as she emerged. He could see the convoy about five miles away to the west being attacked by aircraft, the sky above it pockmarked by the barrage flung up by Verschoyle's ships. Plunging into the darkness once more, they thundered through, to find the Italians shelling the smoke where they'd last appeared, the blast from the exploding missiles dispersing the rolling banks of black even as *Impi*'s guns crashed out.

There was a yell as they saw another flicker of light on the leading cruiser that told them they'd scored another hit. *Impatient* was just disappearing a mile away when Rumbelo called out from the back of the bridge that she was on fire.

'Looks as if she's lost her starboard point fives, sir.'

'What about Nineteenth Flotilla's W/T?' Kelly asked.

'Plenty of traffic, sir,' the signals officer said. 'They all sound like battleships, and they appear to have invented an aircraft carrier. There's been a signal to one, *Incredible*, telling her to be prepared to fly off her aircraft.'

Kelly smiled. Verschoyle was never behind the door when cunning was handed out. He was still watching *Impatient* when Rumbelo's voice came, quietly and unemotionally.

'Torpedo bombers sir. Green-five-oh!'

Every eye on the bridge swung to watch the S79s come in.

They were fast three-engined monoplanes but their pilots seemed as uncertain as ever and the attack was just as half-hearted.

'Torpedoes gone!'

Impi turned to comb the wakes and, as the torpedoes vanished astern of her, the S79s swung away and disappeared from sight, just as high level bombers appeared. But Kelly knew they needn't worry too much about them because they were too near to the Italian cruisers to make that kind of bombing a safe pastime.

'All right, Quartermaster,' he said. 'You can take it easy for a bit. They've gone and we're wearing out the sea.'

As they swept towards the smoke again they saw *Inca* register another hit, this time on the second cruiser. They were dangerously close now, however, and they saw the flashes rippling down the leading Italian's side as she fired another salvo. It seemed an age before her shells crashed into the water round *Impi*, engulfing her in columns of water masthead high. Shell fragments screamed through the air to bury themselves in the ship's sides. They held course a little longer and once again had the satisfaction of seeing the Italian contours change.

'Turning away again, sir.'

The fear of torpedoes was still very real to the Italians and Kelly knew he'd been wise to keep the threat open as long as he could.

'Starboard twenty!'

The next salvo fell short but almost immediately one of the look-outs sang out that the high level bombers were coming in again. None of the bombs struck them, though the whole surface of the sea was stirred up around them. As they plunged once more into the smoke, they saw *Impatient* emerging. She came out like a charge of cavalry, every gun going, but as she swung, they saw a sheet of flame leap skywards near the after gun turret. Snatching a quick glance between watching the Italian ships, Kelly's jaw was tight, but *Impatient* was hidden by smoke and he couldn't tell what had happened to her. As he swung back to watch the Italians, Rumbelo called out.

'She's all right, sir. Midships gun's firing.'

As they entered the darkness yet again, Kelly forced his mind back to the Italians. Smart was an experienced captain, which was why Kelly had given him the rear and most dangerous position, and it was up to him to get his ship out of danger. As *Impi* emerged on the safe side of the smoke, she was followed by *Inca* and shortly afterwards by *Impatient*, still streaming smoke.

He guessed the Italians would be turning on to a more southerly course now, to give them direct access to the convoy, and, outranged and outweighted, it was clear that if the smoke blew clear nothing could save them from their bigger guns. And with *Impi*, *Inca* and *Impatient* gone, it would be the turn of the convoy, because there was little the smaller Hunt-class ships could do.

The smoke was thinning now, torn to shreds by the bursting shells and the swift passage of ships.

'Range two-five-oh!' The range taker's voice came as *Impi* burst clear. The range had dropped dramatically, and with *Impatient* damaged, the Italians would grow more determined and the mere threat of torpedoes would no longer work. This time it had to be the real thing.

'Make "Attack with torpedoes."'

As the two remaining destroyers emerged from the smoke, bunting fluttered to *Impi*'s yard-arm and eighteen missiles leapt into the water like salmon.

'All torpedoes fired and running correctly!'

'Italians turning away, sir!'

The silhouettes of the Italian ships changed once more as they swung from the torpedoes. The Italian destroyers were crashing towards *Impi*, their guns blazing in an attempt to drive the British ships away, but their gunnery was indifferent and, though their shells landed close by in a flurry of spray, stirred sea and shrieking splinters, no one was hit.

They seemed to have been manoeuvring in and out of the bank of smoke for hours now and Kelly glanced at the sky.

'This bloody day seems endless,' he remarked.

'Range two-nine-oh!' The range finder had been calling out the range all the time in his bored, undramatic voice almost as if he were a bus conductor asking for fares. 'Range three-one-oh! Range three-two-oh! Range obscured – !'

The last Italian shells had fallen just ahead of them and tons of water, yellow-tinted by the explosive, fell across *Impi*'s upper works. As the spray cleared, Kelly saw the Italians were still turning, then the contours resolved themselves into steadiness,

151

and he realised they were now heading north.

'I think they're breaking off the engagement, sir!' Latimer's voice was high and excited. 'I think we've pulled it off!'

There was a burst of cheering then Siggis's mad voice rose from the point fives in a chirrup of triumph.

'God bless the sweet little cherub who sits up aloft looking after the soul of poor Jack!' he yelled. 'God bless him and pray for thim Italian admirals. Tryin' to hit us was like tryin' to nail jelly to a wall!'

As Kelly slipped from his stool, the masthead buzzer went.

'Enemy fleet red one-oh. Heading away from us.'

Latimer offered Kelly a cigarette and he lit it gratefully and began to walk up and down, stretching his legs. He only had a space six paces forward and six paces back, but the bridge personnel, grinning in a mixture of pride, freedom from strain, and relief that they'd been spared one of the gory scenes that could be produced from a direct hit, made way for him.

He felt tired, more from tension than exhaustion, and from his deep concern for the ships and men under his command. But the satisfaction about him was powerful enough to reach out and touch. Once again they'd forced the Italians away by nothing else but superior morale, bluff and Nelson's dictum that no captain could do wrong if he put his ship alongside the enemy.

'Make to Battle Cruiser *Verschoyle*,' he said. 'From *Kelly*. "Many thanks. Congratulations to *Incredible*'s Commander (Air) for prompt response. Resume convoy formation and report damage."'

Below the bridge, Siggis was chirruping a song as he helped his mates to shift the empty cartridge cases. Every man in the ship was aware of what they'd done and what it had done to the Italians' confidence. The other destroyers were drawing closer now and the damage reports were coming in.

'*Impatient* reports large hole in deck. Heavy fire midships. Fourteen casualties, nine dead. There may be others.'

It was a simple report, but Kelly knew exactly what it meant. The hole in the deck would be circled by long jagged blades of steel, red-hot fragments would have traversed the bulkheads and the middle of the ship would be a raging furnace with paint, linoleum, bedding, stores, personal belongings and food, all blazing together. He could see the smoke still pouring out of the hole, below which the first lieutenant and his damage control party would be struggling with hoses and axes to put out the fire.

It was now almost dark, that blessed darkness which in these narrow seas was so important. The signals officer appeared.

'I think the Italians should go back to selling ice-cream, sir,' he said. 'W/T's just picked up a BBC announcement that they've lost Keren in Abyssinia.'

'Perhaps our friends over there heard it, too,' Kelly suggested. 'Perhaps that's what knocked the stuffing out of them. Their East African empire seems to be fading away at high speed.'

The signals officer had other information, too. 'Mediterranean Fleet's at sea, sir. Admiral Pridham-Whipple's reported enemy units south of Crete. With the lot we've just seen off, the whole Italian navy must be out.'

Kelly sniffed the air. Over the years he'd developed an instinct and he knew that with Cunningham at sea there was something in the wind.

'Make to the Captain, Nineteenth Flotilla "Conduct convoy to Malta. Am pushing ahead."'

Verschoyle's response was typical. 'Don't pull your poop string.'

'Tell *Impatient* to take *Indian*'s place and *Indian* to join us at full speed.'

The signals officer had hardly disappeared when he returned. 'From C.-in-C., Med, sir: "Report fuel state."'

'Tell him more than enough for Alex.'

A few minutes later another signal arrived.

'"Join Main Fleet."' The signals officer looked excited. 'Rendezvous position follows, sir. The pilot has it. Main Fleet's about seventy miles due south of Gaidaro Nisi on course two-seven-five.'

They clustered round the charts, hands moving as a new course was worked out. They had plenty of fuel in hand because the convoy's slow speed had forced them to steam at their most economical rate, and they could now push ahead throughout the whole night at moderate despatch in a converging direction.

From intercepted signals the following day they learned that the convoy, in spite of running into trouble from aircraft, had reached Malta, while somewhere to the north-west of them Admiral Pridham-Whipple's force from Piraeus, guarding the western flank of the troop convoys heading for Greece, had stumbled on an Italian battleship of the *Littorio* class. In the ensuing fight, Pridham-Whipple had escaped unscathed, though he was once more out-of-touch, but, warned by his signals, torpedo bombers from *Formidable*, with Cunningham's forces to the east, had hit the Italian which was now reported to be making for Taranto at greatly reduced speed.

They had no idea with certainty where the Italian ship was and, judging by the signals they intercepted, she could well be across their course and could even have been joined by other Italian ships, including the ones they themselves had sent about their business.

As they discussed the situation the masthead look-out sang out. 'Ships in sight. Green one-oh.'

'British destroyers, sir,' Latimer said. 'Radar reports more ships behind.'

A few minutes later the topmasts of heavy ships appeared to the east then slowly they were able to make out the silhouettes of four big ships with an attendant cloud of smaller vessels.

'It's *Warspite*, sir,' Latimer reported. 'With *Barham* and *Valiant*. The carrier's *Formidable*.'

'It would be nice to meet our late opponents again with a few big boys on our side,' Kelly observed.

As they thundered by, a lamp started flashing.

'Signal, sir. From C.-in-C.: "Take station to port."'

'Make it so.'

It soon became obvious that Pridham-Whipple's cruisers were searching ahead of the main fleet at maximum visual signalling distance, combing the darkening sea for the first sight of the enemy. As *Impi*, *Inca* and *Indian* took up their positions, the late sun was catching the black, white and grey camouflage of *Warspite*. Behind her, following in line astern, *Barham* and *Valiant* each had a magnificent white bow wave and a glistening wake. Their eight powerful fifteen-inch guns were trained fore and aft, each containing a shell weighing approximately a ton, so that a salvo was enough to destroy a smaller ship at once.

154

Their white ensigns were in sharp contrast to the deep cobalt of the sky and the ultramarine of the sea, and at the masthead *Warspite* wore Cunningham's red cross of St. George. They were all old ships but they still presented a striking display of power, grandeur and majesty.

'Signal from C.-in-C., sir: "If cruisers gain touch with damaged battleship, Second and Fourteenth destroyer flotillas will be sent to attack. Twenty-Third will remain on station. If she is not then destroyed, battlefleet will follow in. If not located by cruisers, I intend to work round to the north and then west and regain touch in the morning."'

Almost immediately, aircraft signals reported the Italian ships some fifty miles ahead on a course of 300 degrees, moving at a speed of between twelve and fifteen knots.

'Four hours or more before we're up with them,' Latimer observed.

Half an hour later, another aircraft message reported that the Italian fleet consisted of one battleship, six cruisers and eleven destroyers.

'I'll bet Cunningham's doing his "caged tiger" act up and down the bridge,' Kelly said.

His eyes felt red with tiredness and his face was raw from the wind. He hadn't had a wink of sleep for forty-eight hours but he was curiously refreshed at the possibility of new action. Ever since 1914 he'd hated the Germans and all they stood for, and he had nothing but contempt for the Italians. It was a narrow-minded, bigoted attitude that had often made him enemies in the thirties when fashionable London had been cultivating the Nazi attachés, but it appeared to be a sensible, no-nonsense approach at that moment.

At dusk, Tenth Flotilla moved ahead of the battlefleet and Twenty-Third Flotilla dropped astern. One of *Formidable*'s aircraft had reported a hit on an Italian cruiser and they knew that the action was drawing nearer. With two ships damaged, it would be hard for the Italians to avoid it. The tension increased. Not since *Graf Spee* had been caught and destroyed in the first winter of the war had there been a major fleet action and every man was itching to be part of it.

They were well to the west of Crete now, with the nearest point of land Cape Matapan. The silence on board *Impi* was marked and as the minutes ticked by an uneasy feeling began to grow that somehow they'd missed the Italians who must be legging it for home at full speed. Then Pridham-Whipple reported unknown vessels ten miles ahead, and the tension became unbearable and, in *Impi*, the doctor abandoned his cypher work and began to set up a casualty station in the wardroom. The excitement grew and the gunnery officer's joy at the possibility of being able to let off his guns again was intense.

As Kelly returned to the bridge after his evening meal, Second and Fourteenth Flotillas moved ahead and the tension became taut enough to pluck at as the two groups swung away, turning and twisting like snipe as they fell into single lines astern of their leaders. Just ahead, the vast bulks of the three great ships were silent in the darkness, without a single visible light, rearing out of the sea like hills, only the faint white foam and phosphorescent trail of their wake visible.

'Intercepted message from *Ajax*, sir: "Three unknown ships bearing between one-nine-oh and two-five-two, distant five miles—"'

They stared at the charts and Latimer jabbed a finger. 'There,' he said.

The weather had improved a lot and the night was calm with just a slight haze that reduced visibility, obliterated the stars and accentuated the blackness of the sky.

'Intercepted signal from *Orion*. Unknown ship two-four-oh degrees, five miles, apparently stopped. . . .'

'Must be the battleship,' Kelly said. 'That'll please Cunningham.'

'Battle fleet altering course to port. . . .'

'Conform.'

The fleet had turned towards the west in single line ahead, Cunningham handling his ships like destroyers. The huge, darkened steel castles hush-hushed through the water, their silhouettes barely visible against the horizon with the long sweep of their foredecks, the banked ramparts of their guns and the hunched shoulders of their bridges. Radar reports were being picked up steadily.

'C.-in-C., to Twenty-Third Flotilla: "Take station to starboard."'

'Somebody's spotted something.'

156

As they came up alongside the darkened heavies, the signals officer intercepted a signal from the destroyer, *Stuart*, ahead of them, that electrified them.

'Darkened ships to starboard. Position –'

'Must be different ships!' Kelly said. 'They're in a totally different place.'

Almost at once, the battle fleet swung again in the opposite direction, turrets swinging round, and *Formidable* began to haul out of the line of fire.

'Darkened ships, green three-one!' Latimer's voice was cracked with excitement. 'Two large ones, headed by a smaller one and followed by three smaller ones – no, four! There's another barely visible trailing astern.'

Almost immediately, Kelly saw the black shapes moving across his front from starboard to port, about two miles away, apparently totally unaware of their presence. As his ships sped on in total darkness, with only the hiss and rattle of the sea and the humming of the turbines to break the silence, he was on edge with waiting for the signal from the flagship.

Glancing to port, he could still see the shapes of the battle fleet, and *Formidable*'s huge bulk dropping astern.

'We seem to be the meat in the sandwich,' he said. 'I think we need to get out of this, or the Admiral will damn soon tell us to. Full speed, Pilot. Bring her round to starboard.'

Impi's stern went down and her bows lifted as she leapt ahead, turning to starboard, followed round like circus horses by *Inca* and *Indian*. Latimer, his night glasses up, called out the identification.

'Big ships are *Zara* class! Others are destroyers – big ones! They haven't the faintest idea we're here! Their guns are still fore and aft!'

It was an awesome moment. The battlefleet was moving into line ahead again and, in the dead silence, it seemed impossible that the Italians couldn't hear the voice of the gunnery control personnel putting their weapons on target. The turrets steadied.

'The Admiral's got his wish,' Kelly observed flatly. 'You couldn't be more point-blank than this.'

As he spoke, a searchlight broke out from one of the British destroyers ahead of the fleet. The beam fell directly on the third ship in the Italian line. With its light Mediterranean paint turned silver-purple, it looked like a ghost ship, its shape reflected on the calm waters. Above, the heavens were full of stars. Just out of the light but picked up by the overspill was another huge ship, the curve of her stern silvered by the glow, and ahead, other ships, just beyond the beam, could be seen in silhouette.

'Sitting ducks,' Latimer said. 'They've –'

What he was saying was lost as the silence was shattered. As *Warspite* and *Valiant* opened fire, great jagged tongues of flame leapt from the rifled barrels of their main armament. Because they were so close there was no pause between the crash of the guns and the arrival of the shells, and the salvos struck the third ship in line just below deck level in a brilliant splash of light, so that she burst into flame from just abaft the bridge to the after turret which was lifted clean over the side by a direct hit. Within seconds both *Warspite* and *Valiant* had started with their secondary armament and, on fire for her whole length, the Italian ship began to list to starboard.

'Poor sods!' The words came from Siggis on the twin Bofors, not because he was sorry for the Italians, but because he was a sailor and he was watching other sailors die.

The great guns of the British ships thundered again and again. The din was terrific and, as the huge orange flashes leapt out, the air seemed to expand and contract to the shock. *Impi*, *Inca* and *Indian* were still swinging to starboard out of the field of fire when searchlights began to blaze out from every ship in the fight. *Warspite* had now shifted her fire to the second ship in the Italian line and in a little over three minutes five fifteen-inch broadsides had hit her. The third ship was a sea of brilliant orange flame by this time and, turning slowly out of line, was already sinking. *Barham*, coming up astern to replace *Formidable*, was firing at the leading Italian destroyer which came alive with brilliant orange flashes obscured by thick smoke. She also turned out of line, burning fiercely, and *Barham* joined *Warspite* and *Valiant* in destroying the second large ship. Completely crippled and burning fiercely, she was listing to port, her bows swinging slowly until she had turned sufficiently to present her starboard side, like a wounded bull facing the goading of the banderillas.

She was a holocaust of flame now, the red glow lighting the cloud of black smoke above her. They could hardly believe their eyes. In ten minutes the British fleet had utterly destroyed three Italian ships. Not a single shot had been fired back.

As they watched, the huge shapes of the British heavies lumbered round to starboard, as if the Italians had fired torpedoes, and *Impi* and her consorts found themselves once more across their course and dangerously close. Turning in a complete circle to pass astern, they saw the Italian destroyers in the glare of the flames making smoke as they scuttled north. But the last of them, trailing behind out of position, swung in the opposite direction as if her captain considered he hadn't the time to follow his comrades. Unaware of the British destroyers hidden by the big ships, he steamed directly across their bows.

There was no need to issue orders and every gun crashed out in a single shout. The Italian destroyer was hit again and again, one moment crashing through the water, the next stopped dead, her bow dipping into the sea to send a wave over her fore-deck.

'By God,' Latimer said in astonishment. 'First time! We ought to have a photograph to present to the gunnery instructors at Whale Island!'

Again the guns roared and a tremendous explosion followed. A vast gusher of black water lifted into the air alongside the Italian ship, then flames lit up the wreckage, the boats and the men struggling in the sea. As the Italian ship heeled over, her bow dipped beneath the water and within two minutes she was gone.

As they steamed over her grave, they could hear an uncanny noise in the darkness that came from drowning men, then they were passing through a flotsam of human beings and wreckage. To port, from the shattered big ship which had been third in the Italian line, there was a terrific explosion and they saw a mushroom of black smoke coming from her vitals. Flames lit the water for miles, showing a desolation of debris and pathetic bunches of men clinging to rafts. The ship looked gigantic in the crimson glow as she slowly turned over to lie on her side so that they could see the whole shape of her deck. Men were scrambling about like ants among the carnage. One turret just wasn't there, and the others were even now still pointing fore and aft.

159

The bridge area was enveloped in a mountainous conflagration with, above, a pillar of smoke, its underpart glowing red. Like some fabulous animal breathing fire, she turned tiredly over and sank.

There was one solitary cheer from aft somewhere then silence. Nobody on the bridge spoke. The death of a ship, of whatever nationality, was always awe-inspiring.

Latimer's words came quietly.

'He that outlives this day, and comes safe home,
Will stand a-tiptoe when this day is named.'

6

Kelly had been into many places but he was always impressed by Alexandria. There were cities which were beautiful in the fashion of regal old women, and profiteer cities like Shanghai which were mere *parvenus*. Alex was like a well-bred old duchess and, just then, she seemed to be enjoying a face-lift. The war had brought a garish prosperity, and among the Jews, Greeks, Syrians, Turks, British and French, there were now the refugees, the grim-mouthed Poles, and Frenchmen hating the Germans, the English and themselves.

As the fleet had steamed homewards there were mixed feelings. They had not found the crippled Italian battleship, which had managed to escape to the north, but they had sunk two eight-inch cruisers, *Zara* and *Fiume*, and three destroyers, *Alfieri, Carducci* and *Alpini*, and Fourteenth Flotilla had run into and sunk the Italian cruiser, *Pola*, which had been stopped the previous night by torpedoes from *Formidable*'s aircraft.

Steaming through the mats of wreckage and survivors, their scrambling nets down, they had dragged aboard the yelling Italians who had proved a pretty sorry crowd, most of them very young and many of poor physique. Some of them had broken into the officers' wine store and were drunk and they claimed they'd not fired at the British ships when they'd been sighted because they were afraid they'd fire back.

The sea had been covered for miles with a film of oil, and the wreckage and the corpses and the clusters of men in boats extended as far as the horizon. In the middle of the work of mercy, a German aircraft appeared and the rescue had had to come to an abrupt halt as the fleet shaped course for safety.

'Report "No damage, no casualties,"' Kelly ordered.

Below him, near the pom-poms, Siggis was singing as they

161

cleared the shell cases.

'On a sailor's tomb no roses bloom – '

'Better add,' Kelly said with a smile, 'that morale also seems to be unimpaired.'

There was jubilation as they slipped through the boom and moved to their buoys because it had been a tremendous victory for the loss of only one aircraft and its crew. The news of the victory had gone ahead of them and the whole of Alex had turned out. Tugs and launches led the ships in, their crews, both Egyptian and British, going mad, dancing, cheering and throwing their caps in the air. Even the crews of the immobilised Vichy French fleet lined the decks to watch. Every siren and whistle in the harbour was going at full blast and every ship cleared lower deck to cheer them in.

'Sounds as though peace's broken out,' Latimer grinned.

On their last drop of fuel, *Impi, Inca* and *Indian* were the first to go alongside the oilers, then every man of every ship's company turned out to store and ammunition. Even the doctors, paymasters, stewards and storekeepers had their coats off to handle the 4.7. shells and boxes of light ammunition and the heavy cases of stores. By just after midnight, they were able to report themselves ready for sea again.

Cunningham received Kelly warmly. They had known each other in the Dardanelles in 1915 when Kelly had taken passage in Cunningham's ship. The admiral's cherubic face, which could be so grim when he was angry, showed the delight he felt at the way his captains had behaved.

'I was pleased to see you,' he said. 'I can do with every destroyer I can get. And every aircraft, too. I expect they'll dish out awards for this, but on the whole I think I'd much rather have a squadron of Hurricanes or another flotilla of destroyers.'

Though the news was good at the moment, with Addis Ababa expected to fall at any moment to bring the campaign in Ethiopia to an end, and more Italian destroyers operating from Massawa in the Red Sea sunk by *Eagle*'s Swordfishes, he was under no delusions about the value of the victory. 'It's come when our fortunes are at a particularly low ebb,' he said. 'And we all know what's ahead of us because the campaign in Greece's not going well. I just hope we've convinced the Italians of our supremacy so that they're unlikely to risk another rough handling.'

Kelly knew what he meant. What lay ahead of them when the Germans went into the Balkans, as they most assuredly would, had surely been made easier by those devastating broadsides from *Warspite, Barham* and *Valiant*.

With the bombing attacks on the troop convoys to Greece growing noticeably heavier and the new German Army in Libya doing far better even than had been expected, it seemed a good idea to Kelly to take advantage of the lull to dine his captains ashore, though it was a pity they couldn't include Smart who was doubtless eating omelettes and bully in hungry Malta with Verschoyle.

As they turned out of the docks into Ras-el-Tin Street, the sun was still hot, and the pavement contained the usual hordes of cringing dogs, blind beggars, shoe-shine boys, fly-whisk vendors, acrobats and snake charmers. After England, it all seemed a little unreal, despite its familiarity, with the native children, their stick-like legs twinkling, crying for biscuits, bully or baksheesh. The restaurant seemed to be packed with army officers, all apparently staff.

'They must be in serried rows at HQ,' Latimer commented. 'It's a wonder they don't trample each other to death.'

Everybody seemed to want to buy them drinks and they ended up at a party in one of the flats overlooking the Sporting Club at Gezira. Who owned it nobody seemed to know, but it was full of officers from all three services, together with a sprinkling of Wrens, ATS and WAAFs.

The Wrens seemed to have the edge on all the others when it came to good looks and Latimer was very quickly busy with a blonde who looked as if she'd once been a film star, while Kelly found himself talking to a Wren Third Officer with a pretty face that seemed vaguely familiar.

'We were expecting Captain Verschoyle,' she said and he smiled, knowing at once where he'd met her.

'You're Maisie,' he said. 'From Dover.'

She smiled. 'Actually it's Hermione Pentycross, but Captain Verschoyle always said it was too much of a mouthful.' She introduced him to one or two other girls and eventually to a First Officer older than the others.

'This is – '

'I know who it is,' Kelly said briskly. 'We've met before.'

Miss Jenner-Neate hadn't changed much since they'd met in Santander. 'Gin-and-It to the girls, these days,' she said with a small smile. 'They consider anybody over twenty-five to be decomposing.'

'How do you come to be here?'

'I married in 1939 but my husband was lost in *Courageous* and I thought I'd better join up. I reverted to my maiden name because we'd only been married a few weeks and I seemed a fraud masquerading as a married woman.'

He decided she wasn't half as bad as she made herself out to be, because she was slimmer and the splendid figure he remembered from Spain was even more splendid than before. In addition, she was undeniably good-looking with thick chestnut hair, wide grey eyes he'd not had time to notice in Santander, a straight nose and a full firm mouth. For the first time he realised that her voice was low and musical and that what she said was to the point, so that it seemed to enhance her character. The habit everybody had of addressing her by her surname seemed to put people off but Kelly decided she could grow on a man, and that but for Teresa Axuriaguerrera he might have noticed her before.

Everybody was still a little euphoric after the success of the convoy and the battle off Cape Matapan and he was just wondering if he could invite First Officer Jenner-Neate out to dinner when suddenly the news worsened. As they'd been expecting, the Germans had gone into Greece and Yugoslavia, and Alexandria suddenly seemed like an ants' nest stirred up by a stick. It looked very much as though the British High Command had been caught with its trousers down, because Tobruk was in danger of being besieged and everybody seemed to be wailing that the decision to send troops badly needed in North Africa to Greece ought never to have been made.

'My centre is giving way, my right is in retreat; situation excellent. I shall attack.'

When Foch had said that, he had doubtless had his tongue in his cheek, but Kelly could see what he meant. Disaster seemed no time to go into a decline and, with everybody in Cairo and Alexandria in a state of nerves, he decided that First Officer Jenner-Neate was the only calm one in view, and he suggested

164

she had a drink with him at the Club.

She seemed a little startled at his interest and flattered that he should wish to see her again.

'Most people seem to prefer my underlings, Captain,' she said. 'Even senior officers.'

She knew his record. 'As a matter of fact,' she said. 'I knew of you in Spain. You were in a book my brother had, called "Best Stories of The Great War". It described Jutland and how you brought your ship home. I was always pinching it from my brother. Perhaps that's why I married a naval officer.'

They were careful not to refer to her husband. Nor even to the news, because the Luftwaffe had caught three ammunition ships in the harbour of Pireaus and, when one of them had been hit, the eruption had flung blazing debris everywhere, igniting buildings and small craft, and engulfing the area with smoke and dust. Eleven ships had been lost, damage had been enormous and Pireaus had ceased to function as a port.

Jenner-Neate was in no doubt about how people regarded her. 'To the girls under me,' she said, 'I'm as old as God. But to the men who come in from the desert I'm the answer to their prayers. You'd be surprised how many of them tell me I'm beautiful. If I were, I'd be pleased. But I know I'm not.'

'You look all right to me,' Kelly said cheerfully.

She gave him a quiet smile. 'Perhaps you've been a long time at sea.'

She invited him back to her flat for coffee and he wondered if she were throwing out invitations. She lived in a modern block overlooking the desert but casting its shadow over a huddle of filthy Arab shanties. Everything was modern and sumptuous.

'Unfortunately,' she said, 'the fittings, which were put in by Egyptian labour, fall apart at the first touch. The bottom floor contains a garage and a cotton broker; the middle floor, offices and what, judging by the girls and the traffic, is without a doubt a brothel; and the top floor, us and the headquarters of the Society for the Redemption of Fallen Women, run, so I'm told by an Italian spy and three elderly English spinsters. I share with another First Officer, but she's on duty.' She gave him a sharp look. 'Which makes us entirely alone. Does that frighten you?'

He grinned. 'No.'

She smiled back. 'It does me. I'd prefer that you got no ideas in your head, because I invited you here for coffee and that's all you're going to get.'

He found he enjoyed her forthrightness and the way she moved. She seemed sparing of effort yet there was a regal swing to her skirt as she went in or out of a door, and he decided that what distinguished her above all the other Wrens was style.

They sat drinking brandy in the semi-darkness and when he leaned over and kissed her, she stared calmly back at him and said nothing. When he tried again, she kissed him back but then she pushed him away.

'That's as far as we go,' she said.

He was faintly disappointed and decided she was playing hard to get, but when he asked when he could see her again, she gave him a sad little smile and shook her head.

'War's a sad time, isn't it?' she said. 'Nobody meets anybody under normal circumstances.'

He remembered Teresa Axuriaguerrera saying something of the same sort in 1937 — years ago now, it seemed. Circumstances were always strained and every meeting had to be conducted as if it were the last.

'In any case,' she said. 'I'm afraid it doesn't depend on me. Your flotilla's due for sea. I saw the signal this afternoon.'

He was silent for a moment and she gave him her sad smile once more, so that he realised she'd probably said goodbye in the last two years to many men, including her husband, who had never returned.

What she'd said proved to be correct and the following morning a signal came ordering *Impi*, *Inca* and *Indian* to Suda Bay in Crete. Even the war in the desert seemed to have edged nearer and it was possible from time to time to hear the grumble of guns to the west.

Despite the suddenness of the departure, not a single member of the ship's company was missing and there were only three drunks, one of them inevitably 'Dancer' Siggis, and they arrived in Suda after a voyage through high seas whipped up by strong easterly winds, to find the place in a panic because everybody knew that if Greece capitulated the next target would be Crete itself.

The place lay like a basking lizard in the sunshine, the brown

166

cliffs lapped by the dark waters of the Aegean. The mountains behind rose in rocky folds, their slopes covered with scrub with, here and there, flowers and small cultivated patches among the olives and cypresses.

Already soldiers were struggling to set up guns and weapon pits. Parties of them tramped along the roads, and staff cars containing worried-looking officers trailed plumes of yellow dust as they hurried past. The tanker, *Pericles*, which had been damaged by Italian frogmen lay touching the bottom, with a tanker alongside her, pumping out her cargo. Not far away, another victim was the cruiser, *York*, which had had to be beached and was serving as an AA battery.

Her crew were already supplying men for landing craft – as good for getting men off beaches as for putting them on – and news had just arrived that the Greek Army of the Epirus had capitulated without informing the Greek government or the British, and it had been decided that evacuation plans must be prepared if any of the Australian-New Zealand Army Corps was to be saved. Military events were moving with frightening speed and changing like a kaleidoscope as the German blitzkreig advanced almost unchecked. Measures and counter measures conflicted. Precautions became useless and, as confusion created more confusion, orders were out of date before they could be implemented.

By the middle of the month, with the situation reaching disaster proportions, commercial shipping was brought to a standstill as military and naval needs took over. The evacuation of troops, with all their military paraphernalia, mechanical transport and equipment, who had been put ashore only a matter of six weeks before, became the top priority, and *Impi*, *Inca* and *Indian* were sent with two assault ships, *Glenbyre* and *Eastern Prince*, to Kalamata.

The evening sun was still above the horizon as the first of the bombing attacks developed almost at the moment they arrived. A large Greek yacht was alongside the pier, a fast-looking capacious vessel due to sail after dark, and civilians, British troops, walking wounded and the nursing staff from an Australian hospital had just finished boarding her when seven Junkers 88s appeared over the hills. Two of their bombs struck her at once and others exploded on the quayside. Within minutes her graceful lines were obscured by flames and smoke and they could hear the screams of men, women and children coming from the inferno.

The guns were roaring at the aircraft as they swung away and one of them spiralled down trailing smoke, but the yacht was already ablaze from stem to stern, and the wooden jetty where she was moored also caught fire as the ship became a blazing trap for hundreds of people. The Greek sailors had not rigged their fire hoses and, manoeuvring alongside, *Impi* managed to turn her own hoses on to a patch of deck to keep it clear enough for screaming people to reach it and jump overboard. As they moved as close as they dared, every man who could swim jumped into the sea to drag the survivors to scrambling nets.

The flames seemed to claw upwards for hundreds of feet as Kelly edged *Impi* still closer. Heads were bobbing in the water, faces blackened with oil, and the whaler was lowered and, with the Sub in command, was left astern as *Impi* moved away to gather in the more distant survivors. Oil had leaked from the blazing ship and was spreading outwards over the surface of the water, and it was a grim race to pick them up before the flames reached them. By this time, dozens of men were jumping over the side with lines and bringing burned survivors alongside. As they moved in and out of the flames and smoke, scattered bombers were still dropping mines by parachute but, apart from the guns' crews whose weapons were hammering into the sky through the smoke, they were all too busy to notice.

When they could no longer see any heads in the water and were just about to return to pick up the whaler, Siggis yelled up to the bridge that he'd seen a man on a raft. As the ship swung, the direction of the smoke changed and they saw an oil-soaked soldier sitting on a tangle of debris surrounded by flames. As they approached, one of the stewards kicked off his boots and, going into the water with a magnificent dive, dragged the man from his raft and swam with him to the after landing net.

It was dangerously hot now and the yacht was a pillar of fire, and black and filthy clouds of smoke were filling the sky overhead. The men on deck were covered with sweat and, with their own load of fuel oil and ammunition, it was growing dangerous.

'We can't stay here any longer,' Kelly shouted. 'Tell him to hold tight!'

168

As the ship went astern, he was certain the two men would be washed away, but the steward had one arm through the net and the other round the survivor's neck, almost throttling him. Whipping them aboard and, picking up the Sub with more survivors, they backed off to safety.

They had seventy-eight people on board, men, women and children, dirt-streaked, wet-through and shivering, filling the ship with the stench of oil and sea water. Tea had been brought for them but as fast as they drank it they were vomiting it up again. Children were screaming with fear and women were sobbing, and among them a hysterical man was shouting that he was drowning as he was held down by two of his friends.

They pushed them on board *Glenbyre* but the incident had wasted hours that should have been used for evacuating troops; and in the harsh world of war, troops were of more importance than civilians, and they were still pouring into the port in their thousands by every means at their disposal from lorries to bicycles and their own two feet. Morale had reached rock bottom and many of them no longer carried weapons. A pall of defeat hung over the place like a leaden cloak, and the only glimmer of light in the gloom was the hope of rescue by the Navy that they all cherished.

Impi finally secured alongside under her own searchlights and without any help from ashore, and within minutes, hundreds of men had appeared, standing in bunches waiting for embarkation. But time had to be wasted rigging clusters of lights and making preparations to marshal them into some semblance of order, things which should have been done long before their arrival. By the early hours of the following morning, the harvest of men totalled over eight thousand, but since they had to leave before daylight it was a saddening experience to know that thousands more had had to be left who would have been aboard if someone had only shown some initiative.

As the convoy assembled outside the harbour just before daylight, a New Zealand colonel appeared on *Impi*'s bridge to say there were two of his companies at a fishing village further along the coast, so, ordering the convoy to leave with *Inca* and *Indian,* Kelly took *Impi* close inshore and found the harbour just before daylight.

As they groped their way through the unlit and deceptive

entrance, the quay appeared to be deserted. One of the Maltese stewards could speak Greek and Kelly sent him ashore in the whaler with Latimer and the New Zealand colonel. They returned half an hour later with only nine soldiers and the New Zealander on the verge of tears.

Apparently nobody had heard of the impending arrival of the rescue ships as the telegraph system had been put out of action and the army radios had failed to pick up any signals. It was growing daylight now and becoming dangerous to stay much longer.

'Sound the siren,' Kelly ordered and the high whooping cry began to echo among the hills. Almost immediately, men appeared about two miles away, popping up like jacks-in-the-box among the folds of ground.

'Keep it going!'

The distant figures were joined by others and began to stream out of the rocky fissures until they clotted together into a black mass of men hurrying down the dirt road to the harbour. They arrived alongside, panting and sweating, and were driven like sheep up the gangways.

As they went astern, more men appeared and Kelly put the ship's bows against the dockside, keeping her there with the engines running slowly ahead. Considering what a reputation he had for handling ships alongside, he thought, he was taking a hell of a chance. Ropes were dropped ashore and, as the men scrambled up them, the ship finally went astern in almost full daylight with two soldiers still clinging to a rope ladder dangling from the bows.

The air attacks started not long after sun-up. It was a clear bright day with a fresh wind which whipped the sea into a short ugly swell. The dive-bombers immediately singled out *Glenbyre*, the largest ship, but *Inca* and *Indian* took station between the two transports to afford them protection while *Impi* moved ahead to throw up a barrage through which the Stukas would have to dive.

It didn't seem to put the Stuka pilots off in the slightest, and within minutes *Glenbyre* was shaken by two direct hits, one engulfing the bridge in a sheet of flame. She swerved, almost colliding with *Inca,* and swung helplessly head to wind so that the flames were fanned along the length of the ship which was soon burning fiercely from end to end.

Kelly's face was taut. He knew they daren't stay and his eyes hardened as he turned to the yeoman of signals. 'Make to *Inca* to remain and pick up survivors.'

As the rest of the convoy continued, the Stukas were still flying over the burning ship, spraying it with their machine guns and cannon and subjecting *Inca* to sporadic attacks. As the noise died and the aircraft disappeared, nobody was under any delusions that there wouldn't be more.

The buzzer went. 'Masthead to bridge. Four ships in sight dead ahead.'

They swung round, wondering what they were in for next. For a long time, with the sun still behind the distant ships, it was impossible to tell what they were, but then they turned slightly to starboard to come up on their port side and Latimer grinned.

'Hunt-class ships, sir. *Chatsworth* in the lead. And there's an I-class ship bringing up the rear. I think it's *Impatient*.'

The four newcomers closed them at full speed, and Verschoyle's signal was a repetition of one he had sent to Kelly up the Yangtze in 1927.

'Fancy meeting you.'

As the four ships crashed past them, *Impatient*'s roughly-patched wounds clearly visible, her light flashed.

'Request permission to escort little sister *Inca* home.'

'Make "Granted".'

Almost immediately, more Stukas arrived and the holocaust of sound started again as the guns threw their barrage of steel into the sky. As they came in, Kelly found himself cataloguing and analysing his thoughts. It wasn't fear that filled his mind but grim fatalism. The muscles of his mouth were drawn taut and he felt that *Impi* was only a minute fragment in the catastrophe of events that were taking place.

They beat off the aeroplanes without damage but as they began to relax, the signals officer appeared alongside.

'Distress call from *Inca*, sir: "Being dive-bombed."'

'It's started.' Latimer's mouth was grim. 'It's going to be murder.'

An hour later the signals officer appeared again. '*Inca*, sir. She requests fighter protection.'

'There is none,' Kelly snapped.

Junkers 87s were dive-bombing the ships in Suda Bay as they arrived, contributing to the growing chaos there with attacks which came with an intensity that stunned the senses. One of their bombs near-missed *Eastern Prince* and she came to a stop with steam coming from her engine-room ventilators.

Out in the harbour, ships were queuing up for the long journey to Alex while personnel ships were waiting to disembark at jetties where others were busy getting rid of their cargoes of men. Already, it was clear *Impi* would be going back to the mainland and the first lieutenant had got his men splicing slings for stretchers and lashing drums together to make rafts because the soldiers were going to have to come out on anything that would float. The doctor had roped off benches for operations and the cooks were baking double helpings of bread and preparing cauldrons of soup. The sailors seemed fatalistic.

'What's the good of cleaning it up?' Kelly heard Siggis say. 'The bloody pongoes'll only come and mess it up again.'

As they put their ropes ashore, the signals officer appeared, his face grim.

'They got *Inca*, sir,' he announced. '*Impatient* reported picking up the survivors of both ships, but then the bloody Germans raked *them* with machine gun fire and killed the guns' crews, and the bombers went in. *Impatient* went in about fifteen minutes, with most of her crew and the survivors from *Inca* and *Glenbyre* they had on board. Some have been picked up by *Ashby*, but not many, I'm afraid.'

'How about the captains?'

'Not among the survivors, sir.'

Kelly's face was grim. Out of his flotilla, he now had two ships left, and ships were not merely steel and guns and turbines. They were living disciplined organisations with officers, seamen and stokers, and death by oil suffocation or entombment in the bowels of a ship was a squalid and terrifying end. And every one of them had a family – parents, wives or children – who were still writing letters in the belief that they were alive. Even when the news arrived, 'Missing, presumed killed' it would still leave a tiny spark of hope. As he looked at his ship's company sleeping off their exhaustion in the sun, he was staggered how young they looked despite the beards they grew, and a great surge of pride and affection for them filled his heart.

Mail had arrived from home and it seemed like a glimmer of sanity in the lunacy of death and destruction that prevailed. Kelly Rumbelo had got his commission and was now in *Repulse*, and Paddy had got her wish and been warned she was to go eventually to the hospital ship, *Anarapoora*, at Scapa, but she was disgusted because Hugh had left Macrihanish on appointment to *Victorious*, which was due for sea. The trivialities the letter contained seemed to make sense just then, after the deaths of Smart in *Impatient* and all the men in *Inca* and *Glenbyre*.

In defeat defiance, Churchill had said, but that was fine if you had the means, and defiance was always a bit more personal when you were the one who was doing the defying. At that moment, every day they awoke to find themselves alive was another day of grace and they were under no delusions as to the future.

Kelly had just put the letter aside when a signal arrived that he was to take over Verschoyle's ships, refuel immediately and be ready for sea within four hours. *Chatsworth* was on the oiler when they arrived and Kelly appeared alongside her with a crash that demolished the whaler.

'It's getting to be a habit,' he said.

Verschoyle looked tired and dark-eyed. 'Next time,' he said, 'I'll have it put in the water and signal you when it's safe to come.'

He was depressed by the disasters, because he'd already lost *Rushden* on the Malta convoy. She'd had to be beached at Marsa Xlokk after being damaged by a near miss and, although he'd brought every one of the merchantmen home, with his ships almost out of ammunition, *Mons Star* had been hit by a bomb eight miles from Grand Harbour. He'd managed to tow her in with *Chatsworth* and *Hallamshire* in a chaos of wires, ropes and cables, with most of her oil intact, but *Clan Mackay* had been sunk by another bomb at her berth with the loss of most of her cargo.

Since then, he'd been operating with his remaining ships and *Impatient* off Volos and had no great opinion of the staff work that had sent him there.

He offered Kelly a drink and a cigarette and sprawled in his chair, his body limp with weariness. 'This is only the beginning, too,' he went on. 'When they start on Crete, we'll have to do it all over again. It'll be like Dunkirk, only worse, because this time we've got to do it across a hell of a lot of sea without the RAF to watch out for the Luftwaffe.'

He smiled wearily and sank his drink. 'It's a bugger of a war, isn't it?' he said.

7

They had brought the army out, but the battle was far from over. Before long the Germans would attack Crete and the British had to hold it as much as the Germans had to capture it.

There was little light in the darkness and British fortunes were at their nadir. Tobruk was besieged now and the situation in the desert had grown worse. Two British generals had been captured – 'It ought to ease the crowding among the staff a bit,' Latimer commented – and most of the armour had been lost. Every gain from the winter campaign had gone.

In Alexandria the anxiety was obvious. With envy in his heart as he saw the delight with which Verschoyle and Third Officer Pentycross greeted each other, First Officer Jenner-Neate became a symbol of calm to Kelly. He found himself investing her simplest actions with something the other Wrens couldn't even pretend to possess – confidence and efficiency when they seemed to be blessed with nothing but the enthusiasm of youth, grace when they seemed as awkward as colts, tranquillity when they seemed to shriek like a lot of disturbed parakeets. It was tragic that they'd met again at the most desperate period of the war. Nothing was normal: everything – associations between men and women, even love affairs – had to be conducted at a frantic pace. Britain was fighting for her life. Now that the invasion scare at home had died, the desperation was all in the Middle East, because if the Mediterranean were lost the whole of British strategy would collapse.

With the North African coast occupied by the enemy, there could now be no air cover for the biggest part of the Mediterranean, and Malta was once more in danger of starving. The respite the destroyer crews had hoped for after Greece – because there was hardly a single ship that was not in urgent need of a refit – never materialised. Tank and aircraft reinforcements had to be pushed through from Gib, because the army couldn't wait for it to go round the Cape, so a convoy was assembled at Alex and, escorted by every available warship, run westwards to Malta where the tank and aircraft convoy was met and brought back to the Eastern Mediterranean. The Luftwaffe tried its hardest but the volume of gunfire was so tremendous it was beaten off without loss, but neither the tanks nor the aircraft, which had been brought at such effort from England, had been fitted with sand and dust filters and the work had to be done before they could go into action.

'Why in God's name couldn't they fit the bloody things before they shipped them?' Verschoyle snarled. 'The whole goddamned lot could be destroyed before they've even fired a shot!'

Desperate for calm, Kelly looked up First Officer Jenner-Neate again, but she seemed wary of him and was so perpetually on duty she began to torment him with her inaccessibility. He could see her and talk to her at headquarters but never alone, and he wondered if she were avoiding him. He knew she had a highly responsible job that demanded dedication and long hours but, by this time, her dullest, most menial chores had become for him an expression of her personality. She was completely mistress of what she did and seemed to tackle her work with a serenity that elevated it beyond a mere chore, and he took to hanging about in the corridor near her office like a love-sick midshipman in the hope of meeting her. When she appeared, which was rarely, she was always in a hurry, however, and in his desperation he wondered if he were falling in love again. Surely not, he told himself. He was too bloody old for that and she was too sensible.

Finally, he grabbed her as she appeared with an armful of papers and was just about to ask – demand even – that she meet him for drinks when the fleet chaplain appeared. Frustrated, he swore bitterly and he saw the chaplain's lips purse. Jenner-Neate's mouth was as firm as ever but as she vanished – as suddenly as she'd appeared – her eyes were smiling.

In a fury, he wrote her a note asking her if he could take her out to dinner but it came back with a scrawl across the back – 'Too busy. And so will you be soon.'

176

She was dead right again and the following morning he heard that the Germans had occupied the island of Milos eighty miles to the north of Crete as a base for the assembly of convoys and that they intended to mount a massive invasion of Crete by air. It needed no great intelligence to appreciate that the targets would be Canea, Retimo and Heraklion, and to counter any such attack naval forces were to be deployed to the west and north-west of the island, while the main fleet remained at Alexandria. Air reconnaissance or fighter cover was not expected to produce much.

Latimer blew up his lifebelt with a great show as they left for sea. 'I expect it's all the air support we'll get,' he observed.

With Intelligence reporting that the attack could be expected any day, Kelly took *Impi* and *Indian*, followed by Verschoyle's three Hunt-Class ships, to Suda Bay before leaving on a sweep to the north. It was a messy arrangement mixing the classes of ships, but it was typical of war when tidiness was often sacrificed to ensure that it went on without interruption.

'It's a bit like Boy's Own Paper,' was Verschoyle's comment. 'Soldiers of the King facing fearful odds.'

Crete was a harsh island, but dawn there always seemed to be extraordinarily beautiful, rising on decks wet with dew or powdered with sand blown from Africa, and it required little imagination to understand why it had been so beloved of Byron and Rupert Brooke.

To the men struggling to build defences, however, and to the nervous sailors with their eyes on the sky on the lookout for aircraft, there was little poetry in a place that was only a temporary refuge from German ferocity. Whitehall was urging that it should be made a fortress, but no arms had arrived and, despite the numbers of soldiers, it remained a base of gunners without guns, drivers without vehicles, and signallers without radios, all mixed indiscriminately together and left to man the defences because there had been no ships after Greece to transport them to Egypt.

On the evening of May 19th, north of the island, Kelly's four ships were found by dive bombers but, thanks to the anti-aircraft guns on the Hunt-Class ships, they were all driven off. Because of their smallness, however, the Hunts were unable to carry a great deal of ammunition or fuel and, as they returned to Suda Bay to re-ammunition, they ran into a fresh series of air attacks which appeared to be directed chiefly at the beached *York*. They were due to head north again the following day but, as they prepared for sea, they could see heavy German bombing south of Canea and towards Maleme.

'Break out the Flit guns,' Kelly suggested to Latimer. 'I'm going to my cabin. Call me if it comes on to bomb.'

He had hardly spoken when aircraft appeared over the mountains and swept over the harbour. Immediately, every gun on every ship burst into flame. The din was terrific and a Junkers 88 hurtled over the bay at masthead height, trailing smoke, to disappear beyond the hills in a great flower of flame.

'That's got one of the buggers,' Siggis yelled with satisfaction.

As they turned from watching the disappearing aircraft, they saw more appearing to the south and west of Canea.

'Junkers 52s.,' Latimer said. 'Transports.'

Almost immediately, they saw objects falling from the aeroplanes and the blossoming of parachutes, then more concentrations of troop carriers and gliders making for Maleme.

'The invasion appears to have arrived!'

Almost immediately, the signal arrived to send them off to the north.

'SWEEPS CANCELLED. GERMAN SEABORNE FORCE NORTH OF CRETE. COURSE 180. PATROL NORTH OF HERAKLION EAST OF LONGITUDE 25 DEGREES GUARDING GENERAL AREA SUDA BAY/ KISSAMO BAY/MALEME.'

As they slipped to sea, it was obvious that the military situation ashore was already confused and uncertain, and more aircraft were already swinging in to attack Suda Bay. As they turned north they could smell the land – the dry breath of rock, dust and rotting driftwood – and in the distance the sky seemed to be full of aircraft and the black pockmarks of shell bursts.

'Aircraft green one-oh!' Rumbelo's voice swung their heads round. 'About twenty of them!'

'They're Junkers!' Latimer yelled. 'Twenty-one, to be exact. And they don't have escorts!'

'Make to all ships,' Kelly said. 'Point blank range.'

As the flags fluttered up the guns remained quiet, and they

watched in silence as the aircraft approached. Since the ships made no attempt to fire, the pilots of the Junkers seemed to feel they were out of ammunition, and made only a slight swing away from them. But then every gun in the flotilla, the 4.7 all-purpose weapons on the I-class ships, the point-fives and Verschoyle's four-inch high-angle guns, burst into flame. The first of the transports was surrounded by puff-balls of smoke and almost immediately its starboard engine began to trail smoke. A door opened and men began to jump, their para-chutes opening as they fell. A second machine just behind ex-ploded and fell in pieces, a wing sidling sideways and downwards in long slicing curves through a sky that was dotted with the falling bodies of men.

Latimer was shouting with excitement as another aircraft caught fire. The transports had run straight into the barrage and within seconds seven of them were falling towards the sea and several more were trailing smoke. The rest swung away to the north, followed by the pockmarks of shell bursts.

'That's stopped the bastards laughing in church,' Siggis yelled jubilantly.

They continued to head north, fighting off a half-hearted attack by Italian bombers and later a force of high-speed Italian torpedo boats which hurtled round St. Nikolo Point at the east-ern end of Los and let go their torpedoes before retiring in the face of overwhelming fire. Throughout the night they sped eastwards, dreading the following morning and the possibility of being discovered by dive bombers.

Latimer appeared at Kelly's side.

'Forces C and D have been attacked,' he announced. '*Ajax* damaged. *Juno* sunk.' He frowned. 'My brother-in-law's in *Juno*.'

'I'm sorry, William. I hope he's safe.'

Latimer shrugged. Tragedies of this sort were common coinage these days and people had grown so inured to them, they no longer had much impact.

Shortly afterwards another signal arrived. 'NUMBER OF SMALL CRAFT HEADING SOUTHWARDS TOWARDS CRETE. BELIEVED TO BE PART OF INVASION FLO-TILLA. CLOSE IN THROUGH KASO STRAIT AND KITHERA CHANNEL TO PREVENT SEABORNE

179

LANDING.'

'Give me a course, Pilot,' Kelly said. 'Revolutions for 28 knots.'

Just after eleven o'clock, the masthead look-out called out.

'Masthead to bridge. Unlighted ship red two-oh.' There was a pause. 'Correction. Several ships. Small ships. They look like Greek caïques.'

'Port two-oh!' Kelly said. 'Full ahead both. Stand by the searchlight. How far north of Crete are we, Pilot?'

'Eighteen miles, sir.'

'I bet they were hoping to make the place in darkness. Searchlight!'

Impi's light blazed out; *Indian*'s followed, with the lights of Verschoyle's ships. Just ahead were about twenty-five caïques, the small wooden cargo boats that operated among the islands. They seemed to be crammed with men among guns and boxes of what appeared to be ammunition. Officers in the bows appeared to be yelling instructions to each other with megaphones.

'My God, what a target!' Latimer said. 'Poor bastards!'

'Save your sympathy,' Kelly snapped. He bent to the voice pipe. 'Fire at will!'

As the searchlights had appeared, the sails of the caïques had been lowered to minimize their size, and as the British ships came round, guns blazing, the little vessels began to scatter.

'Destroyer, sir,' Latimer reported. 'Coming up astern of them! Looks like *Lupo* class. Modern but small. 3.9-inchers and torpedo tubes.'

The Italian ship was making smoke which was drifting towards them as she crossed in front of the caïques. Immediately, *Indian*'s guns crashed out and they saw tall fountains of water lift on either side of the Italian's bows. The next salvo smashed home just abaft the bridge and they saw a large fire break out. The Italian captain was conducting himself with great courage, thundering towards them with every gun blazing. Turning to comb his torpedoes, they swung back towards the convoy, still hitting the Italian destroyer with everything they possessed, and as she swung away, burning, a complete broadside from *Impi* struck her on the stern.

'Oh, Jesus,' Siggis's exultant voice yelled. 'Straight up the arse!'

While *Impi* and *Indian* had been tackling the escort, Verschoyle had made no mistake about the convoy, and as they swung back to help, they saw that most of the caïques were on fire or sinking. Only three or four seemed to be still afloat and trying to turn north away from the withering fire. They were crowded with men, and were flying the Greek flag, and the destroyers tore into them, snapping and tearing like wolves which had broken into a flock of sheep. Every gun was roaring, pom-poms and machine guns riddling their occupants, and German soldiers were leaping into the sea fully-equipped. Between the roars of the guns they could hear the unearthly wailing of drowning men.

As *Impi* turned, a small wooden schooner appeared ahead from the darkness, filled with a sea of white faces.

'Ram the bugger, William,' Kelly said, and *Impi*'s bows swung.

They saw open mouths yelling, and waving arms, and men started to jump overboard, then *Impi*'s bows carved through the wooden sides of the schooner with hardly a shudder, crushing wood and metal and flesh and bone. As the two ends of the vessel leapt up, one of the soldiers was flung in the air and, for a second before he disappeared, they saw him on a level with the bridge, his eyes wide in startled horror, his fingers clawing, his legs working as though he were running. All round the ship, men were rolling and tumbling in the wash of the bow wave and the wake, turning over and over in the turbulence, the air full of their shrieks. The schooner's mast slid along the ship's side, scraping over it with a scream against the steel, then it snapped off and, as *Impi*'s stern came round, they could see only disturbed water, a few broken planks and half a dozen bobbing heads.

Nobody on *Impi*'s bridge spoke. The schooner seemed to have disappeared with all her cargo of men as if she had never existed. It was an appalling slaughter and, as they dragged a few soaked survivors aboard, they realised they had annihilated a battalion of a mountain regiment.

Almost as soon as it was daylight, the dive bombers found

them and they had to fight off a spirited attack which, though it brought no casualties, caused slight damage from a near miss to *Ashby*.

'Ask all ships to report remaining ammunition,' Kelly said. 'We must be running low.'

The replies were disturbing. *Impi* and *Indian* reported forty per cent remaining, while Verschoyle's ships reported only thirty.

'I suppose we're doing some good,' Kelly observed. 'If only by attracting enemy aircraft away from everybody else.'

'I'm not sure we are, sir,' Latimer observed. 'Force A reports being under heavy attack, and *Carlisle*'s been damaged. Force C's also been attacked and they've hit *Warspite*. The two forces are now in company.' He looked serious. 'The war at sea seems, as the fiction writers put it, to have blazed into life. The BBC reports *Bismarck* and *Prinz Eugen* are also at sea and heading into the Atlantic.'

'God help the Atlantic convoys,' Kelly said. 'I'll bet there are a lot of loins being girded up at home just now.'

They were still digesting the thought of the two great ships getting among the merchantmen struggling across from America when they intercepted a signal announcing that the destroyer, *Greyhound*, and the cruiser, *Gloucester*, had been sunk.

'Our turn tomorrow,' Latimer said.

Almost immediately Rumbelo sang out. 'Aircraft! Dead ahead!'

'Earlier than that, William,' Kelly said. 'Now.'

As the ships drew closer together to give mutual support, the Stukas came in. *Indian* was hit by three bombs at once. Two of them blew the after boiler room and the engine-room open to the sea and the third detonated her after magazine. There was a tremendous explosion and as the smoke cleared they could see the ship hanging in the water in two blazing halves, surrounded by bobbing heads.

Their guns still firing, *Impi, Chatsworth, Hallamshire* and *Ashby* moved among them, their scrambling nets down, dragging shocked, dazed and oil-soaked men from the sea. Some of them were weeping and it didn't seem possible that they could take much more without respite. The human system could absorb only so many shocks before it broke down, and courage was a resource that could be drained away by the constant shattering

182

of the nerves.

As they swung south a signal arrived ordering them to sweep inside Kissamo and Canea Bays. There was no time to transfer *Indian*'s survivors and, as they entered the Antikithera channel, *Ashby* began to fall behind.

'*Ashby* has "Not under control" balls up, sir.'

The signals officer joined in. '*Ashby* reports steering defective,' he said. 'Helm jammed twenty degrees to starboard.'

The damage, trivial at any other time, was a portent of disaster and *Ashby* was studied with dismay. With the constant threat of air attack without any effective defence, with every near-miss the bomb with their number on grew mathematically closer, and Kelly could feel tiredness drain away his resolution. It was almost easier to lie down and let things occur as they would.

Ashby's trouble raised the problem of what to do with her and how to protect her and, for safety, he left her at the entrance to Canea Bay. As they probed into the darkness, almost running down a large caïque which they left burning, she reported her steering defect repaired. By this time every man aboard was exhausted and Kelly couldn't remember when he had last left the bridge. His muscles ached and he had smoked cigarettes until his mouth felt charred. Most of the duty men, waiting with slumped shoulders at their guns, had remained at their positions through three watches, sustained by food prepared by cooks released briefly from their action stations. On the bridge they were no different, eating stale corned beef sandwiches and dipping dirty mugs into buckets of cocoa.

As they picked up *Ashby*, they were warned by radio of approaching aircraft and soon after daylight high level Dorniers appeared.

'Gets a bit like those old Douglas Fairbanks pictures, sir, doesn't it?' Latimer said. 'You've no sooner leapt down the stairs and skewered a couple of bandits when you have to swing from the chandeliers on to a table to skewer two more.'

The guns crashed out to keep the bombers high but they were persistent and Kelly saw the bombs falling towards them, a bunch of small black objects coming down in a shallow arc.

'Hard a-port!'

The ships scattered and, as *Impi* swung, the whole salvo fell between them. The aircraft circled for a while and they guessed they were calling up their friends and, sure enough, forty minutes later three more Dornier 215s appeared. Their bombs all went wide but *Ashby* reported that her steering gear had gone again. By this time the sun was well up and it was a perfect day, with the water glittering as the sun caught the waves.

'Fuckin' Mediterranean!' some disgusted and exhausted sailor said below the bridge.

'Christ, man –' Siggis' cheerful voice came up in reply '– old ladies pay 'undreds of pounds to come 'ere!'

'Aircraft green five-oh!' Rumbelo yelled. 'Many aircraft!'

'It gets monotonous,' Latimer said. He was smiling, but it was a smile full of tiredness and strain.

'There they are, sir. They're dive bombers.'

'Enemy aircraft! Enemy aircraft! Green five-oh! Angle of sight three-oh! All close-range weapons load and commence tracking!'

The yammer of the alarm bell mingled with shouts as the distinctive flat W of the Stukas' wings became clear. With their fixed undercarriages, they looked like huge eagles with their claws down, stooping for a kill. Coming out of the rising sun, they were beginning to separate into two groups.

The first group caught *Ashby* as she swung to port, all her guns firing, and Kelly saw the bombs crash into the sea all round her. Then a flight of six separated from the second group and started their dive. Without waiting to give orders, Kelly put the telegraphs to 'Full ahead'.

'Hard a-starboard!'

The turn brought the ship back on its tracks underneath the diving aircraft and two of the bombs missed to port while the third aircraft failed to pull out of its dive and crashed into the sea with a tremendous splash.

'One!'

'Two!' Latimer yelled. 'Siggis got one!'

One of the climbing machines was trailing smoke. A parachute blossomed below it just before it exploded in a flare of flame.

'Hard a-port!'

'They've got *Ashby*!'

Swinging round on his stool, Kelly saw that *Ashby*, on fire amidships, was slowing to a stop and settling rapidly. Her loss would force the rest of them to stop to pick up survivors and every man aboard knew they'd be sitting ducks.

'Here they come again!'

'Hard a-starboard!'

Impi was turning at full speed as the Stuka came in low over the stern. The barrage of flak seemed overwhelming and impenetrable. The guns' crews were working like madmen, their weapons blotching the sky with shell bursts, but the aircraft still came on.

'Midships. Steady.' The navigator's voice was quite calm. 'Hold her there.'

The bomb seemed to hang below the aircraft as it was released, poised over the ship for what seemed an age, growing larger and larger as it came nearer, as if it were a balloon being blown up by a child.

Siggis' guns were hammering away and they saw the Stuka lift away with pieces falling off the wing. With everybody else's eyes on the aeroplane as it began to tilt to one side in a sideslip towards the sea, Kelly was watching the bomb. Half-consciously he saw the splash in the corner of his eye as the aeroplane went in, then the deck jarred under his feet as the bomb struck with a shattering explosion that jarred his spine and made his teeth feel loose.

8

The bomb had landed behind the bridge and burst in the foremost boiler room in a dull eruption of flame. An immense explosion shuddered the ship and wrenched out a vast vomit of twisted steel, splintered boats, sparks, water and smoke. A huge cloud of soot flew up from the shredded funnel with a perfect ring of smoke and came down in a spreading cloud of black. Holes appeared in the bridge-plating, while a man running for shelter was cut almost in two and flung against the bridge ladder to smear it with his blood.

When they lifted their heads, X gun had vanished as if it had never been there, leaving only a gaping hole surrounded by jagged blades of shining steel. The searchlight had also gone and among the debris lay the remains of the crew, the blistered paint of the deck splashed with their blood. Flying splinters had scythed their way through the men on the deck, until the bridge structure looked like a colander. A petty officer, his face soot-black, one eye a pit of blood, was huddled against the scarred plates looking as though someone had fired a gigantic shotgun at him, his body and face full of red holes pumping blood. One of the gunners, his face already the colour of slate, was curled up like an unborn child, moaning, and across his body was draped one of his mates, the top of his head sheered off as cleanly as if someone had used a huge chopper so that his brains were oozing down his face.

The second wave of bombers was coming down on them now, and Latimer's voice, cracked with shouting, lifted hoarsely. 'Here they come again!'

'Midships!' Kelly spoke automatically, knowing that the bombers would be aiming off for a starboard turn but, expecting the ship to right herself as she came out of the swing, he realised that the deck was still canted over at an angle and, though he couldn't see from the bridge how far the bomb damage extended, instinctively he knew that *Impi* was mortally hit.

'Hard a-port!'

Expecting the ship to swing the other way, he knew his suspicions about her wound were correct as she continued to swing to starboard. Then he realised the list was increasing and that she was no longer turning but was heeling over on to her side.

'Stop engines!'

The voice pipe buzzer went and Latimer answered it.

'Coxswain reports ship won't answer helm, sir,' he reported. 'And there's no reply to engine room telegraphs.'

Kelly drew a deep breath. A and B guns and the point-fives were still pounding away and, just to port, Verschoyle's two remaining ships were sending up a terrific barrage. One of the Stukas peeled off and crashed into the sea, but *Ashby* was low in the water now, her stern awash, and men were trying to throw overboard Carley's, wooden rafts and anything else that would float.

In the shambles of twisted steel and torn bodies, sobbing, swearing sailors were trying to clear the deck for the damage party. But it was too late and *Impi* was already settling. Figures were bursting through the smoke, heads down, their arms raised against the flames, when the next wave of Stukas roared down into the barrage that *Impi*'s guns were still sending up. The list was steadily increasing and it was only then that Kelly realised the bomb had wrenched away the starboard side hull plates under the vanished X gun and the ship was taking in tons of water.

The whole of the stern was in flames now, terrible beyond words, and when another bomb struck her, *Impi* seemed to shudder like a tortured animal. The bridge screen was shattered and the compasses smashed. The bridge messenger was still clinging to it, moaning, and as Kelly, struggling to regain comprehension, turned towards him, he saw that smoke enveloped everything aft of the bridge, which was a tangle of bunting, fallen halyards and aerials. Through the voice pipes he could hear the despairing cries of those trapped below. The bridge was already tilting but men were still being dragged from the blaze. As the list increased, the wounded and dying began to slide towards the inferno, then somewhere in the smoke there was another explosion and it suddenly dawned on him that *Impi* was rolling right over.

'Abandon ship,' he shouted. 'Save yourself, William!'

Turning, he saw Rumbelo just behind him, his steel helmet gone and blood on his face.

'Get going, Albert,' he said.

Rumbelo looked stubborn. 'After you,' he said.

'Get going!' Kelly roared.

Rumbelo stared at him for a second, frowning, then he turned abruptly and scuttled down the bridge ladder.

As the sea poured into the broken hull, the water rose – slowly at first, but steadily and quite distinctly – then it came in a roaring maelstrom of water and, with men struggling clear of swinging stays and falling equipment, *Impi* leaned over on her side at a grotesque angle in the sea. Another aircraft came in and its bomb hit the deck over A boiler room and brought the foremast crashing down across the Bofors. The deck lurched and Kelly fell to his knees, then it seemed to slew, one side lifting crazily.

One eye on the sky, he saw Latimer leaning over the bridge rail, shouting to men below, and Siggis and his crew struggling free from the debris and the trailing wires of the aerials to drag the wounded to the side as the deck lurched again, then suddenly he realised there was water all round him and that Latimer, the navigator and the yeoman of signals had all disappeared. Climbing on to the gyro compass pedestal, he stared round him, feeling the ship cant further and further to starboard. Stokers were struggling up from below, bursting out of doorways and hatches, their eyes starting from their heads with their efforts, but there was no panic, only haste, and he could still see men pushing life rafts into the sea.

For a while he clung on, then the sea swept him away like the breaking of a dam. As it roared over him, he kept his head enough to take a deep breath. Finding himself in darkness, his ears filled with the rush and crashing of water, he realised that the ship was upside down, still moving ahead under her own momentum, and that he was underneath her and terrified of dying alone.

It was pitch dark, then, as he fought free of familiar objects and trailing guy wires and aerials that were dragging him down, he saw a faint glimmer of light appear. As it grew, the blackness became green and, his lungs bursting, he forced himself to keep his mouth shut, even clapping his right hand over his mouth to pinch his nostrils together. Slowly the light grew brighter and, in desperation, he had to open his mouth. The water rushed in, choking him, then, with a great spluttering, agonised gasp, he burst to surface, shooting above the water almost to his waist as he broke free. Alongside him, *Impi* was still moving slowly ahead, her stern sticking up, all red lead and weed, her propellers still turning in the air as she slid forward and downward, trailing a cloak of wreckage, wires, and bodies.

Terrified he'd be dragged down with her, he swam as hard as he could to struggle clear. The ship had turned turtle so fast, not a single boat had been launched and there appeared to be only two Carleys in the sea. Everything else had gone with the ship. Then a bulk of timber shot to the surface a few yards away, leaping out of the water like a dolphin in a cloud of spray to slap back with a splash.

Men were clustering round the raft where he recognised Latimer by the stripes on his shoulders standing up yelling at them. His face was black with oil and his hair was plastered across his face. More men were heading towards the raft and the yeoman of signals passed Kelly still wearing his steel helmet. It made him look like a tortoise in the water, then he suddenly became aware of its weight, wrenched it off and tossed it away.

Swimming towards one of the Carleys, he saw a row of splashes cross the sea ahead of him and wondered what they were. Then, with a roar one of the Stukas swept overhead, her machine guns going. As the splashes approached again, he drew a deep breath and dived below the water, and when he came up, the Carley seemed to have emptied of all but lolling men and Latimer had been hit in both legs and was sprawled across the bulge of the side.

Reaching the raft, he saw there was only one uninjured man on board and he ordered him to climb out so they could push more injured aboard. They had no sooner finished when the Stukas came again and half the men they'd just pushed aboard were killed in the new attack. Laboriously, gasping and spluttering, they lifted them out and pushed more aboard. It was an agonising experience because everybody was covered with oil and it was impossible to get a grip on the half-naked bodies. Pulling one of the stokers towards the raft, Kelly found his head bumping against a mat of dead men, and he could see the navigator trying frantically to claw his way over the slimy o l-covered side to pull men aboard. All round him he could hear the choking cries of drowning sailors, and the whole business was made more gruesome by the calm sea and the brilliant sunshine.

A young sailor no more than eighteen clung alongside him. He wore nothing but a vest and his face and body were so charred he looked bald and black and wet-through at the same time. They tried to push him into the raft but he died as they did so and they had to let him float away and save someone else instead.

Wild-eyed and gasping, looking like a nigger minstrel under the fuel oil that stung his eyes, Kelly stared around him. As the raft lifted on a gentle swell, he saw that *Ashby* had also disappeared and that there was another knot of bobbing heads about a quarter of a mile away. Then nearby, squatting on a floating spar, spitting with fury, he saw the ship's cat, its bedraggled fur sticking up in spikes.

'That's it, Pluto –' it was Siggis, black-faced and spluttering but with his daft grin stretching across his face ' – give 'em what for!'

He started to sing.

'Anybody here seen Kelly,
Kelly from the Isle of Man –?'

His reputation as a wag brought the others in and the song seemed to help a little in the exhaustion and fear, and the misery of defeat.

' –Kay, ee, double-el, wye –'

Still singing, Siggis had pushed his way through the gasping, choking, drowning men to where the cat snarled on its little raft, and they were all watching him as he reached up to stroke it and got his naked arm clawed from elbow to wrist for his trouble.

'Some bugger's still full of spirit,' he panted.

Then another Stuka roared overhead and, as the bullets

spattered the water, the singing died.

'Don't seem to like that song,' Kelly gasped. 'Better change it.'

How long they clung to the raft, he had no idea but eventually *Chatsworth* appeared. *Impi* was still afloat, upside down. Her stern had sunk and now it was her bow which was awash. As Kelly was hauled on to the deck of *Chatsworth*, he stood silently, shocked, exhausted and stinking of fuel oil, then Siggis arrived alongside him, wearing only a pair of ragged underpants and clutching the drenched and angry cat to his oil-slicked chest.

'Them bastards'll pay for this, sir,' he said.

'I'm sure they will, Dancer,' Kelly said. 'And I just hope you and I are there when the bastards do.'

As they stood together, staring across the lifting water, *Impi* began to slip out of sight.

'Give her a cheer, boys,' Siggis yelled, and there was a ragged yell that only made them all feel sadder.

Stumbling, black and slimy, to the bridge, Kelly found Verschoyle waiting for him.

'Hello, Ginger,' Verschoyle said quietly. 'I was afraid you might not have made it. I didn't recognise you under the make-up.'

'Thanks, James,' Kelly said gravely. 'It was kind of you to come.'

It seemed odd that the two of them, once the deadliest of enemies, should stand there, one of them dripping and covered with thick fuel oil, the other immaculate in white, greeting each other so formally.

'Sorry to make such a mess of your bridge.'

'Not at all. Make yourself at home. Thought we might try to pick up some of *Ashby*'s people.'

There were boats and half a dozen Carley floats where *Ashby* had vanished and every time they stopped to pick up survivors, Junkers 88 bombers, which had now appeared in place of the Stukas, tried to hit them, dropping their bombs in shallow dives. As they finally vanished, Verschoyle lowered his whaler.

'Good job it isn't undergoing one of its periodic repairs after being smashed by the flotilla leader,' he observed dryly.

As the boat collected survivors and drew alongside the ship to allow them to scramble aboard, *Chatsworth* nosed slowly ahead, moving between the lifting mat of bodies from one raft to another while everybody on deck kept their eyes on the sky for more attacks. It was a long and difficult job because the 88s never left them alone, but with the attacks growing worse, they finally hoisted the last man on board and Verschoyle bent to the voice pipe.

'Half ahead both,' he said. 'Starboard ten.'

It was only then that Kelly realised that *Chatsworth* had also been damaged by a near miss and could only make half-speed, and they would have to limp home to Alexandria at only sixteen knots, every available space in the ship crammed with survivors shuddering with shock, and *Hallamshire* nervously watching the sky astern for more attacks.

A burly figure, unrecogniseable under the coating of oil, pushed along the crowded deck.

'That you, Rumbelo?' Kelly asked.

'Yes, sir. I made it, thanks to you. I wouldn't have if I'd stayed any longer.'

'You're not so young as you were, old lad, and not so bloody slim either.'

With Rumbelo and the yeoman of signals, who was the only other recognisable petty officer left from *Impi*, Kelly sought out the wounded. *Chatsworth*'s deck was as slippery as a skating rink and, with no freshness in the hot, unstirring air, the ship reeked of blood and chloroform and fuel oil. Even the brief visit below was enough to turn the stomach. *Impi*'s doctor, soaked with oil and water so that his shorts clung to him like part of his skin, was moving among the injured men with a sort of desperate devotion, refusing to change his clothes or even stop to swallow a mug of tea. He was pallid with strain and shock but he was full of confidence and vigour. With him was *Chatsworth*'s doctor, a mere boy just out of training hospital whose only claim to fame had been the bright idea during a wardroom party when the alcohol had run short of introducing crushed benzedrine tablets to the sardine sandwiches with riotous results. The two of them were working together as if they'd been in partnership for years.

Latimer was in considerable pain but no bones seemed to have been broken and, though he'd lost a lot of blood, there seemed a good chance of his being on his feet again quickly.

Going round the coughing, groaning men, taking their addresses and promising to write to their families, it was only when he'd finished that Kelly realised that the attacks were still going on and made his way back to the bridge. Verschoyle was sitting calmly on his stool, conning the ship as though he were entering Portsmouth through a regatta. There were a lot of near-misses and at times they were so close the bridge was drenched with the spray they threw up.

'I think we're just about out of ammunition,' Verschoyle pointed out.

As darkness came, the bombers gave up, but before dawn the ship came to a stop through lack of fuel fifteen miles short of Alex, and the tug, *Ruma*, had to tow them in. As they entered harbour, the surrounding ships were crowded with watching men, and as the little *Chatsworth*, her sides packed with survivors, moved past, followed by *Hallamshire*, the ships of the Mediterranean Fleet cleared lower decks and cheered them in.

Verschoyle had lent Kelly clothing but, as Verschoyle was six foot two and Kelly was five foot eight, nothing fitted very well. He had to see the C.-in-C., but Cunningham was busy, his thoughts centred on Crete to the exclusion of all else.

'Anything you're in need of?' he asked.

'Only another ship, sir,' Kelly said. It was largely bravado.

Cunningham's staff were also preoccupied because, in addition to watching Crete they were closely following the Atlantic and it was only then that Kelly remembered that *Bismarck* had escaped through the Denmark Strait and was being sought by half the Home Fleet.

'*Hood*'s sunk,' they told him.

It didn't seem possible. *Hood* was a magnificent ship and her yacht-like lines had made her the favourite of the fleet.

'How?' he asked.

'Same as Jutland. Plunging fire. Only three survivors. Went down with ninety-five officers and thirteen hundred men.'

Kelly drew a deep breath. By what stroke of luck had Kelly Rumbelo left *Hood* to get his commission and join *Repulse*?

'What about *Bismarck*?'

'Gather they've lost her. But they've brought in *K.G.Five* and *Repulse* now from Orkney.'

Kelly Rumbelo's move had taken him from *Hood* and certain

death to be aboard one of *Hood*'s avengers. He could well imagine the mood in the searching ships.

'They've also called out *Victorious* to search for her with her aircraft. They're obviously trying to stop her getting back to her base.'

So Hugh was there, too! Forgetting his own distress in his concern, he hoped to God the weather was reasonable because flying over the cold acres of the Atlantic in the murk of a northern storm could only end one way.

Several of *Impi*'s wounded had died and he had to attend the funerals. He didn't like funerals. There were several thousand men floating about the Mediterranean who hadn't had the benefit of clergy and it didn't seem to make much difference, but he felt the survivors would appreciate it.

It was a heartbreaking affair with white ensigns and the Last Post and a long liturgy about decomposition which, when he thought about it, seemed nauseating and unnecessary. He had to read the prayer but would much have preferred to have said quite simply 'These were our comrades and messmates and we commit them to God.' Instead, he had to deliver a great many words that a lot of the sailors wouldn't understand, and the dignity seemed to disappear in the meaninglessness. Death in a fighting service was not the emotional business it was in civilian life. Because of discipline, it was often surprisingly well borne by men who otherwise might not have been conspicuously brave, and when it was over you became merely a matter of statistics with 'DD' – discharged dead – against your name, and that was that.

Fortunately youth was a help and resilience allowed them to spring upright again after bending to disaster, and perhaps their greatest help was their hatred of the enemy. They couldn't credit the Germans with humanity and there was not much point in doing so, anyway, because they were fighting for an evil cause.

Three days later he said goodbye to the survivors of *Impi* and the few who'd arrived from *Inca*, *Impatient* and *Indian*. There seemed remarkably few of them and they were almost unrecogniseable in hand-me-down odds and ends of clothing, naval, military and civilian. Rumbelo was among them, his bulk crammed into a jersey and trousers miles too small for him.

'Keep an eye on things for me, Albert,' Kelly said. 'I suppose I shan't be far behind you.'

It was almost beyond him to make a farewell speech, and as he went along the line, shaking hands, he saw Siggis, still clutching the ship's cat.

'This is the third ship I've lost, sir,' he said. 'One in Norway, one at Dunkirk, and now this one 'ere. After this, I ain't even 'avin' a bath without tyin' meself to the taps.' He paused and, behind the daft grin on his face, Kelly saw there were tears in his eyes.

'She was a good ship, sir,' he mumbled. 'She –'

'Don't you start, Dancer,' Kelly interrupted quickly. 'Or you'll have me at it, and that would never do.'

Even the news that came in the following day that *Bismarck* had been sunk didn't help much and, to complete his agony, during the evening a telegram arrived from Biddy.

'Hugh missing. Flew off *Victorious*. Not recovered.'

So that was that, and poor little Paddy had never had her wedding. He felt like creeping away into a corner and weeping. Instead, he sought out First Officer Jenner-Neate and got quietly drunk at her flat.

9

Crete was finished by the end of the month. The Navy had not let the Army down, but the cost had been heavy. In addition to the losses off Greece, they had now lost the cruisers, *Gloucester*, *Calcutta* and *Fiji*, with *Warspite*, *Formidable*, *Valiant*, *Barham*, *Orion*, *Ajax*, *Perth*, *Dido*, *Naiad*, *Coventry* and *Carlisle* damaged. The destroyer losses had been enormous – eight sunk and sixteen damaged. It was almost more than the fleet could stand.

First Officer Jenner-Neate remained curiously detached. She had hardly turned a hair when he'd arrived on her doorstep, merely pushing across the gin bottle and going into the kitchen to prepare sandwiches. When he awoke on the settee the following morning, aware that he'd poured his soul out to her the night before, she'd already left for work.

Collecting a taxi, he managed a shave, found himself fresh white drill and, in a borrowed cap, set out to find her and thank her. For a change, her office was empty and she was alone.

'Dinner tonight,' he said at once.

She gave him a little smile. 'Sorry, not tonight.'

'Why not?'

She gestured at her piled desk. Her eyes looked gentle but her voice was steady. 'It doesn't seem to have occurred to you that there's a war on.'

'Having just lost every bloody ship I commanded,' he snapped. 'I think I do.'

Her eyes fell and she looked contrite. 'Of course. That was a silly thing to say.'

'I have to talk to you.'

'What about?'

'I behaved like a frightened midshipman last night. Senior officers don't go into a decline just because defeat's in the air.

196

We're an élite community and in return we're supposed to behave with dignity.'

She didn't seem to think his behaviour at all odd and she gave him another small smile. 'Everybody has to kick the boards loose occasionally,' she remarked.

'Then see me.'

'I'm on duty and if we don't stick at it the whole thing's going to fall apart.'

'Say it's your grandmother's funeral.'

'My grandmother died when I was seven.'

'How about your Grandfather?'

'During the Boer War.'

Kelly scowled. 'Couldn't you stop being an Intelligence officer for a while and be a woman?'

She was flattered but she remained adamant and he had to admit defeat. Instead he headed for *Chatsworth* to find Verschoyle, but Verschoyle was ashore with Third Officer Pentycross and he began to feel there was a conspiracy against him and was desperately lonely. Inevitably he thought of the way it might have been.

'Oh, Charley,' he burst out in anguish to the mirror in the room he'd been given. 'What a mess it all is!'

It was a cry that came from the heart and was rooted deep in his past, belonging to all his hopes, ambitions and disappointments, and had nothing to do with First Officer Jenner-Neate.

Since there wasn't a ship for him, he found himself on Cunningham's shore staff and, a fortnight later, with his own flotilla reduced to two ships, Verschoyle also found himself ashore, while *Chatsworth* and *Hallamshire* were attached to yet another flotilla. Then, on June 21st, a telegram arrived from Paddy. 'Hugh safe. Picked up by Icelandic ship after two days in dinghy. Taken to Reykjavik.'

It seemed such wonderful news, he sought out Verschoyle at once and the drinks they took developed into a celebration at Third Officer Pentycross's flat. In the middle of it, the girl she shared with switched on the radio, her eyes shining.

'I think you'd like to hear the evening news,' she said.

Churchill's voice was announcing that the Germans had invaded Russia and he, the arch enemy of Leftism, was offering help and friendship.

'Well,' Verschoyle said dubiously, 'I suppose it means another ally.'

'It'll also probably mean convoys to Russia,' Kelly pointed out.

'Round North Cape.' Verschoyle shuddered. 'It's bloody cold up there.'

There was one cause for satisfaction. Crete, it was claimed, had held up the German attack, and suddenly everybody was pointing out what had happened to Napoleon's Grand Army in 1812, and was working out how long it would be before the Russian winter set in.

It made them hold their breath. Now surely Hitler was undone. Though nobody in Britain had ever expected to be beaten, it had seemed after the disasters of the preceding twelve months that the war might go on for ever. Now, victory seemed not only certain but even seemed nearer.

First Officer Jenner-Neate still troubled Kelly and her very inaccessibility acted like a goad. Wondering if he could change her mind with a gift, he studied the shops but soon realised he had no idea what might interest her. Trinkets and cosmetics seemed trite and the rest of what there was to offer was appalling and had probably been made in Birmingham. He even looked at nightdresses and underclothes but somehow he couldn't imagine the dignified body of First Officer Jenner-Neate in anything else but a naval uniform. He even tried to imagine going to bed with her but even then he could only imagine it in uniform, and he had given up in despair when, going back to his office, he found a note waiting for him that made his heart leap.

'I'm free tonight. Come and have a meal at my flat.'

He wrote across the back in a square scrawl that seemed as if it would wrench the pen nib from its socket, 'Not half! Will bring booze!'

He reached her flat unable to contain himself. She immediately gave him a drink and said she was going to change into something comfortable. His look of alarm made her smile.

'Sorry,' she said. 'That was a silly thing to say. It doesn't mean what it means in novels.'

She reappeared wearing a dress that surprised him because it was old-fashioned and out of date. She'd also combed her hair out of the somewhat severe style she wore with her uniform and that, too, looked curiously lacking in taste so that he was desperately disappointed.

She caught his expression. 'Women officers are often disappointing in civilian clothes,' she pointed out. 'It's fortunate that most men are, too. Do I bother you dressed like this?'

Suddenly he realised that like so many naval wives she came from a proud, decent family which no longer possessed the wealth it had once had, so that, while she'd probably been educated at one of the best schools in the country, she'd never had money to spend on herself and knew nothing about clothes. It explained so much about her and she was so honest he couldn't resist her. He offered her a cigarette and they sat smoking and drinking together for a while, then she went to the kitchen and started to cook. Growing irritated with talking to her through the door, he joined her to stand by the sink wearing a frilly pinafore which belonged to her flat-mate as he helped to peel the vegetables.

She was a splendid cook and they both drank a little too much wine. Going on to the verandah to smoke their cigarettes, they caught the tang of the burned evening air off the desert, that strange cooling scent that always came at that time of the day.

'This is the best time in the whole twenty-four hours,' she said.

He studied her as she stood watching the light fade, enjoying her simple dignity. The unfashionable dress meant nothing and when she told him about herself, his guess about her background turned out to be correct.

When he kissed her, her cheeks were cold from the night air.

'I love you, Jenner-Neate,' he said.

She smiled at him. 'My name's Helen,' she pointed out. 'And I don't believe a word of it.'

'I have a confession to make,' he admitted. 'When I came here tonight, I intended getting you into bed.'

'I have one to make, too,' she said. 'I know.'

He kissed her again and this time she kissed him back.

'But let's make no bones about it,' she urged. 'You're as

flattered as I am, but that's all. A woman's plumbing's different from a man's and she has to be careful. Besides, I'm not in love with you and you're not in love with me.'

'Of course I am.'

'Try it again. This time honestly.'

He paused, then he smiled. 'No,' he said. 'Lonely, perhaps.'

'So am I,' she said briskly. 'And it's cold out here. Perhaps we ought to go to bed.'

He glanced at her and she looked at him steadily. 'It's a working arrangement,' she reminded him quietly. 'In wartime there's no such thing as a platonic friendship.'

1941 dragged its weary way on. Despite the optimism that had sprung from hopes of a German defeat in Russia, by October Hitler was announcing that the last great decisive battle of the year was about to take place in front of Moscow, and then in November the carrier, *Ark Royal*, was lost. Goebbels had reported her end on so many occasions her sailors even jumped up and down yelling 'We're here, we're here!' as the radio put the rhetorical question 'If she isn't sunk, then where is she?' She was followed soon afterwards by *Sydney* off Australia, then the battleship, *Barham*, and finally in December came the crowning agony of the annihilation of the American Pacific Fleet at Pearl Harbour and the loss of *Prince of Wales* and *Repulse* off Malaya.

It was a shattering blow and to Kelly twice as hard because of Kelly Rumbelo who had escaped death in *Hood* by sheer chance and survived the encounter with *Bismarck* in *Repulse* only to run into this new disaster on the fourth day of a new war. Wiring Thakeham, he did what he could through official channels to find out whether the boy had survived, but the Far East was in a turmoil and it was impossible to discover anything.

Throughout the catastrophes, his only source of comfort was First Officer Jenner-Neate. When the news was at its worst, she was at her calmest and, though he'd never considered the act of love one of the more stately of God's creations – with Christina it had even been riotous, bawdy and distinctly gymnastic – with Jenner-Neate it remained as dignified as she was. It wouldn't have been hard to fall in love with her, he felt, but her attitude seemed to preclude that.

Verschoyle raised an eyebrow occasionally, feeling that Kelly could have had the pick of the Wrens, but Kelly had no wish to be involved with one of the blonde young girls who made eyes at him in the corridors. Verschoyle and his Maisie were all right. They'd known each other a long time and were used to each other, but Kelly couldn't imagine himself going overboard for a twenty-year-old girl. Not that it would have been difficult because some of them were flattered by the attention of senior officers and some of the senior officers were even a little glazed about the eyes as they watched them. Even Verschoyle seemed to be changing.

'It's Maisie,' he admitted. 'I'm thinking of marrying again.'

Despite everything, despite the disasters, Alex seemed not to be part of the war. It was something to do with the warmth and the sunshine and the number of women about, and the wailing of the muezzins from the minarets. But because Egypt was isolated and too far from Hitler's bases for his bombers to be dangerous, it had a curiously detached air about it.

The Battle of the Atlantic was still going on with increased ferocity and almost insuperable losses, but rumours were beginning to reach them that, with the new detection instruments that were being developed the U-boats would soon not be having it all their own way.

The end of the year brought a telegram from Rumbelo to say his son was safe. He had been picked up long after the other survivors from *Repulse* and somehow been taken to Australia, which explained the time that had elapsed before he'd been able to contact his home. But almost immediately, the New Year brought another blow. *Scharnhorst, Gneisenau* and *Prinz Eugen*, sheltering in Brest, had made a break for Germany and a lot of young RAF and Fleet Air Arm pilots had been killed trying to stop them.

The evening news from the BBC always brought a grim silence as they listened to the list of enemy successes. In the Mediterranean, *Nelson* was torpedoed, *Kandahar* was lost, and *Queen Elizabeth* and *Valiant*, the only two undamaged capital ships still available, were put out of action by Italian frogmen.

'Think the blows'll ever end?' Verschoyle asked wearily.

'Yes,' Kelly said. 'We're coming to the end now.'

Verschoyle's eyebrows lifted in disbelief and he tried to explain. 'The Americans are going to react to Pearl Harbour as we did to Dunkirk,' he said. 'And when *they* get going, the war's as good as won.'

As if to back his confidence, news came that the Russian winter had saved Moscow and Hitler's advance had ground to a stop with whole brigades of tanks rendered useless by the absence of anti-freeze and whole regiments decimated by frost-bite in their summer clothing. Hitler, it seemed, had finally bitten off more than he could chew and it was reassuring to learn that even the Germans, with their vaunted skill at organisation, could also be wrong.

Suddenly, too, they became aware that the Americans were no longer friendly neutrals but allies; and American officers, some of them with Italian or German names and outlandish habits which served to stress that they weren't just Englishmen with strange accents but a different nation, began to appear. They were easy-going, anxious to learn and informal to a degree that was startling to the Royal Navy, which had never been noted for its informality.

'I think the war's beginning to be interesting,' Verschoyle said. 'Especially as we've been ordered home.' He flourished a signal. 'What's more, we're in good company, because Cunningham's going home, too. He's going to head the Admiralty delegation to Washington. The Yanks are agitating for action and he's leaving within the week. I've scrounged a lift for us in his aircraft.'

The following day, to Kelly's astonishment, Verschoyle married Third Officer Pentycross. The fleet chaplain officiated and Kelly acted as best man, and they went for a two-day honeymoon up the Nile. When they'd gone Kelly went with First Officer Jenner-Neate back to her flat where he told her the news. She received it calmly and their love-making was almost dispassionate. But while there were no tremendous surges of emotion, he knew there would also never be any heartbreak. Because he owed her so much, and because he was grateful, even because he felt it would work, he asked her to marry him. She refused him without pain and without rancour, though there was a glint of tears in her eyes as they kissed goodbye the following week.

When they left by train for Cairo, the station platform was crowded with officers seeing Cunningham and his wife off, and Third Officer Verschoyle, née Pentycross, clung to her husband's hand through the window.

'I'll be home very soon after you,' she said. 'They've promised me a passage.'

As the train started, Verschoyle sat back, his expression still a little dazed.

'It feels funny being married again,' he said. 'And Maisie's no Christina. Perhaps she'll be calmer, though. What about you?'

'What about me?'

'You're still a bachelor. You'll soon be too bloody old to remarry.'

Kelly shrugged. 'There must be some admiral's daughter who's missed the bus who'll have me.'

Verschoyle eyed him keenly. 'Do you want some admiral's daughter who's missed the bus?'

Kelly smiled. 'Not really.'

'There's still only one woman, isn't there?'

Thinking about it, Kelly knew there was. His affair with First Officer Jenner-Neate had been only a substitute and all along she'd been playing the part he'd written for Charley. He frowned.

'I suppose so,' he said.

'Then why in God's name don't you marry her?'

Kelly gave him an angry glance. 'Because she wouldn't have me,' he said.

Verschoyle studied him for a while. 'I always had a high regard for your Charley,' he observed. 'Even in the days when I was chasing her elder sister. She can't be that barmy. *Why* won't she have you?'

'I'm damned if I know.'

'You're going home. Why don't you ask her?'

'I have done.'

'Ask her again.'

'I did.'

203

Verschoyle's face was long with sympathy. 'Why not try yet again?' he asked.

Kelly exploded. 'How many more bloody times do I have to go through it?' he asked.

Verschoyle was silent for a moment, then he smiled. 'Depends how important it is, doesn't it?' he said.

From Cairo they travelled by flying boat to Khartoum and then across Africa by land plane to Sierra Leone. From Kano in Nigeria, they flew to Lisbon, finally arriving at Bristol in bitter spring weather.

It seemed strange to be back in England after over a year in the Mediterranean. The place looked surprisingly shabby and the scars of the bombing were everywhere. But there was a new cheerfulness that had been missing when they'd left, as if people were at last looking into the future with optimism. The biggest change was the number of Americans who had suddenly appeared and when they went for a drink in the station hotel bar, they found it full of them. They were mostly ordinary GIs and they all appeared to be millionaires, but they made way quickly, eyeing the ribbons on their chests with interest.

'What's that one for, sir?' one of them asked Verschoyle.

'That's the DSO,' Verschoyle said cheerfully. 'I got that in the last war when I was about your age. If you want to see a *real* medal, take a look at my friend. You can't get better than the one he's got.'

Thakeham hadn't changed but for once everybody seemed to be at home. Rumbelo was due to go to a shore job at Scapa and was in a murderous mood at the thought that nobody would let him go to sea. His son was also on leave, wearing the two stripes of a lieutenant and the ribbon of the DSM. He was burly and strong and, untouched by his experience in *Repulse*, had the look to Kelly of a man who was going to go a long way. By contrast, Hugh, wearing a DSC and clutching Paddy's hand with a desperation bordering on intensity, looked on edge, as though his nerves were strung taut. Most of the men he'd joined up with were dead and there was bitterness in his voice as he spoke of them.

'They were killed by admirals who hadn't the foggiest idea how to use aircraft,' he said. 'They think airmen are expendable because they're rough, raffish and lower middle class, and even now they can't accept that a battleship's nothing but an aging matinée idol.'

'I suspect,' Kelly said gently, 'that it's not so much stupidity as that science has pushed their task beyond their competency. People always expect security at the lowest cost and we were never encouraged by the parsimony of a nation at peace to try anything new.'

Because Hugh was still attending hospital after the exposure he'd suffered, Paddy had not yet gone to her hospital ship and was working instead at Haslar.

'This time,' she told Kelly, 'I'm determined to marry him. If ever a man needed a wife he does and I'm going to be her. It'll be a white wedding –'

'White?'

She stared back at him, her eyes frank and forthright. 'White,' she said. 'For virginity. I don't give a damn, myself, but my mother does and being able to stare out her friends will compensate her for the number of times she's noticed me vanishing into Hugh's room.'

Her happiness had a curiously brittle quality and was strangely heartbreaking, because, while Kelly Rumbelo looked as tough and enduring as his father with his thick shoulders and red hair, Hugh had a curious fragility about him, a sort of transparency about his skin that made him look ill. To Kelly he had the appearance of a man with the look of death on him and, dispassionately, grieving, he wondered how much longer he could survive the sort of chances he took.

The following day, determined not to do what he'd so disastrously done before, he set off to find Charley. Hugh's impending wedding seemed a good excuse, because Rumbelo had mentioned that, since she knew everybody concerned, it would be nice if she could be there.

He took the train to Dover, but the woman who opened the door to the flat where she'd lived was a stranger, the wife of a British colonel in training in the area. She had no idea where Charley had gone and, even at the Castle, there was no one who knew.

'She went to London, I think,' he was told. 'Somebody said she was going to get married.'

Depressed by the news, he borrowed a telephone and rang the Admiralty but nobody there knew her name.

'How about Upfold? She might be using her unmarried name.'

There was another long silence. 'No. Nobody called Upfold here except the porter. He wouldn't be any relation, would he?'

'No,' Kelly said slowly. 'I shouldn't think so.'

Determined not to be beaten, he dialled Directory Inquiries and badgered them for a quarter of an hour. But of all the Upfolds and Kimisters available there was none that could possibly be Charley. Finally, he had a brainwave and obtained Mabel's number. If anyone knew where she was, Mabel would. But when he rang the number in North Wales he'd been given, it wasn't Mabel who answered, but another woman.

'She left here over a year ago,' she told him. 'Some time after Dunkirk, I believe. Her husband was posted to some job in Scotland but I've no idea where.'

Still undefeated, Kelly found an army list, discovered what he could about Mabel's husband then, ringing Army Records, learned that he'd been promoted brigadier.

'Where is he now?'

'In India.'

'How about his wife?'

'The last address we've got is North Wales.'

Slowly, flattened, Kelly put the telephone down, then, disappointed and suddenly lacking interest, he took the train back to London. Almost the first man he met at the Admiralty was Corbett. He looked old, as if the work of the last two years had aged him.

'I heard you were on your way home,' he said. 'And I'm glad. Things are beginning to move here now that the Americans are in with us, and I think before the end of the year we'll see quite a change.' He smiled. 'It looks like being an American war from now on, of course, with us as junior partners, but at least they've got all the right ideas and it's become policy to bring home everybody who's likely to be needed for a second front. I hear you're getting the cruiser, *Chichester*.'

'*Chichester*?' Kelly frowned. 'There must be better cruiser captains than me.'

Corbett smiled. 'Perhaps,' he said. 'But you've also got *Sara-*

wak and the destroyers *Marlow, Meteor* and *Morris* to make up a new·group, Force T. You're not *captain* of *Chichester*. You'll be flying your flag in her. You're being upped to Rear-Admiral.'

Part Three

1

It was strange to be consorting with the mighty.

Since there was little point in going to Thakeham, Kelly went instead to Liphook to see Latimer to check on his state of health and, finding him recovered, recruit him for his staff. Using his telephone, he also contacted Seamus Boyle, who was in Bath, and got him appointed as his secretary. Rumbelo went without saying because he'd been nagging at him all week-end to get him out of going to Scapa. It was exciting to be able to work small miracles and pleasant to see his name in print: 'Rear-Admiral Sir Kelly Maguire.' The 'Sir' was a bit of a cheat, of course, because he'd only inherited that, but it sounded good all the same.

He felt he couldn't let the occasion go without informing First Officer Jenner-Neate but he was just sitting down to write the following day when a telegram arrived.

'Congratulations. Just noticed.' The signature, 'Helen Jenner-Neate,' was as dignified as she was herself.

There was a lot to do. He had to call on Gieves to order a new uniform and have all his gold braid changed, and it gave him a lot of pleasure to be asked to a party at the Dorchester that was attended by cabinet ministers, admirals, generals, air marshals and actresses by the dozen.

Hugh and Paddy were married at Thakeham in July. The weather was good but spirits were a little dampened by the continuing Japanese successes in the Far East and the fact that the Eighth Army had just been flung back almost to the gates of Cairo. But Hugh was recovering quickly and Paddy was pulling out all the stops to get herself appointed to a hospital ship in Glasgow, because Hugh had been told he was being given a shore job there.

211

Curiously, there was still no sign of Kelly being ordered to his new command, which was lying at Belfast, and he began to wonder if Corbett had been wrong. Nobody was saying anything, however, and a succession of unimportant jobs suitable for his new rank was found for him at the Admiralty. But none of them seemed to lead anywhere and he began to wonder even if he'd gone wrong somewhere and he was being shunted into a backwater. Corbett was suddenly secretive, too, giving nothing away, and he came to the conclusion that his new command was the shortest he'd ever held. To get his hands on two cruisers and a flotilla of destroyers was what every naval man asked and to have them snatched away again before he'd even seen them was hard to bear.

He was on leave and weeding the garden at Thakeham when a signal arrived ordering him to report at once to the Admiralty with a view to flying to Gibraltar, and he came to the gloomy conclusion that his hopes of a command at sea had finally disappeared out of the window.

To his surprise, he found Boyle waiting for him and, with the Afrika Korps suddenly in full retreat after a massive battle at El Alamein and the Eighth Army whooping after them in full cry under a general called Montgomery who was known to the public only for his odd habit of wearing more than one badge in his hat, they could only assume that their unexpected appointment had something to do with the Med.

At Gibraltar, Kelly was once again sworn to secrecy and informed there was to be a major landing on the North African coast. The date was governed by the need to help the Russians and to avoid the deterioration in the weather. The Americans were running the affair and Eisenhower, the American general in command, despite a lack of battle experience, was proving enormously popular with the officers beneath him.

Cunningham was there, too, and it was he who briefed Kelly. He grinned in his usual way, quite unabashed at having summoned him to his side. 'Sorry about Force T,' he said. 'But this other thing came up and when your name was mentioned we had to hold that in abeyance for the time being, because you're more use here for the moment. This operation's going to provide the second arm of a pincer that'll finish the Germans for good and all in North Africa, make the Mediterranean and

212

Malta safe, and provide a springboard into Europe. There'll be three main landings, at Algiers and Oran inside the Med and at Casablanca on the Moroccan coast. In addition there'll be a smaller landing at Helillah to secure the port installations there for further moves eastward.'

'And me, sir?'

Cunningham smiled. 'There's always a snag, isn't there?' he said. 'The assault was originally to have been entirely American but in the end some of the troops are going to have to be British, though we're keeping 'em well hidden under the American cloak. However, there's still a fear that the French are going to resist and we've laid on a few cloak-and-dagger operations to contact their key men. Mark Clark's being embarked by submarine to land west of Algiers and you're for Hellilah.'

'Why me, sir?'

'Because you speak French and so does your secretary, and we have a Frenchman there who says he can do a deal if he meets a man with the right standing. He mentioned your name. Admiral Buzon. Know him?'

'Never heard of him, sir.'

'Well, he's heard of you and he's hoping to bring his people in behind us. It'll be your job to make sure he knows exactly what we want – chief among which are undamaged port installations. We have a French pilot and a Desoutter four-seater, and he's going to fly you and Boyle to Ain Aflou where there'll be fuel. From there you'll go to Amimoun where Admiral Buzon's car will be waiting for you. Boyle's to know nothing of all this in advance, by the way. He's here merely to make sure no linguistic errors creep in. You'll be flown to your new command as soon as it's over.'

The strain placed on Gibraltar's resources and the organisation of auxiliary craft, tugs, tankers, colliers, ammunition vessels and special personnel by the coming invasion was tremendous, and the staff had established themselves in damp, airless offices under the Rock where Kelly was wheeled into Eisenhower. He was a tall man who explained the seriousness of the task.

'There are a few of our people, I guess,' he said, 'who fancy that the French have only to know that the Americans are running the show to welcome us with open arms, and ships have loud-hailers on their bridges ready to make appeals to them.' He gave an infectious grin. 'So that they won't think it's a Gaullist or an Englishman making the announcement, we've picked Americans who speak French with bad accents. I guess we're hoping it'll have the same effect as Joshua's trumpets at Jericho.'

'Probably attract a terrific fire when they hear their language being massacred,' Cunningham commented.

Eisenhower smiled and continued. 'You have four days, and by the time you get back the convoys should be approaching Gibraltar. They'll need to be assured that it's not going to be too tough, because most of these guys are pretty green and we haven't had the time to give them the final polish. You'll be put on board the United States cruiser, *Tyree*, for the landing.'

The French pilot had a familiar look about him and Kelly recognised him as Leduc, the man who'd flown him into Santander in 1937. They left as soon as it was dark and an hour later were picking up Spanish Morocco. It was odd to look down, with the lights from the dials reflected on their faces, and think they were about to land in neutral, if not enemy, territory. Dimly-seen mountains swept back beneath them as they began to descend and, as the machine rattled to a stop on a stony airstrip, faces appeared in the dark alongside and there were muttered words in French. They didn't leave the machine but they could tell they were at a high altitude from the brisk air. Men were busy on the wings with cans as the tanks were refilled, then there was a bang on the fuselage and a figure appeared in front of the nose to swing the propeller.

Lifting out of the darkness, Leduc turned east and they flew along the edge of the Little Atlas mountains, navigating by dead reckoning, with all three of them checking to make sure there were no mistakes. Eventually, growing stiff and cold, they saw three lights winking at them from below in the shape of an L, and Leduc tilted the aircraft to sideslip in.

'I hope you can do it,' Kelly said.

'I've been doing it for six months into France,' Leduc smiled. 'Dropping agents.'

As the machine rumbled to a stop, there was a bang on the door and a dark face appeared alongside. As they were led to a car they heard the aeroplane swing round and, as the car drew away, saw it moving off into the darkness.

Nobody spoke and they drove in silence for an hour over a road that seemed specially designed to shake the liver loose before eventually pulling up at an unlit house. Escorted between a high hedge of aloes on to a verandah, they moved through a door into total darkness. Then, as the door clicked behind them, the light went on.

Wondering if it were a trap, Kelly stared round him. There were half a dozen men in the room, all obviously French and, judging by the cut of their jibs, all naval men. As he was still blinking, a door opened and a tall man with a lean face advanced towards them, smiling, his hand held out in greeting.

Kelly and Boyle exchanged quick glances and smiled back.

'Archie Bumf!'

'Admiral le Comte d'Archy de Boumfre-Bouzon,' the man who had brought them said indignantly.

There was an enthusiastic and delighted greeting between the three of them, then wine and food were brought and even before they'd finished it they were getting down to work with directions, distances, lists and numbers.

'True Frenchmen are waiting to welcome the forces of freedom,' d'Archy announced. 'There will have to be a fight, of course, because Darlan doesn't like the British and it will be consonant with honour. But it won't last long and, here, it will not take place at all. The lighthouse at Pou will be lit and we shall be holding a practice black-out to make the task easier. But you'll have to be quick and if there's any resistance it will come from the battery at Mersa-el-Fam where the commander has strange ideas about patriotism. A solitary salvo into the countryside behind should be enough to convince him that resistance would be pointless.' Papers were pushed across. 'These are the co-ordinates and we would prefer that the salvo did not land *on* the battery.'

Poring over the maps for the rest of the night, they slept during the next day. Leduc was waiting for them at Amimoun the following evening and the journey back to Ain Afrou was without incident. Leduc asked no questions and they refuelled quickly and were soon crossing the narrow strait in a south-east to north-west direction. Gibraltar, brilliantly lit, was impossible to miss and, as they touched down, they were met by a car and rushed up the winding road to the galleries in the Rock.

'I think you'd better get some sleep,' Kelly was told. 'A Catalina will be leaving tomorrow to meet *Tyree*.'

The Catalina was an American aircraft with a British crew and, squatting in the blisters, they were flown directly northwest. The weather in the Atlantic was deteriorating and there were a few anxious faces. The Eighth Army was still chasing Rommel along the north coast of Africa and British submarines and surface ships were hammering every attempt to carry supplies to him. After three hours, they saw a vast collection of ships plodding doggedly eastwards, and the Catalina landed on the water within reach of a destroyer which put down a whaler.

It was difficult putting out an inflated dinghy and climbing into it in the seas that were getting up, and they even began to wonder if they'd make it. But the destroyer gave them a lee and they were soon on board the whaler and heading for *Tyree*.

The American admiral greeted them warmly. His name was Charles J. Allington and he insisted on Kelly addressing him as 'Al.' He was brisk and no-nonsense but was clearly glad to see Kelly. This was his first wartime operation and he was glad to know the reception was to be favourable because the convoy had been shadowed for some time by aircraft.

'Intelligence says we're believed to be just an extra large convoy for Malta and that the Krauts are massing their aircraft in Sardinia and Sicily,' he said. 'I sure hope they're right.'

He was faintly awed to be surrounded by so much history. Certainly no waters in the world had seen so many maritime engagements. It was here that Drake had singed the King of Spain's beard, here that Rodney and Jervis had won their victories, here that Nelson had commanded, here finally that Cunningham had held the waters.

All round them were troopships, landing craft, escort vessels and covering warships. There was absolute silence and a severely guarded black-out. As the ships passed through the Strait the sea was calmer and conditions were clearly favourable for a landing. Pilotage parties had reconnoitred the beaches ahead and boats with shaded lights lay stationed

216

offshore to assist navigation. Throughout the voyage the troops had been practising going to their landing craft stations, at first in daylight and then after dark, and everybody had an American-prepared booklet on North Africa which contained a great deal of value, chief among which was the sentence 'Do not monkey about with Mohammedan women.'

A cluster of lights appeared on the port bow, sharp against the shadow of the land, which they identified as Talebala.

'There'll be a black-out at Helillah,' Kelly said.

'Fine. What's our position, Navigator?'

'Seven miles offshore, sir.'

Allington pulled a face and turned to Kelly. 'How's about moving in closer? My orders say seven miles and the U.S. Navy's strict about following orders, but I guess *I* wouldn't like to travel seven miles in the darkness in one of those goddam landing craft. What do you say?'

Kelly smiled. 'We have a saying in our Navy,' he pointed out, 'that a bit of Nelson's blind eye never did anybody any harm.'

Helillah was a lucky landing. They could hear gunfire from further west near Algiers where landing craft and the destroyer, *Broke*, were sunk and the destroyer, *Malcolm*, was badly hit in the boiler room, but at Helillah there was only a solitary shot fired at them from the battery at Mersa-el-Fam. A salvo from *Tyree* into the country behind encouraged the battery commander in the belief that resistance wasn't worthwhile, and soon after the troops went ashore a rocket soared up to indicate the landing was unopposed.

The French resistance stiffened the following morning, however, and batteries at Cape Matifu had to be bombarded before they fell into Allied hands and, with a freshening wind, the unloading of stores on to the captured beaches was delayed and landing craft were wrecked. By late afternoon, however, they heard the French were willing to negotiate and the whole coast fell.

Algiers, where headquarters was set up, was beautiful, row on row of white buildings climbing up the hills above the bay, with the white mosques of the Kasbah gleaming in the morning sunshine to make a wavering reflection in the dark-hued sea. The place was full of round-eyed young soldiers newly out from

217

England and America, flamboyant Algerian cavalrymen, piled-up fruit barrows, black shoeshine boys, Arab women in coloured veils, and street vendors offering necklaces and fly whisks.

The French were polite, even if not friendly, but the political stew had been unwholesome for so long the suspicion in the air made the place uncomfortable. The French hated the Allies, particularly the British, and there were thousands of refugees, many of them rich from the profits they'd made supplying the Germans. However, Algiers was considered to be part of Metropolitan France and, with the Allies actually on French soil, they finally discovered they were happy about it and set about making them welcome.

Kelly's share had not gone unnoticed and Boyle caught a glimpse of a letter from Cunningham to Ramsay, '. . . Ginger Maguire did very well and thoroughly justified his choice . . .', but the smell of intrigue and bad feeling among the French was still strong and both Kelly and Boyle were glad when a signal arrived instructing them that their job was done and that they were to report back to the Admiralty.

Back in England, Kelly was given the choice of leave or going at once to Force T, which had been temporarily commanded by the captain of *Chichester*. He didn't hesitate.

Paddy was at Thakeham as he stopped there to pick up his gear. She'd just received a signal telling her to report to *H.M. Hospital Ship Anarapoora*.

'Where is she?' she asked.

It took Kelly only a few minutes to find out. 'Anchored off Lyness. It's Scapa.'

He had expected her face to fall. Most people's faces fell when they heard they were posted to Scapa. But her eyes were dancing.

'Hugh's due up there,' she said. 'I wonder if he pulled some strings.'

Kelly's first job was to learn something about his ships and the captains serving under him. *Chichester* was one of the City-class ships, handsome with heavily-raked funnels and quite capable of her designed speed of thirty-two knots. She had twelve six-inch guns in four turrets of three guns each, two forward and two aft, eight four-inch ack-ack guns, light weapons, and three torpedo tubes on each side. Her consort, *Sarawak*, was similar and slightly faster. Henry Pardoe, Kelly's flag captain and senior staff officer, was a little older than Kelly, somewhat unimaginative but with a solid record and no fear. Cassell, of *Sarawak*, had been in Kelly's term at Dartmouth, where he'd been noted for his intelligence and commonsense, and the destroyer captains were equally experienced.

As the group left harbour for working-up exercises, Kelly was determined that each of the individualists astern of him – and there wasn't a naval officer born who wasn't an individualist in some way – would quickly learn that the squadron was to be a solidly-welded unit. All day they carried out gunnery exercises and at night executed movements in the dark. By March they were as trained as time would allow and every captain knew not only what his brother captains would do, he also knew what his admiral expected of him.

They guessed they were due for Scapa when they'd finished, because Scapa was on the way to Russia and lay across the route of the German heavy ships in the Norwegian fjords, and when, soon afterwards, they were directed to Glasgow to ammunition and store ship, they knew they would soon be off to sea in earnest. As they arrived in the Clyde, Kelly saw *Anarapoora* lying off Greenock. Immediately, he sent a signal asking Paddy to have dinner with him in Glasgow, and her message came back, warm, enthusiastic and as impertinent as ever.

'I'll bet you've got a handsome flag lieutenant,' she said. 'I'd like to bring a friend.'

The flag lieutenant was a donnish young RNVR with a Cambridge degree, and the two girls were excited and obviously delighted to be seen in the company of an admiral. They were happy enough in *Anarapoora*, an old Henderson line ship, and, not a bit disturbed about the loneliness of Scapa, were chiefly concerned with the way the Goanese crew felt the cold.

'They're half-frozen most of the time up there,' Paddy said. 'So we spend all our spare time knitting woollen comforts for them. It's a bit lonely, too, but there's a depot ship, *Dunluce Castle*, and destroyers and patrol vessels come in from the North Atlantic for refuelling or a day or two ashore, so we see a bit of life.'

'What about amenities?'

She gave him her familiar grin. 'There aren't any. Just thousands of sex-starved males. Actually, we get an occasional visit to Kirkwall for shopping or dinner at the Royal Hotel where the Fleet Air Arm pilots from Hatston try to pick us up. Or an occasional dance at the Church of Scotland hut. They send a signal and there's a hair-raising journey in a drifter through the darkness. We're not good dancers but we're good listeners and the inevitable walletful of photographs is always brought out. It's the homesickness of the men that touches you most.'

'It was in the last war.'

'I hear we're going to Rosyth,' she went on excitedly, 'and Hugh's due there, too, in a shore job, so we'll be able to behave like husband and wife at last. He might even manage to make me pregnant.'

Scapa didn't change much. For anyone going on leave, it was still the longest railway ride in Britain and the train, Kelly noticed, was still called 'The Jellicoe Express' after the commander-in-chief in the First War who had initiated it. Though to those reservists who remembered the previous war, the place was bursting with welfare facilities and canteens, there was nothing to attract the townsmen now coming into the Navy, nothing to compensate for being set down in this inhospitable outpost, and the situation was not improved by the fact that many of them had only recently been dragged away from desks and factories. There were no pubs, no dance halls and, above all, no girls, and even the fact that the Women's Royal Naval Service was there operating signals stations made little difference. Scapa was as popular in this war as it had been in the last, yet, when the weather was calm, the colour and cloud effects were as magical as ever; and, when the water was as smooth as glass and the ships were reflected mirror-like in the water, it was possible to believe that it was a nautical valhalla and that the story about the seagulls being the spirits of drowned sailors was true.

As the winter deepened, they made occasional sorties to sea and eventually were sent to Glasgow again to refuel. *Anarapoora* was there once more and once more Kelly invited Paddy out to dinner. She seemed full of spirit and quite undeterred by the isolation.

'It's always exciting,' she said. 'Once we were nearly run

220

down by *KG Five* and every time we go ashore it's a matter of life and death.'

He noticed she'd not mentioned Hugh and, guessing something was wrong, he probed gently. Her expression changed at once to one of distress and he knew that her brightness was only a brittle façade.

'I thought he was going to get a shore job,' she said. 'But it wasn't that at all. He won't accept one.' It all came out in a breathless, agonised rush in her misery. 'Do you think he's trying to get himself killed? Just because all his friends have gone? He's going back on carriers.'

'Well, carriers are pretty big, Paddy,' he reassured her. 'And, since *Ark Royal* was lost, we've learned to take pretty good care of them. Which one?'

'*Parsifal*. He says she's a bit smaller than normal.'

Kelly was silent for a moment. *Parsifal* was a CAM-ship, carrying one Hurricane which could be catapulted off but not flown back on. Trips from CAM-ships were only one way and all the pilot could do was ditch as near to the mother ship as possible. In good weather and good conditions there was a boat waiting to retrieve him but there could be bad weather, bad conditions and probably German ships or aeroplanes about which might cause the captain to sacrifice one man for the safety of the rest.

He saw Paddy looking at him. She was as well aware as Kelly of the risks that naval aircrew took. With a father and a brother constantly talking ships, she had no delusions about their chances of survival.

'Yes,' he agreed. 'A new kind. Bit smaller than *Ark Royal*, of course.' He was telling no lies but he wasn't telling the whole truth either.

He returned to Scapa in a thoughtful mood to find Verschoyle waiting for him with his destroyer group. He was not long back from Russia and he hadn't enjoyed it. After the disaster when the convoy, PQ17, had been ordered by the Admiralty to scatter and been massacred, only one more convoy, PQ18, had been sent and only one had returned home. The presence of German heavy ships in the Norwegian fjords was forcing the old 'fleet in being' complex on the Navy, something nobody liked, and a new scheme was being tried.

'Submarines are being maintained off the north Norwegian coast,' Verschoyle said. 'And we're going to run convoys with a close escort of small ships and a forward escort of fleet destroyers. That'll be me. There's also to be a covering force of light cruisers at Kola Inlet where the Russians are as bloody-minded and unco-operative as possible.' His smile widened. 'That'll be you. You'll hate it.'

2

'CHICHESTER,' the signal said, 'FLYING FLAG OF REAR ADMIRAL DESTROYERS WITH MARLOW METEOR AND MORRIS TO FORM FORCE T TO PROVIDE COVER FOR CONVOYS JW50C, JW50D AND RETURN CONVOYS RA50C AND RA50D. SHE WILL SAIL FOR LOCH EWE TO ENABLE REAR ADMIRAL DE-STROYERS TO ATTEND CONVOY CONFERENCE.'

Latimer laid it in front of Kelly, and gave him time to absorb it.

'*London*'s sailing for Hvalfjord with two American cruisers and an American ack-ack ship and her escort of destroyers,' he said. 'To be on hand if needed. Home Fleet's expected shortly at Seidisfjord.'

'Air support?' Kelly asked.

'Home Fleet's got *Victorious*. Captain Verschoyle has *Parsifal*.'

'And us?'

Latimer smiled. 'None, sir.'

'Watchmen and special sea-duty men close up! Secure all scuttles and watertight doors –!'

In the mess decks and passageways, men lashed hammocks. Communications were tested, and men pulled on seaboots, duffel coats and balaclava helmets. Stokers, telegraphists and artificers groped their way to their positions. Underfoot there was a faint trembling as the engines turned.

As they slipped the buoy just before nightfall and headed out through the Hoxa Gate, Kelly, huddled in his duffel coat, looked back at the long wake dropping behind them. He knew what his ships' companies were thinking because he was thinking it himself. There lay Thurso and the road home. Then the Old Man of Hoy and the other islands fell astern and he turned to face forward. He'd been through it all before – the smell of the salt and its sting on the cheek, the runnels of spray moving along the grey paint, the quiver and throb of the ship as she tossed her head and flung the swell aside.

The merchant ships were waiting at Loch Ewe, the assembly base opposite Stornoway, travel-stained, slab-sided vessels marked with patches of rust and loaded beyond their marks with munitions. Like all convoys, they varied from straight stems and bluff bows to flat sheerlines, and their masters gave their speeds as varying between nine and fourteen knots, though Kelly guessed that their chief engineers, many of them canny Scots, would have a knot or two in hand. Some of them flew the red ensign, some the stars and stripes, and two the pale blue of Panama, the bunting darkened by soot and rain.

The conference was held in a Nissen hut and the merchant captains filed in, many of them wearing civilian clothes. They all had weathered faces and the faraway eyes of seamen, most of them carried brief cases or small attaché cases, and they all looked slightly bewildered and shy. As they took their seats and filled in the slips of papers to give the number of officers, ratings and DEMS gunners in their ships, they were issued with a copy of convoy orders.

The American cruiser captains, present for the experience, looked strange in their unfamiliar uniforms but they were attentive, intelligent and more than willing to conform. There had been a lot of bad feeling when Convoy PQ17 had been lost and a lot of sneers about 'What price the Italian Navy?' but everybody knew the truth now, and though there were still occasional bar-room brawls, for the most part the Americans had accepted that it was a case of interference from above and that there was nothing wrong with the British sailors themselves.

There was still a strange feeling of doubt, however, that was a hangover from the disaster and Kelly tried to be brief and to the point. His cruisers, he said, would provide cover near Bear Island, the danger point nearest to the German bases, and he finished by introducing the convoy commodores and the commanders of the distant escorts, and Verschoyle made clear their chances.

'Darkness will be our greatest ally,' he said. 'And there won't be much else at this time of the year. Attacks by the Luftwaffe should be unlikely and U-Boats should have difficulty finding us. What we have to fear are surface ships, but it's hoped that bad weather will help.'

It was a little like a lecture in a village hall, and Verschoyle was curiously subdued as they left.

'It amazes me,' he said, 'that the poor buggers trust us as much as they do.'

As he waited for *Chichester*'s boat, Kelly saw Hugh nearby, holding an armful of woollen clothing. His face was thin and drawn but he managed a grin.

'Stocking up with warmth,' he said. 'I'm with James Verschoyle's group.'

'Does Paddy know what you're up to, Hugh?' Kelly asked.

'No, sir.' Hugh looked stubborn, as though what he was facing was only too clear to him. 'I haven't told her. But I expect she'll find out pretty soon.'

Kelly had no doubt. Paddy had a high intelligence and her naval background left little question but that she would know where to ask. As the boy climbed into *Parsifal*'s boat, Kelly remained staring after him, thinking of Paddy's anxious eyes. Aboard *Chichester*, he rang for Rumbelo.

'I just met Hugh,' he said. 'He's in *Parsifal*.'

Rumbelo's face was blank. 'Yes, sir,' he said. 'I know. I had a letter from Paddy. She knows, too.'

The following day they left Loch Ewe for Seidisfjord, picking up *Marlow, Meteor* and *Morris* off Cape Wrath. It was known that the Germans had reinforced their heavy ships and, although darkness would reduce the danger from air reconnaissance, U-Boats across the path of the convoys would report their position, while polar ice would force them south of Bear Island so that if the German heavies came out they wouldn't have a very large area to search.

As they arrived off Iceland, there was a thick fog and it was impossible to find the entrance to Seidisfjord. There was no question of the cruisers going in to top up tanks and Kelly could only order the destroyers to wait until the fog cleared, top up and then join Convoy JW50C to help the escorts. It had raised a problem. *Chichester* had to steam almost two thousand miles and, though she carried nearly two thousand tons of fuel, she burned eight tons an hour at seventeen knots and thirty at thirty knots, while the German ships, operating close to their bases, had no such worry. Somewhere just behind him Verschoyle's convoy, JW50D, was still assembling, with its escort of three Hunt class destroyers, four corvettes, two trawlers and a minesweeper, and would pick up Verschoyle's fleet destroyers as the Hunts turned back at the limit of their range.

To the south of Bear Island they ran into severe gales built up by winds roaring across the Atlantic and funnelled into the gap between Scotland and Iceland. As the seas mounted, they had to reduce to ten knots, climbing the huge waves to crash over the crest into the next trough with tons of water streaming off the foredeck.

Round North Cape, the water swirling across the ship began to freeze until it lay in a thick carapace over the decks and super-structure. Turrets, torpedo tubes and radar aerials were kept constantly moving to prevent them becoming solid and, in the worst weather, the forward turrets were trained to starboard to avoid damage. Tompions, the metal caps which screwed on the mouths of the gun barrels, couldn't be used in case they froze solid, and the ends of thick cardboard cartridge cases plastered with grease were used instead. Feet and fingers ached with cold and the north-easterly wind brought flurries of sleet and snow that reduced visibility and periodically obscured *Sarawak* following on their starboard quarter.

Clothing was the special Arctic issue of heavy woollen underwear under two, three or four jerseys, mittens, sheepskin-lined boots and thick woollen stockings – far from enough when it was impossible to eat regularly or obtain hot drinks, and when the wearers had to sleep at night action stations. They weren't much better off on the open bridge, where the cold insinuated itself beyond scarves, gloves and boots, and Kelly's exposed face felt frozen. The men had only just cleared the ice on the decks and upperworks when Pardoe had them out again, working with brooms, paint chippers, hammers, salt and sand, working the capstans and deck winches, rotating the guns, raising and lowering them continuously, using steam-hoses to clear boat-hoists, ladders and doors. There was no labour-saving way of clearing the ice. It could only be done with aching hands and frozen feet. Below, conditions were equally appalling, with all hatches battened down, and scuttles and deadlights secured. With nowhere for fresh air to enter, the atmosphere was stale and unappetising, and life was reduced simply to keeping watch, eating and sleeping.

With Convoy JW50C safely beyond the danger area, Force T dropped anchor in Varenga Bay in Kola Inlet, but Murmansk was a dreary place with a scything wind full of ice particles. In addition to a marked surliness and lack of hospitality among the Russians, the place was less than ninety miles from German air bases so that a permanent aircraft watch had to be kept, and on the only occasion when a German aircraft appeared the shooting was more fitting to a fireworks display. Kelly said so in no uncertain language and his gunnery officers made a point of passing it on.

Because of the bitter weather, liberty men were permitted to go ashore in duffel coats and seaboots but, because there was nothing to buy, nobody bothered with Russian currency. They had to stick to recognised thoroughfares and Russian sentries were posted everywhere. There was no fraternisation because nobody felt like fraternising, no booze, no bars and no shops, and they took ashore their own cigarettes which they were firmly forbidden to offer to the Russians.

The first convoy, JW50C, arrived the following day, with its load of tanks, lorries, guns and aircraft. Probably in celebration, the Russians provided an unexpected concert with a naval male voice choir, who sang until they were exhausted. Since it had been laid on by the Soviet naval commander-in-chief, Kelly had to attend, but he bolted as soon as it was over to his operations room.

The chart wasn't very helpful. About that time Convoy JW50D would be passing the vicinity of Jan Mayen Island where the Hunt-class destroyers would have turned for home at the limit of their range and the escort duties would devolve on Verschoyle's bigger ships. Meanwhile, in the Kola Inlet, the British SNO was assembling the vessels of Convoy RA50C due to leave for home.

Kelly stared at the outline of the land and the bleak north coast of Russia. Somewhere to the west, thirty-odd merchant ships, carrying enough armaments to equip a division, were plodding slowly towards them. They had a long way to go and he was not deluded that the Germans weren't aware of them.

As *Chichester* and *Sarawak* left the following day, it was well below freezing and the land lay under a thick layer of snow and ice. Turning about at a point sixty miles south-west of where Verschoyle's convoy would be, they swept across the danger zone where the German ships, if they came, would appear. There was no sun and they could see very little horizon; with a continuous blanket of low cloud, periods of snow and even elusive and inexplicable patches of mist. The navigator was working on pure dead reckoning, keeping the plot up-to-date with unknown rates of drift and the unsteady compasses of the high latitudes as the ship battled against the heavy seas that made steering difficult.

Deciding that the convoy would probably have been blown off its course by the gale, Kelly made up his mind to head southwards.

'We don't want to be spotted by some Hun pilot out for a blow after lunch,' he said. 'Ask the destroyers what fuel they have left.'

The destroyers reported they were very low and he had just ordered them back to Varenga to oil when Latimer appeared. 'Admiralty signal, sir. "Suspect convoy JW50D detected by U-boat while passing Bear Island."'

Kelly read the signal and handed it back. He was in position. There was nothing he could do but wait.

Sleet and rain were driving in sheets across the bridge structure and the funnel smoke was whipped away to nothing even as it emerged. The wind numbed bare flesh, explored every aperture in clothing and made bloodshot the eyes of the men who had to stare into it.

Gazing over the bridge screen, his gloved hands round a mug of scalding cocoa, thick as liquid mud, Kelly tried to balance the odds. A signal had been picked up from *Lotus*, one of Verschoyle's ships, to *Langdale*, his flotilla leader, indicating that she'd depth-charged a submarine contact, and following this, there had been intense enemy radio activity. In his heart he knew it was the Germans preparing to leave harbour. They

228

must have picked up the convoy on their radar and would know its approximate route.

He was not an emotional man and had never suffered from self-doubt, but he knew that a naval commander, like his counterparts on land and in the air, could make or break himself in a second by a wrong decision. Success would be applauded but failure was never allowed. The men in London who had so conspicuously failed to provide the services with the weapons they needed would not hesitate to demand the removal of anyone who failed to use the little they had to the best advantage. Responsibility was a fine thing to have, he decided, with the rank and power that went with it, but when it included the lives of hundreds of men it could also be a heavy load.

'What's the met situation?' he asked.

'Untidy, sir.'

'Where's *London*?'

'Turned back, sir. They were south of the convoy until two days ago.'

Kelly nodded. He had a feeling that this would be the day when things would happen if they were going to happen at all. He was heading now towards where he thought the convoy was and he intended to cover it by steaming ten miles north of its planned route and fifty miles astern of it. Orders clearly stated that cruisers were not to approach nearer unless the enemy were spotted.

'Oh-four-five, please. Revolutions for seventeen knots.'

He intended to steam across the convoy's wake before turning astern of it so that he would have the advantage of light during the short hours of visibility, and might even avoid air reconnaissance; while, if the German heavies *were* coming out, he ought to be able to intercept them either from ahead or astern. He just hoped his guess at the convoy's position and the navigator's workings were correct.

With the ship iced up, steam hoses were playing on the foredeck to get rid of the ice when Latimer appeared alongside him once more. 'Signal, sir. From SBNO, North Russia: "German destroyer detected off North Cape. U-boats ahead and south of JW50D."'

'It seems to be brewing up, William,' Kelly said.

They continued on their course under darkening skies. It was freezing cold and the heavy cloud and lack of daylight made a depressing scene. Already the ice was beginning to form again on the ship. Soon afterwards, Latimer produced another signal.

'PHOTOGRAPHS OF TRONDHEIM AT 1400/3 SHOW THAT CRUISERS ZIETHEN AND MUFFLING AND FOUR DESTROYERS HAVE LEFT.'

Kelly studied the signal for a moment. Both *Zeithen* and *Müffling* were bigger than his own ships.

'Well, that's that, Henry,' he said to Pardoe. 'I think I'll go and get something to eat. It might be a good idea to let the watches get something hot inside them, too. We don't know when we might meet these gentry.'

Rumbelo was waiting below to take his layers of bridge clothing.

'I hear the Germans are out, sir,' he said.

His mind busy, Kelly grunted an affirmative and Rumbelo was silent for a while before he spoke again, slowly and soberly. 'This is no place to be flying, sir,' he said.

Kelly had no sooner returned to the bridge when another signal arrived. 'Admiralty to C.-in-C., Home Fleet, sir,' Latimer said. '"Further A2 report states warships are expected to attack FW50D between fifteen degrees and – "' It ends with corrupt groups due to interference.'

Kelly found himself wondering. East or west? He was still debating it when a signal arrived from the Admiralty to the Home Fleet and the escorts of JW50D. 'ENEMY UNITS APPROACHING CONVOY. SUBMARINE REPORTS LOSING THEM IN FOG. EXACT POSITION UNKNOWN. ADVISE AIR RECONNAISSANCE.'

Kelly stood in silence, his face taut and grim against the lash of spray as he thought of Paddy's small anxious face. This is it, he felt, and soon afterwards, *Chichester*'s operators intercepted a signal from *Langdale* to *Parsifal* – 'FLY OFF. SEARCH SOUTH.'

He wondered what it had cost Verschoyle.

He noticed Latimer looking at him and he hitched his heavy scarf closer about his neck. They both knew what it meant. CAM-ship aircraft were never catapulted off until things were desperate and, when they were, it usually meant the end for the pilot.

'You might pass the word to the W/T room to keep it to themselves, William,' Kelly said.

As Latimer turned away the bridge voice pipe went. 'Radar to bridge. Echo seven and a half miles to the north-west.'

'Pass it to *Sarawak*,' Pardoe said. 'And sound action stations.'

As the alarm rattles went and the greased cardboard discs covering the guns were removed, below in magazine and shell rooms the supply parties loaded the cordite hoists with flashless charges and the shell hoists with shell.

'Instruct *Sarawak* to fire night tracer to distinguish her fall of shot from ours,' Kelly said. 'Order her to conform to our movements and follow five cables astern.'

'More radar reports, sir! Two echoes steering eastwards. They aren't U-boats.'

'Probably stragglers from the convoy.'

'Or enemy surface ships, sir.'

'Echoes steering oh-eight-nine! Making twenty-three knots.'

'*They*'re not stragglers,' Pardoe said. 'They're too fast.'

'Appears to have possibilities,' Kelly agreed. 'We'll close, to track and establish touch.'

As the ships turned south-east, another report came.

'Blurred object bearing oh-eight-nine.'

As the guns and directors swung to the new sighting, however, the information came that the contact was doing only ten knots.

'Must be a different contact,' Kelly said. 'Follow the first one.'

For half an hour, the strange ships continued steaming eastwards without any alteration of course or speed and without any clue to their identity. Then, unexpectedly, Rumbelo sang out from the back of the bridge.

'Gun flashes to the south!'

As they swung round to stare over their wake, beyond and above *Sarawak*'s swinging masthead they could see a flickering white glow against the clouds.

'Probably ack-ack fired at Russian aircraft,' Kelly decided. 'We'll stick with the contacts.'

But as he leafed through the deciphered signals, he was growing worried. He was still uncertain of the position of the convoy. It ought to be to the east and experience indicated that after the gales there might well be stragglers, while the gunfire might well be from the detached escorts rounding them up.

'More gunfire, sir!' Rumbelo reported. 'Looks heavy, too.'

'Sir!' It was the signals officer. 'Signal from *Lotus* to *Langdale*: "Three destroyers bearing three-oh-nine. My position 72 degrees 35 minutes north, 28.00 east."'

'They can't be British destroyers,' Kelly growled. 'Navigator, prepare a course.'

The ship continued to butt into the seas, *Sarawak* keeping station astern. Aware of a tightening of the throat, Kelly knew that somewhere ahead in the murk there were German ships.

'Signal, sir, from *Langdale* on fleet wave: '"Unknown ship bearing three-two-four, range seven miles, course one-three-nine. Position—"'

A second signal followed, 'THREE UNKNOWN BEARING THREE-TWO-FOUR.' and almost immediately another, 'ONE CRUISER BEARING THREE-THREE-NINE.'

Holding course some minutes longer, Kelly studied the chart. Judging by the flashes they'd seen, somewhere in the murk of the northern afternoon, one or all of Verschoyle's ships were in trouble and it was clearly his duty, as it had been since Nelson's time, to steer towards the sound of the guns. But he had no sure knowledge that the firing came from the convoy because the flashes came from the south and they'd estimated that the convoy was to the east. His first concern was the convoy, yet, judging by the flashes, they still had forty-odd miles to go to reach it, a good hour and a half's steaming in which time enemy heavies – if the firing came from German heavies – could blast it from the sea. It was a disturbing thought.

He decided to act on a hunch. What radar had picked up were stragglers and the convoy *was* to the south.

'What's the course to the gun flashes, Pilot?'

'One-six-nine, sir.'

He turned to Pardoe. 'We'll turn on to that, please, Henry. And make to *Langdale* "Am approaching you on course one-six-nine." Then let's pipe hands to supper. They have twenty minutes.'

The ship was silent as she drove south with her consort, two thousand men hurtling into the unknown, eyes fixed on instruments and counters, hands busy with levers and wheels, bodies moving to the shift of the sea. Many of them had spent all night at action stations, heads pillowed on lifebelts, while inside the ship away from the smell of salt spray and the tang of wet decks the long lines of lights turned night into day with the winking indicators and the steady murmur of machinery. The doctors were laying out their instruments and communications were being checked and re-checked, blank-faced men testing systems and gun mountings, training them from side to side to ensure there was no interference from the ice; while in every corner of the ship, often frighteningly alone, other men watched dials and instruments as they waited.

Pardoe had spoken to the ship's company, telling them the situation as it appeared from the bridge. Provided they knew what was going on, they would accept any level of discomfort and danger, but when they didn't understand morale was affected. They didn't mind the captain blowing his top, or even appearing without his trousers, if that were normal, but so long as he ran true to form life was ordered and they could accept what he asked of them. Nobody liked being shot at or did his job as well when he *was* being shot at, but it was a help to know why it was happening, and made facing the grim music just a bit easier.

'Intercepted signal from *Langdale*, sir!' The report broke into Kelly's thoughts. ' "Have been hit forward." '

So Verschoyle had found the enemy, or to be more exact, the enemy had found Verschoyle.

'Hoist battle ensign!'

The great white jack jerked up to the yard arm, almost obscured in the murk. Kelly's eyes lifted to it and, staring upwards, he suddenly recalled Verschoyle's signal to *Parsifal*. Where was Hugh now? Somewhere out in the stir of low cloud, bad light and lifting seas? By this time he must be out of petrol, and unless he'd ditched right alongside his ship he'd never be found.

He drew a deep breath that was painful in his chest and tried to thrust the thought from his mind. He could see other men about him and wondered what was going on in their minds. Were they, too, worried about sons or brothers? They all knew since Pardoe's broadcast that they were about to meet a

233

superior enemy force, and he knew they, too, were afraid – not of death because you didn't wonder 'Shall I be killed today?' – but of everything that there was to attend to, and of letting down everybody else about them who was dependent on them. What was happening to Verschoyle? What had happened to Hugh? How could he best bring his ships to the enemy so that they could bring the biggest number of guns to bear?

His thoughts were interrupted by Latimer. 'Signal from *Langdale*, sir. "Am retiring on convoy under smoke screen. Forward magazine flooded. Fire in boiler room." They're also picking up *Lindsay* now, sir. She's been holed forward and reduced to fifteen knots.'

Kelly nodded, wishing *Chichester* were faster. She was crashing along now at full speed but it seemed terribly slow under the circumstances. With two ships badly hit, Verschoyle was desperately in need of help.

'We're picking up *Langdale* to *Lotus*, sir,' the signals officer reported. 'It's garbled but the message's clear. Captain D's been wounded and he's instructing *Lotus* to take over for the time being.'

So they'd got Verschoyle, too! How bad was it, Kelly wondered, and how would Maisie take it? Well, he imagined, because she wasn't the type to panic.

He was trying to concentrate when another garbled signal from *Langdale* was received.

'CONVOY COURSE 178. CRUISER CLOSE TO CONVOY . . . CAPITAL SHIPS . . . CLOSING CONVOY.'

What was missing? It seemed that more than one German heavy was doing the attacking and, against odds like that, Verschoyle could be wiped out with all his ships. He'd already lost two of the escort and, if they were retiring, was it because they'd managed to drive off the Germans or because they were being overwhelmed? The only thing he knew with certainty was that somewhere ahead were superior enemy forces. The Germans didn't risk much these days with anything else but superior forces because they didn't appear to like gunfire. He felt a little like someone trying to pluck up courage to plunge into an ice-cold bath, and in the pit of his stomach was the sensation he'd often felt as a boy before starting a race at school. He wasn't afraid but he was terrified of making a mistake that might lose the lives of everybody around him.

He glanced at Pardoe. He seemed calm and didn't look oddly at Kelly, so he could only imagine that he must look calm, too. There would be no failure. The ship had done good service in more than one action and her company had been together a long time now. Just astern he could see *Sarawak* on the port quarter, her bow wave just visible in the gloom.

'Home Fleet's preparing for sea, sir!' Latimer appeared alongside him, laconic as he kept him informed of the shape of events.

'They'll be a bit pushed to get here in time to help,' Kelly growled. 'What ships?'

'*KG Five*, sir, with *Howe*, *Kent*, *Berwick*, *Bermuda* and destroyers. They're heading towards the homeward-bound convoy.'

The minutes seemed to drag. Occasionally they saw the gun flashes ahead, getting nearer all the time, and he was so tense he forgot the cold. The flickering glare in the clouds came again and he hoped his message had been received. It was no help but it might encourage and it would identify his ships as he burst out of the murk, because in the twilight it would be difficult to tell who it was appearing. Still firm in his mind was the need to see the convoy safe to Murmansk and allow the homeward-bound convoy to slip away undetected.

The ship was crashing into the sea at its full thirty-two knots now and, with fuel oil being burned at a fantastic rate, he knew that whatever the outcome, he would have to go back to Kola Inlet when it was over. The boiler room fans were thundering and the noise was such that it was impossible to speak, and suddenly he became aware of the cold as the icy wind drove in his face. Fine spray was lifting and blowing over the deck to add to the ice already there. Above his head the radar aerials moved like the antennae of some great steel animal.

By this time it was possible to pick up the individual gun flashes and see smoke along the horizon, and he guessed that behind it somewhere Verschoyle was probably fighting with everything he'd got for the convoy. Everything depended on Kelly but he couldn't blunder into the fight without identifying the enemy or he might well find Verschoyle's ships between them. And while there was light he had to keep it behind the

235

Germans because the only way he could hope to make up for the weakness of his own force was by keeping to the darkness.

'Radar reports large ship ahead! Range nine miles.'

Almost immediately, another big ship was picked up fourteen miles away on the port bow. The first ship appeared to be steering east across *Chichester*'s bows while the second was steering a course that was bringing her nearer to them with every second.

'Any destroyers?'

'Nothing else shown, sir.'

On their present courses, the two unidentified ships would disappear to the eastward away from the lighter sky to the south, and over there a confused battle was going on with gun flashes flickering against the cloud formations.

'Turn to port on a course parallel with the first target.'

Even as he spoke, Rumbelo yelled. 'Large ship dead ahead!'

The words were like an electric shock and heads jerked up as they strained their eyes for this new opponent. Already the forward turrets were swinging, the muzzles lifting. Except for the sound of the sea, the crackle of orders and reports over telephones, an enormous silence seemed to enfold the ship.

'Two smaller ships in company! Presumably destroyers.'

The big ship they could now just see appeared to be firing to the east and they clearly saw the tracer shells arcing away.

'Firing fast, sir. About seven salvoes a minute.'

'Alter course to the target!'

The unknown ship could now be seen as a dark blur against a rolling bank of smoke which presumably had been put down by Verschoyle's ships. She was still stern-on but as she turned to starboard her silhouette changed.

'It's *Müffling*,' Latimer snapped.

She had presented them with a perfect target. 'Come round to starboard,' Kelly said. 'Make to Admiralty "Am engaging the enemy."'

As *Chichester* thundered round, with *Sarawak* in her wake, Pardoe, his eyes flickering between the enemy ship and the range dial, looked up. 'Permission to open fire?'

Kelly nodded and Pardoe bent over the voice pipe. 'Open fire!'

The crash of the guns shuddered the ship as the twelve huge

shells sped from all four turrets. As the guns recoiled, the smoke was whipped away by the wind with the acrid bitter smell of burnt cordite, and the shells described their endless arcs towards *Müffling*. After weeks of seeing nothing at sea, as always it was an unreal feeling to be firing at the enemy.

'Over!'

The second salvo was short but as the guns roared for the third time, they saw a dull red glow between the enemy ship's funnel and mainmast.

'We've hit her!'

Both ships were firing at tremendous speed now. They had obtained complete surprise. *Müffling*'s guns had still been firing to port and both *Chichester* and *Sarawak* had got off four salvos before they'd been brought round to starboard.

'She's turning towards us!'

They could see destroyers moving ahead of the big ship now, their funnels streaming smoke as they tried to lay a screen to hide her.

'Starboard. We'll keep in step.'

'Range four miles.'

It was hard for Kelly to tell what the German ship was doing now but by conforming to her movements he could keep all his guns bearing and hold her against the light.

They waited tensely for the German ship to come on to a steady course, but she continued her turn towards them and then, in the murk, ran into the growing smoke screen and vanished into the darkness.

'Cease firing!'

Staring ahead, Kelly tried to decide what the German ship was doing. Was she continuing to circle so that she would come out a mile further east, or was she endeavouring to escape to the south? He decided it was safer to assume she was going round in a complete circle and *Chichester* continued to turn herself, with *Sarawak* close behind.

'Ship red one-oh!'

'Looks like a destroyer!'

The oncoming ship might well be one of Verschoyle's ships, but she was in a perfect position to fire torpedoes and it was best to take no chances.

'Steer towards.'

As they turned towards the enemy ship to comb torpedoes, the range-taker calling out the range, *Chichester* was doing over thirty knots. As they steadied on the other ship, Pardoe was straining his eyes ahead.

'I don't think she's one of ours!'

'Funnels are too far apart, sir,' Rumbelo called out.

'Ready to fire!' the gunnery officer reported.

'Make the challenge!'

As the lights were switched on, two white lights came on from the other ship.

'Wrong answer,' Pardoe snapped. 'Open fire!'

The six guns of the forward turrets crashed out at point blank range.

'You could almost ram the bugger, Henry,' Kelly said.

Chichester was still swinging as the shells smashed into the destroyer. Fires broke out at once and several more explosions showed as the second and third salvoes struck.

'I don't think you'll need to ram after all,' Kelly observed flatly.

By the seventh salvo, the enemy ship was smothered in smoke and flame and was falling to pieces before their eyes. She was so close now that the four-inch AA guns opened up and as they heard the rhythmic pounding of the multiple pom-poms, the men running along the destroyer's deck were swept away. She was down by the bows already and a mass of flames but, as they swept past, the after-turrets continued to fire, every gun hitting her so that she was completely overwhelmed, unable to use either her guns or her torpedo tubes. As *Sarawak* thundered past, yellow, red and green rockets soared from the nest of flames and they saw the ship sinking lower and lower in the water.

3

There were still contacts on the radar screen to the south-west, but the threat of the German heavies seemed to have receded. They were far from being out of the wood, however, and the report of more contacts came almost immediately.

'Ships red-nine-oh! Believed to be destroyers!'

'They're in a good position for a torpedo attack. Turn towards.'

The strange ships were steaming a parallel course but were they German or did they belong to Verschoyle?

'Flashing light,' the yeoman of signals called out. 'It's making "R".'

'Repeat it back.'

There was a long pause. The delay caused by the repetition was giving them a few more seconds to approach.

'He's making the letter "G" now, sir.'

'Repeat that one, too,' Kelly said. 'And open fire.'

The flash of the guns blinded them.

'Over! Well over!'

'No, sir,' Latimer said, his glasses to his eyes. 'They're firing at another ship beyond the destroyers. Gunnery control thinks we've seen it, too.'

It was impossible in the murk to tell exactly where the shells fell but then they saw columns of water rising ahead of them.

'*They*'re not short!' Kelly snapped. 'And they're not from ahead either. They're from the port beam!'

As he swung, he could see himself entering a trap. There was a big ship ahead and another one, probably their original target, on the port beam, and in the darkness there were undoubtedly escorting destroyers with torpedoes like the one they'd sunk. As he concentrated, he was hardly aware of the shells bursting in the water around them. The fact that they were under fire seemed of secondary importance just then.

The shells were still falling close and he heard the clatter as splinters flew past and hit the upperworks. His nostrils were full of the smell of cordite as the guns crashed.

'Turn away!'

The ship heeled as helm was applied. Any destroyers there were ought by now to be behind them.

'Enemy ships also turning away, sir.'

'We'll maintain touch. Alter to westward. Let's see if they really are legging it. Reduce speed to twenty-seven knots. If he turns back we'll be in a good position to get between him and the convoy.'

As the ship crashed through the dark seas, eyes strained towards the blank horizon.

'Radar reports contact lost, sir.'

Kelly frowned. 'I think they're going back into their holes, Henry,' he said.

Soon afterwards, with the clouds breaking, the navigator managed at last to fix their position. They had shadowed the German ships, risking another attack by destroyers, until they'd made sure they were heading away from the convoy. By now, the homeward-bound convoy must have reached safety astern of them, while Verschoyle's ships must be coming into their area.

'Signal, sir. From *Langdale* to *Lotus*. "In view of holes in forecastle and deteriorating weather, consider it advisable to proceed to Kola forthwith. Captain (D) concurs."'

So Verschoyle wasn't dead! But it was clear he was out of action and his first lieutenant had taken over.

'Make to *Langdale* that we'll cover her.'

Suddenly Kelly realised he was cold, and was exhausted as much by the bitter air and tension as by the long hours on the bridge. It brought a feeling of depression and with it came the thought of Hugh.

'Make to *Parsifal* requesting information of the pilot she flew off.'

Soon after midnight, they picked up another signal from *Langdale*. *Lotus* had taken over as senior ship of the escort and after the position and course that followed the message

240

continued:

'LANGDALE PROCEEDING INDEPENDENTLY TO KOLA INLET. ESTIMATED TIME OF ARRIVAL 0700, 17TH. APPARENT SITUATION ON LEAVING CONVOY: LINDSAY DAMAGED. WHEREABOUTS UNCERTAIN. REMAINDER OF ESCORT AND 30 MERCHANT SHIPS UNHARMED. TWO MERCHANT SHIPS AND TRAWLER THORN NOT IN COMPANY SINCE 14th.'

It was blowing half a gale now and, as he waited impatiently for *Parsifal*'s reply, Kelly tried to show no emotion. It was his job to appear unaffected and concerned only with his ships.

'We'll sweep to the limit of the Russian submarine area,' he said. 'What's the fuel state?'

His mind was on his ships and the job in hand but, like everyone else he was suffering from the anti-climax that always followed a period of high tension and danger. In addition he couldn't put aside the thought of Hugh's frozen body lolling in his dinghy in the darkness and he wondered if anyone had informed Verschoyle.

'*Parsifal* replies, sir.' The signals officer appeared '"Pilot's whereabouts unknown. Due to action German heavy units obliged to abandon."'

Kelly sighed. So that was that. Hugh had taken a dangerous chance just once too often. He caught Latimer's eyes on him and passed a hand over his face. His features felt stiff.

'I'm going below, William,' he said. 'Pass the word for Rumbelo to see me, will you?'

As they entered the Kola Inlet the following morning, Russia looked depressing and cold, and Kelly wondered if they were right to ask young men like Hugh to suffer for such a bloody ungrateful ally.

His thoughts were particularly bitter when Latimer appeared alongside him, so sulphurous in fact he was surprised to see Latimer was smiling.

'Sir: Signal from the trawler, *Southern Star*.'

He took the message, his mind still on his job, then the words leapt out at him.

'SOUTHERN STAR TO CS ONE. REFERENCE YOUR 2040 TO PARSIFAL, HAVE PICKED UP MISSING

PILOT. UNHARMED. RECOVERING.'

Kelly looked at Latimer. He couldn't believe it. This was Hugh's third escape and his second encounter in a dinghy with the waves and the weather. He must bear a charmed life to scrape through with such a thin thread of luck.

'God's good, William,' he said. 'Better than we probably deserve. I think we'd better let Rumbelo know.'

The battered *Langdale* was already alongside Varenga pier when *Chichester* dropped anchor. At once, Kelly called for his barge and headed towards her.

Her paintwork was scarred and scorched by flames and her funnel and bridge were riddled with splinter holes. Two hits forward had wiped out A and B guns with their crews and almost the whole of the forward part of the ship had been on fire. The hit on the funnel had sent a shower of debris into the engine room and blown open the boiler casing. Aerials had been brought down and the range finder smashed, and because the forward capstan wasn't working, she couldn't move from the pier and the crew had been offered billets ashore in an ugly stone building furnished with little else but pictures of Stalin. They had elected to stay on board.

The first lieutenant was a good-looking man who looked like a younger edition of Verschoyle himself and had probably been picked for that reason.

'With their usual bloody-mindedness, sir,' he reported, 'the Russians refuse to believe we've been in action with anything bigger than a destroyer. I expect it's political, because I've noticed here that only Russians can lick the Germans.'

The hospital was a stone building in which there seemed to be remarkably little heating and the electricity kept failing, but the naval surgeon ashore had rigged up secondary lighting with aldis lamps and a torch. Verschoyle was propped up in bed, his face smothered in bandages. A splinter had smashed his jaw and sliced up his cheek. He was under sedation but was conscious.

'Hello, James,' Kelly said.

'Hello, Ginger. What about my missing ships?'

'I'm afraid you lost *Lutine* and the trawler.'

'Poor old *Thorn*. She wasn't very big and she wouldn't have

242

had much chance.' Verschoyle paused. 'I'm damn sorry about Hugh, Kelly.'

Kelly put *Southern Star*'s signal in his hand.

'I can't see it. You'd better read it.'

Kelly did so and Verschoyle was silent for a long time.

'I must be growing old,' he said at last. 'I feel I'd like to cry.'

Kelly smiled. 'It was a bloody good show you put up,' he said. 'I've been talking to your captains and your first lieutenant. I'll see you get a gong for this. The biggest I can dig out of 'em.'

'Thanks.' Verschoyle's mouth curled under the bandages. 'It's nice when you become sufficiently senior to see that your friends get presents. We ought to operate on a you-kiss-mine-I'll-kiss-yours basis. We could be the most decorated people in the Navy.'

'How do you feel?'

'Bloody terrible. The buggers have spoiled my manly beauty at last.'

'Can you see?'

'Not really. But they say my right eye's all right.' Verschoyle paused. 'How about the ship?'

'We'll get her repaired at Rosta and send her home as soon as possible. You as well. We've arranged for you to be put aboard *Lindsay* and sent back with the next convoy. I'll see if we can't get Hugh aboard, too.'

There was a long silence, before Verschoyle spoke again. 'Wonder how Maisie will take it. Suspect she married me because I looked presentable.'

'I think she's tougher than that. You'll be on your feet in no time and after this you should be well in line for that broad stripe.'

There was a long silence.'But not at sea again.' Verschoyle paused. 'Still, I was always one for comfort, as you know, and a cushy job in some esoteric branch of the Admiralty would suit me fine. I'll leave the battles to bloodthirsty buggers like you.'

Kelly arrived in England long after *Lindsay*. They had been ordered to Iceland to refuel then sent out into the Atlantic where a German raider had been reported near the Azores. Intelligence had it that, with the German heavies short of fuel and apparently despised by Hitler, the menace at sea in future was likely to be only from such raiders, because someone seemed to have found the answer to the U-boats at last, and they were being sunk in unexpected numbers and the Atlantic convoys were suddenly immune from attack.

There were American ships at Scapa when they returned and the picture had completely changed. The Germans had lost a whole army at Stalingrad, while in the Pacific the Japanese were also on the retreat. England was changing constantly, too. The Americans were arriving in force now, taking over the country, stealing all the girls and drinking all the whisky. There was some resentment but also a great deal of admiration because they'd learned quickly in North Africa. Off-duty American naval officers wore clothes that seemed to indicate a round of golf, but for the most part they were the product of a naval school as traditional and expert as Dartmouth, and the regulars knew their job, while the amateurs were enthusiastic and contained some unexpected faces. On one occasion, Kelly found himself drinking gin with a man he'd watched more than once on the screen at the cinema.

Perhaps the most encouraging sign was the numbers of landing craft being gathered in English ports for the invasion of Hitler's Fortress Europe and, with the Eighth Army already ashore in the toe of Italy, Mussolini, defeated on every front, had been deposed.

Hugh was at Thakeham, white, shaken and ill, but slowly recovering and Paddy was on compassionate leave to look after him. She gave Kelly a curious glance that seemed more gratitude than anything, as if she considered him responsible for giving her husband back to her, but privately she confided to him that Hugh was determined to get back into the war somehow.

'What is it that drives him like this?' she said, her small face agonised with worry. 'Hasn't he already taken enough chances?'

Was it his youth, Kelly wondered. The fact that he'd been ignored for much of his childhood and early manhood by Christina? Her own tremendous vitality and zest for life even? Or was it that his father had been nothing but a cypher and he was anxious to prove that he wasn't, too?

At the Admiralty, everybody seemed pleased by the skirmish

off Bear Island, and it seemed clear that Verschoyle, despite his wound, was expected back in uniform by the autumn. Kelly found him at Haslar in excellent spirits, though his handsome face had been transformed. A livid scar ran across his jaw, leaving a deep grove right up to his cheekbone, his nose was wrenched out of shape and his right eye was milky and turned outwards.

'One fixed, one flashing, like a wreck marker,' he said cheerfully. 'Maisie thinks I'm wonderful.'

Kelly produced a box of cigars and a pineapple. 'Got 'em at Punta Delgada in the Azores,' he said. 'The ship was stacked with 'em. The lower deck must have made a fortune.'

Verschoyle was smiling. 'I've got something for you, too,' he said. 'A bit of news.'

'They're giving me the Home Fleet?'

'Eventually. But not yet. No, it's not that. I'm on the track of Charley Upfold.'

'What!' Kelly sat bolt upright.

'Steady on! I haven't got much. I heard it from a chap who was in here till two days ago. She's still with the Navy. Or was.'

'Where, for God's sake?'

'She went to Ops Division Signals Room at the Admiralty. Some lecherous bastard called Lewis had his eye on her and got her there as his secretary.'

Kelly's heart sank and Verschoyle grinned.

'Nothing came of it, old son. I gather he was a bit of a shit and he was eventually sent to North Africa. He's still there.'

'And Charley?'

'Well, she isn't waiting for Lewis, because he turned out to be married with two kids.'

'And now?'

Verschoyle's smile died. 'Well, there I'm stuck for a bit. You see, she left London.'

'Where for?'

'I don't know. And neither does the Admiralty, so she's not a Wren. But leave it to your Uncle Sherlock. When they let me out of here I'll have nothing to do and it'll stop me getting bored.'

Uncertain whether to feel depressed or encouraged by

Verschoyle's news, by September Kelly was back at sea and *Chichester* was full of American officers, naval, military and air. There was little to fear in the Mediterranean now but the Germans were sneaking U-boats past Spain armed with acoustic torpedoes which homed in on the sound of a ship's propellers, and several ships had had their sterns blown off. They were also believed to be developing some sort of radio-controlled bomb, and ships were taking scientists to sea with special receivers to pick up the wavelengths.

Despite the fact that an advance into the Balkans towards Vienna seemed a good idea, somehow the American government was not in favour and they weren't throwing their full weight behind the Italian campaign; but as the summer ended, *Chichester* and *Sarawak* found themselves moving west round Malta and Pantellaria with Force H from Gib, guarding the western flank. Sacks of orders had arrived on board and, though they knew there was to be another landing, they were still in the dark as to where it was to be.

'I'll bet the Germans have worked it out,' Latimer said grimly. '*I* have – and I was supposed at school to be a bit dim. It has to have a suitable beach, it has to be near a major port and it has to be within fighter cover. It's Salerno.'

The hot purple blue of the Tyrrhenian Sea was thick with north-bound shipping west of Sicily and east of Sardinia. Capri was fifty miles away and they were all waiting expectantly when Latimer appeared on the bridge, grinning.

'Allied troops have landed at Salerno, sir,' he said. 'And the Government of Italy's handed in its chips. They've surrendered. They're coming in on our side.'

Kelly smiled. 'If they do as well for us as they did for the Germans, Hitler's got nothing to worry about.'

People were dancing in the squares of the twin towns of Messina and San Giovanni as they passed, with wild festivities, floodlit churches and fireworks, but the fact that the Germans hadn't surrendered, too, was obvious when the Luftwaffe attacked just before midnight.

The first indication that something was happening was the crack of gunfire from the port side of the fleet. Immediately, the alarm sounded and the guns began to bang away. The barrage was too much and the German airmen failed to make much of

246

their attack.

'Timid as a bean-fed mare,' Latimer said.

By this time, they'd learned that the Italian armistice terms included the immediate transfer of the Italian fleet to the allies and the requisitioning of merchant shipping, and during the early hours of next morning, they were instructed to accompany *Warspite* and *Valiant* to meet the Italian ships twenty miles north of Bone.

'Second time round,' Kelly observed dryly. 'I did this in 1919, too, with the German High Seas Fleet. There's nothing quite so dramatic as seeing your enemies coming in grovelling.'

After the dark days of Crete and Greece when Cunningham had run the Mediterranean Fleet on a shoestring, there was a strange emotion running through the ship, and they were off Bone at dawn when the Italians came in sight. As the two forces steamed towards each other at twenty knots, the gunnery officer was comparing their silhouettes with his cards. 'I never thought in 1941 that I'd survive to see this,' he said.

His eyes narrowed and as the Italian ships dropped anchor – two fifteen-inch battleships, *Andrea Doria* and *Caio Duilio*, five cruisers and nine destroyers – he voiced the hopes of every man on board.

'Perhaps we can go home now,' he said.

4

With the Italians out of the war, they had somehow expected to put the Med behind them, but the Americans at Salerno had run into trouble and the squadron was ordered to bring their great guns to bear. The hills were close and full of German artillery shelling the airstrips and landing places, and it was the Navy's job to knock them out.

Observers were landed and in the sunshine they could see the leaping fountains of earth and stones and drifting smoke. How much damage they were doing it was hard to say but the American troops were enthusiastic. A heavy shell made the sound of an express train and the thought of an express train filled with high explosive passing overhead was always encouraging.

They were so close inshore, they could see soldiers stripped to the waist unloading stores, the great fifteen-inch shells from *Warspite* and *Valiant* flinging houses sky-high, and ammunition dumps going up in fearsome explosions of black smoke and debris.

Every hour or so, German fighters roared in with their cannon going, coming in low as they stood off the shore at night. The following morning, they moved in again, blotting out German positions as the Americans consolidated their grip. The thunder of the great guns provided a deep base to the battle, and the smaller armament of *Chichester, Sarawak* and two American cruisers, *Savannah* and *Philadelphia*, a higher-pitched counterpoint.

For two days and nights they hammered the shore, until the possibility of a large-scale disaster changed slowly to success, and for safety, Kelly sent for a copy of the Admiralty report on the new radio-controlled bomb.

'Make to all ships,' he said. ' "In the event of attack by glider bombs, one officer is to do nothing but observe and report on the behaviour of the bomb." '

Almost immediately, Rumbelo sang out.

'High level bombers to starboard! About 16,000 feet!'

Unexpectedly the aircraft remained just out of range, then one of them peeled off and steered parallel to the group's course at a distance of about five miles. As they watched, there was an orange flash beneath its wing and what looked like a smaller aircraft swung away towards them.

The bomb, fitted with stubby wings, was hurtling towards them at tremendous speed, and while it was still in flight, the next aeroplane peeled off and released another. Fighters were being used to distract attention, but Rumbelo, stationed on the bridge as usual, had long since developed a flair for picking out from the approaching aircraft those which were heading for the ship and those which were not.

'Aircraft astern,' he said calmly. 'Coming up fast.'

'Make to all ships,' Kelly snapped. ' "Independent action." '

The navigating officer had a man on either side of him reporting on the progress of the bomb, and they watched it pass overhead. Almost at once, there was a deep thump beyond *Sarawak*, which was turning in a tight circle to starboard, the bright sun catching the curve of her bows, and a column of brown smoke lifted into the air.

'*Morris* hit,' the midshipman sang out.

The next few minutes were extraordinarily exciting, with a calm sea and the spotting plane sitting like a vulture high in the sky. *Morris* was stopped and on fire, but her guns were still banging away, while the bigger guns of *Chichester* and *Sarawak* tried to reach the aeroplanes waiting to drop their bombs. The Oerlikon and Bofors crews were aiming at the approaching missiles and the petty officer telegraphist, knowing the bombs were controlled by radio, had put every set he had to transmit at full power in the hope of disturbing the enemy frequency, and they were all banging out 'Balls to Hitler.'

'*Warspite*'s been hit, sir,' Latimer said. 'She's still firing but her steering seems to be jammed. There's a tug going to her. *Morris* reports she's still underway but her speed's limited to fifteen knots. *Savannah* and *Philadelphia* also report hits.'

'Here comes another,' Rumbelo reported. 'Straight for us!'

Kelly watched the bomb. The missiles were arriving at about four hundred miles an hour but it was obvious the controller in his aircraft could only change their direction and could not prevent them losing height.

'I think a turn to starboard, Pilot,' he said quietly, 'and when it follows, hard a-port. That ought to fox it.'

Chichester was moving at full speed to starboard, and as the bomb followed her turn, the navigator ordered hard a-port so that the bomb, swinging after them again, stalled and splashed into the sea. From the time of sighting to its arrival had been only eight seconds.

With Salerno secure, the squadron was moved to Algiers and Kelly flew ahead, sitting on an uncomfortable bench in a Dakota troop carrier.

Cunningham, who was setting up a new headquarters at Naples, appeared only occasionally, and the supply of stores, repairs and maintenance of fleets and bases had almost broken down, so that Kelly, with other senior officers, found himself involved in reorganising it twelve months too late. He was glad to move to Naples in the New Year.

'Same hard-arse aircraft as last time,' he said to Boyle as they climbed aboard.

Cunningham informed him that his squadron was to move to the Tyrrhenian because there was a new landing at Anzio in the wind and organisation was difficult because the politicians were not prepared to postpone any landings across the Channel.

'Plan seems to be a bit of a dog's breakfast,' he confided. 'Alexander's orders are clear enough but for once the Americans don't seem to have the same sense of urgency.'

As they dropped anchor in Naples Bay, landing ships were waiting with their flotillas of assault craft hoisted at the davit heads. Orders came on board in sealed sacks and the briefings explained what had to be done. The Allies, it appeared, were in serious trouble at Cassino, and it seemed logical to use sea and air power to dislodge the Germans by landing behind their lines.

'I just hope the Germans have been briefed how *they're* supposed to act,' Boyle said.

The destroyers remained underway all night, constantly

dropping small charges because of the fear that frogmen might try to attach limpet mines to the troopships, and on every ship, young Americans were preparing their equipment with the introspective, dedicated concentration of men about to go into action, chewing gum, talking laconically and polishing their sub machine-guns.

They sailed in the evening to join up with the transports, followed astern by long lines of landing craft. Surprise was complete and the assault wave got ashore without a single casualty, but nobody had heard of Suvla Bay at Gallipoli in 1915, and the same sad story was played out again as the troops consolidated, and the whole object of the landing was lost on the first day.

During the evening, Dornier 217s appeared and the defensive pattern of dodging to sea with every gun and radio set going on full power to disorganise the glider bombs began. Alexander arrived from Naples in a destroyer, urbane, handsome and looking as if he'd just come out of a bandbox. He was worried because the general in command at Anzio had concentrated on getting his supplies ashore and had not pushed inland.

'Looks like being a costly withdrawal instead of an advance,' he said as he took a drink in Kelly's cabin. 'And if the casualties are high, the effect on the morale of cross-Channel invasion forces could be disastrous.'

Instead of withdrawing, however, he fired the general in command and put another in his place, and when he returned he looked even more pink, polished and unperturbed than ever.

'Two years ago,' he said, 'the Germans would have pushed us back into the sea, but they seem to have lost their zip a bit and I think we shall hold.'

Anzio was monotonous and dangerous. Throughout February, supplies were poured ashore and the difficulties were added to by the bitter weather. From time to time, they returned to store and reammunition in Naples, which was a festering sore on the face of Italy, packed with narrow streets and mouldering houses all the worse for four years of war. It seemed to be full of starving children and girls of all ages selling themselves to the troops so that their families could eat. The Italian males, both the soldiers and the civilians, seemed to have lost their backbone and, with a vicious black market encouraged by the troops, it was a sick city full of corruption and distrust.

251

Anzio ground on. When it had started, the British had been joking that they'd soon be requisitioning the Coliseum in Rome for the opening of the Flat, but progress remained snail-like and during March Kelly was more than delighted to receive a signal ordering Force T home. They arrived in the same bitter weather that they'd left, with cold winds and sleet. Off Land's End; they were ordered to Plymouth but nobody seemed to expect them, and they were left kicking their heels in the Sound.

'Shore staff seem as efficient as ever,' Kelly observed tartly. 'Better call my barge away, William, and I'll go and tear 'em off a strip or two.'

A boat manned by Wrens who seemed to have been picked solely for their good looks passed them with the mail as they left the ship's side. The acknowledgement to an admiral turned out to be smiles and waves, and Kelly grinned back. They were a joy to see, and the men leaning over the guard rails seemed to think so, too. Sailors were lonely, sentimental creatures and were always ready to give affection to a pet or a girl friend, and the girls were already doing well in the form of cocoa, chocolate, cigarettes, even lipstick and silk stockings bought in Africa, which were tossed down with every kind of lewd suggestion and request to meet them at the dock gate, which they accepted with even wider smiles, language as basic as the sailors' and not the slightest sign of embarrassment.

England seemed to be stiff with Americans. They were everywhere, in every bar, club and restaurant. On every hillside they were practising assaults; farms, estates and whole villages had been taken over. London was on tenterhooks because it was well known that the invasion was coming before long. Nobody knew exactly when but there was no doubt about it now and the Luftwaffe had recently come to life suddenly so that the nights had been almost as noisy as they had been in 1940 and 1941.

Corbett was still at the Admiralty, looking very old and tired so that Kelly became aware for the first time just how much strain he'd had to bear. 'Intelligence said it was the Luftwaffe's last fling,' he pointed out. 'A reprisal for the bomber offensive. But they knocked the St. James area about and a lot of shops and houses, including mine, had their windows blown out.'

By this time, harbours were packed with ships in a way that German bombers couldn't have missed, but the Little Blitz had

252

already petered out and there was now nothing but the occasional sneak raid – most of which came to nothing, because the British and American air forces had made it their task to see that the recce planes should observe nothing but what it was intended they should see.

There were so many men in the south of England now, the coastline seemed to bulge, and still landing craft and small ships were being built to add to the crowding. To produce them in sufficient numbers, the Government had organised industries which had never before had anything to do with the sea, and prefabricated sections of sea-going vessels came together only at the coast for assembly and launching; while men of all types, too old for service at sea, ferried them to the Navy. If they were not always as naval vessels should be, at least they floated and their engines turned and, though their skippers were often young and had never handled anything bigger than a rowing boat before the war, they managed – sometimes with nervous uncertainty, but they managed. Tension was at fever pitch, more with the general public than with the armed forces, who were cool because for them the shouting had long since died. With the Americans, the war had become big business and it *had* to succeed.

Verschoyle, who was now exercising his not inconsiderable charm on Eisenhower's staff, informed Kelly that he was to have X Force, comprising *Chichester, Sarawak, Norwich* and eight destroyers, and that he was to be attached to O Force, which was to attack a beach not yet identified but known as 'Omaha.' As he was leaving, he drew Kelly aside. 'Just one more thing,' he went on cheerfully. 'I know where your Charley is.'

Kelly had been studying the charts and his head jerked round. 'Where?'

'Felixstowe. She needed to get away from the smell of Lecherous Lewis and she's been up there a year now. Captain's a chap called Fanshawe. You'll probably remember him because it seems he served in *Clarendon* with you in 1914.'

The news left Kelly with his heart thumping excitedly. At least now, he thought, he knew where to look.

There was to be no immediate chance of taking advantage of the information, however. By this time there were a million and a half Americans in England and their training centres stretched from South Wales round the coasts of Cornwall, Dorset and Portland. Force X moved to Scapa in May. Considering it was the fifth year of the war and that a battle fleet had been stationed there since 1939, not much had been done to relieve the monotony beyond a drab wet canteen for the sailors. Though there was a great pretence of despising the comforts the Americans provided for themselves, they were all well aware that under the Americans Scapa would long since have been made much more bearable.

Anarapoora was still there and, with Paddy back aboard her, Kelly sent his barge across with a message. They met in Kirkwall and she immediately drew him to one side.

'They've taken Hugh off flying,' she said.

'Altogether?'

'Altogether! Not even training. He's got a ground job – at Macrihanish again.' She gave him a shaky smile. 'I can't tell you how happy I am. It means he'll survive the war and that we'll have a chance of a life together. It hasn't been much of a marriage so far with him in one place and me in another.'

Kelly smiled, pleased for her. 'It's the way things work in wartime,' he said. 'Produces a great deal of ill-will on both sides. What are you going to do, get a posting ashore?'

She grinned, her eyes bright. 'Not likely,' she said gleefully. 'I'm finished. I'll be out of uniform by the time you're home again. I'm pregnant. Hugh's over the moon. We'll be making you almost a grandfather.'

He kissed her. Ever since he'd known them he'd regarded Rumbelo's children almost as if they were his own and he'd adored Paddy from the moment he'd seen her.

'When's it to be?'

She looked at him as if they were conspirators. 'A long time yet, but I've handed in my resignation.'

Kelly was constantly in London to attend the conferences at Eisenhower's headquarters at Bushey Park, to the north of London. Like every other senior officer, he'd long since grown used to long cold trips in transport aircraft or converted bombers. The whole area of Bushey Park was surrounded by endless caravans of drab army trucks loaded with war supplies, huge

dumps of stores and strings of murderous-looking tanks parked
nose-to-tail just off the pavements with heavy guns, ammunition caissons and other military hardware. Headquarters was a
sprawling hutted camp in a wide park where the grass was
already worn thin by hundreds of feet. There seemed to be staff
cars everywhere; and what looked like the whole of the top half
of the army, air force and navy lists for Britain and the United
States – to say nothing of other odd countries like France, Belgium, Holland, Norway, Poland and Denmark – was there.

The conferences showed a lot of divergence of opinion. The
British were inclined to go on waiting until they felt the invasion
would be a walk-over. The Americans, generous, passionate
and eager, were anxious to start at once.

'They aren't scraping the barrel,' Verschoyle pointed out
dryly. '*We're* down to our last army.'

Endless lists of beaches similar to the French ones they were
to assault had been made up, and the names of ancient ships to
be sunk as part of a floating breakwater were carefully studied,
because after the submarine depredations, there were never
enough transports and no one wished to sink something that
could carry troops or munitions. An incredible scheme for
taking their own harbour across and for transporting petrol by
pipeline under the Channel had been prepared, as well as complicated Intelligence moves to delude the Germans about the
direction of the assault.

Landing craft were stuffed into every little harbour of the
south coast as far as Falmouth in Cornwall. The RN Training
College at Dartmouth had become the home of an amphibious
force training programme, and there were sailors in tented
cities in Dartmouth and Salcombe and, as Kelly well knew,
round Harwich on the East Coast. Milford Haven and Penarth
had been assigned to training and maintenance; Teignmouth
to repair; St. Mawes to landing craft; Fowey to the training of
doctors and medical orderlies. Exeter was a supply base; Laun-
ceston a depot for army spare parts; Tiverton a depot for naval
spare parts; Bugle an ammunition depot. Hedge End in Wilt-
shire was set aside for diesel engine overhauls; Netley, in
Hampshire, for a base hospital; Deptford, on the Thames, for
amphibious maintenance.

It was an incredible organisation and British ports were

never so congested. The Americans alone took up an enormous amount of room. Yet their very numbers were reassuring to people who had spent three of the last five years living on a knife-edge between defeat and survival.

Because there was no more space in the south, gunfire support ships, including Force X, moved to Belfast Lough. It was a time not only for training but also for prestige inspections. Eisenhower inspected Kelly's ships, and the King, equally assiduous, visited Portland. High among Kelly's duties was getting to know the Americans. The sailors were always turned out in dress blues and at action stations, but aboard one small craft, as he was progressing solemnly along the deck escorted by American officers, a head appeared through a hatchway and a grinning face asked. 'Wouldja like a cup of jamoke, Sir Kelly?'

A minute later he was in the wardroom drinking a cup of the best coffee he'd tasted since the war began.

'I asked the King and *he* had a cup, too,' the American cook grinned delightedly.

Shoreline sketches prepared to a scale of one in 10,000 were distributed even to the smallest landing craft. They included sun and moon data, beach gradient graphs, inshore current data and tidal curves. They all knew the invasion was growing nearer and they were all beginning to feel that it was going to be a walk-over when the Germans came violently to life against a rehearsal off Slapton Sands at the end of April. Caught by a squadron of German E-boats from Cherbourg, two LSTs were sunk and another damaged, with the loss of nearly seven hundred American soldiers. For a while there was some ill-feeling because the British thought the Americans were expecting it to be too easy, and the Americans pointed out that the British MTBs and MGBs which were supposed to be patrolling the mouth of Lyme Bay had failed to spot the Germans.

'Somebody,' Kelly observed, 'was depending too much on radar and not enough on Mark 1 eyeballs.'

As the spring wore on, the weather became kinder. Destroyers seemed to be working up all over the Irish Sea and round the Hebrides, firing at shore targets, sleeve targets towed by aircraft and surface targets towed by tugs. In the middle of May, they were ordered south again, and they knew at once that the invasion, which had been in their thoughts for so long,

256

was at last not far away.

Invasion headquarters had moved to Southwick just behind Portsmouth in a Georgian house in the Forest of Bere, which had been requisitioned originally as a navigation school and re-christened HMS *Dryad*. It was surrounded by rhododendrons and parkland, but was dreadfully overcrowded, with commanders sleeping in dormitories of twelve and sixteen and Wren officers twelve to a room in two-tier bunks.

To Kelly's surprise almost the first person he bumped into was Helen Jenner-Neate, now a chief officer and married to an American.

'He was a bit bolder than you, sir,' she smiled. 'And certainly he has more money. I couldn't resist.'

From Southwick he went to a briefing conference at St. Paul's School, in London, where Montgomery had set up his headquarters. The room was circular, like a cockpit, with narrow benches rising in tiers and a gallery supported by sombre black columns, all packed with senior officers of all three services, both British and American. The seats were un-comfortably hard but the room was hushed and the tension palpable, and the interest never flagged. It was like watching the completion of a vast jigsaw, with all the pieces fitting into place and the knowledge that if one were missing or broken the result would be chaos and defeat.

It was easy to break the journey back to Portsmouth at Thakeham and Kelly decided that, since there was no immediate prospect of the invasion for a few days, he'd take advantage of the fact to go to Felixstowe and find Charley.

He was just packing an overnight bag when the telephone rang. Frowning, thinking it was a recall after all, he snatched it up. To his surprise, the voice was Hugh's. He seemed to be under some severe emotional strain and was gagging on his words.

'Hugh! What's wrong?'

'It's Paddy!' The voice came shakily over the wires. 'She's dead!'

5

A column of troops on the way to the coast was passing through Thakeham when Hugh brought his wife home.

She'd been released because of her pregnancy and had been on her way to Kirkwall when the drifter had been run down by a destroyer. Eight nursing sisters and three soldiers had been drowned. Hugh had met the coffin at Thurso and had accompanied it by train to London and then by road to Thakeham. The roads were packed with trucks full of soldiers heading south into the invasion area and nothing was allowed to interfere with their movement – neither birth, marriage or death – and the hearse had to wait as they rolled past.

Kelly felt bereft. Standing alongside Verschoyle, staring at the cold wooden box on the hearse, he found it impossible to believe that it contained Paddy. He'd taught her how to sail, how to play cricket, how to use ju-jitsu – suffering a wrenched elbow in the process as she went at it too enthusiastically. He'd seen her grow from an impudent child to a young girl and watched as she and Hugh became aware of each other, their wrestling matches changing abruptly to swimming, cycling and long walks together, both of them suddenly solemn and full of earnest questions.

Had he even unknowingly been a little in love with her himself? It seemed too silly for words, but there had always been a curious rapport between them, a certainty of each other, a feeling that each had always known what the other was thinking, a shared conspiracy of humour and knowledge. Or was it because she was like Charley – the old Charley he remembered with warmth from his youth, not the Charley he'd last seen, angry with him and mourning all the lost years? Was it just that, or was it – could it have been? – that Paddy with her infectious

258

laugh and her immense enthusiasm had meant more to him than he'd realised?

He couldn't believe that he'd never hear her giggle again, or that faint trace of Irish she'd inherited from her mother, and was bewildered that her fey forthrightness had vanished forever. Not long before, he'd been congratulating himself on his luck and hoping, with the end of the war drawing near, that they might all survive. There was no justice, he thought. The clerics could preach about God's mercy and God's will but he was damned if he could see how it worked. And why, he wondered, the lump in his throat big enough to choke him, why did it always seem harsher when the dead were young and attractive and full of joy?

Hugh was straight-backed, showing no emotion beyond his taut white face and clenched fists. Rumbelo's face, like his son's, was wooden, and even Biddy's was unmarked by tears. Naval training was a funny thing; however hard they tried to mock it, it rubbed off.

They didn't have time to absorb that Paddy was dead because, as they returned to the house, Latimer rang to say that they were expecting the invasion to take off at any moment and, while Hugh vanished northwards again, the others drove down to Portsmouth together, the dead girl's father and brother and Kelly, unspeaking, each of them busy with his own thoughts.

The roads were packed with vehicles moving in long brown columns southwards – lorries, tanks, jeeps, ambulances, Scammells, mobile workshops, every kind of military vehicle imagineable. There were no bands, no flags, and no crowds to shout 'Goodbye.'

Latimer had everything under control, and that afternoon Kelly sat in a sealed cinema, its stage set with large maps and blown-up photographs, and listened as the plans for the invasion were laid bare, with the names of their landing points, the men who were to run the show, the ships which were to carry the troops, the warships which were to support them. The secrecy was ended at last and this time they got the whole plan, the exact landing places, the enemy forces opposite and the details for every assault, even the date. Force X was part of an American group, O Force, escorting American troops ashore at Vierville-sur-Mer.

259

As they drove back to *Chichester*, it was hot with a clear blue sky and, by the time they arrived, the soldiers were moving from their camps to the ships and landing craft. Everywhere you looked there were men, well-behaved and thoughtful, sitting on the edge of the pavement eating their rations among the tanks and jeeps and trucks, and drinking tea provided by moist-eyed women from the houses around.

Orders, two large sacks of books comprising thousands of pages, had arrived and been signed for by Boyle, and they had just settled down to read them when another one arrived, containing amendments and appendices. Nothing had been left to chance and, with a bottle of whisky and a bottle of gin on the table and Rumbelo to keep them supplied with sandwiches, Pardoe, the navigator and all *Chichester*'s senior officers gathered in Kelly's cabin, were sworn to secrecy and told to get on with it.

The main points all had to be committed to memory and they finished in the early hours of the morning, only to start again the next day. Apart from a two-hour break in the evening, they went on correcting all night. The following day, as he returned from a final conference, Kelly saw that the dock gates had been closed and, though men were going in, nobody was coming out. Inside, by the police box, an elderly man was arguing.

'Why can't I go 'ome?' he was saying. 'I only work in the canteen and my missis'll wonder where I've got to.'

'Look, Dad,' the policeman said. '*I* don't know why you can't go 'ome. I just know you can't.'

The following day they oiled, ammunitioned and stored ship, and anchored off Spithead. The day was grey with mist and the Channel was cold in the poor light. Three big motor launches crowded with men and equipment began to move slowly out to sea, and in front of them was an incredible panorama of ships and small craft stretching as far as the eye could see, over them a network of silver barrage balloons.

As the hours passed, the wind began to freshen and, as the forecasts became more unfavourable, the atmosphere changed to one of dread. Once in motion, like a juggernaut the invasion could not be stopped and if it ended in bloody catastrophe the war could go on for another ten years.

'Unsettled westerly weather setting in,' Latimer reported.

'Anti-cyclones over Greenland and the Azores, and depressions moving east-north-east across the Atlantic. This could be the most unholy mess you ever saw.'

By the evening the forecasts had become alarming. Outside, the thin rain had changed to a downpour and everybody was on edge and ill-tempered. Troops had been embarked and some ships were even at sea. If the weather worsened and the operation was postponed, they would have to steam in the opposite direction, with all hopes of surprise endangered.

'They'll have to postpone,' Latimer said.

'They can't postpone,' Kelly snapped. 'The plan's tied to the moon.'

From one of excitement, the atmosphere became one of dragging uncertainty and anxiety, and there was a feeling that instead of victory the assault could turn into a disaster. The code word postponing the operation for a day arrived just ahead of Verschoyle. He appeared dripping wet in the war room that had been constructed on *Chichester*'s aircraft deck. His face was grim but he'd brought with him an American colonel called Sarpiento who was to help the bombardment officer with the selection of targets. He was a small man, in civilian life a lawyer, and, to Boyle's startled amazement after a preliminary 'Sir', he immediately started addressing Kelly by his Christian name.

'Forget it,' Kelly murmured. 'If it's good enough for him, it's good enough for me.'

All round them, ships tugged uneasily at their anchors, and ropes and seasick pills were being handed round on the landing craft. With men cooped up in some cases for four days, the strain was beginning to tell.

'Destroyers are chasing back the leading ships,' Verschoyle said. 'They'll be back off Portland Bill by midday. For the small craft it's a different matter. There are no berths available and they'll have to churn it out near the Portland Race until we can find room in Weymouth Bay.'

He crossed to the charts and his hand moved across them. 'The low up near the Shetlands is filling up,' he said, 'and we expect lower seas and less surf for two days starting tomorrow morning. The Met boys won't go beyond that, but I think you'll be going and I thought I'd just come along and say *bon voyage*.'

261

He looked at Kelly. 'Contacted Charley yet?' he asked.

Kelly shook his head. In his grief at Paddy's death, he hadn't had the heart to pursue the matter.

Verschoyle sighed. 'Yes,' he said. 'I understand. If you need any help, just ask. You're such bloody innocents, you seem to need Father's help.'

Curiously, it was Verschoyle's reminder about Charley that brought back once again the realisation that Paddy was dead. He'd always admired Kelly Rumbelo's steadfastness and his stolidness, but the mercurial character of his sister had enchanted him, and he found the thought of her struggling in the night-black water nauseating. Drowning was a fearful and squalid way to die, and he fought to put aside the image of her terror as the cold water filled her throat and eyes and nostrils, and the icy Scapa cold clutched her limbs.

He was thankful for the invasion, for the mountain of work that faced him, because it was the only thing that stopped him thinking.

The gale showed no signs of abating. The rain lashed the sides of the ship and, with the anxiety real enough to touch, it seemed a good idea to hold a church service. The chaplain managed it in the mess flats, with the ship's company sitting on stools and tables and on the floor. As he watched them, Kelly was aware of their desperate youth and wondered if he could ever have looked like that, because they looked like children waiting to go on a picnic.

After it was over, they got down to the maps and charts of the French coast again and the captain of every ship in the squadron was ordered on board.

'Our job's to get these men ashore at Vierville,' Kelly pointed out. 'And then to make sure that our targets – or anything else that fires for that matter – are knocked out. As the troops go in, we're to cover their flanks from attacks by gunfire, tanks, aircraft or infantry. Nothing must divert us from these objectives, not the rescue of men from sinking ships nor anything else. As long as you have a gun to fire, it must be fired.'

It was still blowing the following morning, with white-tipped waves and spray flying over the small boats that fussed about the fleet. The weather was miserable, especially for the soldiers. For the commanders it was one of intense anxiety as they watched fuel states and worried that in the confusion they would lose some of their commands. That evening Latimer brought the met report. Two low pressure systems had joined together in a single low, and moderating winds and a break in the solid cloud were predicted. As the day dragged into darkness, they knew the invasion was on.

It was like taking a city to sea.

They began to move out one after the other in a long line of ships, like a thread unrolling southwards, endless columns converging into a unified whole in the black night, then parting again as they headed for their separate destinations.

With darkness, the wind had dropped a little, and they could hear the drone of aircraft. Thirteen miles south of the Isle of Wight, they sorted themselves into five lanes, one for each assault, and in mid-Channel each lane became two, one for the fast convoys and one for the slow.

The sea was still rough, and the landing craft were bad sea boats, so that it was almost impossible to hold them on course. Those on the inside columns were fighting to keep station while those behind were struggling to hold back and had to keep going full astern to avoid riding up the stern of the vessel in front. Occasionally, because of sheer unmanoeuvrability, the columns kept drawing together, occasionally riding alongside each other, even crashing into each other, then separating and finding station again.

By now the Omaha bombardment group, led by USS Texas, had caught up with the landing ships packed with troops. As far as the eye could see the Channel was covered with ships and smaller craft.

'Light on the port bow!'

'That'll be the control vessel. Starboard two points.'

As Chichester turned, Sarawak, Norwich and the destroyers swung with her.

'Entrance to swept Channel Number Four coming up!'

'Let's have the lighted dan buoys ticked off,' the navigator ordered.

'Almost eight bells, sir,' Latimer said.

'Another few minutes,' Kelly murmured, 'and it's D-Day.'

Voices suddenly became hushed about the ship, and the

bridge became silent. The atmosphere was alive with emotion. Overlaying the tension, there was a quiet exaltation, something more than confidence.

'Divine guidance,' Sarpiento suggested.

'More likely relief after indigestion,' Latimer said.

Above the clattering of the wind and the hiss of the sea, they could hear the dull rumble of explosions ahead where the bombers were plastering the area inland, and every now and then they saw the sky light up to the flashes of their bombs and could pick out the line of the coast as it was silhouetted. Kelly's thoughts were busy, one half of his mind on the job in hand, the other half divided by sorrow at Paddy's death and the knowledge that he knew where Charley was.

'Light ahead, sir!' Latimer's voice jerked him back to the present.

'Point Barfleur,' the navigator pointed out. 'It's one of the world's tallest and most conspicuous lighthouses.'

'What the hell's it doing burning like that?' Sarpiento asked.

'Perhaps to help the E-boats home.'

'I hope there aren't any goddam E-boats out tonight.'

There was a tense silence that was broken by the rattle of the anchor cable. An eighteen-knot wind was blowing off the Cotentin Peninsular and a heavy overcast lay over the land though occasionally the clouds broke to allow the moonlight through. The night seemed hot after the recent storm in England.

Sunrise was due at 0558 and to seaward landing craft loaded with tanks were closing up. Ahead, the minesweepers had swept and marked the channel with dan buoys up to eleven miles off the beach.

'Germans are quiet,' Latimer said.

As the darkness began to pale and colour appeared in the sky, Kelly strained his eyes through his binoculars to the coast ahead. Above them the steady stream of aircraft continued. As the light increased it was possible to pick out the assault craft at the davits of the anchored landing ships. The minesweepers, their job done, were heading rearwards as the sky filled with the sound of hundreds of aircraft. As the thunder and the thud and crack of bombs died away, there was a curious pause and a quietness that seemed eerie.

264

Turning to port, they saw landing craft being pulled out by a naval captain in an LCH and sent to their proper stations. LCTs carrying tanks, and LCMs with demolition units on board dodged among the big ships, frightening themselves to death, but there were no collisions.

The fire support ships were ahead of the confusion. *Glasgow* led the western group with *Texas*. *Arkansas*, the oldest battleship in the United States Navy, led the eastern group, with *Chichester*, *Norwich* and *Sarawak* and two French cruisers, *Montcalm* and *Georges Leygues*, known to the lower deck as *George's Legs*. Every ship was flying a huge battle ensign and the grey dawn was lightened by the colour of the bunting fluttering at the yard-arms.

Round the transports the landing craft were forming two lines parallel to the beach.

Sarpiento frowned. 'Between you and me,' he said to Kelly, 'I think eleven miles is too far out. That goddam wind's coming across eighty miles of Channel.'

But orders had laid down strict adherence to times and places and by 0430 the landing craft were on their way. Behind them others circled, waiting to take their places. As they passed *Chichester*, the men in them looked wet-through, seasick and thoroughly unhappy.

Then, unexpectedly, because in the silence they'd almost begun to expect no opposition, a single gun fired. It came from a light battery near Port-en-Bassin on the left side of the beach. The huge *Arkansas* was just beginning to loom through the darkness like a fortress as the night came to an end and the shell sent up a column of water close by her.

'Cry havoc,' Latimer remarked. 'Here we go!'

Other batteries on the eastern end of the beach began to fire and there was a crash as the destroyers fired back together, then they began to bang away solidly at the shore defences. With a tremendous roar, the cruisers joined in, with *Arkansas*' huge guns providing a deep bass chorus. Within a few minutes the shore batteries had been silenced.

'Start the scheduled bombardment!'

Texas' fourteen-inch guns were already digging huge craters in the Pointe du Hoc, flinging great chunks of cliff into the sea. *Chichester* was thumping away steadily at known enemy positions and exit roads that led from the beaches, with *Norwich* and *Sarawak* thundering away alongside and the destroyers aiming at pillboxes and anti-tank guns and a radar station near the Pointe du Hoc. Watching through his glasses, Kelly turned to Pardoe. 'I don't think enough time's been allowed for this, Henry,' he said. 'The results aren't going to be as good as we expected. Tell 'em to step it up.'

Rockets and shells were dropping on a strongpoint at Les Moulins, then a raking fire started from the German guns on the easternmost exit road and *Arkansas* switched her huge rifles to them.

A thick pall of dust and smoke was beginning to obscure the targets and, as the half-light swelled into daylight, they heard the thunder of aircraft engines again and saw a whole armada of bombers sweeping in.

Watching them with his glasses, Sarpiento looked puzzled, waiting for the eruption of earth and sand on the beaches.

'Where are the goddam bombs?' he asked.

'Inland,' Latimer said. '*Too far inland.* Compensation for crops and cattle follows. So much for the policy of bombing blind through the overcast and delaying thirty seconds to avoid casualties.'

In the last minutes as the troops began to set foot on the beaches, the bombardment reached its peak. Through the shellfire, thousands of rockets from LCRs whistled shorewards in flaming arcs, and tank and machine gun fire cracked and rattled. As it died down, however, the ominous sound of German automatic weapons and artillery could still be heard and they saw columns of water lifting among the landing craft approaching the shore.

'Direct your guns to the shore targets, Henry,' Kelly said.

As Pardoe passed the order to the gunnery control, the long barrels shifted and the shells began to drop just beyond the struggling boats.

By this time the whole shoreline had burst into flame and forward movement seemed to have been lost. As the boats dropped their ramps, the soldiers floundered chest-deep in the water, falling on the sand or in the shallows, while less resolute men crouched behind the beach obstacles, hoping for the gunfire to lift. Those who had crossed the beach were huddled against the

266

sea wall, their officers killed or wounded, enfiladed by German guns which made them sitting ducks. *Chichester*'s guns switched to knock the guns out, but the whole beach was disunited, with confused, leaderless men without officers, cohesion, or artillery support, while the Germans shot up the tanks as they waddled ashore.

An American destroyer moved in closer and Kelly turned to the navigator.

'How far's this bloody channel marked, Pilot?'

'For gunfire support ships up to a ten-fathom line four thousand yards offshore, sir.'

'Tell the destroyers to move in to the limit. And make to *Sarawak* and *Norwich* to keep us company.'

Many of the landing craft had gone ashore in the wrong places and, despite the destroyers moving up, the number of wrecked tanks, smashed vehicles and wounded men continued to grow.

'Tell 'em to get further in,' Kelly snapped.

'If they go much further, sir, they'll scrape the bottom.'

'So long as they stay upright and can fire their guns.'

'Signal from flagship, sir. New firing pattern. We're to help seal off the beaches against reinforcements.'

'There won't *be* any reinforcements,' Kelly said. 'Ignore it.'

Within an hour they began to see a distinct improvement. Two large landing craft steamed at full speed through the obstacles, firing everything they could. Bulldozers drove two gaps through the dunes and with the destroyer fire drenching the pillboxes, the German positions were finally overwhelmed.

'Intercepted message, sir,' Latimer reported. 'It states that troops are advancing up the western slopes of the exit from Sector Easy. Shore bombardment officers ask that fire should be directed further west.'

Kelly drew a deep breath. He felt stiff and tired as he eased the earpads that protected his hearing from the din of the guns. Cold and hungry, he turned away, rubbing shoulders that ached under the weight of his binoculars. Rumbelo was standing behind him with a tray of soup and sandwiches. His face was expressionless and it didn't require much understanding to guess what he was thinking.

They were ashore. The end of the war was in sight and, despite the risks they'd taken, they'd all survived – all except Paddy.

6

Even at sea the sullen smell of smoke came, foul and threatening. Ashore, the build-up continued, lorries, men, guns and tanks moving steadily inland. Only a few German planes had appeared and the worst danger now was from falling splinters from the ack-ack shells. The night had been one of tension but there had been none of the expected counter-attacks, and the men in the orchards and fields ashore had seen only shadows in the darkness as they lay in their slit trenches to write home that they were safe.

The morning had started with a raid by four Me 109s, which had come in low and fast, hit a ship with a small bomb, and flashed away over the hills, while every ship in sight had filled the sky with a rash of shellbursts. When *Rodney* arrived, swinging to the British beaches to the east, they knew the situation was safe, and suddenly the place was less like an enemy coast than Spithead as the great ship ran close along the shore, training her triple sixteen-inch turrets towards the land. Behind her came *Warspite*. She seemed to have been everywhere there had been trouble since the war began and the ship's company crowded up to cheer her. Finally, other ships arrived and throughout the day there was always one of them in the assault area, firing its big guns through clouds of rolling cordite smoke.

Rumours were around that the Germans had improved on their glider bombs and look-outs were alert for rocket-propelled pilotless aircraft. As they headed back to Portsmouth to reammunition, just ahead of them they heard a tremendous bang and saw a huge cloud of smoke and water rise into the sky. Imagining it a ship that had hit a mine, they headed for the spot but found no trace of debris.

'Flying bomb,' Latimer said laconically. 'We've just seen the first.'

Almost immediately the new blitz on London started.

After refuelling, they were back across the Channel, this time to the British beaches where the nights were becoming exciting as enemy planes arrived and E-boats came out, but by the middle of the month the shore was secure; and by the end, with the invasion moving northwards, the need for the big guns off the coast had vanished and they were recalled to England. With *Chichester* due for a major refit, Kelly was ordered to strike his flag and report to the Admiralty for instructions.

It was Corbett who met him as usual – a curiously shrunken Corbett – and he informed Kelly that he was to be given a shore job in Europe.

He held up his hands before Kelly could protest. 'Admirals don't always lead from ships these days, my boy,' he smiled. 'You'll be wanted after the war's over and you need experience of this committee work we go in for nowadays.'

It seemed Kelly's name was being considered for a new task force which the Admiralty was considering for the Far East, comprised of battleships, carriers, cruisers, destroyers, oilers, supply ships and every other kind of ancillary vessel, and he was being ordered to join the headquarters Ramsay was setting up in Normandy.

'There'll be a lot of rebuilding to do in Europe,' Corbett said, 'and you might as well be in on the ground floor.'

It seemed to be time to take up Verschoyle's tip about Charley and, unable to face Biddy at Thakeham, he headed direct for Felixstowe. He still couldn't thrust Paddy from his mind. She'd been all he'd hoped for from Charley – brave, forthright, undemanding, intelligent and full of spirit. He had managed at last to lose the image of her dying or lying on a littered beach with the sand in her hair and in her eyes. Now it was just the ache of bereavement, and a feeling of guilt because it was the Navy, in the end, which had killed her as surely as it had destroyed Charley.

Light Forces headquarters were in a pub, near the small boat basin, overlooking a concrete quay filled with gunboats and torpedo boats, and there were a great many incredibly young men about who made him feel aged. They looked like piratical schoolboys, with shabby uniforms smeared with grease and caps from which the wire had been removed.

The first person he met was Fanshawe. He was a captain now and he'd grown fat and bald.

'They have a habit of entering harbour without lining the decks,' he said. 'They leave their ensigns at the masthead until they're blown to threads. They aren't very good at answering signals and in harbour you can never find them, because they spend all their time asleep except when there's a dance on somewhere. But give them a job to do and they do it with aplomb and a hell of a lot of courage, though they sulk like prima donnas if they're reminded they should enter harbour with their crews in some sort of uniform. In fact – ' Fanshawe grinned '– they remain entirely civilian at heart and nothing on God's earth's going to change their outlook. They belong to a different navy from mine and I love 'em.'

He knew Charley and listened to Kelly's story quietly. 'I thought you married her long since,' he said.

'No,' Kelly said shortly.

'No, I suppose not,' Fanshawe agreed. 'Because she's a widow, now I come to think of it. I heard she'd been crossed in love or something, so she probably came here because everybody here's so bloody young she didn't have to fear one of them making propositions to her.' He smiled. 'Unfortunately, she's just moved to Harwich.'

He laid on a boat and Kelly was driven across the river by one of the most beautiful girls he'd ever seen, so that he wondered again, as he always did, if the Navy, being sailors, always made sure there was no dearth of pulchritude. She gave him a salute that would have done the master-at-arms of *Chichester* justice and then a beaming smile that ruined it as she directed him to base headquarters.

Destroyers were coming in from their patrolling of the D-Day beaches and the place was full of activity. In the Communications Section, Wrens and civilian workers were sitting in front of telex and cipher machines and there seemed to be a constant hither and thither of messengers. There was no Charley.

'She's on leave,' he was told.

'Leave?'

'We're all entitled to a little, sir.'

271

Kelly's heart began to sink. 'Where does she live?' he asked.

'Here,' they reassured him. 'In Harwich. We've got her address.'

He found a taxi but the driver was a refugee from bombed-out London and, short of petrol, refused to cruise round looking for a street he didn't know. Instead, he dropped Kelly nearby and left him to set off walking.

It was dusk by now and his face was grim. This time he had no intention of taking no for an answer. If Charley weren't married already, he was determined to have her.

As he drew near the address he'd been given, the air raid sirens went but he told himself it couldn't be much. The *Luftwaffe* was virtually finished and nowadays there were only the flying bombs. A policeman who saw him striding along thought differently. 'You ought to be going to the shelter, sir,' he said.

'Bugger the shelter,' Kelly growled.

It was only when he became aware of the clatter of what sounded like an enormous motor-cycle engine and heard the quadruple concussion of a salvo of ack-ack shells that he realised the area was more dangerous than he'd imagined and took shelter in an archway, deciding he wouldn't be much good as a courtier if he were dead. A sailor sheltering with his girl-friend stiffened at the sight of his braid and slammed him up a salute.

Kelly's return salute was brief and indifferent and the sailor looked at his girl-friend, pulled a face and started making plans to bolt as soon as he could. Bad-tempered admirals were best left alone.

The guns went again, banging away enthusiastically. The sound of the motor-cycle engine had become shatteringly loud by this time and the sailor and his girl were looking up nervously. Having only just come from Normandy and not being so experienced with flying bombs, Kelly watched them to see what they did.

Suddenly, with a frightening abruptness, the sound of the motor-cycle engine stopped dead, and a workman's bus just down the road emptied at full speed, everybody running for shelter. The sailor's girl-friend, who seemed to know more about what to do than any of them, flung herself down, so Kelly did the same. He landed on top of her and the sailor landed on top of him, so that they were all huddled in a heap by the wall.

For a long time there was dead silence, almost as if the whole of Harwich were holding its breath, then there was a tremendous crash and the halted bus vanished in a sheet of flame. The blast lifted Kelly from the pavement and slammed him down again and he felt a rush of air strike him. Lifting his head, he saw the whole front of a row of terraced houses sliding down in a torrent of bouncing bricks and skating slates, and a vast flattened smoking area of sterile soil where the bomb had exploded.

He was about to scramble up when he realised he could hear another bomb coming and instead he clung to the sailor and his girl. Glass was tinkling all round him and pieces of metal from the bus were slamming and clanging down into the road. What seemed like tons of fragments of brick fell on him as he held his arms over his head, and a tremendous cloud of plaster dust welled up and spread over him. He felt the pavement lurch twice more as the second bomb landed and saw another sheet of flame spring up some distance away beyond the houses and a vast spiral of black smoke rising.

It seemed to be safe at last and he felt the sailor climb off him and in his turn he scrambled off the sailor's girl-friend. She looked scared as she pulled her dress down over her knees.

'You hurt?' Kelly asked.

'No, sir,' the sailor said. 'She's not hurt, are you, Dot?'

He seemed determined not to offend an admiral and the girl shook her head, more frightened of Kelly's rank than of anything else. They dusted themselves down and shook off the fragments of glass and stone, and Kelly lent the girl a clean handkerchief to wipe the dust off her face.

'Better keep it,' he said. 'I'm going to see if there's anything I can do.'

Near where the bus had been, a body was lying in the gutter. It had no head or arms and the stumps were pumping blood out at an extraordinary rate. Another man was vomiting by a wall nearby, a long stream of saliva hanging from his open mouth. Policemen and air raid wardens had appeared like magic, and one of them touched Kelly's arm. 'You all right, sir?'

Kelly stared down at himself. His braid was fouled with dirt and there was blood on his shirt cuff. What a bloody silly thing to do, he thought, nearly getting himself killed just when they'd upped him to rear-admiral.

Smoke was lifting into the air beyond the houses ahead and, knocking the dust from his uniform, he set off again. His stride was firm and his face was grim, but inside he was more uncertain than he'd ever been.

He became aware of more policemen, then he saw an ambulance and crowds on the pavement, and he began to hurry. Unable to get through, he pushed his way past, only to realise with a shock that the crowd was round the address he'd been given. There was a whole area of flattened houses such as he'd just left, with a further fringe of damaged ones where the blast had been less violent. A string of vehicles, fire appliances and ambulances had arrived and what looked like hundreds of men were picking among the rubble.

From among the wrecked houses on the edge of the crater, an ambulance man was just helping an elderly woman away. She was bleeding from cuts made by flying glass, her clothes were torn and were covered, like her face and hair, with a mask of pulverised plaster and soot. The whole street smelled of smoke, old dust and fear. Slowly he picked his way along it until he found the address he was seeking. Like the other houses, it had lost its façade, and the interior looked as though it had been through a shredder. The wallpaper hung in strips and windows and doors were missing. The walls were pockmarked with fragments of stone and hedgehogged with jagged daggers of glass, while in the street below there were sickening splodges on the pavement which a workman was covering with sawdust.

His heart cold, he pushed forward, and was just on the point of asking a policeman whether he'd heard what had happened to the occupants when he saw Charley. She was sitting on a low wall, her face black, her clothes covered with dust, and she was clutching a silver frame which he recognised at once from three years before as the one which had held the photograph of the dead RAF officer. He stopped, feeling that he'd been wrong to come, but then his heart went out to her and as he approached she lifted her face. Tears had made two pale runnels through the dirt on her cheeks, and she looked dazed, but he knew at once that she'd recognised him. She didn't seem in the slightest surprised to see him and he saw her expression twist into anguish.

'Oh, Kelly!' she said, as if he'd seen her only the previous day, as if she'd been in touch with him through all the empty years. Then, as he lifted her to her feet and put his arms round her, she began to shiver and her face crumpled and the tears came. 'Oh, Kelly, Kelly,' she whimpered.

'Thank God you're safe,' he said.

She seemed to recover a little and after a while the shuddering seemed to subside.

'I was at the back when it happened,' she was saying. 'If I'd been at the front I'd have been killed. Everything's gone. There's nothing left worth having.' Her head moved as if she were shaking it to try to put her senses in order. 'I'll have to find somewhere to live.'

'There's Thakeham, Charley.' His arm still round her, he began to lead her away and, when an ambulanceman approached, his expression questioning, he shook his head.

Leaving her drinking tea at the police station, he set out to find a car. There appeared to be no taxi drivers with enough petrol to go beyond the city boundaries, but in the end he found a car hire firm with a load of black market fuel and persuaded them with a colossal bribe to take him to Thakeham. Pushing Charley into the car, he put his coat round her and climbed in beside her. She said nothing, flashing him only occasional glances as she sat huddled beside him, still clutching the silver picture frame to her. It was a slow drive across London because the flying bombs were still coming in, and they were diverted half a dozen times. It was late when they arrived at Thakeham but Biddy was at the door the minute the car drew up. She asked no questions but, as she led Charley inside, she turned to Kelly, her eyes questioning.

'Bombed out, Biddy,' he said laconically. 'She'll be staying here until she can find somewhere.'

She nodded and vanished and he hurried to what had been his mother's room to make sure it was in order. He could hear splashing from the bathroom next door and Biddy's low voice.

His coat, smeared with dust and spotted with blood, lay on the bed. Alongside it was the silver frame Charley had clutched to her all the way from Harwich and he picked it up to put it where she could see it, wishing he could produce in her the same devotion she seemed to feel for this dead airman. But, as he turned it over, he saw that the face staring out at him through the cracked glass was his own, the press picture taken when he'd been to the Palace to collect his CB.

Deliberately he kept out of the way and Biddy, her face still showing her own grief, arrived soon afterwards to say that Charley was sleeping.

'Best leave her alone,' she suggested. 'She'll probably be all right in the morning.'

He ate the meal she set in front of him without noticing it and slept badly, finally falling into a restless doze in the early hours of the morning. When he woke, he bathed, shaved and dressed hurriedly before going to his mother's room. Charley was sitting up in bed, wearing a dressing gown belonging to Biddy. There was a piece of sticking plaster on her forehead and a red weal on her cheek. The ordeal had marked her and shadows like bruises lay beneath her eyes against the mask-like pallor of her features.

'Hello, Charley,' he said quietly.

She gave him an uncertain smile and he noticed that the silver frame was on the table near the bed face-down.

'That's a lovely shiner you've got.'

She nodded, her smile tremulous and doubtful. 'I'm sorry to be so much trouble,' she said, avoiding his eyes. 'I'll find somewhere to go as soon as I can.'

'No! Stay here. The place's enormous and there's nobody in it. Stay as long as you wish.'

He was cheating a little, trying to make her dependent on him so that she'd be unable to leave, but his hold on her was too tenuous and he was determined not to let it slip from his fingers again, especially after he'd seen what was in the picture frame that she'd clutched to her so determinedly.

'I'm grateful for what you did,' she whispered.

'I've been looking for you ever since 1941,' he said. 'I even tried to find Mabel in the hope she'd know.'

Tears welled up in her eyes but she managed a smile. 'You became an admiral after all, Kelly,' she said. 'I'm so pleased.'

'We might have celebrated it together,' he said gruffly. 'But I didn't know where you were.'

'I knew where *you* were,' she said. 'Always. I knew when you were bombed in the Mediterranean. I was watching the signals in the Ops Division when *Impi* was sunk and I followed the fight against *Ziethen* and *Müffling* every bit of the way. I wasn't supposed to read the signals but I did. I told them – '

'Told them what, Charley?'

She was silent for a while. 'I told them that I knew you. I was terrified.'

'Why?'

He sensed an advantage and decided to have it out of her. He believed in himself and, confident now that he'd seen his own photograph in the silver frame, he was determined to push it to the limit.

'Why, Charley?' he persisted.

'I thought you might be hurt.'

'They can't touch me,' he said briskly. 'I'm fireproof. But why should it worry *you*?'

She stared at him with enormous eyes, a black fear like a physical presence in her body. Before she could answer, he spoke again, forcefully, and with no sign of humility.

'Marry me, Charley.'

She looked at him. 'You sound as if you were on the bridge giving orders.'

'I'm not on the bridge,' he said. 'But I'm trying to give orders. I need you. I love you. I've loved you all my life.'

She looked at him wonderingly and he had a sudden uneasy thought that, in all the years he'd known her, in all the years of telling her she meant something to him, he'd never managed to tell her that. His briskness dispersed.

'I have a feeling,' he said uncertainly, 'that that's something I've never said before. I've told you a lot of things – that I needed you, that I depended on you, things like that – but never that.'

'No, Kelly,' she said quietly. 'I don't think you ever did.'

'Well, I do, Charley. Now you're here I want you to stay here.'

She still said nothing and he went on, almost desperately, feeling he was making a very bad job of it. 'When you arrived last night, I happened to pick up the picture frame you brought with you – the only thing you brought. I thought you'd want it where you could see it, but then I saw it was me. Why, Charley?'

She hesitated for a moment before speaking in a whisper. 'Because I loved you, Kelly,' she said.

It didn't make sense because she'd behaved as if she were totally indifferent to him. He'd been desperately jealous at Dover of the other men who'd been in her company, able to see her and talk to her while he was away at sea. He'd wanted to be brutal, violent, demanding that she be faithful to him, a late manifestation of passion that he could only guess had been held back by his ambition and his devotion to the Navy. He'd held it in check because he'd felt it would only have produced coldness.

'Marry me, Charley,' he said again. 'There are such things as special licences and I couldn't bear to lose you again.'

For a long time she was silent and he decided she was going to refuse him again and felt a surge of despair in the uneven stroke of his heart. Then her body trembled as if an electric current had passed through it and there was the sudden bright shine of tears in her eyes.

'Yes, Kelly,' she said. 'Yes. I want to. Please.'

He was bewildered. It was impossible, he felt, to understand women. If he'd asked her before the bomb had dropped, he felt certain she'd have refused him. Yet he knew she wasn't just accepting him now because he was offering her a home and a measure of comfort. Somehow, the flying bomb had snapped some resistance, cleared some final obstacle that lay between them, exposing to both of them their need for each other.

'Stay here, Charley,' he said. 'Don't move.'

She looked up. 'I hadn't thought of going away,' she said.

He went to his room and rummaged in his drawers until he found a small faded red box. He'd almost forgotten it and had never expected to use it.

Returning, he took her hand and slipped the ruby ring on her finger. It looked enormous and he saw her eyes widen.

'Kelly, it must be worth a fortune!'

'It probably is,' he agreed. 'It was given to me in 1919 by the Grand Duchess Evgenia Vjeskov when we fished her out of Russia. I thought then it would make a good engagement ring. It's just taken a long time to arrive.' He paused. 'Christina never wore it, Charley. I never offered it to her.'

She seemed awed by it and she lifted her face to his, a lost look in her eyes, then the tears welled up and she flung her arms round him.

'Oh, Kelly, we've been such fools!'

7

They went to the Lake District to see Mabel, the only relative in the world either of them possessed. Her husband had returned from India and was now running the local Home Guard. As she kissed him, Kelly saw there were tears in her eyes.

'Oh, God,' she said, 'why did it take you two bloody idiots so long?'

They were married a fortnight later at the Esher Registry Office. It was a quiet wedding because Kelly Rumbelo's ship had gone to Trincomalee and Hugh said he couldn't get leave. Since it was so soon after Paddy's death, Kelly suspected he preferred it that way. Verschoyle was there with Maisie, Rumbelo and Biddy, whose face still wore a tremulous expression of her own grief.

In view of wartime restrictions and inability to get petrol, they spent their honeymoon at Thakeham, and almost immediately Kelly flew to Ramsay's headquarters at Granville in Normandy. By September, with all the Channel ports captured, he was told it would be his job to make sure that all the demolished equipment was removed and the ports put in working order as quickly as possible.

'Europe has to support itself as quickly as possible,' Ramsay explained. 'It'll be your job to see that it has the port facilities to do so.'

It was Verschoyle, as usual, who put him in the picture.

'They're looking for an active, alert and determined senior naval officer for Germany after the surrender,' he said. 'Ramsay turned it down on the grounds that the man should be younger and fresher. I suggested you.'

By this time the army was moving swiftly northwards. Paris fell and, soon afterwards, Brussels and finally Antwerp. The perimeter of the German fortress was shrinking every day. By the end of the year they stood on the German frontier and Kelly was in Brussels with Archie Bumf and two Americans as part of the allied committee of recovery, and seemed to spend most of his time flying to and fro between there and London in an assortment of aircraft from old Dakotas to spanking new Liberators.

A Russian Order of Ushakov, first class, arrived, much to his astonishment.

'Who's Ushakov?' he asked.

Latimer grinned. 'Led the Black Sea fleet into the Adriatic in 1798,' he said. 'He must have been good. Even Nelson congratulated him.'

They'd set up headquarters in a large house just inside the French border, handy both for France and Belgium, and had just christened it *HMS Darius,* in accordance with naval orders that all headquarters must be ships, when Boyle discovered his parents-in-law at Ushant. For the next week he virtually disappeared as he arranged for them to travel to England. They were almost destitute, with all their possessions looted by the Germans, but they were in good health, even if hungry.

'Perhaps they're lucky,' Kelly said drily. 'The hospitality since *we* landed's been more than my stomach can stand.'

On Armistice Day, he stood behind Ramsay in Paris at a march past led by Moroccan troops with a large white goat, mounted bands, Scottish pipe bands, French horn bands, and an American band in which the big drum was mounted on wheels and pushed by the drummer. He was travelling long distances by air now, from the Bay of Biscay to the Scheldt, often in freighter Liberators which contained no mod cons and he had to lie in the bomb bays or on the floor. It was cold and congested and he was glad when the trips took him to London.

By this time, the blackout had been partially lifted and they seemed to be waiting only for the last dying kicks of the Nazi regime. Despised by his soldiers, hated by the Germans and succoured only by the sycophants of his court, Hitler clearly hadn't much longer to reign.

Only an occasional German aircraft appeared, sneaking across in the dark to drop anti-personnel bombs, whose sole purpose seemed to be the killing of inquisitive children. There had been a certain amount of euphoric reaction after the race across France and Belgium and a certain slackening of effort, but it had soon been realised after Arnhem, that whatever Hitler's position, the German army at least was far from finished. Short of men and short of fuel, it was still highly professional and still managed to produce resistance where there should have been none; incredibly, in the middle of December, it even managed to launch an offensive in the Ardennes.

Kelly had to spend Christmas in France, and by then the alarm about the Ardennes had dispersed, because the Germans were clearly going to be defeated and with defeat would come the final collapse. Boyle had managed to get his parents-in-law into a house near Amiens and they all went there for Christmas Day, eating and drinking what everybody openly admitted was black market food. For the New Year Kelly flew to London with Verschoyle and went to Thakeham feeling like a bridegroom. He'd seen remarkably little of Charley since his marriage and was pleased to see the house had become gracious once more under her touch.

The New Year went well but on January 2nd, when they were all a little euphoric at the news that the Germans were in retreat in the Ardennes, Verschoyle rang up.

'You've lost your boss,' he said. 'Ramsay's dead.'

'Dead?' Kelly said. 'How?'

'He was flying from Toussus-le-Noble to see Monty. They crashed on take-off. Nobody seems to know why. The sky was cloudless and they got up to about three hundred feet then side slipped in and burst into flames. Perhaps the cold had something to do with it.'

Flying back to France for the funeral, Kelly walked behind Cunningham and Eisenhower. The accident threw more work on his shoulders and he found he had little opportunity to go to England again. Nothing seemed to have come of Corbett's suggestion about the Far East and he'd heard that Philip Vian had got the job.

He felt no resentment. He'd had a good innings. Most boys entering Dartmouth dropped out before they'd reached commander and the number who achieved their broad stripe was very small. He'd been extraordinarily lucky. From being in danger of vanishing into limbo as a passed-over commander in

1936 he was now a rear-admiral. With the war drawing to its end, however, he could expect little more.

Latimer didn't seem to agree. '"Self-love is not so vile a sin as self-neglecting,"' he said. '"Henry V." It's as bad to be over-modest, sir, as it is to be over-bold. You need have no fear. They won't let *you* go yet.'

Kelly grinned. 'When I retire, William, I think you'd better join me – as resident minstrel.'

Latimer grinned back. 'I expect to see you admiral of the fleet before I die, sir.'

As it happened, what Latimer had said came home within days. Verschoyle arrived in a SHAPE car driven by an American WAAC driver who looked as though she'd left a good job as a Hollywood starlet to join the war.

'Where did you pick her?' Kelly asked.

'With the Americans,' Verschoyle said, 'they come in bunches of a dozen. I think they breed 'em in litters, because they always seem to find enough to decorate headquarters.'

He was fishing in his brief case, deliberately brisk and, pulling out a signal flimsy, he looked up.

'Kelly, old son,' he said. 'You're for home.'

'What have I done?'

'Not what you've done. What you're about to do. We still have to sort out those little yellow bastards in Japan. The Yanks have finally agreed to help us organise a task force for the Pacific and Winston's determined to get into the act on political grounds, so that when it's over he'll have some say in what happens to the peace.'

'And – ?'

'You'll be ordered to strike your flag and go home to help set it up. With a step up in rank. I've come to warn you not to get too much involved in this job.'

The promotion came as Verschoyle predicted and with it the news that he was to get a KCB. It brought an immediate signal from Verschoyle. 'Twice knightly. You always were one to overdo it.'

In the same gazette, Kelly was pleased to see that Verschoyle had finally made rear-admiral. With his skill, knowledge and

283

technical ability, it was something he deserved.

He flew home on leave, half-expecting to be called to the Admiralty, but there was no sign that anyone had even noticed him and he spent his leave in a curious frame of mind, tense because he was expecting his new post, and frustrated because it didn't arrive.

'There's something in the wind, isn't there, Kelly?' Charley said.

He nodded, wondering how she'd take the news he brought. She was still not quite the old Charley – as if she'd been too much hurt and was wary of giving too freely.

The pain of Paddy's death was dying at last and it was Charley who was helping it to go. When he felt most stricken and shivering at the thought, she was there to take his mind off her, almost as if she *were* Paddy.

But while the old undemanding warmth had returned, there was something else too. Sometimes she drew a vast breath that seemed to hurt as it filled her lungs, and he never knew whether it was relief or anguish. Women never seemed to have full control over their hearts and even the most intelligent seemed to have a small exposed spot which was never secure. It was a draining, weakening thought that he could still not be sure of her and he knew he was not very patient at studying areas which he knew nothing about.

'You're going back to sea,' she said slowly.

He looked up, unsure of her. 'Do you mind, Charley?'

She stared at him, her eyes frank. 'No woman likes to see her man disappear into the blue,' she said. 'I never did. But it *is* different now, Kelly.'

'It might be the Pacific,' he said.

'That's a long way away.'

'I can turn it down if it's important to you.'

She gave a sudden smile that reminded him with a jab at his heart of the way she'd grinned at him as a young girl, when she'd been the only member of her family able to see any promise in him.

'It would be nice to be the wife of an admiral of the fleet,' she said quietly.

He smiled and she went on. 'The war's almost over, Kelly, and according to what Seamus Boyle tells me, the Japanese won't last long. So go and enjoy it. When the war's over, there'll only be me.'

There was a long silence because he'd been desperately afraid that she wouldn't see eye to eye with him. The relief almost took his breath away.

'I don't know,' he said slowly. 'I thought I'd have heard by now. Perhaps somebody's shoved a spanner in the works.'

But they hadn't. He had no sooner arrived back in Antwerp when a signal came instructing him to report to the Admiralty. With it came another signal informing him he was to leave for Trincomalee where the Far East fleet was gathering. It was personal and it came from Corbett who added his congratulations.

A farewell party was held in Antwerp. The brass was dazzling and a great many people said enough nice things about him to raise a lump in his throat.

They headed for Orly the next morning and as they stopped at the airport, Rumbelo began to pass out the baggage from the boot of the car.

'Am I coming, too, sir?' he demanded.

'No, Albert, old son,' Kelly said gently. 'You're going home to Biddy.'

'I *would* come.'

'I know you would. But I think Biddy needs you more than I do.'

There was an awkward pause because they were both thinking of Paddy, and Kelly hurried on.

'The garden needs your attention,' he said. 'And they'll be starting the demob scheme as soon as the war ends here in Europe. You'll be one of the first out. When I join you, we'll grow roses.'

The aircraft landed at Brize Norton in a downpour and Charley was waiting at Thakeham, smiling in a way that told him the doubts and fears had finally gone.

'You got it, Kelly?'

'I've come home for briefing.'

She stared at him, then suddenly she threw her arms round him.

'I'm so pleased for you and so proud!'

It was the first impulsive show of love she'd shown. It was

spontaneous and full of warmth and he swept her into his arms and began to carry her to the stairs.

'What are you doing?'

'You could say I'm carrying you over the threshold,' he said. 'Something I omitted to do when I married you.' He stopped at the curve of the stairs and looked at her with a serious face. 'It's all right now between us, isn't it, Charley?'

She stared back at him, equally straight-faced, but her eyes were shining. His head was swimming a little as he saw the tears in them, and he was swept away in a torrent of memories which he'd thought had gone for ever. She tilted her head to kiss him. 'Yes, Kelly,' she said. 'It's all right.'

He grinned and began to stamp up the remaining stairs.

'For God's sake be careful,' she warned. 'You'll have a heart attack.'

'Not yet, please God,' he said. 'Afterwards.'

When he went to the Admiralty the following day, for once Corbett was not there to greet him. In his place was Admiral Orrmont, who'd been his commanding officer in Russia in the destroyer, *Mordant*.

'Cuthbert Corbett's dead,' he said. 'A week ago. I think he wore himself out.' Orrmont smiled. 'Now you've got me and I'm to fill you in with everything you're to do. You'll fly to Washington from Bourne and then to Trincomalee where you'll pick up your ships. We're assembling them now.'

Bourne was full of aircraft – Liberators, Lancasters, Dakotas, even a few fighters. They ate a meal at the restaurant which had been set up for transients.

'Better eat plenty, sir,' Boyle warned. 'It's a long trip.'

'I hope you've got us a few comfortable seats for a change, Seamus.'

As they finished eating, they heard the metallic roar of engines and saw a big square-bodied Liberator moving towards them. An American WAAC officer appeared with a list and began to call names. She looked as beautiful as Verschoyle's driver.

There seemed to be hundreds of aircraft on the tarmac and more in the air, landing and taking off in both directions in what seemed a precarious proximity to each other. In the distance they could see the wrecked shell of a Dakota, without engines, the wings charred and black as though it had been on fire.

Latimer was waiting by the aircraft as they climbed from the car. There were three other British naval officers, and three Americans, as well as twenty American air force officers going home after completing their tours of duty. The camera cases over their shoulders made them look as if they'd been on a tourist visit to England.

One of them kicked at the huge tyres of the aircraft. 'I sure hope they put all the rivets in,' he said.

The pilot was already on board, shouting instructions out of his window to a fitter on the ground. Beneath him, painted in white on the aircraft's side, was the name – 'Raidin' Maiden.'

As they climbed in, the WAAC officer gave them all a smile and shook hands.

'Anyone would think we weren't coming back,' Boyle said.

The seats were more comfortable than they'd been used to in the Dakotas but Kelly found he wasn't looking forward to six hours of sitting in them, and the machine was still a bomber with the usual sharp angles and the usual spartan interior.

An American lieutenant appeared. 'The skipper sends his compliments,' he said. 'And says not to worry. It's a straightforward trip. We shall land in Northern Ireland to top up tanks, then go on to Gander and from there to Washington. We're doing it in easy stages for safety. He'd also like you to know that this will be his last trip after fifty-three operational ones, because when he arrives, he's grounded and he's never going higher off the deck after that than his bedroom.'

They were sitting in the waist, each of them with a parachute beneath his feet, wondering how much use it would be if they had to bale out over the Atlantic. The machine had been stripped of everything possible for the trip, every ounce of superfluous weight removed to make the crossing safer.

'Safe as Fort Knox,' one of the American officers observed. 'She's got around a thousand miles safety margin.'

The engines howled as they began to taxi towards the runway. The way the aeroplane moved was far from reassuring and Kelly decided that the pilot was either keen to show off or he'd got used to moving into position fast for the big raids on

Germany. As they waited for the tower, one of the American naval officers moved aft and squatted down in the alleyway alongside Kelly. 'Admiral Maguire, sir?' he asked.

'That's right.'

'Pleased to meet you, sir. Commander Kaysor. I was on the staff of Admiral Allington. He was with you in the North African landings. I never met you but I sure heard a lot about you.' He put his parachute down and sat on it in the alleyway. 'I'm going out to the Pacific, sir.'

'So am I,' Kelly said. 'I'll probably be asking your advice.'

The aircraft jerked suddenly as the pilot turned on full power to swing on to the runway, then without a pause, the engines thundering at full throttle, it began to hurtle down the tarmacadam, the wheels rumbling beneath them, loose objects rattling and clattering.

The centrifugal force as they'd swung had caused Kaysor to slide off his parachute and roll on to his back. He began to get up, grinning, but an unexpected oscillation prevented him and he was still fighting to get to his feet when the aeroplane began an up-and-down motion as if it were bowing over its nose wheel.

They were moving at full speed down the runway when it began to swing to port and starboard. It seemed to be nothing because nobody showed any alarm, but Kaysor's smile had changed to one of bewilderment and suddenly the motion increased and the aircraft began to tilt backwards and forwards in a violent seesaw. Wondering if the controls had jammed, Kelly glanced through the window but the rudder seemed to be moving freely.

'Goddam fly-boys – !'

Kaysor was trying to yell something to Kelly over the din of the engines when there was a tremendous wrench and a bang and Kelly realised he could see pieces of metal flying through the air. There was a yell from up forward and he saw Latimer's jaw drop in a sudden expression of horror as they felt the bulkhead twisting behind their backs. There was a vicious snap and the tail section lifted into the air and fell back again, and still dazed, Kelly realised that for some reason the pilot's final trip was ending in disaster. They were crashing, and he was going to die as Ramsay had died.

There was a colossal bang and the sound of tearing metal,

and they came to a stop with a jerk that flung him on top of Kaysor. Latimer was rolling in the space between the seats, his feet in the air. Of Boyle he could see no sign. He fought free of the tangle of arms and legs and, seeing an opening surrounded by torn metal, realised in an instant that it was his only chance of life.

He shoved Latimer out of the hole in front of him and fell out after him. He seemed to go on falling forever and landed on his shoulder. Something gave with a crack but he knew he had to get clear and scrambled away on hands and knees. Almost unconsciously he was aware of the tail section of the Liberator lying at an angle to the rest of the machine, the nose dipped to the ground, and a torn stretch of tarmacadam, then there was a violent 'pouf' sound and a blast of air lifted him several feet and threw him on to his injured shoulder again as the petrol caught fire.

Violent heat seared his face and he was conscious of a tremendous yellow glare and a new agony in his right leg that he hadn't noticed before. Struggling away on his knees and one hand through petrol that was dripping to the tarmac and made it look as if it were shimmering, he saw that seven men in addition to himself were scrambling about in the flare of flame. One of them was Latimer, dragging himself along by his elbows, his clothes on fire. He was yelling and looked as though he were blind, and Kelly flung himself at him, beating at the flames with his good hand, crying out at the pain because the petrol caused the flames to stick to his flesh. As fast as he slapped at them they sprang up elsewhere and he realised that Latimer was soaked with petrol. Dragging him from the wreckage, he rolled across him, and as he fell back, gasping, wondering where Boyle was and if he ought to have made sure he'd got clear, too, he heard the sound of engines and the shriek of tyres and brakes. Men were running towards him and he felt someone grab him by the armpits and drag him clear then he was being rolled on the ground in a brutal fashion that caused the broken bones in his shoulder to scrape against each other in agonising fashion. Sand was thrown on him, and it was only then that he realised his own clothing had been on fire.

Hurriedly, the survivors were shoved aboard a truck, several of them with flesh hanging from them in charred strips. They were already heading for the hospital as the ambulances arrived, and dazedly, he noticed that the rest of the aerodrome seemed untouched by the disaster and that planes were still taking off and landing as if nothing had happened, flying unheedingly through the pillar of black smoke that was drifting across the runway.

Bouncing about in the lorry, he stared round, still in shock and only half aware of what had happened. To his surprise, he found that in addition to his broken shoulder there was an appalling gash in his thigh that was pouring blood down his trousers. But the other men in the truck looked like burned toast with here and there a patch of clothing or a jagged strip of khaki or navy with gold buttons clinging by a seam or a collar or a cuff to the blackened flesh.

'Christ, what happened?' one of them said, and Kelly was surprised that his voice seemed as normal and unaffected as if nothing had happened.

He began to recognise them at last. Keysor was babbling about the need to inform his wife, and Latimer's blackened charred face was trying to smile at him.

'Fire burn, cauldron bubble,' he said. 'Macbeth, sir.'

'Shut up, William,' Kelly said, struggling to tuck the blanket round him.

Latimer winced with pain, so shocked he didn't feel the sear of the fire but recoiled from the slightest touch.

Someone gave Kelly an injection as the truck stopped and when he came round he found they'd stripped off his clothing and put his broken shoulder into a hideously uncomfortable splint like an aeroplane's wing that supported his arm at an angle of ninety degrees from his body. The ward was full of white-garbed nurses, one of whom told him he'd had twenty-seven stitches in his leg. It was in plaster now and covered by a thing like a kitchen fireguard to keep the weight of the bed-clothes off it. They seemed to have no doubt that he would survive because after six years of war they could judge exactly what the human frame could stand.

His burns had come chiefly from touching the others and were clearly far from fatal. Kaysor, they said, was likely to die that day. Latimer might survive but they had their doubts. In addition to his terrible burns, he had two broken legs, two broken wrists and several broken ribs, but they weren't even thinking about those yet.

'The problem,' the doctor said, 'is that when the burns are as bad as this the serum just seeps through the damaged tissue. We've tried a lot of things but I'm afraid none of them is really effective yet.'

They knew nothing of anybody called Boyle.

Despite the splintered arm and the cage over his leg, Kelly insisted on having his bed placed next to Latimer's. Because he was a vice-admiral, they didn't argue. Latimer was bandaged beyond recognition and was connected to glucose and plasma bottles and was in deep sedation. Later in the day, he came round and looked at Kelly through his only visible eye. His hand moved in a slow floppy movement that rattled the tubes attached to him.

'What happened to your arm, sir?' he asked.

'It's not my arm,' Kelly said. 'It's my shoulder. I broke it.'

'That's buggered up the Pacific, hasn't it?'

'A bit.'

'I'm glad you got out, sir.'

'I'm glad we both did. We were lucky. It broke in two just about where we were sitting.'

'How about Boyle?'

'He doesn't seem to have made it.' Kelly sighed. 'I think you ought to dry up now, William. The nurse'll be after you.'

Kaysor died soon afterwards and then the others one after another. The doctor gave Kelly pills that eased the pain a little and made him doze, and when he woke up they told him Latimer wasn't suffering.

He accepted that this meant that Latimer was going to die but not in pain, and he asked if all their wives had been told.

'They're on their way now.'

The nurses arrived soon afterwards and a bed was wheeled out.

'Who's that?' Kelly asked.

'Not Captain Latimer. Go to sleep.'

Soon afterwards he saw the nurse bending over the next bed, touching Latimer here and there gently with her fingers as if to make sure he was alive. There was only the slightest gasp as he died, and even that was almost lost as an aeroplane thundered overhead.

8

Curiously, it was Verschoyle who was the first to arrive. He appeared at the end of the ward and came slowly towards Kelly, moving cautiously to the bed, his scarred face concerned.

'Hello, Kelly,' he said quietly. 'You all right?'

'Better than most,' Kelly said shortly. 'William Latimer's dead.'

Verschoyle sat down. 'Yes, I heard so.'

'His wife came a few minutes after he went. She walked in expecting to find him alive.' Kelly paused. 'Boyle's wife came, too. I met her first in Russia, you know. She was French. We fished her out of Odessa with her family. Christ – ' Kelly fought to keep the tears back ' – what a bloody waste! What happened?'

'They don't know yet. Charley been?'

'Not yet. What's happened to her?'

'I think there's been some balls-up somewhere. They told me you were at Burn but I knew you were going to Bourne. Perhaps they told her Burn, too.'

'Poor William,' Kelly said. 'All that Shakespeare. What's going to happen now, James?'

Verschoyle shrugged. 'Well, it's obvious you won't be going to Trincomalee,' he said. 'It'll be six months before you're right again and by that time the war could be over. We've already heard that the Germans are making pacific noises. They've all fallen out with each other and they're all trying to grab themselves a bit of security by posing as someone who wanted peace all the time and wasn't allowed to because Hitler was on his neck. I don't think it'll help 'em much because there seems to be a move afoot to bring the whole bloody lot to trial in front of the German people so they can see their guilt.'

293

'Doesn't mean a thing.' Kelly moved his hand. 'If we'd lost, they'd have brought Winston to trial, and, God knows, *he* didn't start the war.'

'You sound low. Fed up about the task force?'

Kelly considered. 'Not really,' he said. 'It'll mean I'll have a bit of time with Charley, which'll make a change, because in the whole of my life I'm damned if we've spent more than a few consecutive days together. Retirement would be nice.'

Verschoyle smiled. 'Who said anything about retirement? This business has caused a bit of switching about, of course, but they reckon you'll be back on the ball in a couple of months, and, knowing you, I reckon they're right. And, since by the time you're out the Germans'll have thrown their hand in, they're suggesting you for that job Ramsay turned down.'

Kelly stared at the bed cover. 'Do they really mean it?' he said.

'Yes. And you'll want a deputy, and that's a job I wouldn't mind.'

Kelly paused, thinking of Boyle and Latimer. 'It's nice to know there'll still be someone around I know,' he said slowly. He managed a smile. 'It's a long time since we half killed each other fighting.'

Verschoyle smiled back. 'It was a good scrap,' he said. 'You'd never have won if you hadn't cheated.'

Charley didn't arrive until the evening.

The nurse was making a brave effort to cheer him up and he didn't want to be cheered up. He felt as low as he'd ever felt and blasted off at her as she punched his pillows.

'Look, sir,' she said finally, 'you may be very important in your ship, but here you're just a patient. And it's time to take your sleeping pills.'

'I don't want to go to sleep,' Kelly snapped. 'My missis hasn't been yet.'

'You'll be no fun for your wife if you're in pain, will you? You've got third-degree burns on your hands, a broken collar bone and a gash as long as my arm in your thigh.'

He took the pills unwillingly and she went away with such an angry expression he made up his mind to apologise and be particularly nice to her next time.

He lay in bed, glowering at the cage over his leg, waiting for the pills to take effect. Poor Latimer, he thought. It had been a long association and it still seemed bloody sad that all that knowledge had been wasted.

Mentally he was calling the roll of the men he'd known. So few of them had been granted his own luck. A few would reappear eventually from prisoner of war camps, a few would recover their health to be useful again, and life would go on. But he wondered how much anybody really knew of what it had cost. They'd spent the last six years seeing their friends whittled away by attrition and even when it was all over, whenever they heard of another one dying it would be like another wound because a war never ended and the grief was never gone while ever there were survivors.

A movement at the end of the ward caught his attention and he turned his head, somehow half-expecting to see Latimer or Boyle. But Boyle had never appeared and Latimer's bed had gone, wheeled away in a hurry after he'd died.

It was the nurse and she was frowning and looked ready to do battle. He forestalled her by smiling and apologising to the best of his endeavour. She looked startled.

'There's somebody to see you,' she said.

'My wife?'

'Yes.'

'Well, wheel her in!'

'I don't know that you deserve it.'

'I'll go down on my knees if it'll help.'

She smoothed his pillow and smiled. 'Just be quiet and calm down. After all, bed's not a bad place to be.'

'It'd be better with you in it.'

She laughed and turned away and when he saw Charley coming slowly down the ward his heart did a flop into his stomach because, somehow, she looked just as she had when she'd visited him in Rosyth after Jutland. She was wearing blue as she had then and, in the same way as then, it made her hair seem darker. She had a paper bag in her hand.

'Grapes again?' Kelly asked.

'Yes.' She sat beside the bed, her eyes on his face. 'I don't think you're the type for flowers.'

She gave a small hiccuping sob and bent to kiss him. 'Oh,

Kelly,' she said. 'I thought at first you were dead.'

'Well, I'm not. Not by a long way. What kept you?'

'They sent me to Burn.'

'Typical bloody staff work! Those buggers get enlarged backsides shining the seats of their chairs! You'd think they'd have managed to get a thing like this right!'

She managed a smile. 'It doesn't matter. They apologised. They said there were so many hurt, they had to rope in anybody they could, to do the telephoning.' She paused. 'Kelly, I'm so sorry about William and Seamus Boyle.'

He grunted. He'd managed to shove them to the back of his mind to be thought about later when he felt he could bear it.

'What do they say about you?'

'Broken collar bone, a gash on my thigh and burns. I did the collar bone diving out of the plane. I must have done the leg inside. The burns aren't much.' He frowned because a lump persisted in coming to his throat every time he thought about it and he had to force himself to be brusque and hearty to keep it back. He held up his bandaged hands. 'This is a damn silly thing to have happen to me, Charley. I can't make grabs at you.'

She gave him a small sad smile. 'You'll not be going to the Pacific now.'

'No.' He managed to smile back at her. 'Verschoyle says they're going to fix me up with a job at the Admiralty. I shall be home a lot. I hope you can stand it.'

She said nothing, her eyes huge and suddenly swimming with tears.

'It's the sort of job that'll get on my nerves,' he went on. 'All those bloody silly office wallahs. I expect I shall be a bastard. Somebody else'll get the task force job and then the war'll end, so I reckon this is the end of seagoing for me. If it doesn't work out, I'll apply for the Chiltern Hundreds and resign.'

'Are you sorry, Kelly?'

He thought about it and found he wasn't. He'd often felt that the old story about the pull of the sea was overdone. He'd probably move to the coast where he could smell the brine in the wind, but he found it didn't worry him really. His mind had dwelt on it a lot in the last few hours. Britain was no longer the super power she had been and in a flash of insight he suspected that the Empire wouldn't survive the fact.

He'd probably had the best of the Navy. He'd known it in its greatest days, when it had kept the peace around the world. It had had a prestige then that it perhaps hadn't deserved, but in future it might well be smaller and somehow he couldn't see himself serving in a truncated version run by penny-pinching politicians.

He looked up to find Charley's eyes on him, gentle, compassionate, understanding – and loving.

'Petty Officer Rumbelo says he's making a corner of the garden where you'll be able to sit in the sun until you're all right again,' she said.

'Good old Albert. I'm glad he wasn't with us. He'd never have got out. He'd have been too fat.' He grinned at her. 'I expect I shall fall asleep on you soon,' he went on. 'They gave me something to send me off. They did last time, if you remember.' He paused. 'Christ, that's a long time ago, Charley! Thirty years, damn' near. Do you mind?'

'Mind what? The thirty years?'

He looked up quickly, suddenly afraid he'd said the wrong thing, but she was still smiling.

'No,' he said. 'Going to sleep on you again.'

The sleeping pill was beginning to effect him at last. His vision was growing blurred and Charley's face seemed to be the only clear thing in the room.

'You know,' he said slowly, 'I think you're the most beautiful thing I've ever seen. And certainly the most wonderful thing that ever happened in *my* life. I don't deserve it – I never did, I suppose – but I'm glad it did happen.' His eyes blurred again and the pale face in front of him wavered. 'And, now, if you don't mind,' he ended, 'I think I shall just *have* to close my eyes.'

She bent over and kissed his cheek. 'Go to sleep, Kelly,' she whispered.

He gave her another grin. 'Yes, Mum,' he said, and the last thing he remembered was her smiling at him.

A SELECTION OF BESTSELLERS FROM SPHERE

FICTION

LOVENOTES	Justine Valenti	£1.75	☐
VENGEANCE 10	Joe Poyer	£1.75	☐
MURDER IN THE WHITE HOUSE	Margaret Truman	£1.50	☐
LOVE PLAY	Rosemary Rogers	£1.75	☐
BRIMSTONE	Robert L. Duncan	£1.75	☐

FILM & TV TIE-INS

FORT APACHE, THE BRONX	Heywood Gould	£1.75	☐
SHARKY'S MACHINE	William Diehl	£1.75	☐
THE PROFESSIONALS	Ken Blake	£1.00	☐
THE GENTLE TOUCH	Terence Feely	£1.25	☐
BARRIERS	William Corlett	£1.00	☐

NON-FICTION

OPENING UP	Geoff Boycott	£1.75	☐
SCIENCE IN EVERYDAY LIFE	William C. Vergara	£2.50	☐
THE COUNTRY DIARY OF AN EDWARDIAN LADY	Edith Holden	£4.50	☐
WHAT THIS KATIE DID	Katie Boyle	£1.75	☐
MICHELLE REMEMBERS	Michelle Smith & Lawrence Pazder M.D.	£1.75	☐

All Sphere books are available at your local bookshop or newsagent, or can be ordered direct from the publisher. Just tick the titles you want and fill in the form below.

Name _____

Address _____

_____

Write to Sphere Books, Cash Sales Department, P.O. Box 11, Falmouth, Cornwall TR10 9EN

Please enclose a cheque or postal order to the value of the cover price plus:

UK: 45p for the first book, plus 20p for the second and 14p for each additional book ordered to a maximum charge of £1.63

OVERSEAS: 75p for the first book plus 21p per copy for each additional book

BFPO & EIRE: 45p for the first book, 20p for the second book plus 14p per copy for the next 7 books, thereafter 8p per book

Sphere Books reserve the right to show new retail prices on covers which may differ from those previously advertised in the text or elsewhere, and to increase postal rates in accordance with the PO.